DESIRE'S DESTINY

"I have sought you out, Aria Dunning." Tynan's voice was filled with the passion she ignited in him.

His mouth lowered by agonizing increments to conquer hers. His kiss was unexpectedly soft and yet commanding. Aria thought only of the pleasure she experienced, warding off unwelcome warnings of what might yet lie ahead. There was nothing here but the magic of what flowed mysteriously between them.

His arms closed slowly about her waist as his lips moved mesmerizingly against hers, testing and tempting her response.

Aria could hardly breathe. The heat from his muscular body made her tremble. Waves of stunning new sensations broke over her—his body pressed against her, his clean, sandalwood scent, his restrained urgency. His last words echoed inside the chambers of her heart . . . *I have sought you out* . . . *I have sought you out* .

REBEL PASSION

Betina Krahn

Zebra Books
Kensington Publishing Corp.

http://www.zebrabooks.com

ZEBRA BOOKS are published by

Kensington Publishing Corp.
850 Third Avenue
New York, NY 10022

Second Zebra Printing: November, 1996

Printed in the United States of America
10 9 8 7 6 5 4 3 2

For SHARON,
sister, mentor, and friend

One

August 3, 1775

"Thomas—stop! What are you doing?!" Aria Dunning stumbled on the sill of the French doors and pulled back against the insistent hand that drew her toward the secrecy of the night-fragrant veranda. But the lean fingers tightened about her wrist, and the tall, familiar form continued across the broad wooden porch, dragging her in its wake. The noise of the party inside receded as both the shadows and Aria's angry confusion deepened.

"Thomas . . . please!"

"Sh-h-h!"

A bit of trailing vine from the trellis brushed her cheek and she shrank from it, recovering her balance just in time to snatch her panniered skirts out of the way of a potted shrub. Then Thomas turned on his heel to take her elbow and pushed her gently into the seclusion offered by other tall greenery.

"Aria, darlin'," his quiet voice rasped with tension as he drew her against him, "I had to see you—"

"Have you taken leave of your senses? Sending Robert Burdette for me the minute I arrive . . . dragging me out here in the dark, without even a civil greeting . . ." She pushed against him, wrestling back in his persistent arms. A late turn of her head avoided his lips, and his kiss grazed her cheek instead.

Her face burned with possible explanations for such stealth. Every one of them added to her growing feeling of dread.

"Don't be angry with me, Aria—" He tried again to pull her closer against him. "How I've missed you—I can hardly sleep at night thinking about you."

"I find that hard to believe, Thomas," she searched his strained face as her eyes adjusted to the dimness, "when you might have relieved your torture with an hour's ride to Royal Oaks. It has been four weeks since you came; but I'd expect after all those months you called on me you'd know the way—" Thomas's chest tightened as her eyes filled with unshed tears.

"Aria—" He stroked her cheek and let his fingers trail down the side of her neck to her shoulders.

"Aria, I couldn't come . . . I couldn't."

"Couldn't? Have you been so busy, Thomas?" she struck back, trying to swallow the hurt that lodged in her throat and threatened to spill from her eyes. "Or perhaps you've simply found the road to Janette Morland's house an easier ride."

"Janette?" Thomas scowled, knowing that now the truth was out and feeling more wretched by the minute. "Aria, I . . . I can explain—"

An explanation . . . not a rebuttal or an apology. It was true then. Aria's fingers curled into knots where they were braced against his arms. He *was* courting Janette Morland. Her tall, admirable Thomas, courting another. She felt suddenly light-headed and a little sick. She pushed his slackening arms from her waist and stepped back, steadying herself by her skirts against the wooden balustrade. She should be furious. She had every right.

"Explain? No, thank you. It all seems perfectly clear." Her voice broke and she bit her lip to stifle a betraying gasp. "No!" She pushed Thomas's hands away when he made to embrace her again. She stiffened and clasped her arms about her waist, trying to pull her reeling emotions back under control. After an excruciating moment, she lifted her chin to him.

"Why Thomas?" she whispered hoarsely, feeling her world tilting under her feet. "Why?"

"Do you think that I would ever look at another woman, much less pay court, if there was any hope for us?" Thomas grasped her shoulders and pulled her close to him. The heat of his hands subdued her initial protest, bringing her bewildered face up to his. "My life is misery to me because of my need for you."

"And so you drown your sorrow in another's arms." Aria clipped each word but hurt quivered in her voice.

"Aria—" he groaned, rolling his head back in frustration. "It was your father . . . he followed me out after that last dinner and forbade me to pay you further court . . . or even see you. He said I'd regret setting foot on Royal Oaks again."

"Father? I don't believe it!" Aria sputtered, but her heart was sinking into her stomach.

"Why would my father forbid you or threaten you, Thomas?" The question was as much for herself as for the hapless Thomas Branscombe. Why indeed? Her father's temper was legendary in the county and for several counties around, if the truth be told. But might it also be made a convenient excuse?

"He's not reasonable, where you're concerned, Aria." Branscombe's lanky frame bent over her and she could feel his hands trembling on her shoulders. "He'd be calling me out right now if he knew we were together like this."

"What possible objection could he have to you?" she charged, finding her defense rang hollow in her own ears. "Why would he bar you from Royal Oaks?"

"He thinks . . . I am . . . we all are . . . beneath you," Thomas ground out as if stung anew.

"That's absurd, Thomas—your family is the wealthiest . . ." Aria paused, then measured her words to staunch the misery that swelled beneath her confusion. "Brantley is the largest plantation in this part of Virginia."

"Then you have named it yourself, Aria . . . absurd. He is possessive with you beyond reason. He has some half-mad notion that you . . ." His voice dropped to a raw whisper. "Aria, you must understand, my family is pressuring me to take a wife. Father's health is uncertain and soon I may have to take up the full reins of Brantley. They want it settled. . . . It does not change what I feel for you." His hands on her tightened as though trying to compel their warmth in her. "Tell me you care for me, Aria."

But in the silence, Aria could find no voice for her warring feelings and no comfort for either of them. Her shoulders rose and her face set like fine marble against any further display of emotion. She squeezed her hands into tight fists at her side and lowered her lashes. She could not bear to look at the pain in his face; it mirrored too closely her own. A long, awkward moment passed.

"Tell me, Aria . . ."

She swallowed. Her emotions were reeling, her reason was in turmoil. But the steadiness of her voice bore testimony to the success of long years of strict training and stern expectation.

"Aria?"

"I can say nothing to you that you do not already know, Mister Branscombe." Her eyes lifted, bereft of all but pride's flame. She could not hold back this last: "I can only ask that in the future, you spare my father's good name in your idle conjectures. And spare me the awkwardness of your attentions."

Filling her hands with the watered satin of her skirts, she fled back into the merciful noise and crush of the gala under way in the great house.

The pale green of Aria Dunning's broad, luxuriant skirts cut a frosty swath through the wine-warmed gathering. She was like an icy winter sea wave, brought to foaming brilliance by the tumultuous forces beneath her surface. Her shimmering gown and honey-colored hair danced with the reflection of the bolder colors about her, making her glow as if some unearthly flame burned at her center.

She was a vision: fine, delicate features, soft, clear skin, and a sweetly voluptuous body that moved with effortless grace. The full bow of her mouth vied for attention with the dazzling green of her eyes. Her clothes were always chosen with her unusual coloring in mind, and tonight, she and the gown that seemed to be fashioned of sea foam were set to enchant. But the conquest of that roomful of noisy and important guests was not her aim this evening, and it would have been little consolation to know how many pairs of eyes traced her passage or how many sighs escaped unguarded lips.

From the corner of her eye, she caught a look of roused interest on her rival's mother. Mayva Morland appraised her with a smug air and Aria saw the woman's sharp, ferretlike eyes fly to the doors she had just entered to discover who had entertained her in the darkness of the veranda. Aria slowed her step and paused to return a stiff greeting to some old friends of her family, praying fervently that Thomas Branscombe would have the sense to enter through another door.

Breathing more easily when the white French doors remained shut, she wound her way through the crush of guests toward the center hall and the grand staircase. Seeing little and hearing less, she had to be out of public view for a while. She had to collect herself.

As she hurried up the steps, her thoughts were consumed by the evening's failure. She had meant to confront Thomas Branscombe with his faithlessness and reclaim what had once been between them. How many times had he sworn his heart, his passion to her? And then came his sudden, unexplained absence from her home, Royal Oaks, during these last weeks. Thomas had long been touted as her match in the county; it was understood by everyone. Well, almost everyone.

Her eyes were downcast and her steps lagged in the broad

upstairs hallway. The loss flooded through her, as she tried to reason it through. Thomas said it was her father; he was the cause. He was known to be protective and jealous of her and her mother. And it seemed since she was sixteen that the young men who showed interest in her found themselves dispatched on family business to other colonies or sufficiently distracted to abandon suit of her. But just before she turned eighteen, tall, well-favored Thomas Branscombe came to call on her and had continued to press his leisurely suit for nearly a year. The Branscombes' name and wealth were coveted commodities among the landed families of southern Virginia. George Dunning's silence was taken for consent, for he was never silent otherwise, and the county assumed it was concluded. Aria Dunning would marry Thomas Branscombe and unite two large and prosperous plantations.

"Well . . . Aria, my dear."

The thin female purr brought Aria's face up abruptly, her eyes crackling with shamed fire. Caught in her misery, standing idly in the hallway, she had not seen the two young women approach and now found herself confronted with one person she was loath to set eyes upon, Janette Morland.

"My dear, you don't seem yourself," Janette said, glancing knowingly at the long-faced Harriet Timmons, who seemed to always trot to Janette's heels as if awaiting a scrap or a pat on the head. "Have you had unpleasant news? Or perhaps something you have had to swallow—eat didn't agree with you? You really should be quite careful at these gay events not to overdo." Janette's dark eyes flashed triumphantly.

Aria straightened with a cool air, taking a deep breath and lifting her chin. "I must thank you for your sage advice, but my health is quite good and I am never tempted to overreach myself." The emphasis she put on the last two words caused Janette's face to tighten. Aria's eyes narrowed suddenly as they focused on something caught in the lace at the shoulder of Janette's dress. She made quite a show of picking the feather from her rival's showy red and yellow brocade and holding it up.

"Well, well, Janette. Counting your chickens before they're hatched again?" With a taunting toss of the feather, Aria nudged her skirts around the others' and sailed off down the hall toward the ladies' retiring room. She would have given a fortune in gold crowns to see if the steam in Janette's face equaled that in her own veins.

The room set aside for the ladies was actually Mistress Stirling's private suite of rooms. The aging Dame Margareth's avowed love of the color blue was evident everywhere—in deep midnight carpets, on sky-blue settee and chairs, in draped azure velvets of windows and bed. The breathtaking rooms justified the gossip that she had sent all over the continent for the means to create a masterpiece for her private enjoyment. In the midst of this splendor, ladies were shedding extra petticoats or ill-fitting shoes while housemaids repaired curls, retied bows, and freshened the powder on wigs. It was the chaos of elegant femininity, closeted from the imperious, disdainful eyes of men.

Aria stood by the door, numbly taking it in. Her hands were cold inside her gloves and she was aching with the combined tensions of two confrontations. For now, all she wanted was a quiet corner to settle in and to slip off her new velvet slippers.

"There you are—Aria! Over here!"

Gillie Parnell was waving broadly and beckoning her to a small knot of girls seated on and near Dame Margareth's walnut poster bed. Gillie's burnished red curls bounced with eagerness and Aria forced a pained smile, knowing she was trapped. Her face felt frozen with self-control, and the iciness was slowly creeping through the rest of her.

There was a time, not long ago, that she had looked forward to these girlish conclaves in the ladies' rooms as the highlight of a ball or party. Now they tested both her endurance and her

Christianity. Gossip was the fare to be had here and Aria knew that of late she had become one of the main courses.

Gillie patted the embroidered blue coverlet beside her, and Aria reluctantly settled on the thick, feather-soft bed. All faces turned to her eagerly.

"Have you seen him? What do you think?"

Aria blinked at Gillie's audacity and her brow crinkled. "Gillie, I have no intention of—"

"I think he's rude and arrogant." Sissy Ruskin broke in, looking to the others for support.

"Only because he didn't stumble and fawn and ask you for a dance the minute you were introduced." Gillie scowled at her and turned back to Aria. "Well?"

Aria looked at the eagerness in the four faces trained upon her and frowned deeply. "I have no earthly idea what you are talking about." She had thought they were asking about Thomas, but quickly realized that even the impetuous Gillie Parnell would never be so crass . . . well, not with an audience. Gillie rolled her eyes and clasped Aria's hands to contain the flighty motion of her own.

"You mean you haven't seen him—the earl?" She was incredulous, staring at the other girls with abject horror. "The Earl of Penrith, all the way from England. He arrived just a bit ago . . . right here . . . as a guest of the Stirlings. He's—"

". . . divine," Celia Marlow finished, looking moony-eyed. "Tall and dark and such elegant clothes. Chinese embroidery on a short waistcoat and his shoe buckles must be solid gold."

"Rubbish," the spurned and stinging Sissy Ruskin objected. "He's rude and full of pretense. We certainly don't need *his* snooty kind roaming about, what with us barreling into war with England. It's an insult, him being here."

"Jealousy hath a spiteful tongue, Sissy Ruskin," Gillie chided her with mischievous eyes. "Alice's opinion has more weight—she danced with him." They all turned to the quiet, brown-haired Alice, who flushed violently at being the center of attention.

"He was very . . . elegant," Alice faltered, then lowered her eyes and finished softly, "and very frightening."

"See—there's the truth of it. He's a vain, frightening boor," Sissy insisted.

"Well, it doesn't take much to frighten Alice, after all." Celia affected a proper sniff as she held up one hand to view it. "And I thought him quite gallant . . . when he kissed my hand."

"O–o–ooh—" Gillie giggled girlishly, her face beaming, "you didn't tell us that! Well . . . I heard old Dame Margareth telling Mama about him. He's very rich and very wicked." She waited while all the others gasped and tittered with horror. Then she turned back to Aria with a loud whisper.

"He's been bounced from court—sent packing. King George won't see his face again, it's said." She paused, savoring this next bit. "He killed someone . . . over a woman." There was a collective gasp. "They say he's here to acquire property and take sport. . . . he's a great hunter. Aria, you simply must meet him and tell us what you think of him. He . . . has no wife."

"Perhaps he killed her, too," Aria quipped, nettled by the obvious speculation in their faces.

"Aria Dunning!" Gillie sat back in exaggerated outrage. "Well, perhaps you're so taken up with your Master Branscombe that you've no interest in other gentlemen." Her sidelong glance at the other girls let Aria know that they had just been treated to an earful from Janette Morland. "But allow us unattached ladies our harmless romantic speculations."

"Speculate all you want." Aria fought the heat rising in her face. "But as they say, you won't smell smoke unless there's fire. If he has such a horrid reputation, then he's done something to deserve it. And we've enough worthless, faithless males on this side of the Atlantic—we don't need to import pedigreed profligates from England."

Gillie's puckish face drew tight. "Proclaim your disinterest all you want, Aria Dunning," she answered with a narrow, meaningful glance at the other girls, "but no doubt, your father will find a titled English gentleman quite interesting."

Aria took the barb squarely, straightening her shoulders. For a long moment, tension crackled between her and Gillie. But it was true . . . what was the use of pretending? Aria knew what these girls and their aristocratic families thought of her father and his lordly manners. His obsession with English nobility and social rank had earned him the nickname of "Squire" in the county. It was well known that "Squire" Dunning never lost the opportunity to associate himself or his English-lady wife with those of noble rank or high military station.

"You're probably right, Gillian Parnell. Sometimes my father shows no better sense than you do." Aria surprised them all into relieved titters and snickers by her retort. "I'm positively parched." Before another moment ticked by, Aria was sailing toward the door.

With sly looks and nods at Gillie, the others jolted up to follow Aria. Each paused before the ornate oval mirrors on the far wall to smooth a curl or pinch a pale cheek into blossom. But Aria was beyond primping and preening; she ached all over from words unsaid and feeling disallowed.

Though the evening was just begun and the party would likely last most of the night, it was already a disaster for all her purposes. Thomas was lost to her, whether by her father's hand or by his own fickleness. Steady, even-tempered Thomas, with his adoring looks and lanky grace. His gentlemanly caring had been easy to accept, then to return. He made everything seem so sure, so comfortable, so contenting. . . . Aria had grown to care for him as she cared for the great stand of regal oak trees for which her beautiful home was named. Now she felt stripped of that security, and she ached silently for the loss she had no luxury to mourn.

Shivering with tension in the drafts of the main hall, she paused to await the other young girls and had to stop herself from grimacing at their giggling and whispering. It had been many months since she was relegated to this flock of unmatched maids. Her presence with them would call attention to the rumored rift between her and Thomas Branscombe. It would be like announcing to everyone that there would be no wedding dance at Royal Oaks in the coming year.

Pausing in the double doorway to fortify herself, she succeeded in drawing the room's attention as well. With a polite, frozen smile firmly in place, she swept past a red-faced Thomas Branscombe to engage their host, the venerable and respected Sir Lowell Stirling, in conversation. No one missed the message intended in her move. As Sir Lowell led her to the center of the floor for the dance, a covert din of speculation broke loose about the room.

One dance was all Aria managed before Howard Parnell, Gillie's father, approached her at the punch table and drew her discreetly aside. When he shoved a cup of the mulled wine punch into her hand, she scowled up into his unsettled face.

"Drink it," he muttered, taking pains to seem quite casual as he paused and glanced about them. She frowned, but sipped from the cup. "It's your father . . ." he informed her.

The strong punch burned her throat, but did not compare with the sudden fire in her cheeks. She set the cup on the nearby table and plied her fan anew to hide her reaction. Little sparks from that heat burned along the nerves in her arms and legs.

"Where is he?"

"This way, in the library." Howard Parnell took her elbow and ushered her from the room. "He's drunk too much and when talk of the conflict up north and independence came up he went half wild. It's out of hand, Aria, tempers are all running high. It'll come to blows."

Hurrying down the hallway, Aria heard her father's drink-hoarse voice raised above a clamor of argument long before they approached the door itself. She stopped, weaving unsteadily as she heard her father.

". . . cowards and traitors who have no sense of their place or duty! We are Englishmen, Robertson, Englishmen first and always!"

She closed her eyes briefly to collect herself and swallowed hard. This on top of all the rest. . . . She had to *do* something. Drawing a shuddering breath, she hurried on to where Howard Parnell stood just outside the half-opened door, nervously adjusting his linen cuffs.

When Aria entered the male bastion of the walnut-paneled library, she was assailed by the heated smells of brandy, cigar smoke, and male sweat. The air was charged and heavy. She steeled herself and pasted an innocent smile upon her features, summoning every whit of feminine guile she possessed.

It was a moment before she was noticed, and several gentlemen rose, hastily rebuttoning their satin waistcoats or resettling their wigs. She stepped farther into the room, flashing a smile about her, but nearly faltering in her pretense when she saw that her father was restrained on one arm by Joseph Ruskin.

"Those who call me a fool for my loyalty to the king do so only to salve their own traitorous consciences. Or perhaps you cannot see how the greedy burghers of Boston play upon your fears. They use you for forty kinds of fools in a game in which we honest, landed folk have no stake!" George Dunning's choleric face nearly matched the crimson of his brocade coat. His eyes were wild and angry and the cords of his short neck were quite visible above his white stock.

He was nearly face to face across the heavy desk with Lemuel Robertson, whose hot temper fully matched his own. And when Robertson opened his mouth for reply, all were astonished that it was Aria Dunning's strong, musical voice that was heard.

"Papa! None here question your loyalty . . . except perhaps your only and quite neglected daughter." Her voice and coquette's smile did not falter as she glided across the wine-colored carpet to her father's side. For a woman to intrude on such a male rite as this gathering was unheard of; for a mere girl, such as herself, to dare it was unthinkable. She prayed they would let her have her indiscretion this once and not hinder her.

"Aria!" Astonishment pulled George Dunning back from the edge of violence and his glare dulled as his eyes fell on his lovely daughter. Ruskin watched the color in his face subside and slowly relinquished his arm.

"Gentlemen, you must forgive my intrusion," she twirled about, sweeping the room with a flirtatious glance, "but your party here has grown quite noisy. And all on account of dreary politics. I cannot fathom what you all find so enticing about such a drab subject when there is gaiety to be had all around you." She whirled prettily at her father's side and slid her arm through his, ignoring his glowering countenance.

"You promised me a dance, Papa, and all I can think is that you've abandoned me totally." Her voice was honeyed and she smiled sweetly up into his florid face. After what seemed an eternity, the tightness about his stubborn mouth eased, letting her have her gambit.

All around the room, muscles relaxed at that subtle signal, and George Dunning cleared his throat testily. "These women, gentlemen—they will have their way with us."

"Vraiment, Papa, toujours," Aria added with a convincing, breathless lilt to her tone as she led him forth. It was the final stroke against his resistance. He had paid dearly to have her tutored in the French tongue and he gloried in her adeptness

at the melodious language at every opportunity—despite the
fact that he could not understand a word she said. Now Aria
had found a compelling application for her learning . . . the
prevention of bloodshed.

Two

Most of the gentlemen in the library were local planters and landowners who had lived in or about Chesterfield County all their lives. They knew George Dunning—his temper, his pretentions, and his weakness for his uncommon daughter. But never had they seen his temper in so dry a tinder. The smallest spark seemed to explode it into full, perilous flame. Indeed, all their tempers were short, each feeling the uncertainty of the times gnawing at their secure, comfortable lives.

George Dunning was among the best-known planters in southern Virginia, famous for his stable of fast horses and for the rich bounty of his fertile lands. While far from being the only royalist about, he was by far the most vocal. He proclaimed and paraded his Tory sentiments at every occasion. Local society had grown tired of suffering his opinions and it was only a matter of time until someone brought him up short and called him to account for his reckless oratory. This evening, disaster had been narrowly averted, and that realization dampened their conversation as they drifted back uneasily toward the main salon.

Soon, only one figure remained in Sir Lowell's library, seated in a deep wing chair that was tucked away to one side of the shuttered windows. A slow smile crept over the square, striking face of the Earl of Penrith and he stubbed out his cigar in the crystal tray on the bachelor chest at his fingertips. He rose and stretched his heavy muscles with sinuous care. Then he straightened his short, embroidered waistcoat and checked the lay of the Belgian lace down his chest. Flexing his shoulders, he set a leisurely course for the main salon.

"Papa, please don't be angry with me," Aria whispered as her father led her to the center of the grand salon and took her hand to join the set of dancers for a lively country reel.

"You overstepped your bounds, Aria," came a curt reply from behind a forced smile. The glow in his eyes might pass for pleasure to another's casual inspection, but Aria read it rightly as indignation.

"Lemuel Robertson always makes you, too angry, Papa—"

"The man thinks like a peasant . . . they all do." George looked at her pointedly. "They haven't the slightest sense of obligation nor care for things of real value . . . like place and distinction."

"Papa—"

"Place, consequence, rank, Aria, everything that truly matters. They would destroy a way of life that has taken centuries to build and refine. It is anarchy they preach . . . worse than stupid, it is criminal!" His face was reddening again and Aria tightened her hand on his.

"Papa, please—" her throat was constricting again with anxiety, "not again, not here. Please just let us dance and enjoy Sir Lowell's evening. Please." The raw entreaty in her eyes finally convinced him and his rigid stance eased.

When the reedy strains of the violins began, both turned perfect, controlled smiles on their fellow dancers. But there was no pleasure in the dance for her; she was simply giddy with relief. And it seemed the crowd caught her mood, for the intensifying noise and laughter had an unburdened quality to it. Talk of rebellion, war, and English oppression was set firmly aside for the time. And the landed gentry of southern Virginia was intent on its pleasures once again.

The Stirlings' grand salon was even grander tonight with the extravagant light of more than a hundred bee's wax tapers.

The costly French furnishings and Persian carpets had been moved aside for dancing and the walls were lined with damask-covered chairs and settees for the ladies. Mirrored glass hung on the massive walls flanking the fireplace, creating the illusion of endless space and unlimited enjoyment. The doors connecting the parlor and dining room to the main salon had been flung back to permit the free flow of guests over the entire first floor of the great house. Wine punch, strong ale, and lemon-spiced applejack were dispensed lavishly with sweetmeats, pastries, and cold dishes, from long tables in the dining room.

The steel-gray eyes of the Earl of Penrith raked the bobbing, weaving figures on the dance floor with detachment until he found the one he sought. As he watched the tilt of Aria's coquettish smile and the innocent provocation of her bare, undulating shoulders, something in those coldly frosted windows of his soul began to warm. He had watched the way she had maneuvered her father earlier—defusing an explosive confrontation. And his worldly gaze had recognized the strength of purpose beneath her soft exaggerations of femininity. The father was a fool, but the daughter certainly was not.

Tynan Bromwell Rutland, Ninth Earl of Penrith, began a slow, calculated circuit of the salon, never allowing his sight to stray far from the captivating young woman who danced with the grace of an ocean wave. It was not her beauty that intrigued him, though she was indeed fashioned to kindle a man's desires. He was a man used to beautiful women of every class, station, and country. And he had come to learn that often there was precious little difference between beautiful women and ugly ones. He sensed strongly that there was more to this slender beauty than silken hair and firm, young flesh. There was something in her that could challenge a man, that could best him if it were not wooed or conquered first.

Tynan Rutland smiled his sardonic best at the ladies who secreted him inviting glances from behind their ivory fans when he passed. Ever a man for a challenge, he vowed silently that he would test that willful beauty in his arms before the night was over.

"I must beg your indulgence, my lord earl." Sir Lowell Stirling made a circumspect nod to his noble houseguest as they stood slightly apart from the dancing. Seeing the younger man's patrician gaze filtered upon him through lidded eyes, the venerable Sir Lowell stiffened. "I received Governor Dunmore's letter only yesterday, and had this event long planned. Otherwise you should have had a more restful welcome to my home."

The earl's mouth curled on one end and his nod of approbation was barely to be seen. His mind seemed to be occupied and he refused to tear himself away from its subject even for his host. Sir Lowell's engrained hospitality was chaffed but not bested by an annoyance like a rude nobleman.

"Then you arrived so late, well after my other guests had arrived . . . when we had looked for you since first light of morning—"

"What pass for roads in this province were clogged with common traffic." Again, the earl's remark seemed addressed to the air itself and Sir Lowell began to redden slightly. Nothing less than a personal request from his old friend, the beleaguered royal governor of the colony, would now make him suffer this arrogant popinjay under his roof.

"I trust my dear wife has seen to your comfort. I fear I was otherwise occupied."

"So I have seen." The earl's tone flattened further. "You show a fine leg in the dance, Sir Lowell." His steel-gray eyes glanced at his host, then away.

Sir Lowell reddened fully at last and squared his shoulders. "I shall introduce a toast to you for all my guests. It will save us both the tedium of numerous introductions."

"Don't bother." At last the earl came to life, turning fully to Sir Lowell. His lounging posture now corrected, he seemed to grow remarkably in both directions. His formidable physical presence was now trained intently upon his host's slightest motion. "I prefer to make my own introductions. It allows me freer movement among your colorful colonial folk."

"But of course." Sir Lowell nodded slightly, a vein in his temple throbbing.

"But do me one courtesy, sir." The earl caught his sleeve as he made to withdraw. "Tell me the name of that interesting blond creature . . ." His sharpened gaze pierced a trail across the salon to where Aria had just finished a set of dances and was plying her fan briskly amid a sea of male adoration.

Sir Lowell shifted about, knowing immediately who it must be that had caught the earl's jaded eye. He drew a satisfied breath and even managed a courtly smile, thinking of the way Aria Dunning would set him down a peg.

"That is Miss Aria Dunning, sir. She is bespoke by Mister Thomas Branscombe, of Brantley House."

"Is she now?" The earl relaxed back again on one leg and peered about the room almost idly. "And who is that fortunate gentleman . . . Mister Branscombe?"

Sir Lowell craned his neck to locate Thomas Branscombe and scowled briefly at the sight of the fellow bending attentively over the Morland girl. "The tall gentleman in brown, near the door, I believe." Sir Lowell rocked down on his heels and noted the way the earl scrutinized the pair while hardly appearing to even look at them. And he made a major adjustment in his estimate of the "popinjay" he now harbored under his roof. The man was more than he seemed. And the thought gave Sir Lowell an uneasy moment as he excused himself.

Standing in a mixed circle of friends with her back to the main body of guests, Aria plied her fan feverishly. Her shoulders ached, her face seemed frozen into a parody of a smile, and her nerves screamed for relief. She gritted her teeth and tried to seem interested in her father's talk of horses and hunting. The last strains of the country dance had just died, and for a moment, the buzz of human voices was all that could be heard. The air was becoming stifling and she passed a warm palm up over her damp cheek, sending it farther up to inspect the outline of her hair. In the midst of the reveler's heat, she was struck with a curious chill that raised gooseflesh on her shoulders and arms. Turning toward the French doors leading onto the veranda, she found Sir Lowell just now ordering them opened.

It was the strain, the tension of this horrid, interminable evening. She simply had to get away for a few moments, to collect herself before she screamed.

She turned for the stairs and found herself confronted by a man, not two yards away, staring at her. The bold intensity of his study took her aback and her fan slipped from her fingers. For an instant she returned his stare. And in that betraying moment, she drank in more about the man than was prudent for any lady to absorb.

He was tall, though not quite so tall as Thomas. But his shoulders were uncommonly wide and his upper body gave him an aspect that spoke bluntly of power. He was wigged with a fine, shoulder-length peruke and his dark blue clothing seemed exquisitely adorned with cording and fine lace ruffles at jabbot and wrists. The last thing Aria saw as she turned abruptly back to her companions was the gentleman's waistcoat—shorter than was customary and adorned with something like Chinese embroidery. She stood a moment, unable to see anything but the dark intensity of his formidable outline as it was lit from behind by the nearby candlestand. And she knew without a doubt that she had just encountered the Earl of Penrith.

She lifted her chin and smiled absently at whoever was speaking, and that unnerving chill possessed her again. Was he the cause of that bewitched sensation? She threaded her tense fingers together and had to stop herself from fleeing the salon.

Her torture was short-fired. His broad shoulder soon appeared in the corner of her eye. She pretended to ignore him at first, but her senses were screaming awareness of his presence.

"Miss Dunning, I believe." His voice rumbled forth, a deep vibration that played with dismaying intimacy across her bare skin.

She stepped back from the edge of her group before turning to face him, buying time to prepare herself for what she instinctively knew would be an assault on her ladylike decorum. And when she looked up into his square, sensual face, she knew it was all a loss. Nothing could have prepared her for the overwhelming impact of his potent maleness, his aura of tightly held control.

"Yes?" Her question sounded almost breathless to her ears. Her mind was spinning. Poor Alice's assessment had been perfectly on the beam. He *was* frightening, though in a way she could never have imagined until now. And instantly she confirmed Sissy Ruskin's observations as well . . . and Gillie's. He was handsome, and worldly, and arrogant, and elegant . . . all those things and one more. It was that something that set Aria's nerves ringing and made her straighten as she felt a curious drawing in her middle.

"Would you do me the honor of joining me in the next dance?"

As he spoke, her eyes fastened on his full, sensual lips and noted the straight, white teeth they hid and the tiny lines at their corners that they could not hide. Those lines spoke of frequent disdain, perhaps of cruelty or indulged vice.

"I am sorry, sir." She picked up her fan where it dangled from her wrist and flipped it open. This time her voice seemed all honey and invitation. She was aghast at the shambles this one man was making of her whole being. "I do not know you."

"You may not have my name, sweet lady, but I'll wager you know me better than any woman here." His tone was not set to flatter. He seemed to be almost taunting her.

Instinctively she stepped back . . . into Howard Parnell, who was holding forth on the virtues of black and tan hounds. The same instant, George Dunning looked up and caught the distress in his daughter's face and the unmistakably personal attentions of that nameless gentleman who had been staring at her earlier. With his usual finesse, George Dunning's pride blew into full gale.

"I hear by your voice, sir, that you are a stranger in these parts," he declared, drawing nearby guests from their own conversation into his. "Here, sir, you do not approach a man's daughter without benefit of introduction."

Aria's heart skipped several beats. *It was happening again.* Furiously she swept the sea of drink-warmed faces leering at the mounting spectacle and slipped between her father and the earl. Grasping her father's arm tightly, she forced him to look down into her face. Her voice came stronger and steadier than she thought possible.

"Papa, the gentleman has only requested a dance. And Sir Lowell thinks well enough of him to have honored him with an invitation." Her eyes pleaded for restraint.

There was an agonizing pause before the earl's voice issued forth. "Tynan Rutland, at your service, sir."

"Well, Mister Rutland." George eased as he evaluated the earl quite deliberately. "It seems one who has found favor with both my host and my daughter should not be denied." He turned Aria about and nodded extravagantly toward the earl. "George Dunning, sir, and my daughter, Aria."

"My real pleasure, sir." The earl's nod was performed as he gazed intently at Aria's pale face.

The discordant strains of tuning strings came together at last in an invitation to dancers.

"Miss Dunning." The earl held out a large, muscular hand to her and she felt as if she were being swallowed up when she accepted it and felt it close over hers. She hoped he couldn't feel how icy her hands were through her gloves.

Holding her hand high, like a trophy, he led her to a prominent place among the dancers and took her other hand behind her back. Aria stared straight ahead, silent and excruciatingly aware of how many eyes were trained upon them. Her insides felt like warm putty as he pressed against her skirts from behind. Her wits were scattering as she felt the heat from his large frame radiating into her bare shoulders. Then they were moving into the comforting pattern of the opening promenade.

Effortlessly, they moved together, hand in hand. She could feel his warm breath against her neck as he held her back against his muscular chest. For his size, he seemed quite adept at the dance and Aria tried to concentrate on her own small steps. But twice the lace ruffle of his jabot raked the top of her shoulder and to her beleaguered senses it seemed like a bold caress. Where moments before her limbs seemed bloodless, now they pulsed with a life of their own.

"How do you find the colonies, sir?" she asked politely as they turned.

"Simply board a ship bound westerly."

She stiffened and his sardonic laughter rumbled forth. "I find them far more civilized than it was rumored." The smirk in his voice remained. "This gathering is a fair counterfeit of a genteel gathering in the country—outside of London."

"Well, if you find us colonists a tedious and dreary lot, there is a simple remedy, sir." Aria poured honey into her tone.

"Oh?"

"Board a ship bound in an eastward direction." She delivered it with a malicious sweetness that caught him off guard.

His smirk became an intrigued smile that hid his further thoughts.

Confusion poured alluring color into her cheeks as they faced one another again and their bodies were brought together after each set of small steps. As they began the second promenade, Aria felt more than heard his laughter.

"Your battle is becoming the curiosity of the room," he murmured low.

"What battle, sir? Am I warring with your lead?" She flushed deeper as she dipped to his far side. "I was not aware of it."

"Your determination to avoid looking at me. You work at it too hard."

But she *had* avoided looking at him, and when her chin raised, she admitted why. His strong features were blunted just short of male beauty, but were all the more sensual for it. Prominent cheekbones and heavy, dark brows gave his face a commanding hauteur. His straight nose was squared at the tip and his eyes seemed chilled by worldly experience. She felt her stomach turn over and suffered a return of that same shocking tingling in her breasts. He was indeed a dangerous man.

"I do not avoid you, sir." Her tension mounted. "I fear my thoughts are elsewhere."

"If you mean Branscombe, he's no doubt sampling that dark heifer's wares in the shadows somewhere about." His voice was low and suggestive as he pulled her closer than the step required.

Aria's spine went rigid and she pushed away. Her pain over losing Thomas was scarcely contained in her straining heart . . . and this arrogant English swine taunted her with Thomas's faithlessness.

"Keep your desultory thoughts to yourself, sir. To leave you standing in the middle of the dance could mean your serious peril."

"Your father?" He snorted half a laugh and succeeded in making Aria's face turn a deeper shade of scarlet.

Her face came up, burning. She was furious . . . and anger was just what she needed.

"Beware, your lordship. I agreed to this one dance with you only to avoid unpleasantness," she gritted out, setting his drifting hand back in place at her waist.

"That is twice tonight you have saved your father from his lower impulses. Are you sure he's worth it?"

It was the final thrust. Aria pulled her hands from his and whirled to drop a brief, angry curtsy before striding from the dance floor. Oddly enough, the music ended just after the earl bowed dramatically in return, making it appear they had only parted a bit early.

The earl marked her destination, and a knowing smile crept over his strong face. He had played this game before.

Aria's sight was filled with a crimson haze that obscured time and place. She sailed through the nearby doors, not realizing they led onto the veranda until the cooler night air brought her to her senses a moment later. She flew to the wooden banister and leaned heavily on it, gulping the night-heavy air and ordering her quaking knees to stop. It was a long, chaotic moment before she calmed enough to take a deep breath and smooth the front of her bodice. Her hands shook as she slid them along the railing, escaping further from the hateful noise of the revelry inside.

She paced until her churning stomach eased. She was sick to death of men and their cock's-pride vanities, their leering and unceasing demands. Thomas . . . her father . . . that loathsome English sw—

"Oh!" Her face came up as she startled back. Her meanderings had taken her to the far end of the house, along the vine-trellised veranda. In the darkness, she had nearly walked into two figures pressed deep into the shadows. Her face turned scarlet with chagrin as she averted her eyes and made to leave. "I'm sorry, I—"

"Aria?" Thomas's voice was strangely hoarse, but recognizable, and his lanky form emerged into the meager light.

"Thomas?" Aria disbelieved it as she said it. His powdered wig was awry, his stock was unwrapped, and his waistcoat gaped open vulgarly.

"But not alone," came a half-slurred feminine voice that jolted Aria's heart back to duty. Janette Morland emerged far enough from the shadows to wrap her arm about Thomas's waist and pull his arm back around her shoulders. Her coif was askew and her mouth seemed bruised and thick. Her front-lacing bodice had been loosened to reveal most of her breasts. Her eyes burned dully at Aria, glazed by passion and drink.

Aria's stomach surged at the tawdry spectacle and she stepped back stiffly to keep herself from falling. Her hand came up to shield her mouth and she struggled for breath. Was this what Thomas had wanted from her earlier? Was this what they would have been like? The dull, accusing pain in Thomas's face stabbed her cruelly.

"Good evening, sir, miss," came a deep voice from behind her. Someone was taking her arm and turning her away. "Come, Aria."

She saw nothing but a broad, velvet-covered shoulder and heavy arm that commanded her along. Stunned, she could not resist and soon found herself halfway around the house and descending the stone steps to the garden. Reacting belatedly to the sting of what she had witnessed, she jerked that unrelenting arm to a furious halt and met its master.

"Let go of me!"

"Not yet." The earl overcame her resistance with ludicrous ease and dragged her out along the stone path into the gardens.

"Stop this at once!" She tried to dig her spool-shaped heels into the path to resist him. He was treating her like a wayward child who tussled and rebelled against an angry parent.

"Please, let me go!" Furious with the pleading in her tone, she clamped her lips shut and struggled in silence as he forced her along behind him.

He released her abruptly and she staggered with surprise. Catching herself, she searched her surroundings wildly. The house was not in sight. They were in a secluded corner of the gardens, surrounded by high topiary hedges and the smell of night-fragrant jasmine.

"Well?" His muscular arms crossed over his broad, luxuriously clad chest and he stared at her tauntingly.

"Well what?" she spat, her breast heaving with the evening's accumulation of rage. Her fists clenched at her sides as she fought for self-control.

"Aren't you going to weep or rant, or faint . . . or something?" His insolent grin perfected his unpleasantness.

"How dare you?" she growled, feeling bolder for the steam in her blood. "What I feel or do is none of your business." She paced toward him, heedless of a prickle of warning. "No doubt you find such humiliation quite amusing." Clasping her bare shoulders with shaking hands, she began to pace, feeling his eyes probing and assessing her.

"No tears." He made a judgmental, *tsk*ing sound. "Perhaps he felt you played too coolly with his affections and sought warmer shores. You've ignored him all evening." His accusation brought her up short and she stalked back to face him, stopping a prudent arm's length away.

"Is loving a game in which a man keeps a tally? He professed to need *my* true love only this evening," she pointed furious again, "on that very veranda!"

"But you did not love him." The earl's voice was low and his tone insistently intimate.

"That's not true." Stung by the implication that she might have ill used Thomas Branscombe, she whirled away, stiffening and tucking her arms about her middle as if to hold herself together. She couldn't think about it now or allow herself to feel the loss. There was the rest of this cursed night to get through—facing Janette and her conniving mother, coping with her volatile, unpredictable father, and being scrutinized by the entirety of their local society. After a long moment, her voice came small and very flat. "I did care. I cared a great deal for Thomas."

It was as though a great weight settled on her shoulders, rounding them and bowing her head. The earl's face tightened and he scowled.

"But you didn't love him as a man." His voice was compelling and surprised her with its nearness. He was directly behind her and took her shoulders, turning her around. But before she could free her hands or protest, his muscular arms had crushed her to him and he held her surprised gaze in the steel trap of his own.

"You didn't love him like this—" His firm lips captured

hers, following the feeble protest of her movements. As her resistance died, his mouth gentled on hers, testing the softness, the curved luxuries of her lips.

She could barely catch her breath. Her head was reeling; her knees were turning liquid under her. The mesmerizing feel of his body against hers blotted out everything but the delicious feeling of his mouth on hers. Starved for breath, she parted her lips and was stunned at the way his warm tongue traced the opening of her mouth. Never before had she dreamt kissing could be like this . . . with open mouths and . . .

She grasped his elegant coat for support. Her lips opened farther, inviting his exploration. Heat poured through her limbs and seemed to lodge in her loins. And in the middle of her, there grew a strange, gnawing ache, like a hunger. She pressed against him, needing, wanting to be closer, to stop this tingling that had begun in her breasts.

His mouth slanted across hers and drifted along her flushed cheek. She could not open her eyes or move as he brought his hand up to touch her face and throat. Half crushing, half lifting her against him, he brought his kisses lower on her skin. He nibbled her shoulder, her throat, then the bare silk of her exposed chest. Trills of new pleasure played on her nerves and waves of heat surged through her, wrought by the hunger of his lips on hers.

She was weakened, pliant under his marauding kisses when his husky voice washed over her and seeped under her skin.

"You could not have loved him like this, Aria." His mouth covered hers possessively and he bound her to him tightly. "If you had returned his kisses as you have mine," his whisper flowed over her face and down her throat like warm honey, "he would never have let you out of his sight."

He pressed her warm, expectant mouth, then kissed her deeply. His breathing became ragged and his body began to heat dangerously against hers.

He crushed her to him with a ferocity that snapped her eyes open. And what she saw stopped her breath. His steel-gray eyes were glowing like white-hot silver in his desire-darkened face. There was no taunt, no coldness, no conceit—only the demand of raw, terrifying hunger.

"Let me have you—now." He whispered as if claiming a right from days of old.

It was as though he demanded her very soul as a sacrifice to his desires. Stunned and trembling, she stared up at him, her green eyes huge and still dark-centered with the aftereffects of his kisses.

"Let me go!" she demanded thickly, an edge of fear sharpening her tone as it finally did her passion-dulled wits. Shrinking and twisting in his grip, she could barely put an inch between them. "If you hurt me, you'll pay for it—I swear—"

She wrestled against his overpowering strength, realizing how little it would tax his strength to take her here, against her will.

"Aria, I want you," he commanded with a deep, rasping growl. "And I'll have you—it's no use fighting it—"

Then with some instinct older than the collective memory of womanhood, she went still in his grasp and felt his straining arms relax slowly, in turn. Alive now with the evening's accumulated fury, she looked directly into his dark, muscular face. For an instant she quailed. He was power, desire, excitement—danger embodied.

She saw the heat of anticipation in his eyes, and knew that once his deed was done, the ice of contempt would replace it. His mouth curled sardonically as he bent his head to claim his prize. Aria had managed to free her arm from his side and now brought a hand up slowly as he covered her throbbing lips with his.

Sharp, jagged pain tore through his face and he was thrown back by a wild explosion of resistance in his arms. The blood pounding in his head temporarily dulled his reactions and it was an instant before he could grab his cheek and react.

But Aria was already well out of reach, flying through an opening in the hedges. The throb in his head brightened briefly into true rage. But long years of military training had taught him to trust little to his first, reckless instincts. And so he stood, holding the side of his face.

Slowly, the tensed masses of his shoulders began to uncoil. He reached almost casually into his waistcoat pocket for a handkerchief and pressed the cool, silky cloth against his burning cheek. There was no stain of blood on it when he drew it, but he stared at it until a slow smile spread over his striking face. He tucked the cloth back into his pocket and pulled his waistcoat down, holding it in place as he drew a deep breath.

He strolled with studied laziness about the secluded court, letting his steel-gray gaze flow over the dark curves and angles of the fastidious greenery. Their grace and symmetry were oddly pacifying. Then at length, he turned languid steps toward the great house, preparing himself for whatever his indiscretion would cost him.

The bright light and the smells of sweat and strong spirits assaulted Aria's senses as she stepped through the doorway into the side hall of Sir Lowell's home. She sagged against the wall and closed her eyes, trying to swallow her turmoil. The entire night had been one disaster after another . . . with injury added to injury, insult to insult. And now she'd just narrowly escaped being . . .

It was suddenly all she could do to remain standing.

She felt her way along the wall toward what she hoped would be the center hall. Somehow she had to make it upstairs, to the ladies' rooms, and repair any damage that might have been done to her appearance. And afterward, she was going home, no matter if she had to walk the muddy miles herself!

"Aria! My lovely daughter." Her father's broad face was beaming satisfaction as he caught her starting up the stairs and clasped her unwary wrist. "I was looking for you."

"No, Papa—" she whispered, her face burning as she resisted his tugs. "I must go upstairs, I simply must!"

"Nonsense." George Dunning ran a perceptive eye over his daughter, and though his gaze narrowed, he gestured to her exquisite gown and said loudly, "You are the picture of loveliness, Aria. There is naught you can do to improve upon perfection. Come, now."

He pulled her behind him to a settee just inside the parlor doors, where Sir Lowell, her mother, and Dame Margareth Stirling were gathered. George's expansive mood was in stark contrast to his earlier dark turbulence, and Aria was experienced enough with his caprices to know there must be a cause. He pulled her to a halt in front of the settee, before her mother and Dame Margareth. She managed a tight smile at the dame and kissed her mother's pale cheek, praying nothing looked amiss.

"We have just had the most startling news, Aria." George planted himself between her and the doorway and gazed at her benevolently. Aria noted that Sir Lowell chose that moment to check his shoe buckles. "Sir Lowell has informed me that the gentleman you danced with a bit ago . . . is the Earl of Penrith." George's eyes gleamed with unabashed calculation. "A real English earl—how fortunate we are to have him visiting with us. And to think that I mistook his attentions to you. We simply must make amends. We cannot have him thinking we Virginians are country clods who do not recognize and appreciate men of quality."

Aria's face drained as she sought her mother's gaze. Marian Dunning caught her daughter's distraught look and allowed a tight, stoic smile to bloom on her face. Dame Margareth's enthusiasm was equally restrained. Neither offered a comment.

"Sir Lowell tells me the family is quite old . . . with fortunes that have fallen, but always managed to rise again. Yes, truly one of the oldest families—"

"Really, father." Aria felt bile rising in the back of her

throat. He was glorying in the importance of the rakehell who attempted her just now in the gardens! If no one else would put a stop to the spectacle of her father's humiliating fawning and groveling, she would. "I find it difficult to believe that any family can actually be older than any other . . . seeing how, as the church teaches, we all had the same First Father. I propose that his family is not better . . . only a bit better documented than the rest. And what a dubious benefit it is to actually know the accumulated sins of generations of one's forebears."

Sir Lowell's guffaw was unstifled, and portly Dame Margareth's shoulders jiggled with her mirth. Seldom did anyone get George Dunning's goat, much less with such thoroughness.

"Aria!" George's drink-merry face had reddened further and he turned on his daughter with indignation. It was her saving that there were not more witnesses to her insolence. "Disrespect for our betters is unseemly. In another time, such talk would have been counted treason and dealt with quite harshly."

"It is fortunate I did not live in another time. I find this one quite trying enough," she bit out, knowing she tested her father's limits. She turned to Sir Lowell, who was examining his shoe buckles again. "I am not feeling well, Sir Lowell. Perhaps that is why I am puckish . . . this late hour of night. I hope you will all excu—"

Her father grabbed her wrist as she tried to withdraw, and when she turned back, his face was a mask of civility. He was gazing past her to the casual approach of the Earl of Penrith, warning her by his savage grip on her arm that she must stay and be silent. Heart thudding in her chest, Aria managed to fabricate a look of polite disinterest and gazed fixedly at her mother, whose sudden preoccupation with her gloves and fan was of little comfort.

"My lord earl." George was bowing a bit too extravagantly, calling the nobleman into their circle. "You must join us, sir, and allow us to welcome you properly to our county. I fear we were not fully introduced before."

The earl's stride was quite leisurely as he slowed and rounded the settee where the older ladies were seated. Drolly, he mused that this did not look like the outraged citizenry, poised to demand a blood-price for his attempt at the wench. As he approached, several other guests on his far side turned to watch him and then returned quickly to their talk with wider eyes.

Aria felt her heart stop as her father jerked her hand, ordering her around beside him to greet the earl. And when her stubborn gaze was finally forced up to confront her tormentor, her legs nearly buckled under her. The earl's cool air was sharp counterpoint to the savage red streaks that marred his cheek from temple to chin. And while all stared at his wound, he affected a pleasantly amused expression that dismissed all their speculations.

"Ah, Master Dunning, I believe." The earl's jaded gaze slid over Aria's tense frame and he smiled fully. While the group was still reeling from the dazzling change in his already handsome countenance, he continued. "But I feel I already know you and your family quite intimately."

Aria's face burned with humiliation at the blatant way he flaunted his degenerate behavior toward her in the face of her family. His smugness, his mocking civility—all while he bore the badge of her resistance before her father's truckling nose and boasted of his "intimacy" with her! The reference was unmistakable to anyone with eyes to see.

She was horrified to think her father so dull-witted where his own daughter was concerned. But in the instant that followed, her father sent her a knowing, appraising look. He knew! He knew and still he played the groveling sycophant! A ringing began in her ears and the blood seemed to drain too quickly from her head. Sir Lowell was saying something . . .

". . . of the opinion that no family can possibly be of greater age than any other—owing that we are all descended from Father Adam."

George Dunning's punitive grip on his daughter's wrist grew tighter, as the earl threw back his elegant head and laughed resoundingly. Sir Lowell joined him and Dame Margareth, and even her mother managed a bit of mirth. All at her expense, she snapped silently.

"Indeed, miss? Are your opinions always so droll and insightful?" The earl stepped toward her, plying that same false but still dazzling smile. Her father released his secretive grip and stepped to one side . . . abandoning her to him.

Aria felt all eyes questioning her response and she could not shrink. "No, your lordship. I fear some of my opinions are not nearly so amusing. But then, perhaps it takes very little to amuse you." Aria practically felt her father's furious intake of breath.

"Ho!" The earl clasped his muscular hand over his heart as if taking another wound. "You cannot think me so shallow, miss, until you know me better." His leering smile was perfectly gauged to ignite her fury.

"I think that prospect rather dim." Aria's fine jaw tightened, heedless of her father's ire.

"Indeed not," George interjected with false congeniality. "Perhaps, Earl, you would do us the honor of having dinner at our home, Royal Oaks, this next week . . . perhaps Thursday. I have heard you are interested in sport and I have a slew of fat birds in my fields."

Aria felt the earl's gaze hot upon her and her stomach turned over. Her father knew the earl had earned the scratches on his face and still he invited the arrogant rogue to dinner. It was as if he were inviting the earl to—

She closed her eyes and swayed, putting her fingertips to her temples. "Excuse me," she breathed, avoiding their eyes and gathering her skirts shakily. "I think the exhilaration of this evening has taken its toll." She swept through the nearby doorway and into the center hall before anyone could move to halt her. Marian Dunning rose immediately and avoided her husband's glare as she nodded silently to her host and the earl, then followed her daughter.

Three

Tempers were boiling like long-watched pots. Angry mutters and low threats beat like a mounting tide of fury against one lone figure in the taproom of the White Stag Inn. Some planters sat on the scuffed and ring-marked tables, while others propped their muddied riding boots on the rough wooden chairs or leaned against the clean, whitewashed stone walls. The smells of saddle leather, tobacco smoke, and spilled ale mingled in the damp, heavily charged air. The intrepid beams of the afternoon sun seemed almost reluctant to enter so volatile a gathering. The assembly of men nearly duplicated the group that had been present in Sir Lowell Stirling's library not quite a week ago. But now, there were no silk shirts, no powdered wigs, and no reason for restraint. Grudges long nursed had begun to surface, loosened by numerous pints of ale and drafts of strong rum.

"We're not treated like true Englishmen," Joseph Ruskin charged, bringing a hard fist down on the tabletop before him, "except when 'tis time for handin' our taxes over or billetin' their lobsterbacks in our houses! I'll be sendin' my boys when the time comes—mebbe I'll go myself!"

George Dunning stood his ground, sweating profusely, his lips foam-flecked and his eyes red with anger and drink. He raised his clenched fists and shook them so that his whole frame trembled.

"Fools! Small-minded bumpkins! You are not fit to be called Englishmen—"

"More like we're sick to death of being *called* Englishmen, taxed like Englishmen, without havin' the rights of 'em!" Lemuel Robertson jumped from his seat beside Ruskin to confront his old adversary. "And we're sick to death of you, George Dunning, an' havin' to suffer your damnable opinions! They spilt the first blood, man—but they haven't spilt the last! Blood'll flow in this county, too," he ground out ominously. "See if it don't!"

"Would they had put a few more treasonous swine beneath the sod—" George spat, then jolted back furiously to avoid Robertson's bone-hard fist. Exploding at last with pent-up fury, George swung back. But the arc of his swing was too broad and laid him open to the younger Robertson's well-placed blow. Flailing back, pain ramming through his midsection, George lost his footing on the damp planking and fell against the corner of a table. His limp body thudded against the bare floor in the abrupt silence. A bright crimson slash opened over his temple and began to spill, and the blood made his ruddy face seem pale by comparison.

The lone sound of Robertson's ragged breathing seemed magnified in the strained silence. Each gentleman present groped through his shock for understanding of what had just transpired. For them it was as though the first blood of the rebellion had just been shed. And the specter of civil war was no longer a distant menace.

"Well, gentlemen," came a coldly amused voice from the side of the taproom, "what have we here? A neighborly dispute?"

The Englishman's voice brought up a host of resentful eyes, many of which narrowed with true anger at the sight of the imperious Earl of Penrith leaning one shoulder against the low door frame. Whether he was a guest of Sir Lowell or not, they had had enough of lordly manners and English pretentions.

"Nothing your lordship would understand." Robertson turned recklessly to face him, still nursing an aching hand. "A dispute over the fight for rights and freedom."

"Sir, in that you err." The earl pushed off from the door frame, entering the low-ceilinged room completely, permitting through the doorway a glimpse of several men behind him, watching, outside in the yard. The earl's broad, muscular frame seemed to crowd the room as he approached the group. His eyes were like chips of gray flint. "Perhaps you have forgotten that little over a century ago all England was torn with strife over these issues you wave about so sacrosanctly. My great grandfather fought on the fields of Moresby when he was little more than a lad. Indeed, the very lands and titles to which I am yoked were bought with a blood-price. The periodic spilling of our blood in some greater service seems to be what we Rutlands do best.

"Let me put it to you gentlemen." A cold smile crept over his face as he relaxed back on one leg and slapped his thigh with his deerskin gloves. "Little of real value in history has been achieved without the shedding of blood. Mankind's progress may be traced in a river of gore. And if you would make something of value here," his light eyes glittered with challenge as he looked straight at Robertson, "you will have to bleed for it."

The unearthly silence raised the hairs on their necks. The earl's piercing stare drifted from one nervous face to another, questioning, challenging. One after one, they looked down or at one another, their faces coloring.

The earl moved to stand over George Dunning's sprawled, unconscious frame. As he stooped to press a hand to George's thick neck, Robertson's anger finally overrode his better sense. He lurched forward, but Joseph Ruskin caught him and held him back.

The earl's dark head came up quickly. Beneath the fine broadcloth of his coat, his muscles were coiled for defense or attack. He seemed almost pleased by Robertson's attempt. Breathing was suspended about the taproom as he rose slowly, letting Robertson feel his peril.

Finally, the Earl of Penrith made a subtle, but unmistakable, display of relaxing his taut body and he straightened his short waistcoat deliberately. "You have not killed him." He glanced about him with sardonic luxury. "But he will need assistance home."

The silence was interrupted by the sound of boot heels on bare boards near the main door of the taproom. First two, then three more men hurried from the establishment. The earl's eyes were lidded and his mouth curled on one end.

"You colonists are a virtuous lot. Where is your Christian charity? Or is it, like your hospitality, in short supply just now?" His sensual mouth broke into a broad, taunting smile and he crouched by George Dunning's body, reaching for his limp arms. In a mere second, the stocky squire's body was hefted up and onto the earl's broad shoulders. Together, they barely cleared the ceiling and the doorway out.

The indolence of late summer floated on the air; the lush, mature green blanketed the woods and meadowlands surrounding Royal Oaks. Aria sat in the windowseat of the upstairs parlor, drinking in the sun's tempered evening light and trying to work on an embroidered hem for a new petticoat. Glancing secretively about the empty room, she kicked off her stiff, new day shoes and pulled her feet up under her skirts to sit cross-legged. Sighing with relief, she put her head back against the wall behind her and gazed out upon the panorama of Royal Oak, her home, her life.

The valley upriver broadened just at the edge of the Dunning estate and swept in a broad plain for several miles before narrowing again through the foothills below them. The Almighty Himself had set his heel down here and flattened out a place for the grandest, richest farmland in all creation. . . . So George Dunning had told his adoring little daughter, long ago. Though grown now and wiser, Aria still recalled that sense of wonder and belonging each time she paused to gaze out over the spectacular valley. She sat in high vantage point in the stately Georgian brick house, staring at the blue-fringed hills in the distance and the gold-rimmed clouds drifting peaceably above them. The patchwork of bounty-laden fields in the distance formed a pattern of flattened diamonds. The smells of drying hay and ripening apples from the orchard below wafted through the open window, soothing her restless heart.

For the last week, she had been in turmoil . . . confronting her father's increasing moodiness by day and battling her own sense of loss and her stubborn desires in her thoughts and dreams at night.

Since that night, her startling reaction to the cynical Earl of Penrith haunted her, pressing her with intense physical memories of pleasures she had never imagined existed. She wondered now why she had never felt such things when Thomas kissed her, when Thomas pressed her to him, when Thomas looked at her with need in his eyes. Perhaps it took a base and sensual rogue to awaken similar feelings in her. Certainly the discovery of this carnal part of her nature could bring no good with it. She shivered unexpectedly and scowled, shaking her head to rid herself of the taint of it.

Her uneasiness with her self-discovery was matched in full by her new and troubling view of her father. George Dunning had always been a doting parent. He had personally taken up the reins of her education from the very first, even before he realized she would never have the companionship of brothers or sisters. The squire had hired tutors from the continent and a stern governess to implement his will; his daughter was to be raised in the strict fashion of the continent's highest nobility. Fortunately for Aria, she had inherited her mother's delicate beauty but not her delicate constitution. Showing her father's robust vigor, she had schooled in riding and the dance, as well as letters, languages, the arts, and music. Nothing was spared, no expense, no trouble, when it came to the preparation of his daughter. And never once did Aria stop to wonder what she was being prepared for.

Her privileged world now seemed to be unraveling through

her very fingers and she was powerless to stop it. The end of her betrothal to Thomas, her best hope for a marriage, was due to her father's intervention—she doubted it no longer. Of late, her father did not act like her father. Increasingly, his laughter had a bitter ring to it, his legendary temper seemed to itch for exercise.

Sequestered in the timeless rhythms of life at Royal Oaks, she had not guessed at the deep divisions that had grown between her father and their life-long neighbors in recent years. The flow of guests to once popular Royal Oaks had dwindled markedly in the last three years; of late, only the staunchest family friends visited. George Dunning seemed entrenched, isolated from the rest of the county by his extreme loyalism to a distant and disdainful crown.

It did not take a great wit to see what her father had in mind for her now. The Earl of Penrith was coming to dinner tomorrow night and Aria knew from that humiliating encounter at Sir Lowell's that her father expected her to ingratiate herself with His Lordship. The earl was wealthy and unmarried . . .

Aria sailed her birch hoop of needlework across the room and jumped up to pace. He was thinking of finagling a match between them! Aria's body went rigid as the details of that degrading scene at the party came flooding back to her. He had invited the earl to dine, even knowing that Aria's refusal of him was scratched into his very skin.

Could her father honestly believe the earl's arrogance and lechery would be curtailed once he crossed their portal and sat in their parlor? She tucked her arms about her waist with a jerk. Her father was a man of the world—he should know better than—

She ran to the windowseat to throw up the window and breathe deeply. Her heart was thudding in her chest and she tried to calm it by taking steady, even gulps of the sweet and tranquil air. A plume of dust rose from the road that wound its way through the fields to the heart of Royal Oaks. She sighed irritably, thinking it was her father returning from town.

She was in no mood to confront him. Likely, he would have been drinking and discussing politics, neither of which was likely to have improved his changeable disposition.

But her eyes widened as they took in two or three horses moving at a fast clip. She squinted and tried to make out more as they rounded the bend and entered the canopy of elms that overhung the road to the main house. As far as she could see through the dust and foliage, one horse was riderless and she did not recognize her father's distinctive seat on either of the other two. Her flushed face was pressed against the window glass and her hands braced against the sash. Through a break in the trees, she saw that the third horse was indeed occupied, by a limp form that was trussed over it sideways. She bolted for the door.

Downstairs, they had seen the riders approaching by now and the house servants were clogging the stairs, craning their necks. Aria pushed by and through them, hurrying down for what she knew would be bad news of some sort.

"Joseph, quickly—" she ordered the aging butler as he hurried from the back of the house into the center hall, dragging his dark coat on as he came. "Get Drucilla—there's been an accident!" Jolted afresh by her own conclusion, she grabbed another servant by the sleeve and sent her into the east wing for her mother. Continuing down the polished wooden staircase, she grabbed handfuls of her calamanco skirts and ran headlong across the inlaid checkerboard marble of the center hall, headed for the massive front doors.

"Help me, Jennie!" she ordered a serving woman, tugging at the great front doors. Then she was running across the small colonaded porch and down the steps into the dirt of the road, where the horses were stopping. Her heart was beating in her throat—the form draped over the saddle was indeed her father. She ran to him, stunned by his slack, reddened face and the dried blood on his head and clothes.

"Papa!" she touched his gray-templed head in horror. When she looked up, it was the handsome and cynical face of the

Earl of Penrith that met her gaze. "What's happened? What have you done to him?" she snapped, incensed by the earl's amused scrutiny of her reaction.

"I? I am the one who brought him home." The earl threw one muscular leg over the front of his saddle and dismounted by sliding insolently down the horse's side. "He was drinking and came to blows with one of your charming neighbors."

Biting her lower lip, she turned to her father and lifted his head to see the wound. Her face drained of color, but she clamped a tight hand on her emotions.

"I don't think there's cause for great alarm." The earl stepped close behind her and lifted her father's dangling ruffled neckpiece, dropping it disinterestedly. "Just a bump on the head. Otherwise, I would have found him a closer sickbed."

Aria's anxiety for her father mingled with her pride and together they produced trembling hands and uncharacteristic silence. She would not trust herself to speak. The other rider had dismounted and began to untie the leather straps that held George Dunning on the horse. They soon formed a chair of sorts with their arms and carried his limp form toward the front doors, waving aside servants' attempts to take over their burden.

"Oh, my God in Heaven—" Marian Dunning met them at the doors and immediately fell back to let them enter. Her beautiful face was as pale as the fragile lace about her bodice. "What's happened?" her hand covered her mouth and her brown eyes widened. "There's blood—"

"It's not as bad as it looks, ma'am," the earl intoned more civilly than Aria had dreamed possible. "A nasty crack on the head is all."

"In here—" Marian started toward the main parlor.

"Perhaps we could just put him in his own bed, madam," the earl suggested. And with a quick look at the other gentleman, he started for the staircase.

"Of course, your lordship." Marian Dunning hurried to the

steps and shooed the servants out of the path as she led the
way up. "But I would not overtax you, for all your generosity."

The earl's mouth curled slightly, though only Aria, hurrying
beside him, saw it.

"It is no trouble, madam." His breath came harder as they
neared the landing. "None at all."

Aria flew past them down the hallway and turned down the
covers of her father's great postered bed. But when they deposited him there, her mother turned to her and blocked her
from returning to the bed. Marian Dunning seemed surprisingly composed as she took Aria's shoulders and stared intently
into her daughter's face.

"Drucilla and I can manage, Aria. Please take his lordship
and the other kind gentleman downstairs and get them a
brandy." Her voice was as calm as if she were ordering the
bolster pillows taken out for airing. "I'm sure they would welcome it, after their labors."

"But Mama—" Aria could hardly believe her ears. The quiet
determination in Marian's eyes stopped her protest. Her mother
was as worried as she was, but Marian Dunning was unwilling
to parade their misfortunes before strangers . . . especially noble ones. George Dunning would never forgive being further
humiliated by having these men witness his helplessness.

Pulling her irritation back under control, Aria nodded. "Of
course, Mama." She turned with her cheeks on fire to lead the
earl and his companion downstairs. She noted the langorous
way the earl sauntered behind her, falling farther and farther
behind as he openly inspected the wide, wainscoted upper hall
with its Adams furnishings. Furiously, she slowed her pace
down the steps and looked back to see the earl stop before a
portrait of her grandfather.

"This way, gentlemen." She tried halfheartedly to keep the
irritation from her voice and only half succeeded. When she
reached the level of the center hall, the coldness of the marble
floor caught her by surprise. Dismay filled her as she realized
that she had left her stiff new day slippers upstairs in her sitting

room. All that stood between her and the cold marble was her silk stockings. She felt positively naked. Slowing so that her slipperless feet would not peep out from beneath her skirts, she tried to stiffen her spine and glide gracefully into the formal salon, where there were thick rugs that might cover her little indiscretion.

Forcing a suitably civil expression, she fought the urge to run back up the stairs to her father's bedside. How absurd that she should be "entertaining" the arrogant earl when her own father lay injured above.

She hurried to the bell pull near the massive, gray marble mantle and rang for Joseph. Belatedly, she realized that Joseph was still with her father and dreaded to think who might come in his place. Joseph was their most polished servant and Aria was determined that the earl would find nothing to sneer about in her domain. Remembering, she curled her toes, drawing them in.

Her eyes drifted inescapably over the earl, even as he paused to inspect the majestic room. His caramel-colored day coat was cut sparingly with narrow lapels and swept back slightly from waist to knee. His short waistcoat was fawn colored, to match his closely tailored breeches, and his Belgian silk shirt bore ruffles at throat and cuff. Tall, straight boots of fine leather covered most of his muscular lower legs. Concentrating on his clothes made it a bit easier to avoid concentrating on him. But as the men approached, she couldn't help the absurd observation that the earl was too broad, too muscular—too coarsely male to be an earl. It further struck her that his clothes were perfectly tailored to obscure that very fact. And Aria's face flushed as she realized that in her mind she had already separated the man from his clothes! What had come over her?

His companion had paused behind him when he stopped at the doorway and Aria made note of it. She had never seen the pleasant young man before this and wondered if he was a servant, dismissing the thought as she recognized the quality of his fine brown broadcloth coat, soft linen shirt, and costly riding boots.

"I wish I were welcoming you to Royal Oaks under more auspicious circumstances." She allowed a feminine lilt to creep into her voice. "Although we owe you much, sir, I do not know your name." She turned her sweetest smile on the unknown gentleman, then looked to the earl for an introduction. He was handling an Italian soapstone carving appraisingly and raised his dark head briefly before setting it back on the table and sauntering over.

"Merrill Jamison, a companion of mine, born and reared in Massachusetts colony." When Jamison murmured something low and returned her greeting with a charming smile and a courtly bow over her hand, the earl's eyes darkened and he set his big hands at his trim waist and leaned back on one leg. His voice dropped an annoyed register. "He's here to take me hunting."

"How fortunate for you, your lordship." Aria let her eyes linger for effect on the reddening Mister Jamison. "My father came to blows," Aria turned to the earl, "with whom?"

"I believe it was a fellow named Robertson that inflicted the damage."

"Lemuel Robertson." Aria paled slightly and threaded her fingers together at her waist. "I might have known—"

"Yes'm?" a female voice drawled from the doorway, pulling Aria's eyes away sharply. It was Levina, the red-haired kitchen girl who had been hired from a destitute tenant family for her adeptness at handling fifty-pound sacks of flour. Aria's stomach fell with disappointment.

"There weren't no one else in kitchen, miss." Levina winced, as if reading Aria's thoughts.

"Levina." She smiled tightly and crooked her finger for the girl to approach. Sliding around the back of the settee toward the girl, she managed a composed appearance. "Do you know where Joseph keeps the brandy?"

" 'Shore do." The girl's hesitant face brightened. "We all know that, miss!"

Aria heard the earl's amused cough and began to color in spite of herself. "Then bring us a decanter of brandy and some glasses . . ." She hesitated to add this last, but surrendered to her better sense. " . . . On a tray."

Levina's eyes widened and her work-reddened hands flew to smooth her heavy white apron. "Oh . . . yes, miss." She started to turn away, but Aria's frantic hand motion, from the end of an arm that was stiff by her side, brought her back, tilting her head and watching intently. Her frown of confusion quickly deepened into a scowl.

Behind the cover of the settee, Aria was lifting her skirts secretively with one hand and was wriggling her unshod toes from beneath the edge of her petticoats. Her eyes flitted meaningfully between Levina's face and her bare foot. Realizing her mistake in trying to enlist Levina's covert help, she let her hem fall.

"Yes'm?" Levina shook her head, and to Aria's horror, she lifted her homespun skirt high and waggled her coarse, homemade shoe questioningly.

Aria widened her eyes desperately, pursing her mouth forbiddingly in hopes of making Levina stop. But the backwoods girl put her rough fists on her ample hips and scowled again.

"I cain't understand, miss." Then she repeated her imitation, this time with obvious stealth, more like her mistress's.

A free rumble of amusement came from one side and a bit to the rear. Aria spun about to see the earl leaning one bent knee on the settee and staring down his nose toward her hem.

"I think it's her slippers she wants, girl. Fetch them for her." The command in his voice, and the taunt, pricked Aria into a royal nettle.

"Oh!" Levina grinned with belated comprehension. "Did you give 'em a toss under your bed agin—an' cain't get 'em out?"

Coloring furiously, Aria glared at the earl's smug expression then turned back to Levina. "The brandy, Levina . . . and on a tray," she ordered curtly.

The servant girl withdrew hastily and Aria turned brusquely back to the settee, pointedly ignoring the earl's hand of assistance. How dare he be so snide while her father lay helpless in a sickbed just above their heads?

She ignored the way Jamison's face was puckered oddly and made a show of smoothing her already silk-smooth skirt as she collected her composure.

"Again, I must thank you for bringing my father home, sirs. I'll not trouble you for further details . . . they will be out soon enough. What is your quarry, Mister Jamison?"

"Quarry, miss?" Mister Jamison sat forward a bit uncomfortably, shifting his muscular hands idly on his knees. His pleasant face knitted with momentary confusion.

"You are hunting, I believe." Aria phrased it sweetly, wondering if all the world was thick between the ears today.

Mister Jamison nodded a smile tinged with relief. "Yes, of course." He glanced at the earl, who was occupied totally by staring speculatively at Aria's skirt hem, and decided to answer himself. "We're going to try for bear and some mountain cat. Of course a stag here and there—"

"But Mister Jamison, there haven't been mountain lions in these parts for the last fifteen years." Aria tried to attend to her conversation and say something intelligent despite the quivery feeling she was getting in her middle. The earl's dark head was lowered and he studied her expertly under lidded eyes. When he looked at her like that, she felt hot and cold all over.

What was she thinking? Her father lying abed, hurt and bleeding just above her, and her base and wayward thoughts turned inescapably to that night in the gardens when he had held her to his broad chest and tortured her with her own responses.

". . . into the hill country . . . to the west." Merrill Jamison slowly ground to a halt, made painfully aware that his conversation, his presence, was incidental to whatever was happening between the earl and the lady. He shifted uncomfortably in his chair and became preoccupied with a splatter of dried mud on the side of his boot.

"Here you be, miss." Levina's voice cracked the strained silence and Aria shot up from the settee like an uncoiled spring.

Turning quickly about, she froze to the spot while the earl's deep laughter boomed uncontrollably about her. Levina stood halfway across the room bearing a huge tray containing an elegant hand-cut crystal decanter and glasses and a pair of stiff leather day slippers.

"M-miss?" Levina would go no farther, seeing her lady's embarrassment and the earl's ungodly mirth. She knew she had trespassed some genteel boundary, and stood with conflicting emotions warring on her hapless face until she could figure what it had been.

Fearing a greater catastrophe, Aria held her head high and hurried to accept the tray from Levina and dismiss her gently. She could certainly bear the embarrassment of an ill-trained servant with grace, even if his lordship made a royal fool of himself. She placed the tray on the table and poured two large brandies, forcing her hands to obey with a semblance of calm as she handed them to the earl and Merrill Jamison. She stood stiffly by the table and felt the earl's steel-sharp eyes raking her as he subdued his high amusement.

Merrill Jamison finished his brandy in silence and in record time and rose, declaring that a pressing engagement in town was all that could tear him away from Royal Oak hospitality. And he had no more cleared the arched doorway when Marian Dunning's voice was heard in the center hall. He politely made the same excuses and was on his way again.

Aria felt the earl's eyes upon her and found it hard to swallow as she knotted her fingers together and greeted her mother anxiously.

"He will be fine, Aria, thank the good heavens." Marian

took Aria's hands and pulled her back toward the earl. "He has awakened briefly and is now sleeping again. I cannot thank your lordship enough."

"Truly, Mistress Dunning, it is an honor to be of service." The earl had risen and nodded benevolently, giving his strong features a noble cast that Aria found perfectly loathsome.

"You must stay for dinner with us, my lord earl." Marian held her hand out to him, gratitude making her soft expression serene. "My husband would never forgive me if you left without seeing Royal Oaks and tasting our hospitality. You were to have dined with us tomorrow night, after all. What difference will one night make?"

"I cannot refuse such a charming invitation." He put one big hand to his chest and smiled with something quite akin to warmth.

Marian grasped Aria's cold hands tightly. Telltale lines of worry were visible about the older woman's doe-soft eyes at this close distance. "I shall arrange it with Drucilla and then I must see to your father. You must entertain our guest, my dear, and show him Royal Oaks."

Aria was left standing in the sunlit salon with the one man in the world that she despised, feared, and yet longed to touch. Feeling trapped, she turned to find the earl staring at her thoughtfully, his hands clasped behind his back. His sardonic grin soon reappeared as he produced her slippers from behind his back.

"You'll need these, I believe." He held them out to her and his sensual mouth curled on one end. "Shall I help?"

Groaning, she snatched them from his hand and turned her back on him. She steadied herself on a nearby chair and jerked up her skirts into an unladylike wad about her knees as she pushed her feet into the stiff shoes. Gone was her ladylike pretenses, and gone it would stay. He seemed intent on stripping her of every shred of feminine coquetry or device. Then he would see her at her plainest . . . and the devil take him!

She was almost to the front doors before the earl dropped

his hands from his dapper waist and erased the image of her slim ankles from his mind. A shaft of desire shot from his loins up into his chest and seemed to explode there, making his chest feel tight. The raw sensations unnerved him. Then he shrugged them off with a displeased roll of his very broad shoulders and strolled after her.

Four

Outside in the lowering afternoon sun, Aria paused on the brick path leading toward the stables to get her bearings. The cluster of brick and stone barns were gathered about the side and rear of the main house in a crescent shape. In many ways they were the pride of Royal Oaks, for they housed the prized breeding stock of a line of horses that was famous throughout the colonies. Whatever else was said of Squire Dunning, it was fairly said that the man had bred and raised some of the finest horses on this side of the Atlantic.

Now those busy stables seemed the very refuge she needed. She unconsciously smoothed her polished, moss-green bodice and ran her hands down and around the unpanniered drapes of lighter colored wool at the sides of her hips. She ran her tongue over the front of her teeth and sent a hand to tame any stray wisps of her tawny hair. Why did he unhinge her so? What was there about his insolent maleness that caused her heart to beat faster and made her skin tingle when he looked at her?

The soft sound of his footfalls alerted her and she turned, chin raised, determined to do battle on whatever front he attacked.

"A tour of the famed Dunning stables?" He seemed more delighted than Aria felt he had a right to be. He pulled a scented lace handkerchief from his waistcoat pocket with deliberate slowness, readying it for his nose. "That would have been second on my list of entertainments." His lusty smirk and insultingly free gaze made his first choice in entertainment plain.

Her throat tightened and she raised her chin another notch. "I do not want you here, sir. I shall honor my mother's request until supper this evening, then I pray you, have the decency to go quickly. And we shall *not* expect you here to dine tomorrow evening—or ever again." The spool-like heels of her shoes pounded hollowly on the uneven paving bricks as she headed for the stables.

She was talking quietly with the stablemaster, Franklin, as the earl caught up with her. The stocky, brown-haired stableman's face was stern, and as his gaze fell on the lord, it darkened markedly. The earl nodded extravagantly as the stout man was introduced to him, but there was no hint of mockery in his manner this time. The two men stood a moment in silence, appraising each other, before the stablemaster stepped back and to one side and waved them into his domain.

Aria watched the earl's elegant handkerchief flutter toward his nose, to ward off the expected of stable smells. Her green eyes narrowed vengefully and her mouth tilted with ill-disguised pleasure on one end. Purposefully, she paused and breathed deeply of the smells of clean straw, sweet hay, freshly waxed leather, and horses. Ladies did not ordinarily venture too near stables, and when they did, they usually pressed scented handkerchiefs to their delicate noses to blot out the coarse odors. But Aria had come to enjoy the strong smell of her family's immaculately kept stables; she had been raised with it.

The earl caught the disdain in her look and immediately lowered his lace-bordered handkerchief. The air was unexpectedly fresh and one of his heavy brows lifted in surprise. He began inspecting the broad stable alley in which they walked, keenly aware that the stablemaster's careful eyes never left him. When they paused by the box stall of a great bay stallion, his arms swept the sides of his coat back as he clasped his hands behind his back and leaned back on one muscular leg. He visually examined the magnificent horse, the polished wood of the stall, and the handcarved name plaque hanging on the stall gate.

Aria's narration of the beginnings of their present line of breeding stock began in a terse, clipped tone. She was careful to stand more than a full arm's length away and allowed her rigid posture to speak her annoyance. But as they passed stall after stall, led by her recounting of bloodlines and anecdotes, her voice and prim posture were warmed by her interest in her subject.

Her clear, rounded tones washed over him and he ceased attending to the parade of excellent horseflesh to concentrate exclusively on her. He drank in the pride in her voice, the sensual promise of her cupid's bow lips, the light that danced in her eyes as she talked of the heritage and hopes of their line. She spoke of the unusual color of a mare and stroked a glossy flank, and his hands itched to stroke her bare, creamy shoulders. She spoke of the haughty temperament of another mare and tossed her head in sympathy, and he wanted to grab her and bury his face in the saucy arch of the nape of her neck. She spoke of the fierce black stallion who had filled their barns with his progeny, and he was seized by the urge to take her beneath him and plant his child in her. His blood was pounding in his head and his steel-gray eyes were lit with silver sparks by his need for her.

Then as she passed through the dusty shafts of light from a window near one end of the stable, he felt as if he'd been dealt a blow to the gut. The light turned her honey-colored hair into spun gold and her skin became Venetian marble. The curious lighting faded her square-bodiced gown to amber. She seemed like a jewel set in sunlight, glowing with unearthly radiance. She turned about with a quizzical look to see what was keeping him.

Her lips parted and her cheeks flushed like golden peaches. She was a goddess, a temptress, with eyes that glowed like Persian amber. Her breasts seemed to rise and fall faster as he caught her gaze and held it in the swirling depths of his. All clues of time and place were snatched away. They stood, suspended, enwrapped by waves of passion and promise. His heart thudded strangely and seemed to pause, quivering, as he felt her desire for him match his own. He could not remember wanting any woman as he wanted this girl.

When the stable foreman stepped between them, his first instinct was to smash whatever had dared intervene. Some small, but tenacious remnant of civilization made him check his primal reaction and in a moment the stablemaster's glowering image finally focused in his reeling mind.

"Ye'll not want to be wastin' the light further in these dreary stables, Miss Aria." The man turned to his startled and embarrassed mistress. "Perhaps the *gentleman* would care to see the grove or the ridge." The stablemaster winced as if the word "gentleman" fouled his mouth. He clearly didn't approve of the earl or of his undisguised desire for the young mistress of Royal Oak.

"Of course, Franklin," Aria managed, collecting her skirts with trembling hands. Her heart was beating in her ears and her breathing was erratic. She walked unsteadily past the earl with eyes downcast, heading for the nearest door. Outside, she wrapped her arms about her small waist and tried to reclaim her stumbling senses. She took a deep breath of the fresh air and heard the crunch of the earl's boots on the gravel behind her.

Then the odd thought comforted her. The earl might have powers that could unlock the secret desires of her heart, but that did not mean he commanded her will, as well. She could not prevent or undo her desire for him. But she didn't have to act on those desires. She was, after all, a lady and a moral being with strength and purpose of will.

At the sound of his deep voice, she looked up, steadying herself on her feet. He stood beside her, his dark hair framing his square, masterful face and his rich coat accenting the size and power of his broad shoulders. But his face was calm, almost relaxed. And his eyes had lost that faintly cynical hint of amusement that never failed to goad Aria's sense of pride. Their gray was clear of the smoke of contempt and the sparks of desire.

Relief flooded through Aria, rushing to her head and leaving her feeling giddy. It seemed as though a truce had somehow been struck and the prospect agreed with her more than she expected. He was saying something about *her* list . . .

". . . but, what is this 'grove' and 'ridge' your stableman mentioned?"

"Ah." Aria colored a bit as she realized she was caught staring up at him. She lowered her face and began to walk along a rutted path leading away from the stables. "The grove is a cluster of great oak trees near the top of the ridge." She pointed ahead toward a gently sloping hill that wore a crown of remarkably large white oaks. "They're the 'royal' oaks that give our land its name. Wait until you see them." She quickened her pace, feeling him fall in beside her with his long, easy strides.

Twice, on their trek up the hill, he took her elbow to steady her across a muddy spot in the worn, grassy track. But as soon as his assistance was no longer needed, she withdrew as quickly as possible. There was no sense in tempting fate.

The gentle grade of the hill was enough to quicken Aria's heart, and as they neared the great old trees, she realized it felt the same as it had earlier when she had caught the earl staring at her. She lifted her skirts slightly and stepped into the tall grasses, wading through them with her eyes fixed on their destination.

Pausing before the first of the massive trees, Aria smiled, her heart thumping oddly and her eyes bright with wonder. If she came here a million times, the next would still seem like the first for her. "Aren't they magnificent?" she breathed.

The great tree stretched awesome branches out in all directions, its top seeming to spear the dappled, evening sky. A light breeze ruffled the large, lobed and rounded leaves into a shushing sound, almost like running water. Occasionally, a branch would yield to the wind in its leaves and would dip as if in greeting. Jays and sparrows circled and landed and chattered in the branches far above. The sounds of nature swirled contentedly about them, but Aria's heart did not slow its pace.

"These are the real Royal Oaks." She turned toward the earl and was faintly relieved to see him standing in his customary, hands-on-waist pose, staring up into the great, trunklike branches. She stepped to the trunk of the huge oak and ran her hand over the wrinkled bark as she circled it. On the other side she stopped and looked out over the fields along the river below. Though it was only a small rise from the stables and main house, this was one of the ridges that defined the fertile valley. And the view seemed to reach exotic, azure worlds in all directions.

Lost for words, Aria heard the earl join her and pause to take in the view. She ventured a sidelong glance at him, catching his strong profile silhouetted against the turquoise of the evening blue. Her wayward eye fastened on the rugged squareness of his jaw, accentuated by the rolled curls at his temples and the sweep of his dark hair on the nape of his neck. A chill coursed through her and she hugged her shoulders, blaming the rising breeze.

She turned back to the shelter of the great trees, stepping gingerly over their gnarled, exposed roots. "I used to come here to play when I was a child. My old governess usually fell asleep. Then I'd lie on the ground and watch the trees swaying overhead." She picked up a twig and traced it with her fingertips, as if reading her memory in its nodes and shriveled bark. "I used to think they were like old men—solitary old brothers—whispering secrets to one another. I always listened so hard, trying to hear what they were saying." She looked up through the pattern of branches to glimpse the sky beyond. Wandering farther among the massive old trees, she spoke as much to herself as to him.

"It's strange. Most childhood things seem to shrink as you

grow up. But these trees seem just as big now as they were to me years ago. I wonder why that is."

The earl watched her lithe young form weave in and about among the trees. Her slender hands caressed the rough bark, her face was wistful and girlish. Locks of her long hair fell across her fashionably revealed breasts and stuck in the stiff lace about her neckline. She pulled her hair away and tossed it back carelessly. Shivering and hugging her shoulders, she pressed her full, young breasts even higher above her ribbon-rimmed front lacings. His loins ached suddenly, putting his desire at war with his reason. She wanted him; he had seen it in the stables. It was but a matter of time . . . and her father would present no problem. But if he took her now, without her full consent, he might never taste the full promise of her tempting passion.

Watching her, he plucked an oak leaf from a low-hanging branch, and when she turned his way, he studied it as though it consumed him. Its sinuous curves and lobes recalled her softness, her lips, the swell of her ripe young breasts. Rigid with self-control, he listened to her words and wondered at the curious way she had of making things seem more than what they appeared. She was rare, this one, and her uniqueness piqued his desire for her anew. She was worth any risk. He wanted her and he vowed to have her, to take her—here, in this cathedral of nature.

"On my family's lands," he said, following her casually, "there are woodlands that have stood for hundreds of years, but there is nothing to match these." He passed a calculating hand down a gnarled bark wound. "Do you know, my grandfather had a man flayed alive for felling two trunks far smaller than this in our forests." Seeing a frown flit across her fair face, he paused and smiled quite apologetically. "It may sound extreme, but it was his outrageous zeal for our last bit of nature that kept our lands from becoming a barren waste. Now they are a treasure that many parted from that land still carry in their hearts."

The tenor of regret in his voice touched something in Aria's heart. She leaned her side against the tree trunk near her and tilted her head, viewing him from another angle. Could there be in that cold, arrogant man a heart that carried and treasured things? As he continued to speak of his home, he seemed to take on more human dimensions of pride and past and need. In the lowering sunlight he seemed no more than a man, a man used to commanding and ordering his world so completely that it had lost its value for him.

In the thoughtful pause that overtook them, Aria felt the chill of the wind again and wrapped her arms about her waist, thinking that they should return to the house soon.

"You are cold." To her surprise, the earl peeled his elegant coat from his shoulders and approached her. Heedless of her step of retreat, he unfurled and settled the huge, silk-lined garment about her shoulders, allowing his hands to linger on her now-protected shoulders. His eyes were murky and unreadable.

The heat of his body still clung to the coat and flowed into her tense frame. Her skin trilled and her fingers dug into the waist of her dress as she tried to calm her jittery nerves. When his hands moved away, Aria felt an awkward sense of intimacy lingering between them. Much as it disturbed her, she could not bring herself to remove his coat, even to reject whatever she suspected might come with it.

The gathered white silk of the earl's shirt sleeves was caught by the breeze and forced to sculpt itself about his muscular arms. If possible, his shoulders seemed more powerful under the expanse of white. His waistcoat wrapped snugly about his lean middle, tapering inescapably down over his snug breeches. Aria's eyes slid surreptitiously over his heavy, solid form, drinking in a thousand tiny details. With heat rising in her face, she looked down to the sparse litter of old leaves and dead twigs at her feet. What was it about him that excited her so? What made her want to absorb every detail of his frame, touch him with her hands, and hungrily feast on his every move, his every word? Belatedly, she understood the stares, the glances of longing, she had often garnered from the young men of the county. For the first time in her life, she was entranced, fascinated by a man. Why, she groaned privately, did it have to be *this* man?

The earl looked up into the canopy of branches overhead and then toward the grassy hillside around the grove. His strong features were sober.

"It is too bad your old 'brothers' have no heirs. Aged though they are, they will not live forever."

The thought had never crossed Aria's mind and her eyes flew wide with alarm as she searched the grove of great trees for evidence to the contrary. But there were no saplings, no seedlings . . . no children for the old "brothers." A pang of intense loss stabbed her. He was right. The dominance of the old trees was so overpowering that no tender offspring could exist near them. Why had she never wondered about it before? And it seemed the grandeur, the nodding benevolence of the aged aristocrats was somehow diminished.

In the quiet that followed, Aria clasped and unclasped her hands in front of her, seeming unable to find a comfortable position for them. And neither could her mind find any comfort when it seemed a surviving bit of childish innocence had been so completely swept away. And why did he have to be the one to reveal it to her?

"My lord," she said in a low voice that betrayed her inner confusion, "you do have a way of making even the most magnificent things seem . . . less, somehow."

The softly made charge sent a cool shiver of pain through his side and he stiffened. Without thinking, he planted himself before her and took her shoulders in his hands. "Is truth not counted a virtue here? It is nature's aim that the cycle be unbroken, parent to offspring to parent. Even in men, is it not right that a man should seek out a woman and plant his seed in her that he may have children about him in his old age?"

Aria's knees were melting beneath her as the heat of his

gaze poured down over her. Her cool green eyes were dark-centered and her lips parted to vent her shallow, uneven breaths. Her senses seemed to hum with expectation. It was nearly impossible to string a logical rebuttal together. "My lord earl—"

"Tynan," he interrupted, staring down into her upturned face and feeling uneasy that the sweet wonder it held could so completely blot out all the rest of existence for him. "My Christian name is Tynan; I would have you call me by that, Aria."

"Tynan." She breathed it softly, not knowing that she sent it pounding through him like a cannon barrage. And in that brief space she had forgotten what objection she had been about to raise. All that mattered was the nearness of his hard, fascinating frame and the bright, hot flame that burned at the center of him, its danger veiled by eyes of cold, hammered steel. Helplessly, she was drawn to him, vulnerable to him, hungry for him.

"I have sought you out, Aria Dunning." His voice was filled with the smoke of the passion she ignited in him.

His mouth lowered by agonizing increments to conquer hers. The contact was unexpectedly soft and yet commanding. Aria's mind began to curl about the singular awe of the pleasure she experienced, warding off unwelcome warnings of what dangers might yet lie ahead. There was nothing here but the magic of what flowed mysteriously between them.

His arms closed slowly about her waist. His lips moved against hers, testing and tempting her response. When her lips parted under his, he indulged in the warm nectar of her mouth by intimate degrees. And when at last the full measure of her was yielded to him, he withdrew slowly, enticing her to her own exploration. The sensitive tip of her tongue traced the sensual outline of his firm lips with tantalizing thoroughness, then met the shocking velvet of his tongue as his lips opened.

Aria could hardly breathe. Dizzying, she threaded her arms

about his waist for support. The heat from his muscular ribs sent gooseflesh up her slender arms and into her breast. Waves of stunning new sensations broke over her, defying her attempt to experience them all in full. His body pressed against her skirts, his clean, sandalwood scent, his restrained urgency, the tension of his ribs and back against her arms. She was insensible to anything but him and the sensations his tender caressing produced in her. His last words echoed inside the unopened chambers of her heart . . . *I sought you . . . I have sought you out . . .*

". . . to love you like this," he uttered against her sensitive, passion-reddened mouth. His hands traced the hollow of her back, the fan of her shoulders, then the slender column of her neck. "I have sought you, and yet I still seek you . . ."

To Aria, the words were a charm of binding, speaking their mutual need. And she rose on her toes to kiss and press her eager young breasts against him in affirmation. There was no future or consequence or pretense. There was no fear of the unknown paths of passion's maze, only the truth of her desire to be with him, whatever that involved.

A cool draft swirled about her as he pulled his coat from her shoulders and spread it on a grassy spot by their feet. His fluid motions seemed slowed in time, consuming her attention until he reached for her hand and helped her to a seat. Unresisting, she obeyed, grateful for the relief to her unsteady limbs. He settled beside her, taking her warm, curving form into his aching arms and slowly lowering her to the silken bed he had spread for them.

His shoulders filled her arms as his intensifying kisses filled her senses. She held her breath when he left her mouth to press his hot lips against her temple, her ear, her neck, and her shoulder. Heat poured through her, lodging in her loins and producing a hungerlike pang that made her moan softly and press closer against his half-sprawled length. Instinct guided her bands along the formidable muscles of his shoulders and back. She pulled him closer to her, crushing her tingling breasts against his hardness.

His kisses ranged lower on her skin and his big hand trembled over the laces at the front of her bodice. One of her slender hands hovered uncertainly as his finger slipped over the top of her square neckline, then tugged downward slowly, forcing the laces to yield their long-held charges. His molten kisses flowed over her and into her as he brushed aside the last barrier, her gossamer lawn chemise. His breath caught as he stared down at the bounty of her creamy, rose-tipped breasts. They were like mounds of pale, silky rose petals, topped by tight, tantalizing buds of a darker hue.

Aria stared wonderingly as he gazed first at her breasts, then into her eyes. Then, closing his eyes, he rubbed his cheek over a sensitive, rosy nipple, then turned his head to repeat the motion with the other cheek. His hot face made lazy circles over her breasts until she could watch no more and shut her eyes, gasping when the feelings overwhelmed her. He returned to spend lush, mesmerizing kisses on her lips before exploring her breasts with his lips.

Aria had never guessed a man might do such things to a woman, but sensed that the tingling she had felt in her breasts was in anticipation of just such delight. It somehow validated her raw new feelings, freeing her upon the sea of her awakening. She soared and floated, feeling each new wave carrying her higher. And when his hard weight bore down upon her, she welcomed it.

Her skirts were drawn slowly upward, baring her tapered silken thighs and firm, rounded hips to his questing hands. Aria moaned with unexpected pleasure. Baring her breasts was not so far from the proper fashion of revealing nearly half of them; but baring her calves, her thighs, her hips, her secretmost womanly places—it was a shock that penetrated the nearly inviolable cocoon of pleasure he had woven about her. Aria felt her knees parted by his hard, irresistible legs and moaned helplessly, giving herself up for the moment to the flood of yearning that surged in her loins.

His hard body wedged itself between her upper thighs, pressed against her lower abdomen. Gradually, his deep, wondrous kisses relaxed her belated guard and he pressed his bulging manhood against her warm, pliant flesh. He lavished attention on her lips and closed eyelids, stroking the damp chaos of her hair. One swift, practiced movement removed the last barrier of his breeches and his flesh met hers. Pulsing, eager, and sensing the long-awaited fulfillment, his shaft entered her slowly, while he trapped her gasp of surprise in her throat.

Pleasure mingled with dull, throbbing discomfort to capture her besotted mind. A fierce maelstrom of pleasure and pain, of horror and delight, seized her, shaking her physically. He lay above her and in her, still and intent upon the nuance of her changing response.

"Aria, love—" he whispered, stroking and kissing her face, "you are so beautiful, so desirable." When she suddenly lay still beneath him, he began to move slowly inside her, aware of nothing but the mingling of their breaths and bodies.

But Aria heard it like a cannon shot, the unmistakable snapping of twigs nearby. That singular sound smashed through the now fragile idyll that had held her, enwrapped, to him. And she felt herself struggling for breath, as if surfacing from immersion in some beautiful, but deceptive and deadly sea. Awareness of her bodily state crashed in on her from all sides. She lay on the ground in the darkening royal grove, her clothes loosened to expose her shamefully. The earl's hard, insistent weight bared down between her spread and naked legs, moving, bending, thrusting, as his hot, desire-darkened face bent over hers. And each of his movements produced a lush, instinctively rhythmic response in her lower half. She felt a tightness, a fullness that burst with full horror upon her beleaguered mind. They were joined! They were—

The sound, snapping twigs and rustling dead leaves, was

nearer now. Aria's heart nearly leaped from her chest and her arms and legs began to flail and push frantically against him.

Her resistance, so late and at so crucial a time, was more an annoyance than a cause for alarm. Her hoarse, frantic groans and sharp physical struggle merely fueled his spiraling desire for the shattering completion. He tried to hold her still, but his senses, his reactions, were drugged by passion and were too sluggish to cope adequately with such surprise.

"Someone's coming!" She pounded his shoulders and pushed furiously at his chest, "Get off me—get away from me!" Wriggling and rolling, she succeeded in tossing him to one side. His flesh left hers abruptly and within her horrified sight. There could no longer be any doubt as to what had actually occurred between them. Before he overcame his surprise, she was sitting up and clutching her gaping bodice as her skirts quickly swallowed the vision of her bare legs from his sight.

She scrambled up onto her knees, just out of reach, her heart pounding in her head. Searching frantically, her large, green eyes lighted on the intruder. A large mongrel dog stood not eight feet away from them, near the trunk of an adjoining tree. In the distance a man's voice was calling and it seemed to grow louder. The animal started toward them, but stopped and sniffed the air. It regarded them blankly for an agonizing moment, then turned and trotted off, stopping to sniff here and there.

Aria gulped a breath, and closed her eyes with relief. She heard a rustling and her eyes flew open to fasten inescapably on her own hands as they clutched her bodice together shakily. She felt her stomach surge.

"Aria," the earl's voice was tight with unfulfilled desire. "Come to me."

Her head snapped up. Anger charged into the empty core of her and lit a blaze in her eyes. "How dare you?" she breathed, putting a further step between them. He lay sprawled on the ground by his traitorous coat, propped on one elbow. His taut face seemed arrogant, carved of base, licentious bronze. She swayed, feeling her body screaming complaints from every quarter. How could she have succumbed to his coarse, profligate lusts?

"Look what you've done to me." She cast a glare of self-loathing down over her rumpled and littered skirts and released her grip on her bodice to begin jerking furiously at her laces. "Now I must trust my virtue to the mercy of passing mongrels—"

The earl's sardonic laugh cut deep into Aria's heart. He was on his feet in an instant, making a swift adjustment to his own apparel. "I have done nothing to you that you did not want me to do." His voice was full of gravel and his words were tightly clipped as he silently cursed that mongrel's untimely birth.

Aria stopped tugging at her laces, stepping backward as he approached. Her eyes blazed, but he was to see that hurt was mingled inseparably with it. She wanted to scream at him and hate him, but the liquid that pooled in her sea-green eyes betrayed her vulnerability. His steely eyes seemed to blue, gathering her gaze inescapably into his. For a moment, he probed her, certain of sorting the artifice of the lady from the genuineness of the woman. His chest tightened as he realized the lady he had thought to beguile was indeed the woman he had wanted, needed, so badly.

Swallowing hard and writhing inside under his relentless examination, Aria finally tore her eyes away, jerking her lacings into submission despite her clumsy fingers. When he stepped closer, she shrank back, a flicker of fear clouding her eyes.

With exaggerated slowness, the earl raised one big hand to pull a dried leaf from her hair. Her tight breath of relief raked through his insides. She ducked quickly around and started for the path down the hill.

"Aria—" his deep voice boomed, halting her.

She paused only a moment, casting him one look back over

her shoulder. He was watching her, his dark face troubled, probably angry. Then she hurried on, breaking into an uneven run that reminded her painfully of his intimate use of her.

The earl stood, watching her go, feeling each step she took as though it were made on his heart. That last glimpse of her face lingered in his gaze; her bruised, pouting lips, the wild toss of her hair about that pale, delicate oval, the cling of unshed tears in her luminous green eyes. Damn! he swore softly, why wouldn't her tears just fall—like other women's? Grinding one fist into the other, he watched her fleeing figure grow smaller. And for the first time in his life, he knew what it was to feel powerless.

Five

When Aria reached the house, her first instinct was to charge through the great front doors and slam and lock them after her. She wanted to strike at him, to charge him openly with the foul seduction he had practiced so callously on her. She wanted to rally her father, her house, against him and make him regret that he stole from her the one thing each woman has to give but once.

But her sense of shame over her eager participation in her own ruin was too great. How could she claim he ruined her, but that he had needed no force? And what punishment would her father exact on her? Shivering, she recalled the calculation in his gaze that night at the Stirlings' party. He knew she was the source of the angry red scourges on the earl's face, and still he invited the rogue into their home to dine. Did the earl assume her father's ingratiating manner extended to his only daughter's virtue? Choking her tears back, she knew that her only course was to conceal what had just happened to her.

She slipped through the rear servants' entrance, praying silently that they would all be about their evening routine and out of their quarters. Taking the steps a few at a time and pausing to listen between, she recognized the devastating change already wrought in her. Now she slunk into her own home like a common criminal, flinching at shadows and fearing to hear even a parlor maid's voice.

Only when she was behind the bolted door of her own room did she allow the full implication of what had happened to sweep over her. She had walked into his jaded embrace like a lamb to the slaughter. How it must have amused him to take her in a place of her own choosing, a place she held aloft as the focus of her family pride and heritage! Shame colored her face hot scarlet and she bit her passion-tender lips savagely.

She had finally encountered the full measure of lordly prerogative that her father had taken such pains to associate himself with. How could any good come of such vile, corrupting contempt for the dignity, the rights of others? How could a man be more "worthy" than others if he treated other men with contempt and women with debasing lechery? What was so "noble" about men like the Earl of Penrith? Her ambivalence toward her father's values and politics was suddenly shattered. She knew now he was wrong . . . *wrong!*

New fear intruded into the turmoil of her emotions. Where was the earl now? Her mother expected she was "entertaining" him and fully expected to see him at their table for supper in another hour!

She jerked open the door of her handcarved armoire and stared into the oval mirror that hung inside the door. The haunted face that stared back at her from a tousled mane of honey-colored hair was that of a stranger.

She touched the silvered glass disbelievingly with her fingertips and fresh tears coursed down her cheeks. His treacherous kisses, his vile whisperings and degrading caresses—they had worked this transformation in her.

Grabbing her ivory brush, she began to drag it furiously through her tangled mass of hair as though she could purge it of the taint of his touch. Then she poured cool water in the Oriental basin to wash her tear-streaked face.

She must collect herself. . . . she must find him before dinner and send him packing. Fragments of grass and leaves still clung to her skirt and she swiped at them viciously with her brush. Quickly, she whirled before the mirror, checking over her shoulder and sending a cautious hand up the front lacings of her bodice. Her knees weakened suddenly and she was all too aware of the evidence of their encounter that still remained on her lower body. She vowed to rid herself of that too, as soon as *he* was gone.

Tynan Rutland stepped soberly into the gracious center hall of Royal Oaks House. Before he had taken half a dozen steps, an erect, white-haired houseman in smart black livery approached him.

"Yes, my lord?"

"Joseph, I think. Is it not?" The practiced manner of a faraway court exerted itself quite naturally.

"Yes, my lord." Joseph permitted himself a tersely gratified smile as he straightened his aged frame.

"Joseph, I have just had a message from my host, Sir Lowell Stirling. It seems I am needed at Sutterfield this evening. Please convey my deepest regrets for supper this evening to your lady . . . and Miss Aria. I cannot imagine how I could have lost her on so short a trek about the grounds."

"Very good, sir." Joseph retrieved the earl's elegant tilt-brimmed hat and escorted him regally to the door. "Have a safe journey, sir." The butler watched as a groom brought the earl's horse around and his craggy face softened with admiration as the earl mounted gracefully and reined off expertly. He was halfway up the staircase when Aria suddenly appeared before him.

"Ah, Miss Aria." His face lit, then scowled at the sad tidings he bore. "His lordship, the earl, bid me send his regrets for supper. He was called back to Sutterfield, suddenlike." He sighed ruefully at the distressed surprise on his young mistress's face and permitted himself the familiarity of reaching out to pat her hand reassuringly. "I'd best get back to kitchen and tell Drucilla. She'll be peevish now she can't show off her cookery for a fine nobleman."

* * *

Aria tossed and turned, her hair tangling about the damp skin of her face and throat. In her sleep-clouded mind, those damp tresses became a man's strong, tantalizing fingers. They stroked and teased, pulling from her deepest recesses, responses she did not realize she was capable of making. But the fingers gradually lost their gentleness and began to clutch at her, to pull and prod her—hurting her. She struggled to get free from the faceless, foglike horror that held her, but the grasping fingers seemed to grow stronger to match her struggles. She twisted and pushed, writhing and being slowly choked by their tightening grip and by her own fear.

She shot up abruptly in the darkness, heart pounding as if to escape her chest and eyes wild with fear. Her nightdress was soaked and her skin was burning hot. Gulping several breaths, she sagged with relief in the dim, familiar surroundings. It was a dream, only a dream, she told herself. Pushing back long strands of hair from her neck, she pulled her knees up to clasp them with her arms, resting her cheek on them. The movement recalled the tenderness in her lower abdomen and she gritted her teeth. She knew the reason for her disturbing nightmare and it was no less difficult to deal with awake.

Nothing was the same . . . not her father, not her future, not even herself. Once their home had flowed with guests, gaiety, and good feelings. Now it was a somber place that seemed to wait upon the next venting of her father's mercurial temper. Once her future was secure and her dreams at night were of placid and genteel married life at Thomas's side. Now she had no marriage prospects, and because of the changes worked in her only hours before, she could never have an honorable future. By the exalted standards her father had tirelessly drummed into her, she was ruined, useless in the marriage trade that structured both lives and fortunes.

She lay back limply on her pillows and stared up at the crocheted canopy above her bed. Her thoughts would not be held from him any longer. The earl, that huge, cynical, world-weary beast. Her pulse raced when he was near, her skin tingled when he caressed it with his rapacious eyes, his deep voice vibrated her body like a harp string. Was it the sin, the taint of her soul, to return his desire? And was her punishment for her sin the ruin of her life for all time to come? Surely God would not be so cruel . . .

Perhaps, the voice of her deepest self responded, it was not for that sin that she was tortured so, but for the desire that still lodged tenaciously in her heart.

A tear traced a burning path down her temple and back into her rumpled hair. Minutes later, she opened her eyes and fixed them on the canopy above, watching the dance of the tree shadows from the unshuttered window growing steadily brighter. In the distance, she heard horses whinnying.

Suddenly more alert, she stared at the brightening light on her canopy and concentrated on listening to the night sounds around her. Something prickled her skin as she realized that the horse sounds grew louder and more frantic.

She threw back the coverlet and slipped from the bed to look out her window. Bright tongues of orange and golden flame licked at the corners of both stables, and in its eerie yellow light she could see smoke boiling from the more distant barns. *Fire!* The blood drained instantly from her head and her limbs, robbing them of strength temporarily. In the flickering light, she glimpsed men on horseback darting between the buildings. The grooms must already be driving the horses and other stock from danger.

She jolted into motion, running for her door and pulling it open. Joseph in breeches and half-tucked nightshirt was hurrying down the hall toward her rooms, calling her name breathlessly.

"Fire . . . in the stables . . . miss . . ." he huffed, his worn face seeming ashen in the light of the oil lamp he carried.

"I know, Joseph! My father—"

"Just roused him and the mistress— Hurry miss—"

But Aria was off down the hall, her nightdress billowing

above her bare feet. As she passed the staircase down to the center hall, she could see servants scurrying about in the half-lit entry below.

George Dunning emerged from his rooms, half dressed in breeches and boots and jerking a shirt unsteadily up onto his arms. He glowered furiously beneath his bandage.

"Papa! What—"

"See to your mother, Aria," he ordered angrily, pausing only long enough to glare disapprovingly at her thin nightdress. "Get dressed, girl, and stay out of the way!" He pushed past her and hurried for the front doors, grasping at the railing for support.

"Aria!" Her mother stood in the doorway of her separate suite of rooms, calling her name. "Aria, get dressed, daughter! Hurry!"

Startled, Aria again ran the length of the upper hall and began to tear off her nightshirt as soon as her door closed behind her. Not stopping to light a lamp, she threw open her wardrobe and pulled out petticoats and what felt like a woolen dress. She jerked on petticoats and hauled the dress over her head, settling it about her waist. She didn't bother with stockings, but searched the floor of her wardrobe for shoes and shoved her feet into them.

Outside, the crackling of hot wood and the popping of burning timbers was louder and the sound of shouts and panicky hooves rose in sickening accompaniment. She ran to the window just in time to see two figures on horseback disappear toward the front of the great house. Frowning, she whirled and hurried back down the hall toward the main staircase. She stopped at the top of it, realizing that both the massive front doors had been flung back. She paused, seeing her father's stocky figure silhouetted by the light-filled haze on the porch just outside.

He was standing there with her grandfather's saber in his hand, caught up in a turbulence she could make no sense of.

There were horses and men—torchlight. She was halfway down the stairs when her mother caught her and tried to drag her back up the stairs.

"No, Mama! What's going on?! Papa needs us—"

"Aria!" Marian Dunning's face was pale, but determined. She shook Aria hard by the shoulders. "Listen to me! We can do nothing for him now! Nothing! Get back to your rooms and stay there until I send for you."

"No!" Aria shook her head, trying to twist away from her mother's desperate grasp. "What's happening?! I have to see what's happening!" She broke away and was down the steps when her mother caught up with her and pulled her to a halt.

Together in the smoky air, they stared at the scene just outside the front doors. Anxious horses reared and plunged as men with covered heads and faces shouted at the imperious Squire of Royal Oaks.

"This is your last warning, Dunning!" a frenzied voice railed amidst a swell of muttering and shouts of "Get out!" and "Death to the English pigs!"

"We don't want Tory filth around here no more. You take your high and mighty English whore and get out!"

"You yellow-bellied bastards! You are afraid to face a man in daylight, but crawl about on your bellies in the dead of night like the maggots you are! Hide your faces, you stinking cowards—I'll find you out!" George raised a furious, white fist. "Do you think I'd let putrid scum like you drive me off my lands?" His body shook with towering rage.

"Get out, or be burned out!" another voice from the pack of jackals barked.

"Damn you sons of Satan! You come here, bearing your master's devil seal—burning my property and threatening my home! I'll show you how I deal with evil, murdering scum!" And he rushed headlong down the steps at the lead rider with his saber raised and eager for blood.

His blade slashed wildly admist the scattering horses, and in the confusion, a scream howled from one of the riders. A sharp crack sounded and George Dunning's blade was no longer visible. The horses thrashed, wild-eyed from the smoke and panicked by the smell of blood. There were shouts and curses in the melee, and suddenly the frenzied cry went up— "Torch the house! Burn 'em out!"

Aria had seen it all, huddled with her mother in the center hall, staring blankly toward the fury breaking loose in the ghoulish light outside the main doors.

"Merciful God!" Marian's agonized voice seemed torn from her soul. "They're firing the house!" Something in her seemed to snap and she shook Aria's shoulders in an attempt to rouse them both. "Aria—go to your rooms and gather what you can—clothes, what jewelry you have. Hurry, girl!" She took her daughter by the chin. "Aria! Now! There's no time to waste!" She whirled and issued orders to the gaggle of servants pressed against the side of the stairs behind them. "Levina, go with Miss Aria. Drucilla and May come with me!" She grabbed the aging Drucilla's hand and pulled her along toward the stairs.

Time seemed suspended in the insidious, seeping smoke that burned their lungs and stung their eyes. They worked by the eerie light of the burning stables, pulling clothes and shoes and linen from beds and wardrobes, shoving leather satchels and sheet-covered bundles through the open windows. Outside, there was no longer the scream of horses, only the dull, encroaching roar of raging flame and of crashing, splintering beams. The hot smoke gradually thickened and darkened, driving them from Aria's rooms and down the back servants' stairs.

The acrid air hit Aria like a kick in the belly. She doubled over, coughing and half blinded by heat and smoke. It was some minutes before she could make sense of what was happening around her. Then Joseph was pulling her back away from the blaze and checking with the servants to be sure no one was left in the burning house. The little butler soon was wetting blankets and setting the men who were not overcome by smoke to collecting things that had been tossed from the windows and bringing them to an area of safety.

Aria pushed herself up from the stone garden wall where Joseph had put her. Breathing was a bit easier and she stood, getting her bearings. She swiped her sooty, bedraggled hair back from her heat-reddened face with the back of a dirty hand and self-consciously smoothed her half-laced dress.

She walked mindlessly, but somehow knew where she was bound. Giving the fire-engulfed house a wide berth, she made her way round to its front. She paused and scanned the hoof-plowed and trampled front lawn and the road that led up to the house Finally, her eyes located the two figures she sought.

Marian Dunning sat on the ground under a huge old elm just to one side of the front lawn. She was holding George Dunning's head in her lap. No one else was around and there was no sound except the groan and crackle of the flames as they devoured the house. The roar of destruction seemed to recede, blocked by the certainty of a greater loss.

They seemed almost serene sitting there, Aria thought, like a summer's day picnic she recalled in the Royal Grove. She walked closer, her hands dangling at her sides, her face expressionless. How good they had always looked together—ruddy fair and delicately amber. At last she dropped to her knees beside them and sat back on her heels. Her spine was rigid and her hands lay limp in her lap.

Marian glanced at her through a veil of unspent tears. "He's at peace now. He doesn't have to fight anymore."

Six

The week that followed the fire rambled through a haze of confusion and pain. The night of the fire, stablemaster Franklin had caught one of their horses and ridden to lawyer Howard Parnell's house to rouse him and tell him of the fire and George Dunning's death. Within two hours their old friend had arrived with coaches and wagons and a small army of servants with tools to help.

Taking charge, he had bundled Marian and Aria off to his house and had overseen the final stages of combatting the fire and the dispersal of servants and staff to various temporary lodgings. At daylight, he had personally driven the wagon bearing George Dunning's body to the undertaker's.

Howard Parnell and his dutiful round wife, Elizabeth, staunchly insisted that Marian and Aria stay with them. And daily, Joseph and Franklin brought word of the state of affairs at Royal Oaks.

The news was often mixed. They had managed to round up most of Royal Oaks's prize horses and stock, but some were still missing and some had died in the fires. The fire was late spreading to the drying barns, and between the servants of Royal Oaks and Howard Parnell's people, they had managed to save the newly harvested crop of tobacco and most of the recently threshed grain. The remaining field crops could still be harvested, but would be sold at a loss because of lack of storage.

Most distressing was the visit from Sheriff Andrew Gilbert.

Marian and Aria were asked to recount and relive each fearsome detail of that awful night. Lean, hawkish Sheriff Gilbert cocked his head and nodded from time to time, asking few questions and scarcely hiding his eagerness to be done. His slightly bulged eyes blinked too seldom and lighted over and over on Aria's comely, black-wrapped form with irksome speculation. As he left, he held out little hope of capturing those responsible for the tragedy, but promised to question the servants for further clues.

From that first night, Marian Dunning dealt methodically with the details of the catastrophe that had befallen them. She had managed to save some monies from the small vault in Royal Oaks House and set about determining the extent of their losses. She took pains to detail each step to Aria, who wanted to hear none of it and seemed always to dissolve into tears or flee the room in anger. Only when they called on the dressmaker for final fittings of their mourning clothes was the subject of money not raised. Marian said tightly that George would not have his widow and daughter mourn him in rags.

The funeral was yet another trial they had to endure. George Dunning's memorial was sparsely attended and Aria sat staring distractedly at the empty pews behind her, unable to fathom why. Her world was slowly constricting into a whirling eddy of ever smaller circles, and her preoccupations seemed to echo that. Why would their neighbors fail to pay last respects to a man who had lived and worked among them all his life, a man who had lent them aid and shared their good years and lean years? It was beyond her comprehension. Added to the obsession her mother and the Parnells seemed to have with things and money, it was overwhelmingly depressing. Everyone seemed all too eager to bury George Dunning and then get on with their lives. But Aria felt her life had all but stopped on that fateful day.

Howard Parnell set the date for the reading of George Dunning's will in his office two days after the funeral. Aria had tried to escape what she was sure would be a morose business . . . settling the provisions and conditions of distributing what her father had left behind him.

"I can't see why I must be there—ciphers and numbers were always my worst at studies. I have no head for figures," Aria remarked testily when they sat down for tea the afternoon before the meeting.

"Then develop one quickly, girl!" Marian had snapped tersely, her face uncharacteristically bright with heat. Then, as if clamping an iron hand on her unusual display, she lowered her voice and eyes and busied herself with the china cups on the silver tea tray. "There are many aspects of death that are disagreeable—mostly for those left alive. Your father would have wanted you to take your place by me."

Aria had sat staring at her mother, feeling like she observed a stranger in a familiar skin. And she chilled briefly at the way her father's unbending will seemed to reach out from the grave to direct her life still. Since that horrifying night, nothing she saw, nothing she felt seemed to offer the mundane comfort of the familiar. She nursed the hope, in her heart of hearts, that some morning she would awaken from this horrible dream to find herself back at Royal Oaks, safe in her own bed. And each morning proved her hope was false.

When the will was read, Aria was there, veiled in her exquisite black, reluctant but dutiful. Two gentlemen representing Richmond concerns with whom Aria's father had conducted business were also present. In the will's succinct phrases and expressions, Aria heard her father speaking as if he stood beside them. Not surprisingly, the bulk of the estate fell to his beloved wife and daughter. But to their unpleasant surprise, there was more.

"Debts." Marian breathed in sharply as she said it. Then her chin lifted tautly.

The way her mother had said the word "debts" skewered Aria's attention and her heart began to thud. She gripped the carved arms of her chair and felt as though she were emerging from a fog into painfully frigid air

"George borrowed . . . several large sums in the past three years—" Parnell busied himself with a stack of papers from the leather folio on his polished desk. "These creditors have already contacted me via these gentlemen. I know this must be a shock to you, but I know the claims to be legitimate. I helped arrange the loans myself . . . in Richmond."

"Richmond?" Aria blinked as if trying to clear her mind.

"He was . . . unable to secure loans from closer sources," Howard admitted gravely. "I had hoped to spare you that."

"George spared us . . . many things, it seems. And none to our benefit," Marian responded bitterly, drawing Aria's surprised stare.

"No!" Aria jumped up, glaring at her mother. "I won't listen to any more of this. They envied him enough to refuse him credit. They stood by while he was murdered and then scorned his funeral . . ." Sputtering, she snatched up her cloak and rushed from the lawyer's office.

Out on the cobblestone and brick street, she settled her wrap about her with a swirl and began to walk, anything to spend the anger in her. Her father was stubborn and sometimes pompous, but he had lived his life here, in this county—and he deserved better from these people. Her steps pounded angrily as she strode the brick path across the town square.

The activity dissipated her anger and she raised her veiled head to look into the faces of those she passed. Their stares were guarded, uncertain, or mildly curious. She recognized some of the people—Mrs. McClellan, the seamstress; Potter, the shopkeeper; Smithson, the baker; Josh Harrow, an independent farmer who had sometimes done carpentry at Royal Oaks. To each, Aria nodded a tentative greeting. But their reactions were the same as they passed, hurrying by or distancing themselves after a curt nod or acknowledging glance.

Aria's steps slowed and finally stopped as she looked around the town square with dry, aching eyes. The trees on the green, the neat whitewashed shopfronts and solid brick and stone buildings, the brick and cobbled streets—all should have looked comfortingly familiar. This place had been her home . . . these people were her neighbors and yet they looked at her as if she were a hideous stranger. Was it guilt she saw in their faces . . . or disgust?

When Howard Parnell's carriage drew up beside her, she scarcely saw it for the tears in her eyes. And the blood pounding in her ears nearly obscured the sound of her mother's voice, calling her name sharply. When she took the coachman's hand and boarded the closed carriage, she could not meet her mother's eye or answer her mother's terse anger. All she could think was that now she truly had no home.

After the reading of the will, Aria kept to her borrowed room the rest of the day. She knew her mother was cloistered with Howard Parnell in his study and knew from what little her mother had revealed in the carriage on the way to the house that things must be desperate indeed. But for some reason, the money didn't seem to matter. All she could think of was the loss of her father and the hostility of the town and the county that had always been her home. In two short weeks her entire world had been turned upside down. She felt rootless and abandoned.

But at least she was no longer enshrouded by that numbing fog of grief. She would need her wits about her to try to make sense of her situation. And for the first time, she allowed herself to contemplate what seemed a bleak and forbidding future.

The next day, midmorning, Gillie rushed into Aria's borrowed room, her eyes wide with expectation.

"Aria! Come quickly! You've a caller . . . you and your mother."

"A caller?" Aria looked puzzled and rose, putting the hoop of needlework on the boudoir chair beside her. "But who—"

"Hurry!" Gillie grabbed her arm and pulled her along, reaching up to pinch her cheeks to redden them.

Aria waved her insistent hands away irritably. "What are you doing, Gillie? Have you lost your senses?"

"It's the earl!" Gillie breathed, jerked back by Aria's sudden stop. "The Earl of Penrith," she twittered, "he's here to see you."

"I don't want to see him." Instantly Aria's hands were cold and her face drained of color. The Earl of Penrith. She seemed to have locked thoughts of him away since that night. But she knew now that part of her overwhelming grief was for what she had lost before the fire, before her father's death. Her feelings about it had roiled about, becoming hopelessly entangled in a maze of subsequent loss and hurt. In an instant now, her emotions seemed to untangle and the separate hurt of the loss of her innocence was all too easy to identify.

He had taken her virginity as if it were a trifle, then rode away without even the conscience to face her afterward. That night her regrets had seemed to be for her future, but now that her future had been swept away by a greater catastrophe, she still felt a horrible sense of shame and loss. How could she face the one who had awakened the carnal, lustful side of her nature and used it for his own base satisfaction?

"Aria?" Gillie's scowling concern reached through her swirling thoughts. "Aria, your mother sent me for you, she said she needs you. Sometimes I don't understand you. If it were me he came to call on, I'd be running downstairs."

Aria straightened her shoulders and managed a tight smile. "How do I look?" It was a small concession to Gillie's excitement. She smoothed her snug-fitting bodice as Gillie grinned and puffed her gathered black lutestring sleeves. Aria pulled up on the stiff black tatting that rimmed the straight neckline of her bodice. Suddenly the memory of a big, square hand on the creamy skin of her breast leaped into her mind's eye and her lungs felt as if they were being squeezed.

"I wish I'd look so good on my wedding day," Gillie retorted wryly, seeing a stunning color rising in Aria's cheeks.

Aria felt her whole body reacting to the prospect of seeing

him, and she loathed herself for it. Her mouth was dry and
her hands chilled. Her knees weakened with each step and her
heart pounded in her throat as if trying to separate her dizzy
head from her shoulders. Gillie squeezed her hands one last
time when they reached the doors to the parlor, then watched
longingly as Aria entered alone.

Marian Dunning sat on the Parnell's tapestry-covered settee
looking dignified and serene in her elegant black. But when
the earl rose from the wing chair near the fire, Aria had eyes
for nothing else.

He filled the room with his powerful presence. His dark
hair was neatly pulled back at the nape of his neck and he
was dressed in an elegant dark blue coat and caramel-colored
breeches and waistcoat. The snowy whiteness of his stock and
lacy jabbot contrasted sharply with the hard bronze of his skin.
His square, sensual features contained that slight hint of
worldly disdain that both fascinated and infuriated Aria. She
had honestly prayed that she would never set eyes on him
again. But her first glimpse of him threw all her resolve into
humiliating turmoil. How could she feel like this when she
knew the depths of the rogue's degradation?

"Miss Dunning." He reached for her unoffered hand.

Only her mother's narrowing gaze made her risk his touch
again. The brief flicker of remembrance in his eye and the
warmth of his hand shocked Aria's heart into a faster beat.
She pulled her hand back hastily and cradled it in her other
one at her waist.

"As I have just told your mother, I was deeply grieved to
hear of your loss, Miss Dunning." The earl turned gracefully
back to the fireplace, resting a hand on the mantel as he absorbed every detail of her form. Her honey-gold hair flowed
in a mesmerizing veil of maidenhood across her creamy shoulders and down her back. The lustrous oval of her face was
paler than when he had seen her last and her eyes that seemed
like beckoning tidal pools were smudged beneath by sleepless-
ness. Set in black, coarsely woven lutestring silk, she was like

an exquisite pearl that he ached to acquire and enjoy. His eyes followed her waist as she settled on a parlor chair by her mother and they drifted upward over the bounty of her ripe young breasts. Need was growing, spreading its relentless tendrils through him.

Aria didn't trust herself to answer, but looked down at her bloodless hands on her lap. Marian scowled fleetingly at Aria's stubbornly demure behavior and watched the way the earl stared at her daughter.

"It is most kind of you to call, your lordship," Marian responded for the both of them. "We are grateful for your interest and your sympathy."

"Are you indeed?" the earl mused openly, still staring at Aria, who raised her chin abruptly, but still would not look at him. "Then I must confess to another, though completely secondary, motive in coming." He turned to address Marian Dunning with his hands clasped behind his back. "I understand Royal Oaks's excellent breeding stock of horseflesh is now for sale. I was most impressed with what I saw that night at Royal Oaks . . . before I was called away." His double entendre rasped against Aria's already chaffed pride. "I have come to tender an offer for the lot of them."

"Then you are sadly misinformed, sir." Aria rose angrily, meeting his surprised look. "Our horses are not for sale, now, or ever."

"If you had kept to your place yesterday, Aria, you would have heard as I did, the final accounting of your father's estate." Marian clipped her words closely and sat rigidly on the edge of her seat. "The horses and the land itself are now all subject to offers." Her brown eyes now glowed with determined sparks as she caught Aria's gaze in hers, daring her to interfere again. It was a command Aria was compelled to ignore.

"This is absurd," Aria paced to the windows, rubbing her palms together. She turned to the earl and charged, "Even if we must sell the Black Warrior and Rondelay, Little Dancer and the others, you have no stable, no means to keep them." But to her dismay, he waved his hand and seemed not the least bit daunted.

"Oh, perhaps I had forgotten to mention it," he smiled a bit too graciously at her mother. "But I have just acquired some land in the northern Carolina. I would simply transfer them there. I fancy the notion of a handsome stable." He leaned one shoulder back against the marble mantelpiece, keeping Aria in his warming gaze. "I am most keenly interested in fine breeding stock." This time he made no attempt to conceal the desire for Aria that registered in his striking face.

Marian straightened her face, carefully concealing the pain in her heart. She knew now what the earl had really come for and she rose with as much dignity as she could muster. "Then it is settled, to my mind. I am sure your lordship will provide well for them." She walked purposefully to the doors and pulled them firmly shut after her.

Aria stood for a moment looking at the doors, unable to fathom her mother's mild acceptance of their fate or her abrupt withdrawal that would leave Aria to the earl's questionable intentions. His movement brought her shame-stained face around defensively. She faced him and watched guardedly as he slowly approached her. He stopped just before he touched her skirts and stood, touching her with his eyes, stroking her in his thoughts.

"Your father's horses aren't all I'm interested in acquiring." His deep voice invaded Aria's skin again with its hushed tone. He caught her gaze in his and the cold steel inside him seemed to become silver. "It seems he had a positive talent for breeding—daughters as well as horses. Name *your* price, Aria. I'll meet it."

Stunned to silence, she widened her eyes and her lips formed a noiseless "oh." His bold gaze, as much as his bold proposal, had knocked all hope of rational rebuttal from her mind for the moment. His sensual bluntness sent a noticeable shiver up her back that brought a sardonic crinkle to the corners of his silvery eyes. He was so close she could almost feel his breath on her face, and fingers of warmth were creeping from the heated skin of her breast throughout her body.

"You'll be well cared for, lacking in nothing . . . and well satisfied. I am the only man in the region that can mate your pretentious Tory blood and provide adequately for your richly cultivated tastes. And my protection will extend to your mother, as long as she agrees." His eyes broke their hypnotizing hold on hers to dart toward the doors. "I think she is wise enough to see the mutual benefit in such . . . an arrangement."

Unable to forestall his need to touch her any longer, his big square hands reached for her shoulders and he pulled her stiffened form against him. He read her lack of resistance as a herald of victory and his carnally carved lips descended on hers with a curl of satisfaction.

His touch set sparks to the perilously dry tinder of her passions. But it was the passion of pride, not of flesh, that he finally unleashed. Her hands came up quickly and shoved him sharply away. Surprise loosened his hold on her arms enough for her to jerk her shoulders and slip free. Her eyes danced with pent-up light, and angry color filled her skin.

"How dare you come here under the guise of respect to make your vile, disgusting suggestions?" Her melodious voice pulsed on its lowest register, hitting square into the middle of him. "You unscrupulous rogue! You thought after what you did to me I'd have so little decency and pride that I'd come gratefully into your bed. Well, you were wrong." She witnessed the quick and skillful recovery of his disdainful composure and she stepped farther back, putting the round parlor table between them. His eyes became flinty so instantly that Aria realized the change had taken no effort.

His coldness, his calculation, the hardness of his gaze were always there, just below the surface. When it suited his purposes, he covered them briefly with a sham of civility or concern. But the true, the real man was the one she saw before her now: carnal, arrogant, grasping. And that realization made her body's traitorous excitement and responses all the more loathsome.

"You thought to capitalize on our misfortunes," she charged anew, lifting her chin and narrowing her eyes with contempt.

"I came to offer you a place with me, comfort, and security." Red was rising under the tight skin of his squarely sculptured face and Aria counted it a score.

"How noble of you to offer me the chance to earn my keep by a whore's part." Her fists clenched before her waist as if to constrain some urge to physical violence. "I don't care if we are penniless. If I am constrained to work like a drudge for an honest living, so be it. I'd rather starve with hunger and freeze with cold than warm your knees in a harlot's bed."

The earl's body was coiled and set as if warding off blows. His face was tight and as hard as red granite. Again he called on the far reaches of his self-control to keep him from his first instincts.

In truth, his anger was as much for himself as for her. Damn! he thought. He had underestimated her and it had been a long time since be had miscalculated so. His exploitation of the lordly role he played had finally crossed into his very judgment. And he mistook the womanliness that had captured him so utterly for softness. This country-bred wench with the body of a courtesan had cast some charm about his better senses. And suddenly he was furious that she should be able to resist what he could not.

"A glib retort," he mused sardonically, forcing his muscles to relax, "from a spoiled, pampered wench who had never known honest toil, nor cold, nor hunger." His eyes glittered dangerously "We shall see how firm your resolve remains in times to come."

"My opinion of you will never change and thus my answer is not subject to change." Aria felt buoyed up suddenly by this small moral victory. Her chin tilted and she stood firm as he approached. Nothing he could do to her now would change the tide of her victory.

"Never?" He paused beside her and slowly picked up his hat from the table. He looked into her eyes and he ran the back of one finger down the side of her face, her throat, and across the revealed part of her breasts.

"My offer shall stand open, for a time. But my generosity has limits. See you do not exceed them."

As he left the Parnells' parlor, Aria felt the skin he had touched burning. She closed her eyes and steadied herself on the table. Her legs were weak and she quaked with unspent tension. The sound of his leavetaking wafted back to her through the open parlor door and she released the breath she held.

Marian Dunning reentered the parlor, her face ashen and tight with anger. Aria raised a stricken face to her and held out her arms as she rushed to her mother's side.

"Oh, Mama—"

"Spare me your pretty tears, Aria." Marian turned from her daughter's outstretched hands, feeling a painful twisting in her chest.

"Mama?" Aria's confusion at her mother's coldness carried on a tremor in her voice. Her arms lowered to her sides and she felt like a scolded little girl again.

"You rejected him." Marian turned on her heel to face Aria. "Your one remaining chance for a future and you—" Anger choked off the rest and she turned from her daughter to put distance between them before she would trust herself to speak again.

"Your father did this to you." She gripped the back of a

stuffed parlor chair until her fingertips were white. "In my heart I knew I would rue the day I let him have his way with your upbringing. I turned you over to him and he filled you with his pretensions, his nonsensical notions of superiority, his abominable pride. And in the end his pride killed him as much as a barn burner's lead ball."

"I can't believe this——" Aria breathed, her eyes stinging and her head beginning to spiral. "He offered me a place in his bed for as long as it pleased him—nothing more! I'd rather toil honestly with my own two hands than——"

"You little fool!" Marian declared hotly. "I heard what the earl said and he was right. You are a spoiled child. What do you know of the privations of common folk? You were raised to culture and ease——" She pushed past the table toward Aria, her eyes fixed on Aria's shocked face.

"We have no resources, Aria." Her slender hand pointed to the spot by her feet as she blazed with long-held resentment. "We are penniless from this very hour. Where in this county could you sell your charms for a future better than what he offered you? Your pride, your father's high-minded principles, they'll do nothing for you!"

Aria's jaw worked, her lips moved, but no sound came out. The hurt, the betrayal of this last known in her world was too devastating. It was all crashing down upon her . . . everything . . . everything was gone. She whirled in a cloud of black silk and ran.

Collapsing on her borrowed bed, she gave way to her chaotic emotions and sobbed uncontrollably. Her virtue, her future was gone. She had nothing to rely on but the charity or the lusts of others. Now her mother expected her to sell herself to the highest bidder—a discredited rogue who hid his debauchery behind the doubtful nobility of a diluted title.

The world was spinning about under her feet, tilting precariously with each passing breeze. There no longer seemed any wrong or right . . . only survival. How quickly the fabric, the noble ideals of her home and family were destroyed under the relentless onslaught of misfortune. What virtue she could yet call her own was now labeled foolishness, ignorance, or pride. What was left to her that really mattered?

Seven

Marian Dunning stood by her daughter's bedside, her eyes misted with forbidden tears. For only a minute, she watched the deep untroubled breathing of her lovely Aria and she felt a wrenching deep inside her. The puffiness of Aria's eyes told eloquently how she had spent the evening. The knowledge that she had inflicted part of that hurt upon Aria bore heavily on her. Marian tightened and drew a shuddering breath. There was no time now . . . for amends or regrets. She set the dim candlestick on the small table by the bed.

"Aria!" she grasped her daughter's shoulders and shook her gently, rousing her. "Aria, wake up! We're in grave danger here, you've got to rise and dress—we have to leave—now—tonight!" She continued her litany of awareness and danger until Aria finally sat up under her own power, frowning with confusion and blinking against the light.

"What—?"

"Aria." Marian grasped her shoulders again and forced her to understand the importance of what was being said. "There are riders gathering near the town hall. One of Franklin's men brought us word—they're coming to the Parnells'—probably because of us! Do you hear me, girl? They're coming for us like they came for your father. We've got to leave—to flee!"

". . . *like they came for your father* . . ." It rumbled about in her head until she righted it and absorbed the terrifying sense of it. Fear smacked her awake and instantly she was pushing her legs from the bed, her eyes wild.

"Aria." Her mother grabbed her quaking shoulders. "We cannot take much. Pack the warmest and sturdiest clothes you have. Wear several extra petticoats and put a second dress over the top so it needn't be carried. Take only your sturdiest shoes and wear your riding boots. We must leave in minutes. I'll be back for you soon. Hurry, girl!"

As her mother hurried out, Aria jolted into action, pausing only a second as a queer chill overtook her. This was just like the night of the fire. Only now, they were fleeing for their very lives.

How she managed it all with no assistance, she could not later tell, but when her mother returned, she was wearing her cloak and stuffing the last of her things into one of two bulging leather satchels.

Marian forced a wan look of encouragement and pulled the hood of Aria's heavy black cloak up to cover her distinctive light hair. She paused and lifted a wayward strand of that silky mass, letting it slide between her fingers. She brushed Aria's cheek tenderly as she tucked it in the hood.

"Come." She took Aria's arm and pulled her down the darkened hallway toward the back servants' stairs. "Howard and Elizabeth will pretend they're asleep and will rouse the house slowly when they come. That will buy us time to make a double trail and get well away before they can figure which way we've gone." She paused near the stairs and sent one hand out in the murky darkness to find the handrail. Aria nodded, knowing Marian could not see her, and followed in like manner.

Marian halted in the stairway landing as she spied the glow of a single taper near the door at the bottom of the steps. "Joseph?" she whispered loudly.

"Yea, ma'am, 'tis me," came the reply and both women breathed again.

They hurried down the steps to find Joseph and his gray-haired Drucilla waiting for them with four nondescript, saddled horses and a fifth that bore only three large bundles. Joseph had loaded his mistress's bags and now took Aria's from her aching fingers and loaded them swiftly.

They all seemed to move as if in a dream. A tall figure stepped from the shadows behind them and Marian greeted Howard Parnell with pain in her voice.

"I pray they won't harm your household, Howard," she struggled for words. "I cannot say what your loyal friendship has meant to us. We had nowhere else to turn."

"God go with you, Marian, and with you, Aria. When you are settled, send me word and I shall try to send you what help I can." Howard's voice was choked with emotion. He took Aria by the arm and led her toward her horse, helping her mount into the unaccustomed astride position. Then he helped Marian up and smacked the flank of Marian's horse to send it off. Aria followed, clutching the reins of the third horse. She looked back over her shoulder and saw only the dim, darkened outline of the house and the bushes and trees. When her mother urged her horse into a gallop, Aria followed suit.

Well out onto the rutted and muddy Richmond Road, Marian and Aria left the road, while Joseph and Drucilla proceeded on. They walked their horses through the shallow, muddy Duck Creek for quite a while. When they left the creek bed, they followed the stream still, skirting in and out of the shadowy trees. Neither spoke. Aria sensed that her mother had purpose in the direction she had chosen, and was afraid to risk detection by asking questions.

They paused on a hill in the shadow of a ridge that Aria recognized. Looking back over the valley that had been their home, they glimpsed a flicker that might have been dancing yellow light near the edge of town, in what would be the location of the Parnell house.

"Do you think they'll be all right?" Aria breathed, barely able to speak.

"God knows," Marian murmured. Then she reined her horse around and continued in silence.

The four or five hours they traveled before sunrise put them well away from the edge of the county. Her mother paused on the rocky crest of a hill to survey their location, just as the gray dawn broke. She slumped back into her saddle and stretched her aching shoulders. Turning to Aria, she pointed to the valley below.

"I believe that's the road we need, down there. But we need to stop awhile and rest the horses." Marian wearily swung her leg up and over the pommel and slid down the side of the saddle.

Aria copied her method of dismount and found her legs weak beneath her. Never had she spent so long in a saddle. Her back and buttocks throbbed, her legs felt as if they'd been stretched and burned, and her fingers cramped from hours on the reins. She tied the horses near her mother's and made herself walk back and forth to work the soreness from her muscles. Her gait was heavy and unwieldy and she felt stuffed like a trussed-up fowl. She wore six petticoats under two heavy woolen dresses that each bore a quilted bodice. A fitted jacket was pulled on over the dresses and her heavy, winter cloak weighed down atop that. She gave in to the overwhelming downward pull of their combined weight and sank down on a big rock nearby.

Even in the cool dampness of early morning, she was miserably hot. Her ribs felt sore as she breathed. But her body's aches and complaints kept her from focusing on even more painful realities. She untied her cloak and let it fall back onto the dew-wet rock she sat on.

She watched her mother's tired face and recognized the quiet strength it masked. Strange, she reflected, how she had always thought of her gently born mother as fragile and somewhat too pale and elegant for ordinary living. Just now she seemed anything but soft or weak. Perhaps it was the overwhelming personality and opinions of her robust father that had eclipsed the quieter presence and fortitude of Marian Dunning.

"Where are we going?" Aria finally spoke, rolling her shoulders and wincing with relief.

Marian sat up on her rocky seat and propped her elbows on her knees. Her forehead rested in her hands. For a long moment she didn't respond, then lifted her head to look at Aria. Her light brown eyes seemed distant and sad. "I have a cousin living in the hills of western Virginia. Perhaps he'll take us in."

"A cousin?" Aria frowned. "You never mentioned you had relations in the colonies. I thought all your family were in England."

"I have a cousin at a settlement, far west of here," she said with finality. "Rest now. We're safe here only for a short while."

The subject was closed. But it did not seem to matter. They had nothing but the clothes on their backs and they rode toward an uncertain wilderness and an uncertain welcome. Knowing their destination wouldn't change their immediate danger or the emptiness inside her.

They rode hard that gray, forbidding day and most of the next, before stopping to rest for more than an hour or two. Though they had walked and led their mounts at times, the horses were exhausted and so were they. Aria could hardly string a coherent thought together by the time they pulled off the rutted path that served as the road west.

They followed a small, clear brook upstream and stopped when they came to a grassy clearing in the thickening forest. There they pulled the saddles from their horses and, with screaming backs and arms, pulled some dried grasses to rub the animals down. Aria stumbled over to a tuffet of dry grass at the base of a nearby tree and slumped into a stuporlike sleep.

How long she slept, she could only guess, but the sun was high and bright in the sky when she awoke to an avalanche of aches and throbs. She moved first her pounding head, then her screaming shoulders and arms, and lastly, her stiff, lifeless legs. A great gnarled root had somehow worked its way up through the grasses where she lay and located the lower part of her spine unerringly. Gritting her teeth, she rolled to one side and sucked in her breath as she sat up. Something hot in her head seemed to burst, showering white-hot sparks down through her shoulders, arms, and body. For a moment, she thought she was going to fall over and pushed her arms out stiffly to prevent it.

"Are you all right?" Her mother's voice was clouded with sleep and came from nearby.

Aria looked around quickly to find her curled on her side at the base of the next tree. Marian's face was drawn and her brown eyes were ringed with exhaustion.

"I'll survive." Aria could not keep the bitterness from her voice. She fought to stand up and took several experimental steps. It seemed to get better as she moved about. She removed her soft, black leather gloves and curled and uncurled her swollen fingers. Faintly surprised that they still worked at all, she sighed raggedly and headed for the nearby bushes. When she returned, her mother had managed to rise and was opening one of the leather pouches that the Parnells had packed with food.

Aria took the battered tin cup from the pouch and walked to the water's edge, kneeling on some rocks by the brook to fill it. She drank gratefully, then filled the cup a second time and carried it to her mother. Marian knelt on the ground by their bags. Her exhausted expression of gratitude and trembling hand troubled Aria.

"I would guess it is safe now to make a fire and cook something. There is some bacon in the satchel and a small pan . . ." Marian's tone was flat as she opened the other pouch and stared into it. "There's flour and oats and a small tin of tea." She looked up at Aria, who stood over her. "We'll have to gather some wood. . . . I'll have to build a fire."

"Mama," Aria said, untying her heavy cloak and letting it

drop to the ground behind her, "I'll gather the wood, there's plenty of it around. You . . . rest."

Marian stared up at her daughter and shook her head as if just now awakening. "There's no rest now for either of us, don't you see?" She clamped her jaw shut against whatever she was about to say and touched Aria's skirts reassuringly. "Just go and collect some dried branches. I'll cook us something to eat."

Aria puzzled over her direction, but did her mother's bidding, returning in a few minutes with a small armful of wood. Marian smiled ruefully when she saw it and remarked that they would need twice as much to make even a small meal. Aria flushed and returned to the undergrowth, bringing back a substantial armload the second time. She saw that Marian had cleared a spot where there was not much grass and had begun to make a ring of stones. Without being asked, Aria began to collect more stones from the stream bank to complete the circle. Then she watched as her mother laid the fire, then pulled grasses and piled them with dried bark chips, setting flint to steel to set them alight.

Marian tended the small yellow flame until it caught the larger branches. And soon she was slicing the side of salted pork with a sharp knife, then mixing oats and flour into some of the water Aria had fetched.

Aria watched her mother's movements carefully, her surprise growing at the skill with which she made the fire and cooked their food. As they sat back in the dry grasses and ate the fried meat and hot oat cakes, Aria sighed with satisfaction. She couldn't remember food ever tasting this good. She sipped from the cup of strong tea her mother had made by setting the tin of water down in the glowing coals and she wiped her greasy fingers on the grass beside her. She watched her mother pop the rest of an oat cake in her mouth, then lick her fingertips daintily.

"How did you know what to do?" Aria pulled her sore legs up and rested her head on her arms, across her knees. "You made a fire and cooked our meal," Aria watched fully five different emotions flow through her mother's face. "How did you know what to do?"

Her mother faced her and read in her insistent look that the time had come for truth . . . the truth she had dreaded all her married life. She raised her eyes to the clear autumn-blue sky as if searching for words.

"I was born to such a life, Aria." Marian's face was stiff and braced. Over the last week she had rehearsed the words over and over in her mind, but now they seemed strange on her tongue.

"Aria, I was not born in a wealthy, noble house in England. My father was nobly born, but a third son and not favored with any particular talent, except perhaps for begetting children. My mother was a squire's daughter. In short order he produced seven children on her, then had the good sense to die early. He was spared the slow dwindling of our modest fortunes." Marian's soft eyes were transported to another place and time.

"I grew up fetching wood, starting the morning cooking fire, tending geese, helping in the kitchen, milking—" She drew a hard breath and shook her head, as if shaking free of the hold of those painful, early memories. She smoothed the folds of her heavy woolen skirt and stared at her small, pale hand, now bruised from the chaffing reins. The air about them became thick and charged with mounting tension. Somewhere a dove was cooing, and the sound of water breaking continuously over rocks beat out the passage of time as surely as a clock.

"George came to England seeking a lady-bride to reign over the empire he was building. But his money was not the introduction to society that he had expected it would be. He was not accepted in the truly noble houses of England. He had bragged in the county that he would bring back a real 'lady' as his bride and he was determined not to return home empty-handed. He visited the penniless Baron of Wrenwyth, near my family's home, and asked to be introduced to the prettiest girl in the area. Fate had favored me with that distinction." She laughed ruefully and dropped her eyes to her fidgeting hands.

"There were too many feet beneath my mother's small table and she was eager to rid herself of a daughter honorably . . . if it can be called honorable to be sold like so much hanging beef—" She stopped, unable to hide the bitter glare that leapt into her eyes, and looked away from Aria's shock. "On the trip back to Virginia, George polished my manners and invented a genteel background for me, involving his friend, the baron. All these years, I lived the lie. When my cousin came to the colonies to live, George was furious. He refused to let me receive him in our home or even acknowledge him. The two times I have seen my cousin, Lathrop, we met secretly at the edge of Royal Oaks. I aided him with household money, but it was not much." She looked warily up at Aria. "Now we must hope that his charity exceeds our own."

Aria stared at her mother, caught up in this new flood of truth and buffeted by clashing waves of sympathy and despair. Tears welled in her green eyes as she struggled to cope with the truth of her background. Her mother's gentle nobility—it was so basic to everything in her life. It was her father's pride and the tone and substance of their household manners and customs. It was the model held aloft to her to guide her own development. She thought of how the blending of two heritages had produced family stories, named their champion horses, dictated her rigorous education, and even shaped their social alliances. And it was all a lie.

"Those stories of your home, your father, your introduction to society . . ." Aria tried to swallow the lump of emotion that threatened to suffocate her. ". . . they were all lies?"

There was a long pause before her mother's quavering voice answered. "Some were stories of my true home and family . . . and some were of the way things might have been. One lie begets another. There was no place to stop."

"And Father . . . was your life with him a lie, as well?" Aria's face heated with disbelief.

"I was scarcely seventeen when George married me and brought me to Virginia. Once I was installed at Royal Oaks, he kept everyone at arm's length from us. I never spoke with another woman without his supervision and approval. He selected my clothes, lest I come to confide in a lowly dressmaker; he selected old Elspeth for my personal maid and she reported to him regularly. When she died, God save me, all I felt was relief at gaining some small bit of freedom at last. All thought George was distracted by his jealousy for me, when in fact he lived in fear that I would give us away." When Marian stopped, Aria raised her head and scoured her mother's pale face with reddened, stinging eyes. Marian stiffened, turning her gaze away and saying the truth as she knew it in her heart.

"I . . . came to care for George, but my life with him was never easy. He was a hard man to live with as a woman. He took you from me to raise his way and, although I often wanted to, I never protested." Marian reached for her daughter's hand and took it despite Aria's resistance. "I wish now I had done many things differently. Your father raised you to wed nobility. Even as he died he was making plans to take you to England and see you introduced socially there."

"England?" Aria wrung her hand free and rose on unsteady legs. Her world was heaving and whirling even though her contrary senses reported that the ground under her feet lay solid and unmoving. "I don't believe you!"

Marian got to her feet, her shoulders quaking with tension and unaccustomed anger. Blue flame crackled at the back of her eyes. "I have spoken the truth, to you, Aria. Why do you think he forbade Thomas Branscombe to see you again? He saved you for the satisfaction of his noble pretensions. He hated the colonial revolt so bitterly because he feared it might hinder his plans for you in England!"

"No—"

"Perhaps it is difficult for you to recognize the truth, having been raised in the midst of so much deceit," Marian gasped, "but I speak the truth. I was sold into a loveless marriage by my mother's need; now you are sold into a life of labor by your father's damnable pride."

Scalding tears were searing burning paths down Aria's cheeks, dripping onto the dark wool of her bodice. Wheeling, she ran in the jumble of undergrowth at the side of the creek. Branches clutched at her heavy skirts and roots rose to trip her booted feet. Blinded by grief, she fled, shoving leaves and branches from her face with panicky hands. She stumbled over and over again, grasping the dragging weight of her skirts and jerking it frantically from underfoot.

Fatigue finally turned her muscles to stone and dragged her down to her knees under a small break in the forest canopy. She fell on a hummock of grasses and sank, face down, giving herself over to the earth's mercy. Small, soblike moans issued from her lips in dry, heaving gasps that seemed to go on and on.

There would be no relief for this despair upon tomorrow's waking. She had lived a dream, a lie, a pretty masquerade that had not been meant to end. Perhaps it had displeased some omnipotent maven of truth, who spread the Dunning name upon the wind and let it be caught by the thwarted, vengeful fates. Or perhaps she had lived only in a house of cards, built high and grandiose on a perilous foundation. It had come crashing down about her, and dwelling in those ruins, she felt as if there was only one thing she had never had in her privileged life. *Truth.*

She saw now that truth, and the human virtue of honesty, were basic to everything of value in life. Suddenly it seemed the only standard of value that mattered, the only comfort she could hope for as loss upon loss eroded all else from her life. She would face the truth of her situation, whatever her circumstance. She vowed from that day forward, she would have truth, if she had nothing else in life.

* * *

The sun was setting when Aria rolled onto her back and stared through aching eyes up at the gauzy, rose-struck sky. A pocket of warmth that had huddled deep within her to weather the tempests of raging emotions now emerged to spread throughout her. For now, she was beyond hurt, beyond shame. She was alive. She had the use of her senses and a strong, healthy body. Her wits were quick and she had an education besides. She must put her dishonor and her family's shameful deceits behind her. She would make her way, with truth to guide her.

A cloak of dry-eyed determination spread itself about her as she rose, ignoring the complaints of her abused body. She found her way back to the brook and followed it upstream until she smelled drifting smoke and saw the leaping orange-gold light of the fire.

Marian rose stiffly from her seat on a fallen log near the fire and wiped her hands anxiously down her skirts. Her face was thickened about her red-rimmed eyes and she hurried to Aria's side. Her attention fastened on a small briar scratch on Aria's fair cheek.

"Are you," she paused just short of touching her daughter and drew her hand back, "all right?"

Aria could not answer or meet her mother's searching gaze. Desperate for something to fill the awkwardness between them, she began to look about for the battered tin pot. "I'll draw some water for tea to ward off the chill."

"Ah, your lordship—" Howard Parnell had hurried into his parlor, mopping his balding brow with a handkerchief. His lanky legs went suddenly limp beneath him from relief. "I had no idea it was you, sir—I was only told some men—" He gripped the mantelpiece for support.

"I have come to learn what you know of the whereabouts

of the Dunnings." The earl spread his boot-clad legs and tapped the back of one knee impatiently with his riding crop. His steel-gray eyes raked Parnell thoroughly, watching for the symptoms of a nervous man's lies. The incident at the lawyer's house four nights ago had clearly unhinged the poor bastard. "Well?" He flicked a hard glance at stone-faced Merrill Jamison, who was watching the proceedings with a tinge of disapproval.

Parnell straightened, hauling his waistcoat back down into place and puffing his chest out, striving for some semblance of dignity. "As I told that rabble who threatened my home, I have no knowledge of their whereabouts."

"I, good sir, am not rabble." The earl's squarely carved features were disquietingly calm and exquisitely insistent. "And you will most certainly tell me."

Parnell's eyes narrowed with a bit of calculation and he strode the width of the broad room to a small liquor cabinet, opening the black, japanned doors to reveal a stock of crystal decanters. "I do not know their whereabouts, sir. May I offer you and your companions a bit of libation?" He swept Jamison then the cabinet with a hand and then eyed the two burly young men lounging outside in the front hall. This had to be part of the "hunting" party it was rumored the earl had installed at Sir Lowell's home.

"I am waiting, Parnell." The earl's tone made it plain that he would not suffer that state for long. "You befriended them; they stayed here. I will not believe that you have no knowledge of them at all."

"I have said," Parnell's long face began to color, "I do not rightly know where they are to be found, sir." His sharp chin raised defensively. "What concern is it of yours where they might have fled?"

The earl leaned back on one muscular leg and allowed his cool smile to rise into his eyes. "I have business with them. I had agreed to purchase their breeding stock at a generous price and am now prepared with a draft from my banker here in the colonies. It took a few days to procure, and I am . . . anxious to take possession." He reached out a hand, palm up, to Jamison and received a folded, sealed parchment wrapped in red ribbon without looking away from Parnell's narrowing scrutiny.

"There is no difficulty, then." Parnell forced a cordial smile. "I am attorney for the Dunnings and administer the estate. You may properly leave the document in my hands and I shall see it is included in the settlement."

"You expect to see them in the near future, then." The earl's eyes lidded as he glanced at the silent Jamison.

"No, sir. I cannot say when or if I might ever hear from them again. But I have been bound over to settle their debts and this sale is necessary to that end. I have been given authorization to act so in their behalf. If you need to see the documents—"

With a peremptory wave of the document, the earl moved to lay it on the table beside him. His movements were langorous and had an air of consciousness about them that irritated Parnell roundly. Slipping his elegant black gloves over his muscular hands, he pursed his mouth in thought. " 'Tis a pity, then. I confess, I had looked forward to seeing Miss Dunning again. I shall leave the business to you, sir."

Parnell watched as the earl bid courtly respect to his wife and daughter and then departed. It had gone well enough, he mused, he had kept their counsel staunchly. But something in the earl's manner at the end made him wonder if he had given more away than he had intended. The blasted English peacock! He lifted the parchment from the table and frowned. No mere peacock possessed such talons . . . or displayed them so openly.

The earl and his companions charted a silent course along the road toward Sir Lowell's Sutterfield. From experience, they

knew that he did not take the thwarting of his desires lightly
and none risked drawing his free-floating ire upon themselves
by speaking. His face was set like granite and his strong chin
jutted combatively under eyes like bright stones.

Merrill Jamison turned in his saddle to better glimpse a
rider coming quickly toward them from across a field to their
left. His eyes widened at the sight of the copper-haired Gillian
Parnell approaching, her flowered day skirts billowing to reveal
the hems of embroidered petticoats and a bit of ankle. He
reined up abruptly. "Well, well. What's this?"

Gillie Parnell reined her horse to a walk and swallowed hard,
trying to catch her breath as she approached the earl's party.
"My lord," she addressed the earl as Jamison leaned down to
take her mount's lead and hold it steady.

"Miss Parnell." The earl nodded extravagantly, his hot displeasure instantly submerged beneath a generous layer of
charm. "How may we be of service to you?"

"I could not help but hear your business with my father."
She glanced somewhat nervously over her shoulder and then
caught Merrill Jamison's warm gaze on her and lowered her
eyes in confusion.

"Will you ride with us a piece, Miss Parnell?" The earl
corrected his mount's course to permit Jamison to lead her
horse between theirs.

"Why did you want to know where Aria and her mother
have gone?" Gillie watched the earl's aristocratic profile and
felt overwhelmed by his air of tightly controlled sensuality and
power. It was exciting, almost breathtaking to be in his company, but it was not altogether pleasant.

"I sought to . . . deliver payment for the animals I purchased from their stables." The words were carefully gauged
as he watched her wistful young face. His voice lowered and
softened. "And I confess," one hand came to rest on the bottom
of his lacy jabot, over his heart, "that to find the trail so cold

was most distressing. I had hopes of seeing Miss Dunning again. Now I must continue my search for her blindly."

"You still seek her?" Gillie lowered her chin, filtering his formidable impact through her lashes.

"I do, Miss Parnell." He scowled at Jamison above her head and Jamison dropped back a stride. "It is easy to see that you are a young woman of uncommon insight and compassion, Miss Parnell. If I may confide in you . . ." Her sober, wide-eyed nod brought a perfectly calibrated smile to his sensual mouth. "I have made Miss Dunning a . . . proposal and I shall not rest until the matter is settled to my satisfaction."

Gillie's mouth dropped open with astonishment and her eyes jolted wider before she checked her reaction.

"I am greatly grieved that she did not accept my offer of protection that very night," the earl continued. "I fear she may think that such an ugly incident may have injured her in my estimation."

"The Dunnings are an uncommonly proud family, your lordship." Gillie nodded, wrestling openly with her thoughts. "Perhaps I can provide a meager bit of aid . . . for I know Aria would do the same for me."

"Anything you may know, my dear Miss Parnell." The earl leaned slightly toward her, flashing a dazzling smile as he caught her timid glance and held it. Confusion rattled Gillie, washing her milky skin with a becoming color that betrayed her powdered freckles.

"I can say with certainty that they traveled west when they left." She spoke urgently and in hushed tones, suddenly preoccupied with the glove buttons at her wrists. "And I am equally certain they were bound west, though I am loath to explain why. They were to send word to my father when they were settled, but who knows what destination they might have had in mind."

"West. Um—m—m . . ." The earl turned it over in his mind. "It is not what I might have expected, but then that is the delight of a woman's mind." He smiled engagingly and drew Gillie into his expanded humor. "The unexpected, the unpredictable."

"You make us sound a capricious lot, sir." Her lashes fluttered with coquettish embarrassment.

"I would never call *you* capricious, my dear Miss Parnell. You are . . . a true romantic."

The way the word "romantic" rolled from his lips sent a pang of intense longing through Gillie. But the guarded look in his eyes when she raised her head chilled it. "I must return." She pulled her horse to a halt abruptly and smiled tentatively as the gentlemanly Jamison moved up beside her.

"Mr. Jamison will see you back—"

Gillie could not resist one last glance at the earl's handsome young companion. "Thank you, good sir, but I'd best return alone . . . and soon. Father would be livid if he knew I had come."

"My eternal gratitude, Miss Parnell." The earl bowed from the waist in his saddle and leather creaked on leather.

"My lord." Gillie nodded, coloring again as she turned toward Jamison. "Sir."

She reined off and shortly was racing full gallop across the field in the direction from which she had come.

The Earl of Penrith rocked back in his saddle, flexing his broad shoulders and resting his crossed wrists on the pommel of his saddle. He looked decidedly pleased with himself.

Jamison scowled and tilted his head skeptically as he watched. "I take it you learned what you wanted to know."

The earl only smiled broadly, transforming his aristocratic features into a glowing mask that was fit to beguile any who beheld it, regardless of age or sex. "We're going hunting, Jamison."

"You're going after her," Jamison surmised.

"I'm going hunting." The earl smiled rakishly. "Isn't that

what idle English noblemen do in the wilderness? Only this time, the quarry is far more interesting."

"But, Rutland, we have a mission—"

"Indeed we do."

Eight

Aria stood in the muddy yard outside the rambling log and mud-chinking structure that served as the hub of this outpost of civilization. Nestled amid the rolling hills, the settlement looked small under the press of the surrounding forest on all sides. She eyed the rough tavern-trading post uncertainly as she avoided staring at the unsettling reunion going on before her. She took a deep breath of resignation and her fingers tightened on the two sets of reins she held in her hands.

A gray-blue haze hung over the clearing in the trees and everything visible was either gray or brown, or some diluted mixture of the two. Aria counted eight or so log structures, which seemed to have sprung up, higgledy-piggledy, from the land itself—cabins mostly, with oiled skins covering the windows and hardened clay and stone chimneys, slash-planking roofs, and crooked split-rail corrals. Muddy paths wound in a disorganized fashion around the structures. She looked back at her mother's tearful face and at her newfound cousin's tightly contained emotion and tried to be thankful for the unexpected warmth of their greeting.

"Come in, please! We mustn't have you standing about in the chill!" Lathrop Glover took them both by the arm and helped them over the peeled-log doorsill and inside. "This is it, my life's work." He stood a moment in the center of the large cabin, sweeping his arms about him and breathing deeply of the wild jumble of assorted smells that greeted them. They stood on a worn puncheon floor in the midst of a great, open room that seemed too large to fit inside the modest building they had just entered.

Aria glanced about her, but returned quickly to her newly discovered kinsman. She assessed his wiry person as he turned to them with a trace of moisture in his sensible brown eyes. His dark hair was bound with a leather thong at the nape of his neck and he wore a well-stitched shirt of buff-colored homespun and linsey-woolsey breeches of bark brown. His feet and lower legs were covered by hand-stitched boots of fringed deerskin and about his middle was tied a belt of the same stuff. His clean-shaven features were refined and Aria thought with guilty relief that he was a far cry from the lout she had imagined when she prepared herself for the worst eventuality.

"This is the store." He waved to an assortment of rough planking shelves containing a bewildering assortment of goods spilling from tins and jars and open wooden boxes. Barrels topped with planks displayed more wares: buckets and baskets, tinware, and bolts of woven goods. Strings of dried onions and dried plums and apples and bunches of dried herbs hung like a forest of potent pomander from the open beams of the roof. Barrels of pungent vinegar preserves and tangy sour cabbage stood in a singular row below shelves of open flour, sugar, and coffee bags in which crude wooden scoops waited. Worked iron tools were jammed into barrels and hung on pegs on the rafters, and oil lanterns and candles hung wherever the meager wall space permitted.

"And this, of course," Lathrop took one giant step in the opposite direction and declared, "is the tavern. I never open up until midafternoon and I close when I'm good an' ready." Aria blinked and realized he referred to the two rough planking tables and numerous crude wooden stools that occupied part of the other half of the cabin. A makeshift bar had been created from barrels and planks before a bank of shelves bearing crockery jugs, small kegs, and flasks of spirits. Crockery steins and tinware cups sat in tipsy stacks on the lower shelf behind the bar . . . right below a boldly displayed flintlock musket. Antlers set in wood decorated the log walls surrounding the great stone fireplace and the windows sported wavy, bluish panes of real glass.

"Evelyn will be overjoyed that you're—" Lathrop grasped Marian's hands and started to lead her toward the cloth-draped door at the rear, stopping suddenly. "Evelyn . . . is not well. The consumption, I trow. It's got worse over the last winter and now she no longer tends the store nor cooks for the trade. There's days she cannot get herself over the edge of the bed." The sudden graveness of his face made him appear years older. "She will be glad of the company . . . and I of the help."

He led them through the low doorway into the adjoining two-room cabin, where a hearty fire in the massive stone fireplace was overheating the main room. The cabin was bright with the light of the fire on the whitewashed walls, and as her eyes adjusted, Aria could see that the wear-smoothed puncheon floor was covered with woven rag rugs. The furnishings must have come from eastern shops, probably hauled at great inconvenience and expense to this out-of-the-way place. There was a table and four comb-backed chairs, a Dutch carved settle to one side of the hearth and a low, spindle-backed rocker to the other side. The small windows that flanked the door to the outside were glazed with real glass, and evening light would be provided by a simple wrought-iron chandelier hanging from a beam above the table. A carved sideboard and tin-fronted cabinet completed the cozy room.

"Sit, sit!" Lathrop pushed them toward the cushioned settee and disappeared into the other room. "Evelyn!" They heard his voice floating back as they shed their heavy cloaks. "Come and see—Marian is here!" Soon a thin, stooped woman emerged, wrapped in a heavy knit shawl and wearing a plain white linen cap over her gray-streaked hair. Aria's first thought was that Evelyn must be much older than Lathrop, but as she saw her cousin's wife embrace her mother, she wondered at her estimate. Aria smiled gently and was silent as the rail-thin woman embraced her and pulled her closer to the fire, to squint into her youthful face.

"She's beautiful, Marian," Evelyn's thin voice rasped. "Takes her fair color from her father, I suppose." One thin hand reached out to touch the unbound flow of Aria's hair. "Like silk—" Then Evelyn was seized by a coughing spasm and Lathrop helped her to the rocking chair, tucking a brightly colored yarn-tied throw about her lap.

Aria intercepted the worried look Lathrop sent Marian above his wife's head and knew it was not only blood ties that assured their acceptance; it was need. When their supper was done that night and Evelyn had been bundled off to bed, Lathrop took a wooden splint from the pipe box hanging near the fireplace and lit it from the fire as he listened to the details of their escape. He toyed judiciously with the burning splint, scowling or nodding occasionally, then finally set light to the pipe he held clenched between his teeth.

"So you've no idea what you've left behind you?" he mused, taking his pipe out to check its cheery red glow before blowing out the splint.

"There can't be much, Lathrop. George's debts were so large, they must have taken the bulk of the estate." Marian looked down at her hands and inspected their new roughness. "We've put the land up on the block, but who knows how long it will take to find a buyer."

"The land?" Lathrop eased down into one of the comb-backed chairs and let out a breath that made a whistling sound. "That was mighty good land, Marian. Surely there's some other way to pay the debts. A man parted from his land—"

"We've not made this trek lightly, Cousin Lathrop." Aria's clear voice sounded stronger than she felt. "We barely escaped with our lives and we could never return to Royal Oaks . . . even if the debts could be settled."

"Marian," he reached for her hand and squeezed it, "many's the time I meant to write or to send word of my thanks. Without your help, the money you gave me, none of this would have been possible. You're welcome here, for as long as need be."

"Thank you, Lathrop." Marian lowered her face and flicked a tired glance at Aria. "We expect to work for our keep I'm not sure what we can do . . . perhaps cook a little, see to your house . . ."

Lathrop's lined face broke into an extraordinary expression of pleasure. "God is good, Marian . . . I'm so sick of my own cookin', I could spit!"

"I cannot say mine will be any better at first—it's been a long time. But I'll work at it."

"And Aria, lass . . ." Lathrop turned to her and frowned in thought.

"I . . . can't cook, Cousin Lathrop," Aria said stiffly, feeling red creeping into her face. No woman of her station would deign to set a hand to a pot or rack or spit. But now her world was turned upside down and those skills she had deemed unworthy were now the ones to be prized in this harsh new life.

"Perhaps Aria could help in the store." Marian sat forward anxiously. "She's . . . good at figures." She cast a tight, meaning-filled smile at Aria, who flushed furiously.

"So?" Lathrop turned to Aria. "I'd be glad of the help there, all right. And with somethin' better'n my old puss to look at," he pointed to himself and made an awful face, "trade'll be up sharply, I trow."

Aria sat, stunned by the lie, and lowered her reddened face, hoping her reaction would pass for maidenly modesty. But inwardly, she was appalled. Their first minutes in this house, embarking on their new life, and already her vow of honesty was severely tested.

"Now," Lathrop slapped his thighs and pushed up from his chair, "we'd best get to sleep. I wish I had a better place for you to—"

"No, no, cousin," Marian shook her head vigorously, "the loft will do fine. After a fortnight in the open, this will be heavenly! Think of it, Aria—a real pillow!"

Aria nodded mutely, hurrying to bank up the coals in the great fireplace as the housemaids had always done in her room at night. She tucked her skirts between her legs and felt her face glowing beet-red from the heat. When she turned back, Lathrop had disappeared into the other room and Marian stood watching her with a curiously soft expression on her tired face. Aria dropped her eyes to the floor and hurried to the ladder.

The loft wouldn't permit them to stand fully, so they moved about on their knees, settling their things back under the eaves. Aria tested the straw mattress laid on the rough planking floor, and she discovered it was soft and fresh. Near it, Lathrop had set a rolled feather ticking and two wool-stuffed, tied quilts and a heavy feather-filled comforter. Feather pillows completed their bed and Aria ached all over at the sight of it.

For the first time in days, Aria untied her laces. Weariness such as she had never known before overtook her. All her energy and concentration was focused on the simple acts necessary to remove her layers of clothes. She didn't want to think about the new lie . . . or what other tests tomorrow might bring.

The loft was warm, and in the light of a meager candle, she removed all but her thin chemise and slipped into her warmest nightdress. She pulled her ivory-handled brush from her leather valise and drew it through her hair with leaden, unconscious movements. Even the jerks of the brush in her tangled hair did not encroach on the reverie that settled over her.

The next thing Aria knew, a voice was calling her name through the darkness and something—someone—beside her stirred. Alarm grew inside her, but her sleep had been so dark and so deep, that she had difficulty shaking it off. Rising up on her elbow, she squinted into the gloom under the eaves and saw her mother silhouetted against a light from below.

"Yes, Lathrop," she was saying softly, "we're awake. I'll be down shortly."

Aria dropped back upon her pillow, her heart thumping wildly in her chest. Her mother's hand touched her shoulder.

"Hurry and dress . . . we'll need water first thing."

Still moving in a fog, Aria rose to her knees, blinking and rubbing her eyes. Her mother was already dressed and descending the ladder. She dressed hurriedly in the growing light from below, banging her head on the low, slanted roof and muttering furiously to herself. Her mother met her at the base of the ladder with a shawl and a wooden bucket.

"Lathrop says there's a spring just down the rise in back."

And before she could speak, her mother had turned back to the hearth and was tending and feeding a new flame carefully. Aria stared at her briefly, wondering at her seeming acceptance of their fate, then slipped the heavy shawl over her shoulders and headed outside with the bucket. She found the place where the spring bubbled up out of the ground to form a small brook and steadied herself precariously on the rocks that surrounded it, dipping the bucket into the cold water. When she pulled the bucket aright, it was only half full, and she huffed, scowling with disgust. The spring wasn't deep enough to allow the bucket to fill.

It was a minute before she thought to go farther downstream and finally found a deeper pool that yielded a full bucket. This time, she also got down on her knees on the rocks beside the water, finding it a much steadier posture for drawing water. And yet another lesson was in store for her as she carried the full bucket back up the slope toward Lathrop's cabin. It took every bit of strength she had to carry the huge bucket—and every bit of grace she possessed to keep from sloshing the hard-won water over the sides. By the time she set the bucket on the floor by the hearth, she had developed a profound respect for the strength and endurance of the serving girls who had tended her cultivated penchant for cleanliness.

Dread crept up Aria's spine the next afternoon when a hillside farmer and his work-worn wife came into the store to trade for supplies. Lathrop called her over and handed her a slate, telling her to mark the value of the man's selections as he called them out and to tally them up. At first she tried to figure each sum as it came, but then Lathrop called out several things at once and she had to copy them all so as not to forget any. Her heart thudded harder with each addition to the list and when their trading was done, she had a list of fourteen figures to add.

Lathrop tied a last string, around the bag of coffee, then came to stand beside her to watch her ciphering. She grasped the slate nervously, making moist clouds on it where her warm fingertips touched it. The farmer and his brown-faced wife came to watch as well, and Aria could hardly swallow as she watched the slight trembling of the chalk in her fingers. After what seemed an agonizingly long time, she finished the sum and Lathrop straightened, raising one brow quizzically.

"That's it, then? Four and seventeen?"

Aria felt her tongue growing thick. "I'd best do the sum again." She managed what passed for a helpful smile at the wary farmer. "We'd want it right for you, sir." She set to work with her chalk and added each column a second time, finding it a bit easier and breathing a sigh of relief when the second total matched her first.

"Four and seventeen." She nodded toward Lathrop, avoiding his pleased scrutiny. The farmer and his wife seemed relieved and Lathrop told her to subtract it from the value of the wheat and corn and the price he had allowed for the man's several animal pelts. Aria wiped the slate with the heel of her palm and felt again as if she were at disaster's very door. She copied the figures and felt her heart leap back into her throat. If her addition was unreliable, her subtraction was downright capricious. She smiled a sickly smile as the couple peered over the makeshift counter at her slate and she went to work.

The tireless lessons of long ago struggled to the surface and in a while she produced the sum, showing it to Lathrop, who whistled low and cast a good-humored frown at the scowling farmer. "Much more of this and I'll be done in."

The farmer shifted from one heavy shoe to the other and glanced at Aria. "Ain't she goin' to do it twice?"

Lathrop sobered, but retained the glint of amusement in his eyes. "Sure." He shrugged and looked expectantly at Aria.

Aria sighed quietly and set to work again. Miraculously, the difference in the sums remained the same and she held it up for all to see. Her face colored at the satisfied smiles of both Lathrop and the couple. The farmer was so pleased, he stuck his thumbs in his rough belt and strolled around the store, eyeing the goods judiciously. He stopped by a bolt of blue flowered muslin and lifted it, running a hardened hand over it. He lifted it up and brought it over to the planking and plopped it down before his startled woman's eyes.

"A dress's worth, ma'am," he proclaimed regally.

Some time later, the couple packed their new belongings on their horses and set off. Aria thought of her fear of being discovered and of the lie her mother had thought might help her. It weighed heavy on her and she thought again her resolve on the trail. So much of her life had been predicated on lies . . . and look where the falsehood and pretense had gotten her. Truth was a hard master, but deceit was crueler, even to those who served it best. Nay, she would never deal in lies and she must not allow this one to go forward now.

She approached Lathrop as he finished serving a pair of local patrons in the tavern and she asked to speak with him. Her spine was straight and her hands were cold as he turned his perceptive gray eyes upon her.

"Cousin, I cannot allow you to think that which is not, when it is in my power to correct it."

He squinted and cocked his head, setting his hands to the waist of his damp apron. "What are you saying, girl? Speak plainly."

"I . . ." She took a deep breath, tempted strongly to let things stay as they were. But a pang of conscience spurred her sharply and she blurted out, "My mother was wrong to say I am good with figures. They were always my worst subject at my studies."

Lathrop's eyes widened and Aria braced herself for the gale of his anger. But he threw back his head and his hearty laughter washed over her crimson face instead.

Taken aback by his derision, she stepped back and muttered, "I thought you ought to know, Cousin. I can . . . help you in the tavern, still."

He snatched her arm to stay her when she turned away.

"No!" He wiped his eyes, trying to calm himself. "Wait . . ." He slowed and took a deep breath. "Take no offense, Aria, none is meant." He pulled her to one side of the bar and smiled at her. "Whatever your skill with figures, it will outstrip mine. Do you know, that until today, I have had to bring my customers into the tavern and treat them to a few rounds of ale whilst I worked to total their bill. Heaven above, girl—even with your 'worst' you'll save me a fortune in free brew!"

Aria stared at Lathrop, and when his shoulders began to shake again, a grin crept over her face that slowly turned to laughter. It was the first time she had laughed in weeks. And she knew that her vow to live only by truth had been validated.

Even though the sunlight was shortening daily, the days seemed to stretch on interminably. From the moment they rose each morning to the moment they settled into their snug bed, they worked almost constantly. The straw broom, the water bucket, the tied-feather duster, the paring knife, and the scrub brush became extensions of Aria's self. In addition to her duties in the tavern, she fetched morning water, scoured cookpots, tidied up the tavern, and dusted whatever seemed dusty. She learned to pluck chickens, to dry beans, apples, and onions for stringing, to milk a cow, to keep an inventory ledger, and to appreciate the luxury of washing, even in cold water.

In the evening, Lathrop took her into the tavern with him,

where she tended the fire and served the food her mother prepared and heavy pitchers of dark, pungent ale, applejack, and
noggins of flip. She kept her hair pinned up inside a white
linen cap and wore one of Evelyn's generous, long aprons that
hid the fashionable depth of her eastern necklines.

She thought she'd never get used to the sea of rough, unshaven male faces that followed her every move about the tavern. She spoke little and could hardly keep from wincing if
there was a sudden move or an explosion of laughter near her.
But after a fortnight, she began to relax and managed an occasional smile when she was paid a rough compliment or was
lent a helping hand by a regular patron.

Little by little, her arms slowed their pinging and her shoulders eased their throbbing when she lay down in her bed at
night. Her stiff fingers regained their mobility and the sore
red spots on her delicate palms toughened into pale callouses.
With only small variations, each day seemed to follow on in
the same pattern. Aria would have lost track of time altogether
if it had not been for the periodic interruption of the Sabbath,
which Lathrop kept strictly as a day of rest.

Glover's Station, as both the trading post and the settlement
were known, was a center of social life and information as
well as trade. When a circuit preacher passed through, Lathrop
set up his stools and benches for a Sabbath meeting. People
stopped in to relate a birth or a death and to read, or have
read, one of the Richmond papers that arrived about every
fortnight.

Aria watched her cousin with his patrons and she learned
much about both. Not only had Lathrop set himself up in business, he had developed a way of life for many people in the
surrounding hills. His stock of goods determined what tools
they might buy, what they wore, how they lighted their homes,
what spirits they drank. His desire to know what was happening in the larger world brought those papers from Richmond
with news that was duly shared, and his charity and imminently

practical religion shaped the moral tone of the area. These hardy people sought his advice and brought him their news.

Aria could not help comparing her cousin and her new existence with her father and her life of empty luxury she had narrowly missed. These were good people, sturdy and hardworking. Their speech and manners were often crude; they were sometimes stubborn or quarrelsome. But Aria felt their determination to succeed here as the very pulse of the land. In their daily struggle for survival, there was no room for deceit or falsehood.

Here was the true life of the colonies, strapping bold and deservedly proud of its survival. This was the expansion, the opportunity the colonial patriots now fought for. Here was the fullest expression of the freedom to speak, to grow, to build . . . unhindered by fetters of empty loyalties and traditions and subservient to none.

Lathrop had made a life here, and in time, she prayed she might make one, too. That hope strengthened her flagging endurance when she realized the long days of grindingly hard, "respectable" toil ahead of her.

Then one night, when they had been with Lathrop nearly a month, a trio of coarse, stringy, over-the-mountain men burst into the nearly deserted tavern late in the evening. Their buckskin jackets and breeches were filthy and they bore long knives in their belts and long muskets over their shoulders. They spent a long, raucous while haggling with Lathrop over the price they were to get for their pelts and hides. Then they sat down in the tavern and consumed the last scrap of Marian's food and began to drink.

They called for more ale and Aria glanced warily toward the store, finding it dark. Alone in the tavern except for one sleeping patron, she drew a pitcher from the large keg and carried it to them, careful to keep to the far side of the table.

"What be the matter, girlie—you don't take to the likes of us?" The burly one laughed, showing his decayed and missing teeth. "Come on around here." He swung one arm wide, beckoning. "Ol' Thacker won't hurt ye none."

"We'll jes' have a bit o'fun." The scrawny one's eyes bulged at the prospect. "We got us a smart bit o' coin an' part of it's yours if'n you treat us right."

Aria clamped her jaw and turned quickly to go. But Thacker's meaty hand snaked out to grab her arm and jerk her back. Twisting cruelly, he pulled her half across the table toward him, shoving his revolting face into hers and smirking drunkenly. "You won' do better'n us tonight, girlie. We'll show ye some real fun."

"Let me go!" Aria spat, green eyes wild with fury. She twisted defiantly in his grip but gasped with pain and groaned, "Stop it—let me go!" She tried again to pull away, but found herself hauled up onto the tabletop by three pairs of greedy, probing hands. "No! No—" Her protest was silenced by a grimy hand, clamped mercilessly over her mouth so that it dug painfully into her cheeks.

"Come on, girlie, don't fight. Ye'll make ol' Thacker sore—an' mean." He pushed her down on the tabletop with his belly as he mounted her on the table. Her thrashing fists were held by the others and the pain in her face pounded through her, making her see dark, blurred spots. She tried to scream, but the sound died a strangled gurgle in her throat.

They pulled off her apron and Thacker tore clumsily at her laces, while his excited accomplices pushed her twisted skirts up her bare legs, fondling them. In the brief second he released her mouth to rip at her bodice with both hands, she drew a starved breath and screamed with all the terror in her. He rocked down on her to silence her with his own spittle-flecked mouth and his accomplices laughed. In their drunken state, they were oblivious to the scuffling behind them.

A heavy stool crashed down over one man's head, dropping him to the wet floor. The other two raised stunned faces to confront the muzzle of Lathrop's flintlock musket, inches away.

"Get away from her!" Lathrop's order was raw and furious. "And get out of here afore I drop you where you are!" The muzzle inched up exactly even with Thacker's bloated face. "Get off her!" He pulled back the level and the click punctuated his command.

"We was jus' havin' a bit of sport wi' yer uppity girl—"

"I ought to kill you here and now," Lathrop blazed as Thacker slid to the floor and stumbled into his inert friend. "If you ever set foot in here again, so help me God—I'll do it!" He burned with contempt as they dragged their unconscious companion to the door and scrambled onto their horses in the darkness.

Marian slipped around Lathrop and gathered the quaking Aria into her arms, murmuring soothingly and leading her into the cabin. Marian helped her up the ladder and held her trembling form until her sobs quieted. All was deathly quiet in the loft as Marian stroked her honey-colored hair and winced at the sight of red marks the brute's fingers had left on her cheek. In a while, exhaustion overtook Aria and she slept, but for Marian, release was not so quickly had. She watched her lovely daughter and her heart shrank within her. What would become of her, here in these rough and dangerous backwoods?

That night the dreams began. Twice Aria was roused from sleep shaking cold and yet wet with sweat. She dreamed again of those fingers, touching and loving her, then grasping and hurting her. And the second time, it was a face that haunted her—a bold, square masterpiece of masculinity that bore a carnal smirk of disdain . . . a face with eyes that burned for her.

The evening's narrow escape only heightened the memory of the time she hadn't escaped—or wanted to. The earl's fascinating face, his mesmerizing loving, pressed her physically once again. In her mind, each detail of her sweet surrender was revived and relived, leaving her warm and aching . . . and shamed.

The sun was well up when Aria descended the ladder the next morning. Her mother and Lathrop and Evelyn were sitting over breakfast ruins at the table.

"I'm sorry I'm late . . ." She flushed and hurried for her shawl on the peg by the door. "I'll fetch some water—"

"Aria, please." Lathrop beckoned her to a seat with them. Stricken by the seriousness of his tone and the graveness of her mother's face, her legs went weak and her mouth dried. She sank onto the edge of the chair, bracing for the worst.

"I'm sorry about what happened last night, cousin. I swear I did nothing to provoke it—"

"No, Aria." Lathrop glanced at Marian, whose gaze searched her lap uncomfortably. "I know it was not your fault. You cannot help the beauty with which you have been blessed. Our attempts to hide it under a bushel have not been very successful. It should be an asset, a blessing to you—a joy. But in this backwater place, it may prove more a bane."

Aria's face burned and she lowered her eyes, praying Lathrop wouldn't order her to leave to forestall more trouble.

"That is why you will help in the store and the kitchen . . . and leave the tending in the tavern to me."

Relief flowed visibly through Aria and she would trust herself only to smile weakly and nod in affirmation. Hurrying to the door, she grabbed the big water bucket and fled.

Nine

The coming of the next Sabbath ushered in their fifth week in Cousin Lathrop's house and dawned unseasonably balmy. With the store and tavern closed, there was little to do but enjoy this respite from the cold and damp. After a morning of unaccustomed quiet that chaffed the edges of her nerves, Aria slipped to the pole barn and managed to saddle her horse.

With the help of an empty nail keg, she mounted and rode out without telling anyone. She knew Lathrop would have sound reasons for his objections and she was determined to have a ride, however brief.

She had forgotten the discomfort of riding astride; now it reminded her poignantly of their perilous flight from their home. But soon she caught the rhythm of the animal's movements and relaxed into harmony with it as she struck out along the road.

The early leaves were starting to turn colors and the bright sun enhanced the growing variety of nature's palette. The gray haze had lifted on the breeze and revealed the true lushness of the forest on the sides of the road. Aria drank in the sight and the musty, sun-warmed smell. She kicked the horse into a gallop and raced exultantly down the rutted road, feeling utterly free.

The exertion brought blood up under her fair skin and she slowed, removing the shawl tied about her shoulders. Still the sun's heat plagued her and she untied the linen cap that contained her hair, shaking it free. A vague sort of contentment nestled in the center of her.

The heat of the sun and the aching in her thighs finally drove her to dismount and to walk her horse into the woods in the direction of the stream. She knew there was a meadow somewhere east of the tavern, near the stream. It would be a good place to rest after she let her mount drink.

Soon a faint droning sound caught her ears and she held her breath briefly, concentrating on it. The sound of water running . . . the stream. Relieved, she led the horse along through the twiggy undergrowth, weaving about to avoid the snags and trees.

She emerged from the canopy of trees onto a small cliff, well above the rocky streambed. Just where she stood, the valley widened dramatically and the small stream that ran by Lathrop's tavern joined a much larger stream to flow swiftly through a tree-lined bed for as far as her eye could see. From her vantage point, Aria could see there was no approach to the river for some distance. She turned the horse and led it in and out of the edge of the trees, following the edge of the cliff as it lowered to meet the small river.

It was pleasant, walking through the wisps of dry grass, feeling the sun's warmth trading places with the trees' shade as though they danced a slow reel. Some distance away, she saw a huge, flat boulder jutting from the shore into the water and headed for it.

She knelt on the rock and lifted water to her lips with cupped hands, drinking thirstily. "It feels good, doesn't it, boy." Her mount had waded in to his knees and shook the water from his nose as if agreeing. "I had no idea there was a river here. I suppose I have much to learn about our new home, eh fella?" She sat back and pushed her feet out before her, pulling off her boots to stick her feet into the cold, inviting water.

The movement caught her eye as she slipped to the edge of the rock, and at first she dismissed it. A drifting twig or branch, she assumed. But it came again and she turned to scour the far bank, feeling disturbed. She caught the outline of a horse, standing in the shade at the edge of the trees. She stiffened, concentrating on the area around it. There! Emerging around the edge of the rocks, thirty yards away—someone in the water . . . a man. She jerked her stocking up and shoved her boots back on, trying to keep herself from looking. Scrambling up onto her knees, she shaded her eyes with her hand and scoured the other bank, for signs of others.

The man was bathing . . . no, swimming. His shoulders glistened like the water's white foam whenever they emerged from the water. His shoulder-length hair was dark as it clung to his head and his shoulders seemed uncommonly broad. Watching him secretively sent an unexplainable shiver through her. For some perverse reason, her limbs refused to obey her when she made to leave.

Her heart picked up its pace as the man plied the water with long, fluid strokes of quite muscular arms. And that moment's contrary admiration obscured the fact that he was swimming in her direction. By the time she realized he was coming nearer, he was already too close. As she slunk back on the rock, he stopped and found shallow footing on the mossy rocks barely twenty feet away.

Aria's eyes widened as his big, heavily muscled form emerged from the water in the nearby shallows. Her eyes stared with terrible fascination as the water lowered from his waist, down over his bare hips. He was totally naked.

Shame infused her skin with scarlet and she felt something squeezing at her throat. She watched, hypnotized, as he stretched his arms out, then up, where he raked his fingers back through his dark hair. His back was to her, but he began to turn about, gazing at the trees on the bank as he rested.

Desperately, Aria forced herself to move back toward the bank, praying she might escape his notice. But the movement only caught his eye that much sooner and his startled face came about defensively. He whirled fully around to face her, coiled and braced.

Aria's heart stopped completely. For what seemed an eternity, she was frozen by an icy gray stare from eyes she had seen nearly every night in her sleep. It was the same square, muscular jaw, the same straight, blunted nose, the same disdainful cast around his carnally carved mouth. And now the rest of him, fully revealed, burned its way into her brain. His upper chest was deep and heavily muscled while the tight skin over his ribs tapered to a lean waist and hard, tight abdomen. He was powerful, magnificent, terrifying. Sunlight danced in the water that clung wantonly to his skin. His arms were corded like a fine Grecian sculpture, and his legs—

"You!" The cold tension in his face melted into a beguiling half-smile as he eased his defensive stance. But he made no move to cover himself, standing insolently at ease as if taunting her to inspect him. "Imagine finding you here," he said, laughing and setting his hands to his waist.

The sound of his voice jolted her into action, and she scrambled from the rock, heading blindly for her mount. He waded a few steps toward her, but his foot hit a sharp rock and he stopped to grab it angrily. By the time he straightened, she was mounted and riding furiously along the bank, heading upstream.

"Damn!" he swore, turning back to the water and wading out enough to dive in and swim hard for the opposite shore. He was shouting as he rose on the other shore and climbed out on the rocks. "Jamison! Jamison!" He reached for his towel and hastily rubbed at the water on his body. He would never dry and dress in time to catch her. "Jamison!" he bellowed.

Merrill Jamison came running through the trees, his shirt tail flying. He stopped dead as the earl's shouting became intelligible. He was pointing across the river, upstream.

"There she is—grab a horse and follow her, Jamison!"

Immediately Jamison was in motion, running back toward the tie line of their horses. He jerked at a set of reins and swung up into the saddle. He rode straight into the river shallows and forged out into midstream, scanning the bank upstream for the earl's personal quarry. Motion betrayed her position as she rode up on the cliff and instantly he set his course to follow.

Aria looked back over her shoulder as she started up the rise onto the cliff. He had crossed the river quickly and was emerging onto the rocks. She swung her burning face around and urged the horse on, as fast as prudence would allow. At the top of the ridge, she turned suddenly into the trees and bent low over the horse's neck, avoiding branches and hurrying around the logs and stumps that blocked her way. Her chest was tight and she gasped for breath as the animal jolted nervously below her. It seemed to have caught her panic and she strained to keep it from bolting recklessly through the woods.

What if he followed? Even if he couldn't follow the broad trail she was leaving, how difficult would it be for him to find the road and then Glover's Station? She pushed on, her mind whirling as she fled the haunting past that seemed to reach out for her.

After a short eternity, she spotted the road and kicked her horse into a full gallop on the dusty, rutted path. Her throat was dry and her eyes burned from the wind, but she ran full tilt until she felt the horse slowing with exhaustion beneath her.

Slowing to a walk, she struggled to regain her grip on sanity. What made her think he might come after her, search for her? She shivered in the bright sunlight and pulled out her white, ruffled cap, stuffing her hair into it with hands that shook violently.

Seeing him like that . . . naked . . . it was natural to feel unsettled, even frightened, she reasoned, dealing only with the topmost layer of her churning emotions. Like as not, he'd enjoy a repeat of their shameful encounter . . . but he wasn't the kind to go out of his way to seek one woman out when he probably had a bevy of fawning strumpets—eager to cater to his lusts. Even in the backwoods, a rake of his caliber wouldn't be inconvenienced by want of a partner for long. He seemed to have a nose for finding a woman's vulnerabilities. He certainly had found hers and played masterfully upon them.

By the time Aria walked through the door of Lathrop's cabin, she was outwardly composed. Inwardly she was grimly apprehensive about her own determination. It should make no difference to her if he found her here at Lathrop's tavern, earning an honest living by serving others. But it angered her that some part of her still felt shamed and disgraced by their circumstances. The only real humiliation, she chided herself, was knowing she had allowed him to work his wicked, hypnotizing lusts upon her. And that was long past, probably forgotten as easily as his last evening's supper.

She set about peeling and paring potatoes as if nothing had occurred. Being near the hot fireplace, sharing common tasks with her mother and Evelyn, her tension abated, leaving her feeling slightly silly. What ill could intrude on so common and uneventful a scene? The afternoon's shocking encounter seemed more like a dream with each minute that passed.

"Aria," her mother said, turning to her sometime later, "we'll need water for coffee. Likely we'll have patrons to feed, even on the Sabbath."

Neglecting her shawl, Aria grabbed the bucket readily and headed for the stream. Her steps were light and quick across the worn grass and down the path to the stream. But at the sight of the rippling, bubbling water, she felt her bones weaken and shook her head to dispel the sight of *him* from her mind. She hissed and forbade her contrary thoughts to extend farther than her growling stomach. Despite her resolve, that peculiar weakness continued to plague her knees and curled its irresistible tendrils up into her abdomen. She sat back on her knees on the dipping rock and forced herself to swallow against the tightening in her throat.

The sun was lowering earlier now and already the trees at the edge of the clearing blocked its final rays before supper. She thought about what the coming of winter would mean, trying to avoid the one thing that seemed to override her consciousness. *He* was here . . . nearby . . . somewhere . . .

She was halfway up the hill, concentrating on the brimming bucket and her own panicky thoughts. Her head was down and she might have run right into them if one of the horses hadn't snorted and edged sideways into another. Her head snapped up and she jerked to a dead halt. The dread that she had battled these last hours now succeeded in freezing her to stone.

She was confronted by a veritable wall of horseflesh. Nearly a dozen men sat staring down at her. And it was a paralyzed moment before she recognized the rider of the huge bay stallion directly before her. The earl leaned an arm on the pommel of his saddle and let his steel-gray eyes roam over her in a leisurely fashion.

Blood rushed to her cheeks, washing them crimson as the details of him seared their way into her mind. His rugged face was half shadowed beneath a flat beaver hat, and his broad shoulders were encased in a soft deerskin jacket. His muscular legs were covered by tall, polished boots. She swallowed, unable to move, but just able to force her gaze away from his. Her eyes flashed with sudden anger at the smirk of amusement on his face when he took in the bucket of water she carried.

They blocked the path back to the cabin. A bolt of ire ran up her spine, stiffening it and jarring her frozen limbs loose. Furiously, she pivoted and started off across the threadbare clearing around the back of the cabin, heading for the front of the tavern. The creak of leather and the thudding of hooves on the packed ground followed her.

"That looks heavy. Would you like some help with it?"

She could hear the smile in the earl's taunting voice and she quickened her step. She gritted her teeth, feeling her body and her senses spring to life under his scrutiny. She heard a shooshing and a thud and could see his deliberately casual dismount in her mind. When he grabbed the bucket from behind, she refused to let it go and turned on him, eyes glowing green fire.

"Let it go!" she demanded, realizing as a chorus of rough laughter broke out from the men behind him that it was probably just what he had expected her to do. His satisfied smile was canted a few fascinating degrees but she was already in high dudgeon and refused to succumb to it. "Let it go," she ground out huskily, her voice a purring threat for his ears alone.

But his smile just broadened. "Always eager to be of assistance to a 'lady.' " His hands relinquised it just as her green gaze narrowed vengefully.

Once she felt the weight of it again, she moved back a step and dropped it, right on his polished feet. The water splashed up, wetting his immaculate pants and shocking him back with its coldness. Let them laugh at that!

Aria would have been pleased by the flare of ire in his lordly face, but she could only imagine it as she ran around the corner and burst in through the tavern door. Lathrop was checking the depth of the ale in the barrels with a stick and looked up.

"Did I hear riders?"

"Yes." Aria headed straight for the doorway to the cabin, shaking and breathing in panicky gasps. What could she do? Where could she go?

Her mother looked up from a great iron roaster set just above the coals and straightened, wiping her hands on her long apron. "You can set the coffee on . . . what is it, Aria? You look like you've seen a ghost, girl."

Evelyn rose, clutching her shawl about her, and came to take her cold hands. "What is it, Aria? Your hands are like ice."

"There are," Aria swallowed hard, "riders. Several. And the

Earl of Penrith is with them." She looked at her mother, and Marian's face drained slightly.

"The earl? Are you quite sure?" Marian stopped and let her eyes drift the room as though collecting her thoughts from its corners. She looked at Aria and chewed the corner of her lip. "Well, he cannot do us harm, nor would he, I think. What would be his motive?"

Aria groaned inwardly as several sprang to mind.

"He is a gentleman," Marian continued haltingly, as if trying to convince herself. "We will bear ourselves properly and he will do no less."

No sooner had she spoken, than a fist pounded at the planking door to the cabin. They could see horses through the small windows, but little else. Aria's mouth went dry and her heart began to thud agonizingly. All three women looked at each other, and finally Marian started to the door.

But the door flung open. "Excuse me—" The earl stepped inside and stopped, eyeing the women with a controlled politeness. His breeches were half soaked and his boots had water beaded on their toes. "I daresay, someone dropped this." He held out the wooden bucket on two fingers as if it were an exhibit. He looked first at Aria, then at her mother, and affected gentlemanly surprise.

"Why Mistress Dunning, Miss Dunning . . . imagine seeing you here." He set the bucket down and swept his elegant beaver hat from his head.

Aria saw red at his unmistakable reminder of their meeting earlier in the afternoon. She watched him take her mother's hand and graze it delicately with his lips and she worked hard at loathing him.

"Your lordship," her mother said, smiling, "this is indeed a surprise. What brings you here . . . to . . . this remote part of the colonies?"

"Oh . . . hunting, madam." He leaned back on one leg and

smiled. "I was led to believe that the game to be had in these parts was rare and worth the chase."

"The game is certainly rare in these parts, sir." Evelyn managed a small laugh. "So rare as to be gone."

The earl turned to her expectantly and Marian stepped closer. "Evelyn Glover, your lordship, my cousin Lathrop's wife. They own and run this trading post and tavern."

The earl took Evelyn's hand gently and attended the same irksome devotion upon it. Aria was curling inside at the mockery of his attentive manner.

"And of course, you know my daughter, Aria," Marian's smile thinned as she watched Aria shrink slightly, then stiffen as he approached her. The earl claimed her hand, though she did not offer it, and turned it over to place his lips against her open palm. Marian dropped her eyes, pretending not to see. Something in her chest dropped heavily.

Aria jerked her hand away as if he had scalded it and glared wordlessly at him as she moved past him to the dish shelf.

"We were preparing Sabbath supper." Marian tried to smooth the jagged atmosphere that engulfed them. "If you and your companions have not eaten, you're welcome to eat with us. I think there'll be plenty, we usually plan on extras."

The earl tore his eyes from Aria's stern back and smiled delightedly. "That would be a boon, indeed. We've been camping for several weeks and my companions crave a bit of comfort. Then perhaps tomorrow, we can replenish our supplies from your stores." This last he addressed to Evelyn, whose pallid face brightened.

"You can eat with us, here at our table, and your men can eat in the tavern. How many are with you?" Evelyn inquired, smoothing her apron self-consciously under his eyes.

"Twelve, madam." He smiled with an engagingly wicked twinkle in his eye. "I've a penchant for biblical numbers."

Evelyn laughed and inserted her thin arm through his, leading him toward the tavern. "Then you must meet my husband,

Lathrop. He prices his goods much the same way you number a hunting party . . ."

Aria turned with dishes in her hands as they cleared the doorway, and she glared after them. Marian saw her resentment and understood it.

"Aria—" She moved to put her arm about her daughter.

"I loathe him, the arrogant swine. He's come to gloat over our misfortune since I refused to—" She stopped abruptly, furious with herself for letting him make such a jumble of her feelings and thoughts. She turned back to her work, smacking the pewter plates and mugs down hard as she set an additional place at the table. She scrubbed more potatoes almost viciously and sliced carrots on the board with unholy relish.

Marian watched surreptitiously as Aria vented her steam. The earl still wanted her and she was bound to have nothing to do with him. Marian's brows knitted as she tested the great roast of pork on the spit above the coals and turned it. Despite his arrogance, he was wealthy and strong and a fine figure of a man. She postponed further thought of it and attended her cooking.

She rose later and set her hands at her waist, stretching her shoulders back. "Aria, all will be ready soon, and we still need water."

Aria colored and reached for her shawl. "I'll get it." Just as she reached for the bucket, the earl's form filled the doorway from the tavern. Quick to seize an opportunity, he crossed the modest room in a few long strides.

"Allow me to help." He reached for the handle and Aria released it instantly.

"Then I'll tend the warming oven and get out the platters." She turned quickly away, shrugging out of her shawl.

The earl sent an appealing look toward Marian. "But I don't know where the stream is," he lied.

Marian turned back to her pots and kettles. "Aria will show you."

The order was clear enough and Aria's eyes narrowed briefly at her mother. She spun the shawl onto her shoulders and jerked up the latch on the door.

Ten

He caught up with her and fell into an easy stride beside her. Her arms were crossed over her chest, trapping the ends of her shawl down over that fair expanse of chest that made him fairly itch inside. Since he had seen her that afternoon, he had thought of nothing else. The cold water of his swim had awakened his senses, set them humming, and when he saw her poised on the rock above him, they absorbed her into his very body. Everything about her had pounded through him at once: the creamy perfection of her breast, the sun-kissed silk of her unbound hair, the luminous green emeralds of her eyes, the rosy pout of her generous lips. Until that moment, he had not known the full fury of a desire that consumes all segments of a man's being—his body, his mind, his very soul. Until that moment, he had nearly convinced himself that his pursuit of her through these backwoods burroughs and primitive camps was a diversion, something on which to focus his restless energies and exercise his luxury-dulled faculties. She was a challenge to a jaded palate, a fresh and utterly appealing taste of sensual awakening. It was natural that he try to reclaim and hold the territory he had once conquered so memorably.

But as he stomped and paced and rumbled orders through his camp, waiting for Jamison to return with word of her, he felt as though something had invaded his skin and crawled and twisted mercilessly about in his guts. His excited nerves seemed to catch fire when he thought of how close she had been and how it felt when her unforgettable eyes had flowed helplessly over his bare body. He had eaten well only a short while before, but his stomach felt achingly empty. He knew no common food could assuage this familiar and yet unaccustomed hunger. Aria Dunning was what he wanted and he vowed by everything he still held sacred to have her.

When Jamison returned with word that she had returned to a settlement, not an hour's ride away, he felt a determined calm settling over him. The turmoil of his passion was not subdued, simply constrained beneath ruthlessly practiced self-control. He knew at last where she was, and in a short time, he would see her again. This time he would do whatever was necessary to see that Aria Dunning would be his.

Aria watched him from the corner of her eye, careful not to let him know. The worldly and disdainful earl had never troubled to temper his mockery around her. Even now, he made the simple act of carrying a wooden bucket a calculated taunt. She reached for it irritably and pulled it toward her. "I'll take that now."

But he refused to part with it and, instead, used her grip on it to pull her a bit closer. "I said I'd draw the water . . . to replace the bucket you . . . lost. You'll find my determination not easily thwarted." He engaged her wary eyes and smiled beguilingly. Aria felt as if she'd been doused with warm oil. "You preferred this 'honest toil' to a life of ease and nights of pleasure at my side, I thought perhaps I'd try it myself . . . to discover what about it enthralls you so."

Feeling the heat of his hands near hers, she pulled them back and tucked them across her chest once more. She was unnerved by what seemed genuine humor in his irresistible smile. There seemed no end to his treachery.

"You've come a long way to mock me and my circumstance."

"I would go even farther," his features sobered and his voice grew a velvety coat, "to learn what else might enthrall you."

Aria drew a sharp, nervous breath and set off on wobbly legs, berating her own willy-nilly responses to him. She forced herself to recount his arrogance, his lecherous demands, his dismissal of something so shattering as the loss of her virtue. His coldness, his calculation were suddenly too well hidden to suit her. He was too attentive, too accommodating to her humble relations . . .

She broke the taut silence, stopping abruptly at the water's edge. "You play with us in a mean sport. Since when do King George's earls draw water like kitchen maids and spend courtly kisses on the hands of tavern keepers' wives?" She could feel his eyes roaming her as though they were a second set of hands and braced herself to resist his physical advance.

"When they have something else in mind." He paused on the slope beside her, resting the bucket on one bent knee. "Are you sure this honorable toil is quite to your liking? I swear it seems to agree with you." His eyes blued and crinkled mischievously at the corners. "You are as tempting as ever, Aria Dunning."

"A dubious distinction, since it takes very little to tempt you," she bit out nastily, forcing herself to realize that he fully expected to charm his way into her arms and bed . . . probably this very night! Even the potent spell of his nearness, his maleness, could not obliterate the feeling that it was wrong, even dangerous, to be so near to him.

"*Um*-m-m . . ." He maintained an infuriating insouciance as he deflected her barbs. "Hair like flowing honey . . ." He reached out one finger to touch the bit of her hair that her cap did not hide, then let it slide down her temple and along the sweet curve of her cheek before withdrawing it. "Skin like cool satin, eyes as green and depthless as fine emeralds, ripely rounded breasts, trim, shapely ankles, and—"

"Stop it!" Aria felt her anger and her resistance to him threatened seriously by the warm honey flow of his outrageous words. She stepped back jerkily, reminded that even distance was no safeguard against his intoxicating tones and seductive speeches.

"—such are all it takes to tempt me to ride about for weeks

in a godforsaken wilderness—" He stopped abruptly and straightened, his captivating lecher jerked unceremoniously back beneath the commanding aristocrat. "My offer to you is still good. And seeing your charming privations and rustic circumstance, I shall not hold your former obstinance against you."

"You are as bold as Satan himself," she stated in angry wonder at the scope of his lordly conceit.

"Ah, but much better looking. And, I think, after this afternoon you have the experience to judge me correct." His head tilted and his arm extended slightly at his side, inviting her to resume her inspection.

Mortification nearly purpled Aria's face and she whirled, grabbing up her skirts and running back up the path toward the cabin.

"Damn!" the Earl of Penrith swore under his breath and started after her. But the bucket in his hand hit the ground and he muttered another unholy epithet as he collected it, then dropped to one knee by the water to scoop the bucket full.

Several long, climbing strides and she was within sight. Her shoulders were squared proudly and her skirts twitched beguilingly as she half walked, half stomped, across the clearing. He hurried to catch her, even as she approached the cabin, and grabbed her wrist to pull her about to face him. She tried to wrench free, but quickly surrendered to his superior strength.

"I've not heard your answer." His breath came fast as he looked down into her hostile beauty, but whether from exertion or from thwarted emotion it was hard to say. He pulled her stiff hand up and glanced from her face to the pale, yellowed calluses at the base of her work-reddened fingers. "Come with me and share my bed and you need never suffer these again." Her hands closed defiantly against his gaze and he pressed his case more adamantly. "Enough of these games . . . name your price and I'll see you have whatever you want." He stiffened as if he spoke to himself as well. "I have never offered such terms to any woman before now."

Aria stared angrily up at him, fighting the insistence of his resonant voice. It suddenly struck her that he thought her resistance was calculated to extract a better arrangement from him!

"You insufferable swine," she whispered. "You think I barter for better terms?" The righteous fire in her eyes made him reconsider the course he had pursued. When she yanked her wrist hard, he released it. "You think of women as pleasuring chattel to be bought and sold, used and discarded like an outmoded coat. Just make the offer high enough and you get whatever you want. Well this time, *your lordship,* you go without. I don't want you or anything you have. There isn't enough gold, enough ease, enough luxury on this side of the ocean to buy you what is left of my honor. What you've had of me already," her voice cracked humiliatingly, "I can never replace. It was more than you had need or right to take."

Feeling her eyes burning suddenly, she backed away from him. "Just go away!" She meant to fire one last volley, but she choked as she uttered it and angry tears pooled to douse the fire in her eyes. "Please—just leave me alone." Humiliated by her traitorous, swelling emotions, she whirled and ran for the safety of the cabin door.

Aria's aim was better than she knew. The persistent Earl of Penrith felt like a hole had been blown through his midsection. He had rather face a full cannonade than the desperation that coaxed her tears to defy nature and refuse to fall. He felt that miserable twisting in his gut again and clamped his jaw together savagely as he sought to control it. It was a long, uncomfortable moment before he could follow.

"I insist, Lathrop." Aria pulled a heaping platter of roast pork from his hands, forcing a false pluckiness into her voice. "I'm not hungry and I'd be poor company at supper." She caught his dubious scowl and smiled as she pretended to read his concern. "I've met Mr. Jamison before; he's a gentlemanly fellow. I won't come to any harm. Just bring the bowls and platters through for me." Before he could raise another objection, she turned and carried the platter down between the long planking tables of men and sat it down before the startled and somewhat uncomfortable Merrill Jamison.

"Mister Jamison, how good to see you again." She smiled with genuine pleasure and pushed him back down by the sleeve as he sprang up.

"Miss Dunning—"

"No, truly . . . sir." She cast a demure look about her at the roughly clad group of men. They were dressed in skin jackets, breeches, and wrapped leggings, though a few wore woolens and boots. They were of mixed age, though tending to the younger; some bore weathered faces, while others showed the paler countenances of city life. Most were unshaven, though clearly they had washed at least face and hands in preparation for a real meal. And they all scrutinized her with bald curiosity. "I hope you've enough ale, I'll draw more when you need it."

"This lady is Miss Aria Dunning," Jamison said, and rose anyway, sweeping the lot of them with a meaningful look, "late of Chesterfield County and Royal Oaks. She is our . . . hostess this evening."

Aria colored at the delicacy of his wording and would have corrected him, but she saw nods of recognition and murmurs all about her. These men seemed to have heard of her family, no doubt because of the villainous acts perpetrated upon them. Well, it was small enough wonder; the whole county had been awag with the story . . . and likely the tale was carried.

Merrill Jamison watched her lithe young figure uncomfortably and several times entreated her to take his seat and join them, but she declined, claiming she had had her fill. His wary eyes returned over and over to the short hall and doorway to the owner's cabin, where the earl was dining. He half expected his friend to burst, outraged, into the room at any second.

Occasionally, she ventured to ask about the success of their hunt or the settlements they had visited. Under Jamison's watchful eye, she was answered in respectful tones and gradually her stiffness abated. The time passed quickly and she returned to sit on a stool beside Jamison several times, trading talk of small matters, including her cousin's trade and the local Indians.

But the Earl of Penrith's meal was far from enjoyable. When Lathrop announced that Aria had insisted on serving their guests, he had ventured a raised eyebrow and a question about the propriety of it. Lathrop had simply shrugged and murmured something noncommittal about Aria's determination as he took his place at the table. Aria's empty plate was often the focus of surreptitious glances and talk grew strained as the laughter and noise wafted in from the tavern increased.

The earl's face grew tighter and twice, when Aria's voice became recognizable, he turned restively in his comb-backed chair and the muscles in his jaw could be seen to work. The atmosphere in the well-warmed main room of the cabin chilled perceptibly as he tossed furtive, irritable looks toward the draped doorway.

The tension was hardest on Evelyn, who was seized by spasms of coughing and was helped by Lathrop into their modest room. He soon escaped as well, stating that he needed to check the stores for what the earl's party needed. That left Marian to clear up after supper.

"Perhaps I may be of assistance." The earl's boot hit the floor with a heavy thud and he rose. "Manual labor seems to be the fashion these days."

Marian protested as he began to stack the plates, but an imperious look stopped her and she grimly set about her usual evening tasks. The air about them crackled with expectation and Marian felt her nerves as dry as tinder.

"Why . . . have you come, sir?" she finally screwed up

courage enough to ask, though not enough to face him for his reply.

He stopped midstride with an empty platter in his hand and his head tilted to study Aria's mother closely. She stood over a basin in the dry sink, her hands hanging and still in the gray, tepid water. Her once genteel skirt was spotted here and there with grease and gray smudges of ash from the cooking fires. He recalled the quiet elegance of the woman as she had presided over the gracious Royal Oaks. A new light flickered in the flinty gray of his gaze.

"I am hunting, madam."

"Hunting what, sir?" She turned slightly, listening intently.

The earl's mouth pursed as he considered his response and he stated boldly, "Your daughter, madam."

Marian dried her hands hurriedly on her apron and stared unseeingly before her. "You have spoken with Aria of your . . . intentions?"

"I believe you know that I have, madam," he intuited, watching her more intently. "And she shows a marked aversion to my . . . generous offer."

"And just what did this 'offer' encompass, sir?" Marian's voice was soft and she held her breath as she clasped her hands before her.

His had tilted and his eyes narrowed as he contemplated what to say. "I offered her a place at my side, comfort, security."

"In return for?" Heat flooded Marian's face as she forced herself to bear the shame she was feeling for her unholy thoughts.

"I believe you know that also, madam. She would share my bed." He saw her flinch as if struck, but she stiffened and turned to him.

"And what else?" Marian's gentle eyes were trained on his sharply squared features.

"What else?" he echoed, surprised by the turn of the woman's mind. Honestly, he had never thought beyond his bed, where Aria was concerned. Then he thought he recognized the direction of her thoughts. "If she bears a child, it will be cared for accordingly, with generosity."

"You mistake me, sir." Marian surprised herself with her boldness. "What would she be to you besides a courtesan? And where would you house her? My boldness shames me but I . . . must know." Her eyes lowered to her tightly wound hands and the earl nodded, unseen, in recognition of the difficulty of this topic of one of her background.

"Such conversations are not uncommon on the Continent, madam. There, 'Mama' often negotiates for her daughter's future. Aria would live with me, of course." He felt himself coiling inside as he answered things he had not yet fully considered.

"And receive your friends and manage your house?" Marian lifted her chin, forcing herself to study him.

"Most likely . . . in time to come," he admitted after a while, hoping to pacify her and telling himself it was possible. With Aria's beauty, grace, and genteel background she was indeed fit to preside over his house as well as warm his bed. Then he swept such considerations aside. "Perhaps if you spoke to her, madam . . ." he ventured.

Marian now studied him through narrowed eyes. His bold, sensual features and extreme male presence sent a shudder through her. "What manner of man are you? What kind of life would my daughter have with you?" There was a trace of sadness in her voice that pricked something near the center of the earl's well-protected chest.

He looked thoughtful and offered her his hand to lead her to a seat near the fire. She refused it, making her own way to the settle. The earl's rueful smile seemed to acknowledge: like mother, like daughter. And Marian rose yet another notch in his hard-won estimation.

He stood before the fire, pondering her question, and looked at her perceptive face, feeling that she had already drawn her own conclusions.

"I am a man of considerable resources, and not without influence. I am strong enough to take what I want . . . even Aria, should it come to that. But I am a man of education and background, without brutish habits. I would prefer she come to me willingly. She will have possessions, comfort, and pleasure, madam. She will have all she can possibly need or want. Here," he glanced pointedly about the modest cabin, "she has no future at all."

Marian shivered involuntarily, knowing that everything he spoke rang of truth—Aria had no future here and he was certainly capable of taking Aria against her will.

"She hates you, you know." Marian's thoughts shamed her as they escaped her lips. "Perhaps she would find her . . . duties . . . with you loathsome."

The earl smiled with animal-like satisfaction that nearly stopped Marian's breath. "I know exactly what Aria feels for me." His eyes gleamed briefly with memory. "And it is not disgust, nor loathing. She may find me hateful, but she wants me as a man . . . that is all that matters to me."

A silence settled between them, growing more weighty as it lengthened, and the muted sounds of the tavern seemed a grating intrusion. Each considered the other, and as if something inside her had wilted, Marian's shoulders sagged and she buried her face in her hands.

The earl shifted from one leg to the other, feeling an unaccustomed pang that reminded him of a conscience long subdued. He wrestled with himself, trying to harden himself against the tears he expected when she raised her face next. It struck him that this might be a ploy to elicit some benefit, some payment for her cooperation, and he tested his supposition.

"I have no desire to drag her from her mother's side kicking and screaming. I could see that you were well provided for in the bargain."

Marian's face came up, drawn, but unstreaked by tears. Her

soft eyes glistened with extra moisture that soon faded under anger's heat. "You would be willing to buy her, then?"

The earl snorted disagreeably, mistaking the light in her eyes for self-interest and calling himself seven kinds of a fool for not seeing it before. "Name your price, madam," he ordered curtly, "and I shall render it to you."

"It will be high, sir." Marian clipped her words as sharply as he had his.

"Name it, madam, it is yours!" he commanded irritably, not caring to hide his contempt for her shameless greed.

"Then you will speak the vows with her." Marian straightened slowly, then rose before his mistrustful scowl.

"What?" He jerked his head back and glared at her, but she held her ground.

"That is my price . . . that which you have just agreed to pay me. You will speak the vows with my daughter, sir, or you will take her only after my last breath is spent." Marian's face glowed like translucent stone.

"Take her as my wife?" He was incredulous; the astonishment melted his sternness thoroughly. This woman was as full of twists and turns as her tempting and tempestuous daughter. He had never considered she might require such a thing of him.

"You find the prospect so odious?" Marian tilted her chin imperiously and folded her arms about her waist.

"Indeed . . . it had not entered my mind," the earl snorted. "I thought . . . to provide you with an income or—"

"*That* is my price." Marian's voice lowered by serious degrees. "You would take my daughter to your bed, beget children upon her whilst she entertains your gentlemanly friends and runs your household. Whether you realize it or not, sir, you want her to wife you. She has received education and upbringing befitting the finest of ladies, and would grace a greater household than even yours. Agree to speak the vows with her or find yourself a doxy to warm your knees and let us hear no more of your wants!"

The earl's mouth drooped slack. How widely his judgment had missed the mark with the mother gave him pause to wonder if he could have misread the daughter as well. But it was only a momentary twinge, soon buried by the onslaught of his keening pride.

"I shall think on it," he mused, stiffening.

As if by some insidious conspiracy of the fates, the tavern curtain lifted and Aria entered, holding it aside for two young men of the earl's hunting party. They bore stacked platters to the table and were thanked prettily for it. Their admiring smiles, as they nodded toward Aria on the way back into the tavern, raked cold steel fingers through the earl's belly. Her eyes were crinkled with genuine delight as she smiled at them, then turned to look at her mother. Her face flushed as she felt his hot gaze upon her and struggled to avoid returning it. But her eyes betrayed her and fluttered inescapably to his direction, deepening the color in her cheeks to a lovely scarlet. The sight was all the confirmation Marian needed; the earl knew well the drift of her daughter's yearnings, even if Aria did not.

Aria had seized a rag and wetted it, then hurried back into the tavern before she could be halted or delayed. The earl's eyes moved with her, absorbing her movements with a possessive hunger. The wry smile that stole over his face was self-deprecating. He ought to have had better sense than to touch her that first time, let alone actually take her. Arrogance makes a good crown for a fool, he had heard it said, and now he paid handsomely to learn the truth of that old saw.

"You have no vicar, no priest, here," he said, still watching the final sway of the door drape.

Marian's face drained as her head snapped toward him. Her heart stopped. "Then you agree to my price?"

There was a pause. "I agree to it."

"Then swear you will speak the vows before the first available parson or preacher . . ." Marian stepped toward him and clutched his arm, staring up into his hooded eyes. "Swear it to God himself."

The pain in the woman's face tightened his chest disagreeably and he dismissed it, reminding himself that it would be some time before they were likely to encounter a colonial parson or "preacher." And if he were forced to speak the vows with the wench, what of it? It would finally settle the question of his marriage and would handle the potential fruit of their union. Marriage need not really change much for a man of means, except to regularize his pleasures and to give him a home, a fixed point about which to move freely.

And there was Aria herself and the deep, intriguing awakening of her pleasures that he had tasted so briefly. He had sworn to have her, to end this odd restlessness that plagued him and interfered with his other pursuits. A strangely amused expression stole over his features, causing Marian to wonder if he meant what he said. But he was thinking that it might be the wench would prove as fertile as she was desirable and he would have long droughts of her pleasures ahead in which to rue this bargain.

"Swear it before God." Marian tightened her hold on his muscular arm, feeling its strength and hoping it would be used to uphold and protect her daughter, never to abuse her.

"I swear it," the earl uttered slowly, looking at the jumble of emotion in her face. "I will speak the marriage vows with her at the first opportunity."

Nodding weakly, Marian released his arm and sank on the settee, clasping her hands in her lap as though they pained her. "Leave tomorrow at first light, then, and take her with you."

The earl watched her internal struggle keenly. "Aria is not likely to welcome that idea . . ."

"Leave the matter in my hands," Marian said softly, her voice dull with pain and resignation. "She will go with you tomorrow morning. Keep to the woods yet awhile. Once you are far enough away from here . . . and she has . . . grown used to you, she will come to accept it."

A soft, insistent voice called Aria back from the dark comfort of oblivion. She floated toward it, unwilling to obey and yet unable to resist. Her mother bent over her on their pallet bed in the loft. In the dim candlelight, Aria could tell she was already dressed.

Marian touched her daughter's face and pushed back a lock of hair that had escaped her nightcap. She sagged slightly at the sleepy smile that bowed Aria's generously curved lips, recalling that same soft innocence of waking from years ago.

"Time to rise, Aria. We'll have guests to feed this morning—hurry." She gave Aria's shoulder a gentle shake and rose. "Dress quickly. I've already laid the fire."

Aria stretched her arms out in the chilly air and kicked the cover aside wearily. Shivering, she pulled her petticoats and her green woolen dress up under her nightdress and fumbled to right them while still on her knees. She was nearly dressed when Marian appeared at the top of the ladder with a crusty roll and a mug of tea.

"I know you didn't eat a bite of supper. It's not good for you to go without eating, Aria," she chided, handing them over. "Here . . . and hurry down to the smokehouse for a side of saltpork."

Aria watched the top of her head disappear from the edge of the loft and bit hungrily into the crusty roll. Marian had slipped a wedge of creamy white butter inside it and she groaned mutely as she savored it. The tea was slightly bitter, but the heat spread lusciously through. her body. She finished pulling on her shoes, pulled up the covers of their bed, and started down the ladder. By the time she reached the bottom, she felt a bit strange . . . lightheaded. She turned toward the fireplace, putting her hand to her forehead. Her mother was

weaving about the fire with her kettle and settling her griddle
on the coals.

Aria blinked and swayed, feeling her sight narrowing into a
long, ever-darkening tunnel. She reached for a nearby chair,
grasping its back with one weak hand. Marian was coming
toward her saying something to someone she couldn't see . . .
then all was soft, warm darkness.

Eleven

Tynan Rutland twisted in his saddle, shifting his delicate burden onto his other aching arm briefly. His shoulder muscles were contracted into knotlike bunches and small rivulets of fire raced up his arms with annoying frequency. Pushing his body's complaints from his consciousness, he looked down for the hundredth time that day on Aria's sleeping face.

Her dark lashes feathered softly into crescents against her cheek and her reddened lips parted invitingly as her unconscious movements nestled her even closer against him. It was those enchanting little movements that produced the keenest agony for him, the misery of untimely arousal that underscored his growing weakness for the woman in his arms. At such moments his face was a glowering mask of displeasure that confounded his companions and sent most of them riding on ahead, ostensibly scouting the area.

Late in the day, he fell to the back of the party, asking Jamison to scout for a suitable campsite and glaring down his questions before they were even asked.

Rutland always had reasons for what he did, Jamison told himself, and eventually the full circumstances of this mad flight from Glover's Station would come out. Never predictable, the earl had truly shocked Jamison when he appeared outside Lathrop Glover's cabin bearing the delectably unconscious Aria Dunning in his arms. Just as Jamison started to protest, Mrs. Dunning had appeared behind his noble friend, bearing two small leather satchels. Dumbfounded, Jamison had taken them and stowed them on a pack horse, as he was bade. When he returned, they were already in motion and Rutland's only explanation had been an oblique reference to a betrothal, spoken loud enough for several of the men to hear. Shortly, every man in the company had observed the possessiveness with which he held her before him on his mount, and wordlessly the understanding was passed that the earl had indeed claimed the girl as his.

The light was dimming fast and Jamison found a suitable spot for several days' camp near an uncharted stream that trickled through a secluded little valley. When he carried word back to the earl and pointed out the approximate location from atop a rocky rise, he was sent immediately back there to supervise the setting up of a base camp. The amiable Jamison spurred his horse irritably and charged recklessly off into the trees below.

The earl's face broke into a pleased smile and he let his mount set a leisurely course down the gentle treed slope. His strong, square hands roamed the silhouette of her cloak, feeling the luscious bend of her waist and the elegant curve of her hip as she leaned against him. Her head fitted neatly in the corner of his shoulder as he held her on the saddle before him, reaching about her to grip the reins. The hard pillow of his chest was warmed by her cheek as it lay against him. That small spot of warmth seemed to promise the sharing of greater warmth yet to come. His breath moved wisps of her soft hair as he looked down at her, willing her to awaken and entwine her lithe arms up about his neck and to press her tempting lips against his. And for the first time since before dawn, Aria stirred, moving her head such that her cheek rubbed the soft deerskin covering his chest.

The earl stiffened, realizing the lulling effects of the day's counterfeit intimacy. There would likely be retribution when she awakened and he tensed in anticipation of a veritable tempest of fury. Then he reminded himself that for him, the reckoning could only end sweetly. A taut, knowing frown creased his brow as he felt her stir and he determined his course with the precision of a thorough, amorous tactician.

Aria's throat was parched and her body swayed and jostled about in an incomprehensible jumble of half-recognizable motions. A dawning gray awareness pervaded her. She was heavy, so heavy, and something confined her to a strange leaning position. She snatched at reason, full consciousness, as it came near, but it seemed to veer off just out of reach in some strange spiraling orbit. It came to her that if she waited, it would eventually complete its gyrations and its ever-decreasing circles would bring it to her eventually. Relief spread through her at this semicoherent bit of deduction and she stirred slightly, awaiting its leisurely descent.

Her eyes fluttered open, but refused to negotiate a common direction and thus shut without providing her meaningful sensation. The force that held her began to feel like . . . arms . . . and the swaying became understandable as the familiar rhythm of a horse in motion. She pushed her eyelids open sternly and glimpsed trees, leaves, patches of dim sky, before they slammed shut again. She tried raising an arm. It was as limp as a noodle and dropped to her side with a plop.

A sound rumbled about in her head and she concentrated her efforts heroically on lifting her head and opening her eyes simultaneously. And it worked!

But what she saw made no sense at all. She knew the face that stared down into hers . . . it was *his* face . . . the earl's handsome, faintly cynical. . . . And as she turned her cheek against his chest, she saw that he held her in his muscular arms and that they were indeed seated on a horse . . . in that forest she had glimpsed.

She closed her eyes again, waiting to awaken fully and half wishing that the dream would continue so that she might learn what would happen next. She snuggled her face back into her firm pillow and sighed dreamily. Her lips bowed with a secretive smile as in her mind's eyes he tilted her face up to his and pressed her lips gently with his own. The sensations were divine . . . all hard and soft at once, just as she recalled them. They produced in her that strange, hungry, drawing feeling she had experienced before only in *his* arms.

Then his circling arms clasped her tightly to him, pressing her softness against his hard body. Beneath them, the rhythmic motion stopped. Her neck hurt as his kisses deepened and began to demand, but it seemed a small sacrifice when this sublime, uncharted excitement was blossoming inside her. His hand took hers and set it up and about his neck, then he returned to stroking her side, her back, her shoulders. Each sweep of his touch was a tender mercy upon her strained and aching muscles.

Her fingers lingered wonderingly over his corded neck, then wound their way upward to his ear and explored the surprisingly soft texture of his dark hair where it gathered at the nape of his neck. Everything about him felt solid, firm, sensual . . . even the supple deerskin that covered his shoulders. Deerskin . . . she shuddered unexplainably.

Her eyes flew open as a stark flash of jagged reality tore through her. This was no dream! He held her . . . in his arms . . . on a horse! Stunned, she pulled her heavy arms from him and he released her, staring with desire-darkened eyes into her dazed expression. He loosened his hold on her and swung his leg over the horse and down to the ground, while steadying her on her seat. He reached for her and his hands slipped inside her cloak to grasp her waist and pulled her down. The heat from his hands flooded into her through her clothes. She stood shakily, and shook her head, trying to clear it. The hood of her dark cloak fell and her hair tumbled about her shoulders in mad disarray.

"You're weak yet. Lean on me." He pulled her against his side with one arm. His deep voice was husky and vibrated Aria's very fingertips. "Or would you rather I carried you?"

"Where . . ." She managed to speak with a tongue that seemed twice its normal size. "Where am I? Where . . . are we?" Her main thought was to be rid of his dangerous, compelling hands and so she pushed against his side with all the force she could muster.

"Whoa—" He caught her before she fell and his unrestrained amusement rankled her fully conscious pride, rousing the rest of her with it. "You're with me," he answered, as if speaking to a child, "and you're safe."

"That's . . . a contradiction in terms," she managed as she planted her feet farther apart and then shook his hands from her arms. This time she stayed upright and his chuckle stiffened her thoroughly. She scowled and looked about them for the cabin, the settlement . . . anything familiar. Her wits were returning and the unbroken expanse of trees and scrubby undergrowth about them gave her an awful feeling of alarm.

"I want to go back . . . where is Lathrop's cabin?" she demanded, cringing inside at the way her voice cracked. She didn't like the way he seemed to be inching toward her . . . with that strange, animal-like look on his aristocratic features. "What am I doing here?" she demanded, risking a step backward and locking her knees. "What's happened to me?"

"You're with me, in the woods." His gaze seemed to spear her and hold her as he approached. Only the rustle of leaf litter on the forest floor marked the passage of time. "And your cousin's establishment is a good two or three days' ride," he pointed over his shoulder, "in that direction." Then he pointed to his left, "or perhaps it is that direction." He smiled knowingly and straightened, pointing behind him casually, "Or perhaps it is that direction . . . it is so difficult to tell direction in the deep woods."

"I don't believe you." She turned her head and glared at him from the corner of her eye as she scrutinized their surroundings desperately. "What am I doing here? Take me back, at once!" A twinge of hysteria entered her voice before she could curb it.

"No," he stated coolly, easing within arm's reach of her. Her cheek still bore the imprint of the soft fringe on the shoulders of his jacket and her green eyes seemed large and luminous, inviting. He could still feel the lush warmth of her pliant mouth under his. "You're with me because this is your place now. You're mine, as I said you would be. You'll travel with me from now on . . . and provide me with your . . . unique comforts." His silvering eyes seemed to strip her of her cloak and her arms came up to clamp it tightly about her.

The impact of what he said came crashing down on her and she staggered, causing him to put out a hand to steady her. She jerked away from it as if it were poisoned.

"You've abducted me." she whispered hoarsely. "You've stolen me from my family—they'll search for me! They'll track us down . . ." she threatened wildly, building a bit of hope for herself that it might be true. Her mother especially would know that she would never—"They know I would never have come with *you* willingly. They'll search for me."

"On the contrary," he said, seeming calm in the face of her growing panic. "They know I have you . . . and have quite agreed to the arrangement."

The news slapped the last bit of dust from Aria's faculties. She heard the birds overhead, smelled the leafy musk of the forest floor, felt the raw thumping of her heart and the full, aching misery of her bones. Everything was excruciatingly clear now. *He* had taken her from her home to be his—

"Liar," she charged, trembling with fury. Her fists clenched into cold knots and her legs seemed like frozen logs. "They would never give me over to a man I despise as I do you!"

"Give? Never suppose they might be so generous with their only prize. You were bought, wench, and with a sufficiently high price that it will take a long time to recoup upon your delightful person." The silver of his glowing eyes seemed to have chilled into bright stone.

"I don't believe you." She clamped her hands up over her ears. But in so doing she only trapped the awful echo of his words inside: *high price . . . sufficiently . . . high price . . .* "My mother is a woman of honor." Aria felt her stomach sinking even as she yelled it out. "She would never sell me into whoredom with you." As she spoke, she recalled vividly the cold fury in her mother's face the day she had refused the earl's degrading proposal. Was it possible?

"She knows how much I hate you . . . hate your arrogance, your smug pretense of civility, your lechery. She would never have betrayed me into your vile—"

He lunged forward and grabbed her shoulders, his fingers biting cruelly to stanch her tirade. "What you think of me is of no consequence. I've told you the truth . . . you're with me now because you belong to me . . ." He struggled with her thrashing, wriggling form, finding it no easy task to subdue her.

"Stop it!" she screamed, struggling to bring her hand up toward his face, her nails bared. He jerked her hard and pulled her full against him, pinioning her arms at her sides and half lifting her feet off the ground. She kicked at his boot ineffectually and wriggled in angry horror. "You low, disgusting—"

"What more proof do you need," he ground out, "of your mother's collaboration than your strangely prolonged sleep? It was her idea to secure your cooperation herbally. Did you enjoy your early morning tea?"

To his surprise, she slowed and managed only to push feebly against him. He could not say whether it might still be the effects of the sleeping powder or whether she heard the truth of his words.

It was the brutal truth of his declaration that wounded her beyond the scope of her struggle. "I don't believe you," she choked, pulling at the back of his jacket.

"She is quite an interesting woman, your mama. Quick to see the practicalities of life and unafraid to seize them. And I think in time you, too, will show promise in making the most of your situation."

Aria was melting inside, unable to absorb all he was making her hear. All she could think was that her mother had sold her into whoredom—just as she had been sold, young and defenseless, into a prison of a marriage. Was it possible? She reeled at her only answer . . . she had learned that she knew very little of her mother . . . but thought she was coming to understand more as their days together passed. Behind her mother's stoic facade, was she so desperate to return to a life of comfort that she would sell Aria into such depravity? And the motherly gesture of concern that morning . . . the tea . . .

"No!" she thrust wildly at him and won her freedom unexpectedly. "You lie," she charged, trying to convince herself of it. But as she backed hurriedly toward the horse, she tripped over a dead branch and found herself falling flat on her back.

Even as her arms flailed to break her fall, he was in motion. And she had barely thudded on the ground before he was atop her like a springing cat. He pushed her arms out to her sides, pinning them there as he eased his heavy body down on her stunned, breathless form.

"Accept it, wench, accept that you are mine now," he growled with a growing huskiness. His face, above hers, was dark with displeasure.

"Accept your abuse? Let you make me your whore?" she spat, fighting for her breath under his crushing weight. "Has the mighty Earl of Penrith sunk to this . . . wheedling and niggling like a penniless sailor to satisfy his lusts?" His face darkened at the cutting accuracy of her assessment.

"I paid a high price for you, wench, and I have you . . . that's enough for now. You have no life back there." He renewed his offensive. "If you escaped and somehow found your way back, they would only return you to me with all haste. You have no place in the world, except with me."

"You cruel, heartless bastard," she rasped, realizing the awful truth he spoke in the ache that was twisting her heart in two.

"I've told you the baldest truth," his deep voice came with tormenting intimacy, "so that you might realize your situation and reconcile yourself to it. It is not so bleak, nor am I so unbearable as you might think just now."

His hand released her wrist briefly and he quickly trapped it beneath his elbow as he reached up to push back her tangled hair from her face. Something inside him was turning over, crowding his chest annoyingly. He watched her teeth savage her lower lip and turned her face up to run his finger over it in a spell of release. The blood-red marks that scored that perfect curve seared their way into his memory.

"Look at me," he commanded furiously, forcing her face back to him when she turned it away. "Look at me."

He stared into the liquid crystal of her haunted eyes and felt a blast of flame shoot upward from his loins. He trapped her gaze mercilessly in his. "I'll see you're cared for, wench. You have nothing to fear from me." He saw the defiant sparks that were struck in her eyes and added, "It is your pleasure I seek, not your soul."

His lips descended on her hungrily, pushing her head back into the leafy carpet below and easily subduing her panicky twisting. She finally lay still beneath him, surrendered to his overwhelming power. Bitterness welled up in the back of her throat.

The calamity of this final and most horrible loss left her too empty, too barren inside to withstand. She didn't want to breathe, to live anymore— She was falling, deeper and faster, in a yawning, black pit that seemed to threaten oblivion. And in desperation, she clutched at something, anything to check her terrifying fall.

Her hands moved over the reassuring solidity of what she had grasped. Her arms circled it and pulled it closer against her. Her eyes opened and she knew she had embraced *him,* the source of her pain and now in a strange way, her only comfort. Giving herself over to the wild sensations surging through her, she returned his kiss as deeply and passionately as her experience would allow.

He made a guttural, animal-like sound deep in his throat and shifted above her to open her heavy cloak. His head left her bruised, throbbing lips to burn their way down across her shoulders and breasts. His arms slipped behind her waist, arching her back toward him as he rubbed his hot face against the refreshing cream of the tops of her breasts. He kissed them and traced the restricting outline of her square-necked bodice with his warm tongue. Aria could hardly breathe, caught up in a whirling dark maelstrom of feeling.

Helplessly, she clasped his dark head to her breasts and wrapped her arms about it. But soon he moved higher on her and kissed her in that deep, penetrating way that mercifully obliterated all else from her mind.

It might have been seconds, it might have been minutes, she had no way of knowing. His muscular arms withdrew from her waist and flexed. Suddenly, he was up on his hands and knees, astride her, staring down at her dazed and vulnerable form. She was like a pale, shimmering pearl set in a tangle of silken hair and dark velvet. And after all he had ventured and risked to bring him to this moment, he was strangely reluctant to press for its inevitable conclusion. He had taken her first beneath a canopy of trees . . .

Her eyes fluttered open, their centers dark with expectation and question. Her breath came in uneven little gasps that matched the wild pulsing of her blood. Cool evening air invaded the space between them, pouring over her well-warmed skin and setting it atingle. A chill invaded her limbs as she watched him above her, taut, poised like a hawk ready to strike. The muscles in his square jaw worked and the light in his eyes dimmed. A curl distorted one end of his bold, sensual mouth as his eyes roamed her. He raised above her so that he stood on his knees, then got to his feet.

"We'll save this play for later." He straightened his hip-length jacket casually and made a show of brushing leaves and twigs from his sleeves.

Disbelief screamed through Aria. She almost cried out to him not to go—to stay and touch her, and hold her. For when he stroked her and fondled her with his taunting, mesmerizing tenderness, he drove the pain, the losses from her mind for a while. She couldn't move. The loss of this last comfort was too cruel, too cutting.

He caught the horse's dangling reins and checked the saddle cinch. Aria turned her head to numbly follow his movements. It was as though she suddenly didn't exist . . . as though only seconds before he hadn't filled her arms, her universe.

If she hadn't already been lying on the ground, she would have dropped with the shock. He hadn't intended to make love to her. She felt the bubble of her despair shattering, sending its cold slivers slicing through her. She had berated his lechery, his callousness and arrogance openly, but until now she had never guessed his capacity for cruelty as well. He used her body's responses to cruelly demonstrate his dominion over her. He wanted to show her how easily he could take her, whenever, wherever he pleased. He wanted her to know how completely she was in his power.

When she opened her eyes, he was standing over her. When he reached down to help her up, she smacked his hand away and pushed up by herself. She stooped gingerly to retrieve her cloak, and felt the blood rushing to her head. She swiped the leaves and twigs from the heavy, dark velvet and refused to look at him.

"Are you recovered enough to go on to camp?" His question seemed an unnecessary taunt.

"I'll live," she spat, as if the prospect revolted her. But when she raised her lovely face to him, her green eyes were strangely pale, burning with hatred, fueled by pain. She straightened and pushed her hair back over her shoulder as if it were loathsome to her. When her cloak settled about her, she strode on unsteady legs to the horse and waited with seething patience.

When he made to lift her up, she jerked back, eyes blazing. "Just . . . get up," she uttered tightly, "I'll ride behind."

"Astride?" He was taken aback by the violent change in her.

"Why not?" She tilted her chin up defiantly. "*You* certainly do."

He threw back his head and deep, resonant laughter purged his tension. "Indeed I do, sweetest." He followed the curve of her cheek with the end of the leather rein. "And tonight I shall demonstrate just how pleasant a position it can be." She reddened and tore her eyes away, fastening them on the stirrup.

In a single fluid movement, he was mounted and he reached an arm down for her. She wanted to ignore it, but with him in the saddle, there was nowhere else to hold. Hauling her skirts shamefully high, she managed to slip her foot into the stirrup he had vacated and with one arm in his and the other on the rear lip of the saddle she pushed up and swung onto the big bay's rump, just behind him. How keenly he watched her every movement was revealed in his low, taunting comment.

"And while we're demonstrating my riding seat, perhaps we'll examine your lovely legs as well."

He kicked the horse into motion and she was determined to hang on without his assistance. But after several twists and jolts that nearly sent her flying off, she yielded when he halted the horse and pulled her arms about his middle, imprisoning them with his arms. Then every bump that brought them together ground her teeth together as well.

The base camp Jamison had set up consisted of three canvas tents erected under the shelter of the trees, a tether line for the horses, and a ring of small boulders set up in the center of a small clearing to serve the cooking and heating needs of the hunting party. A clear, shallow stream meandered quite near the edge of one of the tents, which seemed to be set apart from the others. And the evening's fire was just being lit as they approached. The earl's burly men moved about purposefully, each doing his preordained tasks efficiently, while casting a curious eye toward the approaching riders.

Aria managed to free one hand and pull the hood of her cloak up over her tousled hair as the camp came in sight. She was acutely aware that everyone in camp would know of the debasing role she was to serve here and she hardened herself against that expectation. Theirs might be the first, but certainly would not be the last scorn she would suffer. She might as well accustom herself to it now. Even if they treated her with a modicum of courtesy, it would be a loathsome game, played out only to appease the imperious earl. It was no good pretending honor where there was none. She would deal with her situation as honestly as the Lord would give her grace to do. But that did not mean she must accept her condition or bear it with meekness.

Sandy-haired Jamison came loping over, a wry expression on his face. He stopped, propping his hands on his hips and waiting for the earl to rein up before him. The light of speculation burned brightly in his boyish face and Aria felt her face turning crimson.

"Well, I was about to send out a detail to search for you." He grinned, searching Aria's stiff form intently enough to draw a glare from the earl. "Good to see you're awake at last, Miss Dunning." He nodded to her, little chastened by the earl's displeasure.

"Have you scouted the area?" The earl frowned and swung a leg up and over the pommel of the saddle and made a sliding dismount.

"Of course . . . nothing." He stepped around the earl and raised a hand to Aria, "May I be of assistance, Miss Dunning?" He smiled knowingly.

"No." The earl turned and cocked his head, as his lidded gaze warned Jamison away.

"I'd be grateful, Mr. Jamison." Aria's eyes narrowed as she put out both arms to embrace Jamison's assistance. The man could not help but lift her down, but was hasty at removing his hands from her waist. An awkward silence greeted her as her feet touched the ground and she stood with her hands clasped loosely before her. She missed the looks exchanged above her head.

"We looked for you to be right along." Jamison took in the bits of leaves and twigs that still clung to her cloak and his eyes widened with his own conclusions about the reason for their late arrival. The earl read his friend's thoughts and allowed his mouth to curl into a rakish smile. Seeing that Aria now watched between them, he reached out a square, sinewy hand and pulled a dried bit of leaf from the shoulder of her cloak, dropping it before her horrified eyes with a flourish.

"We . . . rested a bit. The lady was . . . tired."

"Then perhaps she'd like to lie down before supper." Jamison walked around them to grab the reins and gestured to the far tent, the one set closest to the stream, well away from the others. "I had your tent put over there. I thought you'd like . . . some privacy."

"Then you read my mind." The smirk was evident in the earl's voice. "The lady and I are indebted to you."

Aria's face went to deepest crimson as the earl took her arm and ushered her along beside Jamison in the direction of the tent.

"His lordship speaks for himself," she uttered loud enough for both sets of ears. She smiled grimly as Jamison turned a startled look upon her and the earl's hand tightened on her elbow.

"The wench found the journey a bit taxing." The earl's words were clipped with a warning tone she was bound to ignore.

"No doubt, it is some dread constitutional weakness of mine . . . not holding up well under betrayal and abduc—"

He jerked her arm nastily to stop her as he turned a stern look of imperial displeasure to Jamison. "She is too fatigued for company, tonight. We'll have supper in my tent."

"I'll see to it myself." Jamison glanced knowingly between his friend and the lady. He allowed an amused, insolent grin to surface as he turned away with the horse.

The earl glared down at her, then thrust her along beside him and through the opening flaps to the tent. He had to bend his head when standing upright, even in the center ridge of the otherwise spacious shelter. In the dim light, he captured her shoulders easily and pulled her around to face him. He hovered over her like a great, wrathful specter.

"Let me set a few things straight at the outset, wench." One dark brow rose. "This is a camp of men. Your protection is assured only in this tent and within the range of the firelight . . . nowhere else."

His intensity dissolved the retort on her tongue. She swallowed and shifted her feet to a firmer stance and raised her chin silently.

Seeing his message lodged, he straightened and eased his grip on her shoulders. One hand left her to sweep the dim interior about them. "You will make yourself at home here. Your things have been brought . . ." He nodded toward two dark lumps on the ground in the middle of the tent, drawing her gaze to them. Her bags. They were confirmation of her mother's conspiracy against her; he would not have them if he had simply abducted her in the heat of a moment's passion. Her knees weakened suddenly.

"You will call me by my name," he ordered tightly, "both before the others and in private. 'Your lordship' is too . . . formal, in view of the intimacy we shall soon enjoy."

"How generous of you . . ." she bit out, "to allow me such liberties. But I believe I've forgotten your name, *your lordship* . . . just as you seem to have forgotten mine. Or do you call all your whores 'wench'?"

Even in the dusky light, she saw a spark in the flint of his eyes as her steely taunt struck.

"Right now, you're the only one I have," he uttered slowly and deliberately, "and you will call me by my name . . . Tynan Bromwell Rutland." He leaned back on one leg and watched the determination in her gaze. Remembering his purpose for the night ahead, he added, "And you will be Aria to me."

He took an oil lantern from the folding table nearby and lit it. He set it back on the table, and instinctively, she backed against the closed tent flaps as he turned to her.

"I'll send some warm water to you. Get some rest now . . ." His mouth curled insinuatingly and he felt no need to complete his statement. What was meant hung between them on the air . . . she would have little chance to rest later.

He turned and pushed the canvas flaps aside, stepping out and letting them fall back into place of their own leisurely accord.

Twelve

Aria stared about her in the dusky golden lamp light. Beneath her feet was not the bare ground she had expected, but a warm, woven-rag carpet. There was a folding leather chair, a small table, a handsome wooden chest, and an unfolded cot, meant to sleep one. Atop the cot were a feather pillow and a thick down comforter. The smells of recently cleaned leather, waxed wood, and burning oil enveloped her. The blending scents spoke of well-tended male possessions and for some reason the sensations comforted her. She turned around in the center of the tent, looking with sad-eyed wonder at her new home. She sagged down onto the cot and closed her eyes.

With wooden fingers, she untied her cloak and pushed it from her shoulders. Her mother . . . sold . . . how could it be? The pain of dwelling on it was too sharp. She forced her eyes open and rubbed the moisture from her eyes with the heels of her palms. She wouldn't think about it. She couldn't think about it. She had to have all her strength for . . .

Her next thought was to escape; the one that followed was of the practical impossibility of carrying out her first one. She checked the rear of the tent and found tent flaps, identical to those at the front, tied neatly together. Deftly, she undid them and slipped out into the murky evening. She hadn't taken three steps before she heard him behind her.

"This isn't within the circle of firelight," he growled.

"Oh-h!" She startled about, forcing her fright into the cast of anger. One hand covered the skin of her chest as if to protect it from his sardonic gaze. She felt her heart thumping and drew herself up as tall as she could manage.

"There are some common duties that may not be performed in the public glare of a communal fire," she declared regally. "As you have noted . . . this is a camp of men." She tilted her face up to his in a show of reckless defiance and was surprised to see that it carried the day.

He relaxed back on one leg, setting his hands to his waist as he nodded wryly. "I grant you that . . . but I shall accompany you all the same. Your security may prove my entertainment."

Stung, Aria plowed through the underbrush behind the tent and heard him follow. When she was again installed in the tent, with the canvas flaps securely retied, he left her once more. Soon a short, grizzled man appeared with a copper basin of hot water for her, calling out to her from outside the door of the tent. She admitted him and watched as he fished into the wooden trunk for a fresh bit of linen toweling and soap and set them down on the table beside the basin. She remembered him from Lathrop's tavern.

"*He* said I was to see if ya need anythin' else, miss." The stout, ruggedly dressed man stared at the toes of his handmade boots as if embarrassed by his errand.

"No . . ." Aria felt his chagrin creeping into her face as well. "I have . . . all I need, thank you." She spoke softly. "But you can tell me your name."

He looked at her guardedly from beneath a silvering set of bushy brows. "Ac-re, miss . . . jus' like an ac-re o' land." He shifted feet, not knowing what to do with his empty hands, except let them hang at his sides. "I . . . do the cookin' here, miss. And see to the wood an' water an' such."

"Thank you, Ac-re . . . Acre." She smiled tentatively.

Then he was gone and she knew what was expected of her. . . . She was to prepare herself . . . for *him*. She balked at the thought, crossing her arms adamantly over her chest and glaring at the soap and toweling as if she could set them alight with the sparks from her eyes. But the warmth radiating from the basin was too tempting, too seductive to resist for long. It had been weeks since she had the luxury of warm water for bathing and washing.

She edged nearer and finally succumbed, hastily scrubbing and washing the grime of toil and trail from her. It was as soothing and comforting as a full, warm tub. Ruefully, she realized that this was but the first of the earl's tricks to win her cooperation. No doubt his vast, worldly experience made him know exactly what comforts a well-born lady would appreciate.

Well, she mused, as she knelt and opened one of her leather satchels, just knowing his purpose would nullify the seductive effects of his loathsome little bribes. She found her carved ivory comb and began to drag it through her hair, wincing as it snagged in the tangles.

He found her there, on her knees, trying to bring some order to her honey-colored cloud of hair. Her back was to him and he stood in the doorway a moment, appreciating the slenderness of her waist and the ripe roundness of her hips as she flexed and raised her arms. His mouth curled slightly as he recognized the stirrings within him.

The draft of cool air from the open doorway drew a chill along her arms and warned her of his presence. She startled about to find him staring at her above two heaping plates of food.

"You might find the chair or the cot more comfortable," he observed casually, entering and depositing the plates on the table. He paused, regarding the color blooming in her cheeks and the soft frame of her hair about her delicate, oval face. He smiled to himself as he picked up the cooled basin and carried it to the tent door and tossed the water out.

She held her breath as he set the empty basin down outside the tent door. Then he approached her, holding his hand out. She spurned his aid and rose stiffly under her own power. Clutching her comb savagely, she tucked her arms about her growling middle and lifted her shoulders. The delicious aroma of the roasted meat and biscuits and potatoes invaded her senses, wilting some of the starch in her spine. She felt as if she hadn't eaten in days.

He probed the inside of his cheek with his tongue as he let his warming eyes glide over the promising ripeness of her curves. She resisted him now, but in the morning . . . they would see how her feelings might warm.

He pushed the table closer to the cot and drew the chair up opposite it. Easing his big body into the chair, he waved her to a seat on the cot and watched her as she eyed first the tempting food, then the seat he offered her.

"It's not poisoned . . . nor stuffed with love philters. You've had a long fast." Reading her refusal fluently, he altered his approach. "But don't gorge yourself. I can't abide a woman who isn't dainty with her food . . . or eats so much she's dulled for other pursuits. Come to mind, it wouldn't hurt you to lose a bit of that colonial roundness of yours." He stroked his chin with one finger, as if appraising her, then propped his head on his knuckles. "It's charming at first, but heralds a quite unfashionable spread in days to come." He sent one finger across the table to hook her heaping plate and draw it toward him.

She snatched it out from under his poised fork and glared hatefully at him as she plopped down on the cot and stuffed a full half of a biscuit into her mouth at once. He winced for effect, but Aria knew he was toying with her. Chewing the dry bread seemed to take forever, and when a cup appeared before her, she dismissed all questions and drank thirstily. It was wine, a rich red liquid that filled her head with beautiful vapors. Her eyes closed and she sipped it again with a practiced study, appreciating its several merits. After her third mouthful of food, she sighed silently with the physical pleasure of eating and forgot all about the rapid demise of her resistance. That pleasant state might have endured to the end of the meal if he hadn't spoken.

"I usually enjoy a bit of conversation with my supper." He was sitting back in the chair, clearing his mouth and drifting his cup beneath his nose with lazy appreciation.

She swallowed a bite of the savory roast venison and glared at him wordlessly.

"You southern colonials put such a 'charming' variation on the king's tongue . . ." He straightened, fixing her with a taunting stare. "You're certainly in no hurry to be done with speaking. When I first landed in Virginia, I thought I had disembarked by mistake in a colony of the slow-witted."

Aria's sea-green eyes clouded with an impending storm and this time she hurried to swallow. "It would benefit most Englishmen to be slower with their tongues . . . it might give them time to consider the idiocy of their words *before* they are spoken and spare us much listening."

His grin infuriated her. She knew he baited her and still she hurried into his traps. Whatever was the matter with her? She found herself staring at the creases formed in his lean cheeks as he smiled. Her stomach flipped annoyingly and she scowled, turning back to her food.

"Of course, since then, I have become accustomed to the slower pace and now find it quite agreeable," he continued, swirling the wine in his metal cup about judiciously. "Especially the ladies' speech."

"Oh, especially," she echoed irritably. "You think we are a common, vulgar lot, we 'colonists,' but like most Englishmen, you are more than eager to overlook our churlish ways when you sniff some profit to be made. Churls we may be, but we are not duped by your sly smiles and indulgent manners. You English hold us in contempt and I for one would rather see it honestly, openly displayed than suffer this endless, patronizing sham of niceties and civility." She paused, breathless, surprised by her own virulence and nettled by his unruffled calm.

"I believe your northern neighbors are of a like mind. And I believe they have already put an end to the 'niceties' with lead ball and shot." He pulled her gaze into his and she felt him moving forward in his chair. "Pity," he mused, "there is more benefit to be had in cooperation than in conflict."

"The line must be drawn somewhere," Aria shot back, feeling he had shifted the focus and somehow had drawn them into his meaning as well. " 'Cooperation' bought at the price of pride and principles will never bear true benefit."

His shoulders shook with amusement. "Perhaps I was misled . . . I thought you were a cudgeled and branded Tory . . . loyal to the court and enamored of all that is English."

"Perhaps you mistake me for my father, *your lordship*. He labored under the misguided impression that the term 'nobility' implied life on a higher plane . . . nobler motives, superior actions."

"Nay, I'd never mistake you for a man, *wench*." He toyed disinterestedly with his fork then looked up at her from under lidded eyes. "Have you forgotten my name again so soon? Perhaps I shall have to tutor you more sternly."

"I, on the other hand, harbor no such illusions about the nobility." She clasped her cold hands tightly in her lap and continued evenly, ignoring the warning that tingled up her back. "I have learned how callousness and depravity may masquerade as privilege and superiority."

"Indeed?" His eyes darkened a shade. "You colonials have been too long separated from the enchanting vices of civilization to appreciate them fully. I shall make it my personal crusade to see you are properly introduced to them. And there is no better time to start than now. Come here." His voice rumbled low and compelling, vibrating things in Aria's middle.

She reached for her cup with a tremor in her hand and finished the rich ruby liquid. She rose slowly, feeling his eyes already undressing her. She stepped around the table and made an impulsive dash for the opening of the tent.

"No, you don't!" He had seen the telltale darting of her eyes toward the doorway and sprang from behind, grabbing her arm tightly and hauling her back.

"Let me go—" She twisted and pushed in his tight grip,

straining to turn her face as far from him as possible. "You have no right—"

"It's not a matter of rights, sweetest, it's a matter of power." The sudden exertion to subdue her made his voice husky. "I want you and I'll have you . . . now. But it is up to you how many of my men hear your struggles. I have no wish to provide them with such entertainment while I take my own, but neither will it bother me greatly." Beneath his voice ran a low rail of steel that brought Aria's face up in horror.

He was towering dark and powerful above her, holding her clasped against him with arms like unyielding oak beams. The golden light was transformed by reflection in his steel-gray eyes and glowed like quicksilver. She knew he spoke the truth . . . he would take her kicking and screaming if necessary. And it was also true that none here was likely to try to come to her aid against him, not even the pleasant, boyish-faced Jamison. She gradually lessened the force of her shoving against him and, in the silence, stood woodenly still.

He relaxed his bruising grip on her arms and returned to his seat in the chair, pulling her between his muscular legs and imprisoning her between them. His voice softened seductively as he lifted a strand of her hair from where it had fallen across her chest.

"You have such beautiful hair . . . a rare color and with the texture of silk." He rubbed it between his fingers and thumb appraisingly.

"Give me some shears or a knife and I will make you a present of it," she muttered defiantly, her knees beginning to tremble. She was succumbing to that mesmerizing spell of his and it frightened her.

"Nay," he chuckled harshly, "I'd rather have it on you—and then have you. When you venture outside my tent, wear it under a cap from now on." The tone was gentle but the command was ruthless to her ears.

"I will wear my hair as pleases me—" she flashed back briefly, only to have her protest smothered firmly by his quick, hard kiss. He held her head between his hands and his lips slowly gentled over hers, melting her determined frostiness. When he released her, she was dazed by the swiftness of her own response to him. She was trembling and felt as if her insides were dripping into warm little puddles. Panicky shivers ran down her limbs and the dark centers of her eyes grew larger with each wild pulse of her heart.

He must have sensed what was happening inside her, for he smiled knowingly and pulled her closer, trapping her between his thighs. His hands ran up the sides of her waist and met over the bow at the top of her front-lacing bodice. Catching her luminous eyes in his, he pulled the string and undid the bow. He hooked a finger over the top of the laces and pulled gently. She felt the laces slide and knew that a part of her resistance slid also. Then he repeated the action, lace by lace until her bodice was completely loosened.

As each lacing gave, Aria saw the flame at the back of his eyes glow hotter. She could barely swallow; something squeezed at her throat. She tried to make herself recall his arrogance, his cruelty . . . the shame of what he was doing to her. But it all became embroiled in the slowly swirling excitement that was building inside her. This must be the same magic, the same enchantment that had bewitched her in the grove and made her submit willingly to his desires. The memory of those delicious and forbidden sensations had become so entangled with the pain and upheaval of the fire and her father's death that it was no longer separable. And without those potent memories, she had come to loathe herself for her weakness. But she realized that she had no more defense against it now than she had that day, weeks ago. His power over her senses, over her responses, was as complete as it was irresistible.

His hands slipped under the shoulders of her dress and slid downward over her bare skin, carrying the fabric with them. Slowly, he peeled the bodice from her until it seemed to catch on the tips of her breasts. Her hands fluttered up to hold it in place, but he pulled them away and pressed one of her palms to his mouth. His tongue ran over the lines in her palm and sent a quiver of sensual delight through her.

"No," he murmured, holding her hand to his hot cheek and catching her gaze in his, "let me see your beauty. Surrender it to me." As his hands pulled the bodice down, his gaze remained locked in hers, pulling at something within her. His hands ran up her fully bare sides and over her ripe young breasts and his eyes then followed.

Aria was frozen, flushed crimson with embarrassment but feeling a current of excitement that immobilized her resistance to him. She should be ranting or struggling—but part of her wanted him to touch her, to caress her where no other's eyes had even ventured. And when he pulled at the waist of her dress and sent it sliding into a heap about her feet, a jolt of raw pleasure sent jagged tongues of fire through her body.

Then she wore only one petticoat and his big sinewy hands poured downward over it, following, exploring the outline of her hips and buttocks. His face was dark now and set with glowing white coals as he touched her body and felt it tremble beneath his hands. The excitement, as much as the evening chill, raised gooseflesh along her bare arms and set the rosy tips of her breasts atingle.

"You're cold," he murmured as much to himself as to her. He set her away slightly and rose, enfolding her against the heat of his chest. She trembled even more violently as his generous heat invaded her. It was all she could do to remain motionless, to keep her arms from closing about him. He filled her senses, her mind, her . . .

"Come, let me warm you properly." The command was spoken with hoarse effort as he drew her along to the cot and reached for the thick down comforter to draw it about her. He pushed her gently down onto the cot and lifted her feet around onto it.

Aria's head was spiraling dizzily and she lay back upon the feather pillow, unable to quell the hunger in her loins. Her lips were reddened, parted by her uneven breaths, and her eyes glistened with rising desire. She watched him peel his jacket and linen shirt from his broad shoulders and could not tear her gaze away as he shed his boots and unbuttoned the flap of his breeches to shed those as well. The golden light of the lamp cast a bronze glow over his emerging form and the breath caught in Aria's throat. He was huge, marvelous, terrifying . . .

He spread himself over her partly wrapped form like a great, heavy blanket that drove the breath from her. Slowly he replaced the down cover with his own hard, warm skin, pressing her down into the cot and forcing her softer frame to yield and mold to his. He saw the flicker of fear that shot through her face briefly and he smiled, stroking the borders of her oval face almost tenderly.

"I won't hurt you, Aria," he purred from deep in his throat like some great and dangerous cat, "You are more beautiful than I thought . . . even more desirable." He shifted lower on her and rubbed his smooth, lean cheek against the creamy mounds of her beasts while his hands traced the sinuous curve of her bare waist. "This bargain is not so unbearable . . . I'll show you the delights of your own body. And you'll have everything you want of me."

He rose suddenly and covered her lips with his, kissing her in that way that seemed to disturb and uncoil something warm and sensual in her loins. In one last bid for sanity, she gripped the edges of the cot with her hands to keep them from seeking him. But the urgency of his mouth on hers, the intimacy of his hard body fitted against her bare, vulnerable skin wrecked that last desperate bit of resolve. Her arms slowly wound themselves up and about his broad back and she felt him respond to her hesitant caress along the entire length of her body.

His mouth traced a now familiar path across her cheek and down her throat to her breasts and fastened there with tantalizing persistence. His tongue darted across her taut, budded nipples and she felt the rippling vibrations reaching into her loins and between her legs. His big hands teased and massaged her breasts and moved down to her waist and the flat plane of her belly.

She moved under his expert touchings, a low moan of helplessness escaping her throat. Everything he did to her seemed to fill some need she had not realized until its tantalizing fulfillment. His hands scorched the cool satin of her skin, sending their heat spreading through her. He caressed the silk of her inner thighs and she writhed, drawing a ragged breath of shock.

Her lips seemed swollen, sensitive . . . bare without his. Her arms urged his head upward until he possessed her again with his wild and thorough kisses. This time, she returned his ardor fully, opening herself to him, seeking him as he had taught her. Her fingers threaded shamelessly through his dark hair, pulling off the leather thong that bound it. One raven lock fell like a whisper against her face, caressing it.

His spell was so securely woven about her that when he slipped his knee between her thighs, she parted them willingly. As he poured over and against her, she welcomed his hard weight between her legs. Somewhere in the deep recesses of her mind, the shock and discomfort of that first time bloomed forth into tension. But his pulsing shaft entered by slow, pleasurable degrees and soon her anxiousness was lost in the strange, rapturous fullness of her woman's body.

She panted for breath, gasping slightly as he began to move within her. But his movements were languorous and beguiling, calling her to her own movement . . . to meet his thrusts again and again. She clasped him to her tightly, instinctively wrapping her legs about him, responding to his deep, sure possession. His hands stroked and tantalized her body with increasing demand and he charmed her senses further as he repeated her name, over and over.

"Aria, Aria . . . Aria . . ." He held her face between his hands as he thrust and twisted inside her. His eyes were black with ripened passion as he groaned hoarsely, "Say my name, Aria . . . say it—"

"Ty–Tynan . . . Tynan." She wetted her swollen lips and

closed her eyes against the explosion of desire those few syllables set off in him. "Tynan—" She let it roll over her tongue again, tasting the sweetness of it, and was soon lost to everything but the hot demands of his arching, plunging body. Though she couldn't know what came next, she felt the tension gathered unbearably in her loins. As he arched and pressed into her fully, she felt his racking spasms all through her.

A sudden draft of reason swept her as she lay beneath his hot, shuddering body and she knew his cold anger after that first encounter must have been for this last part, his explosive release that he had missed.

He withdrew reluctantly and wedged himself down onto the cot beside her, slipping his arm beneath her head as her cushion. His breathing slowed and the wild thunder of his heart against her face tamed. He pushed a damp, tangled strand of her hair back from her face and dropped a kiss on her temple before laying his head on the pillow beside her. His other arm threaded loosely over and about her waist, stroking her side assuringly.

Aria tilted her head back to look at him. His face was always a raw, male square, his features were finely chiseled, then blunted just short of perfection. A full, sweeping curve, his lips were formed with a faintly disdainful sensuality about them that warned of his unyielding complexion. But now, drained of sensual fire and seeming softer in repose, he was male beauty personified. His eyes were purest silver and the arrogance that often tightened his mouth was gone, leaving his face younger and glistening with the dew of amorous exertion. The ends of his black hair lapped lovingly about his neck, beckoning her, and she reached up to stroke them. Her hand stayed to trace the line of his collarbone and the smooth cap of his shoulder muscles.

Her touch was feather-light and filled with awe. His eyes closed, but the image of her, love-tousled, pliant, soft with passion, remained in his mind and lodged in his chest, crowding his breathing. He pulled her tighter against him and felt her wriggle about under his arm until she faced him and her hips rested lightly against his belly. The tips of her breasts nestled sweetly against his ribs. His eyes flew open to look at her.

She lay on her side with her head on his outstretched arm, fitting her curving form snugly against his harder one. Her eyes were closed, her skin was flushed like ripening peaches, her slender hand rested innocently on his chest. He tensed suddenly and every nerve in his spent body came alive. Elegant courtesans worked arduously to ply the provocative innocence that seemed to come to this wench naturally. Naked and pressing her voluptuous young body against him intimately, she somehow remained innocent . . . vulnerable. And she roused in him a tightness, a protectiveness that he was compelled to extend from himself around her. Only he must be allowed inside that barrier, plundering and reveling in her delectable charms, discovering and commanding her passions, claiming and owning her fierce loyalty. She was his and he would brook no interference with his full possession of her.

Her breathing had slowed to a restful rhythm that brushed the hair of his chest softly. The muscles of his jaw worked slightly as the strength of his arousal became uncomfortably clear. It was not usual for him to feel such need so soon after. . . . He looked at the peaceful cast of her features and felt a sharp, unaccustomed pang of self-reproach.

"Good God, man," he groaned, silently, "you're as randy as a stripling with his first woman." His brows knitted irritably as he forced his muscles to relax one after another. But his agonzing need for the woman who nestled so trustingly in his arms was already beyond his control.

Aria was warmer than she had been in weeks, totally, satisfyingly warm. She moved experimentally and found it somehow produced a heavenly stroking sensation up her side and across her belly. Lips covered the pleased, drowzy bow of her smile. Her eyes fluttered open in the dim gray morning light, focusing on a cheek, a temple, a shock of rumpled dark hair. She knew instantly what was happening and responded languorously to his kiss . . . Tynan's kiss . . . and soon to the warm, heavy weight of his chest pressing down against her breasts. It was one of her beautiful, sensual dreams of him . . . only so much more real.

His hands stroked and explored her body with a thorough intimacy that should have horrified her but, instead, produced a sweet, budding anticipation in her loins and a marvelous tingling in her breasts and lips. His attentions seemed to flow naturally from her lips to her breasts, her belly and buttocks, then to her thighs, calves, and ankles. And then the pattern was reversed, bringing her desires higher as his splendid kisses and caresses rose on her body.

She kissed him with all the aching hunger that throbbed deep within her. Time and place were suspended as he eased his weight onto her belly and fitted himself against her intimately. She welcomed him, gasping with pleasure as he slipped inside her, filling her, completing her. And as he moved, she obeyed his sensual command and moved with him, arching and clasping him closer with each thrust. She wanted him to merge with her, to join irrevocably with her in this sublime and savage union that pushed her to higher and wilder planes of pleasure. Something inside her tightened with each powerful thrust and her nails bit into his back as the bright unbearable tension stretched her nerves toward some unknown breaking point. She could scarcely breathe . . . and didn't care. She could exist only for whatever would happen to her in this storm of spiraling passion.

"Aria—" Her name seemed to flow into and through her from a great distance away. "Aria . . . say my name. . . . Say it—"

Her tongue flicked out to wet her lips and she groaned it from the depths of her tortured soul. "Tynan . . . Tynan . . ."

He erupted into her, shattering some bright and brittle barrier that sent white-hot shards slicing everywhere through his body, convulsing and racking it utterly. He was exploding inside her, inside himself, being ripped from the fabric of his own identity to pour into her with his sweet, salty fluid.

Aria clung to him, carried on the power of his massive climax into unchartered regions of self and experience. She lay beneath his huge, hot spasms of pleasure and felt choked, stunned. Her body throbbed, her nerves were screaming . . . she was afraid she'd burst and afraid of what would happen to her if she didn't. Her heart pounded savagely in her head and the pressure all but obscured her vision. She felt Tynan slide to one side, shifting his weight from her to the cot and hot panic enveloped her.

She lay in his arms, trembling and frightened by what was happening to her. She drew several shuddering breaths and her heart gradually moved back into her chest. The fire in her limbs dampened, replaced by a vague, steamy sense of frustration. What was happening to her? What had he done to her?

Humiliation flooded through her as his hands traced lazy circles on her bare breasts and down over the damp skin of her belly. He nibbled the dewy skin of her shoulder and dropped butterfly kisses on her face. He nuzzled the side of her neck and murmured her name with smoky exhaustion in his deep, invading tones.

Aria squeezed her eyes tighter and clenched her teeth. When the swelling cloud of her emotions finally burst, the flood filled her throat and rose higher, seeping out through her eyes. She was tense, exhausted, humiliated by her abject surrender of her body's intimate secrets to a ruthless, stone-hearted rakehell who purchased and exploited young girls with stunning proficiency. Deeper still was her shame for the way she responded to him, arching, wriggling, gasping, sighing. Even now her breasts ached to feel him pressing down on them again and her woman's hollow throbbed with emptiness.

Tears rolled back from her eyes toward her hair and she doubled her fists and clenched them in sudden anguish. She tried to swallow and struggled to keep the tempest inside her. How he would enjoy this turmoil he had bred inside her!

"What's this?" he murmured, his mouth close against her ear. His hand came up to touch the rivulet of liquid flowing back along her temple. She shrank slightly from his fingertips as if they burned her and turned her head away, her eyes clamped tightly shut.

"Are you . . . hurting?" His head came up suddenly, his lassitude ripped rudely away. His hands sought her shoulder beneath the cover and caressed it lightly. She lay utterly still, her face turned from him. In the dim light the tears glistened like a glassy ribbon against her skin. "Tell me . . ." His tone was level now and insistent. "Are you hurt?"

The overwhelming pleasure of release, which had driven him past the point of mere experience only minutes before, vanished like a quixotic vapor. He had never known such consuming pleasure on a woman's loins and had abandoned all restraint, all control as she responded beyond the erotic promise of his dreams. Now he felt drained, cheated, and somehow accused by her mute tears. He turned her chin toward him.

"What is my name, Aria?"

She winced as if struck and jerked her face away. She wrestled to turn onto her side away from him.

Screaming and shouting could not have made her rejection of him more plain. He stiffened, pulling his chin back. Then a tight knowing look crept over his face and he sent a hand beneath the cover to stroke her shoulder and trace the swaying curve of her waist down over her hip. She had been a virgin, for all practical purposes . . . albeit a very eager one. No doubt she suffered some physical discomfort for her night's work . . . and perhaps a pang of remorse.

"As you grow used to me, this . . . discomfort will pass."

She shuddered under his hand and her shoulders began to shake silently.

"You made it easy to forget your . . . inexperience, sweetest. I shall try to be more gentle with you tonight."

She curled her legs up, becoming a tense, trembling ball.

His tight, wary expression became a creditable scowl. He pushed the comforter off his warm body and rose, naked, into the morning chill. The bracing air shocked his senses no more than her rejection had done. He stood watching her strange, silent weeping, his powerful arms hanging uselessly at his sides.

His throat seemed crowded and his tongue felt thick and clumsy. He turned and reached for his stockings, breeches, and boots, shoving them on harshly. Then, standing half dressed in the center of the tent, he dragged his fingers back through his hair and rolled his shoulders to exorcise this nameless bad feeling. His mouth opened and worked soundlessly, then closed.

"You'll have the day to rest . . ." His thought sounded crass as he spoke it and he let it trail off, unfinished. He turned to the trunk and retrieved his shaving articles and snagged his shirt from the chair on one finger.

Audible sobs now issued from the curled form on the cot and his jaw muscles worked spasmodically. He had never allowed women's opportunistic tears to sway him . . . and the cynical part of him sneered at his own wavering grain. He was not about to weaken to them now because of one night's romp. He strolled over to the cot and stiffened as he saw her bare shoulder, above the cover, quaking. Her slender hands came up to clutch the comforter higher and she buried her face in the pillow, away from him.

"In future," he uttered slowly and with unshrouded annoyance, "I desire my passion seasoned with a good bit less salt."

By the time the words had seeped through the haze of Aria's misery and brought her up furiously on the cot, he was well gone from the tent.

The morning sun pierced the live canopy of trees with intrepid golden shafts that spread into broad, dappled beams. All around the stone-ringed center of camp, Tynan saw his men rising and stretching off the cold stiffness of the night. He paused with his hand propped at his waist and assessed the orderly scene. He had more to think about than just a woman's tears.

Acre was weaving about the morning fire and Tynan sought him out, giving him terse, explicit instructions. Then he turned and strode through the dew-laden grasses toward the bank of the stream that flowed by camp.

Choosing a rock that jutted out into the water, he plopped down heavily and pulled one knee up to rest an arm on it. The musical laughter of the rippling water mocked his blackening mood. He wetted his shaving soap and rubbed it savagely over his scarcely bristled cheeks.

"Well, well," came a familiar voice from behind.

Tynan twisted at the waist and leveled a warning glare at Jamison, whose bright expression belied his just-wakened state.

"Shaving again?" Jamison sprawled on the rock beside Tynan's and leaned back lazily on one arm.

"I always shave of a morn," Tynan answered curtly, picking up his razor and holding the small, silvered glass up to begin his work.

"But not always of a night," Jamison observed offhandedly. "You shaved last night as well. A man who shaves two times a day has a story to tell."

Tynan stopped midstroke and bent a full, murderous glare at his friend. And to his mounting frustration, Jamison's boyish face broke into a surprised grin. He followed Jamison's wide eyes to himself and contorted to look over his own shoulder. His face darkened another shade at the fading but unmistakable nail marks on his smooth, tight back. He straightened, mustering his lordliest mien and shrugged casually into his shirt. His eyes were tight, and ringed, and his usually impeccable hair hung in disarray as he turned a cautionary look on his friend.

Jamison let out a low whistle. "God, you look awful . . . plum exhausted . . ." And he erupted into peals of laughter, nearly failing off his seat into the stream.

Tynan's face burned beneath the razor's pitiless edge and he had to force the scowl from his face to save his flesh further punishment. He flung the soap savagely from his razor and refused to look at Jamison again.

The Bostonian straightened, wiping his eyes and chewing his lips to squelch his mirth. He knew better than anyone how dangerous a line he trod . . . and he still couldn't resist.

"I've seen you level a bawd house and come out looking better. I hope she was worth the trouble you put us all to." He paused and looked at Tynan, cocking his head quizzically. When Tynan's deadly shaving technique continued uninterrupted, he prompted, "Well?"

"Well what?" Tynan turned slowly, his eyes alight with a warning Jamison was hell-bent to ignore.

"Was she worth it?" The reckless colonial leaned forward conspiratorially.

Tynan's nostrils flared as the flame in his eyes fanned brighter. Inexplicably, Jamison's face was before him, but it was Aria's that registered in his mind. Suddenly her tumbled hair, her moist, eager mouth, her warm marble breasts appeared before him just as they had been last night . . . alluring, maddening, yielding. The startled expression on his face heated quickly, and the strength of his reaction set fire to the steel of his remarkable eyes.

Jamison's mouth drooped. The look on Tynan's face made him pull back, abashed by the outcome of his prurient interest. His stomach dropped precipitously at the thought of what it would take to bring the Earl of Penrith to such a state. Perhaps he had seriously underestimated the sweet-faced, unaffected Miss Dunning. He had trouble swallowing. His mind conjured images of paradise that roused his venal curiosity unbearably.

"Damn you!" Jamison scrambled to his feet, berating his own meddling as much as his friend's carnal appetites. "I won't get a decent night's rest until we get back to civilization and—"

Tynan shook free of his entrancing sensual apparition in time to hear Jamison's complaint as he stalked away. He watched the colonial's jerky, irritable stride and his mouth curled sardonically. The prying bastard deserved whatever nightly torture he had in store for him.

Thirteen

The front flaps of the tent were pulled back and tied to admit a pyramid of dusty light and a refreshing draft of cool air. Aria watched Acre go about his routine from rote and she said very little, trying not to seem in the way.

"Thank you for the hot water this morning." She finally stepped forward to lend a hand with the table he was moving into the warmth of the morning sun and was waved brusquely aside.

" 'Tweren't nothin' . . . just my job, miss," he observed tersely, turning back for the folding chair.

"I wouldn't put you to any trouble on my account—"

" 'Tweren't nothin', miss," he repeated adamantly, producing a folding stool from just outside the tent opening.

"From now on, I can wash in the stream," she persisted, feeling his gruffness as a condemnation of her state.

"I have orders, Miss—hot water for ye of the mornin' . . . ever' mornin'. An' I'll be seein' to it, no matter where ye . . . wash." His leathery face reddened to bronze. He turned and strode back toward his fire at the center of the camp, the fringe of his skin shirt swaying feistily.

Aria sighed heavily and closed her eyes. It was no more than she should have expected. Her shoulders ached, the muscles of her arms and legs ticked with tense fatigue, and every step sent spears of pain through her abdomen. In all her young life, she could not recall feeling more wretched. She was like a stiff new shoe, stretching and wearing . . . being molded helplessly to the wearer's stride. The comparison was too apt and she jerked her arms up to rub her shoulders and neck and paced back to the cot. She sank down gingerly, bracing herself with her arms to spare her sore bottom as she settled.

She would not think about it . . . what was happening to her. It only made her feel worse. If she must accept it, at least for now, then she would deal honestly, openly, with it. No pretty lie would sweeten the bitter disgrace that weighed upon her heart. And if she must live constantly with the shameful truth of her situation, then . . . *so would he.*

There her thinking stopped. The earl's figure appeared in the stream of sunlight at the door of the tent and he bent his dark head, entering. He paused, watching her and allowing his eyes to adjust to the dimmer interior of the tent.

"You are up and about." He coolly assessed her fresh-scrubbed appearance and neatly brushed hair. "Acre has breakfast prepared and I'm famished." He lifted one hand regally, as if expecting her to rise with it.

"Especially after such a taxing night's work," she muttered under her breath, rising. It was not meant for his ears but he heard it all the same and his spitefully pleased smile rankled her pride as thoroughly as it had been intended to.

He pulled out the stool from the small table and watched with unsuppressed amusement as she made a stiff crossing toward it. He settled in the chair across from her and watched her fidget surreptitiously to find a more comfortable position. Any sympathy he might have felt was immediately overwhelmed by a warm flood of sensation as he looked at her.

Sunlight bathed her in soft brightness, burnishing her hair as it lay alluringly on one shoulder, gathered and twisted loosely into a soft, obedient rope. She had changed into a fresh dress of rose-colored velvet, inset with a heavy, flowered brocade in the bodice and puffed sleeves. The bodice was low, but rimmed with tatted lace that allowed winks of the tender flesh within. She would not meet his gaze, but he could see that her face bore traces of the night's strain: a slight puffiness about her eyes and a drawn, pale quality about her cheeks and lovely jaw.

"Did you sleep well? I gave order you were not to be disturbed too early." He nodded approvingly as Acre arrived and set two plates of food on the table before them and shed the tin cups he had threaded on his fingers. He ambled off to retrieve the coffee pot and the earl repeated his question. "Did you sleep well?"

"No," she answered bluntly without looking at him. On her plate were fresh-baked biscuits, layered with generous pieces of sugar-cured ham and topped with melting golden cheese. Her stomach growled furiously and she pounced on the feast with knife and fork. She heard a tsking, clucking sound from across the table. Let him order daintiness, she lifted her chin in defiant rapture . . . she'd give him what he deserved . . . raw appetite.

Silently, methodically, she demolished her plate, stopping only to smile gratefully at Acre as he refilled her coffee cup.

The earl toyed with his fork and knife and sipped the strong dark brew occasionally. "I never realized a woman's appetite for food could preclude her love of talk."

She sat straighter and managed to look squarely at him. The swine! Again he commanded her to perform for him! "I've hardly eaten for two days. And my supper was interrupted last night . . . by another's appetite."

Tilting his head, he stroked his chin with one finger and grinned with lecherous delight. "So it was. Take care or I may interrupt your breakfast the same way. But you could occupy me otherwise . . . should you decide to talk."

She took a deep breath, licked her fingers daintily, and wiped the corners of her mouth with her fingers. Her expression was a banal pleasantry meant to mock her words: "I didn't know conversation was included in the bargain. But I can hardly be expected to know the full scope of a whore's duties . . . seeing I have only just embarked on such a career . . .

and most reluctantly." He was perfectly still for a moment, then she saw him relax determinedly.

"Oh, I think you'll learn quickly enough, if last night is any sample." The slight crinkle at the corners of his eyes seemed vaguely menacing and she dropped her gaze to her hands in her lap.

"Then what are my duties?" She braced herself without knowing just why.

"Duties?" He laughed shortly and leaned back. He looked at her from under his brows and his mouth twitched at one corner. "To pleasure me and please me . . . what else are women for?"

Aria's jaw slackened, then jutted stubbornly. "It is difficult to say which is more appalling, your arrogance or your ignorance."

"What a marvelous bright morning it is today!" It was Merrill Jamison's words that sallied forth into the tension stretching between them. He approached with long, energetic strides and a disgustingly cheery mein.

"It *was.*" The earl pushed his plate back onto the table and scowled meaningfully at him. "Don't you have some scouting or . . . something to do?"

"How nice to see you so recovered, Miss Dunning." Jamison ignored the earl's forbidding look to squeeze past him into the tent. He dragged the wooden chest over to the table and sat down on it with a flourish.

"Well, my appetite is recovered at least," she demured, lowering her eyes and flushing becomingly.

"Since you seem bent on intruding, perhaps you *can* be of assistance, Jamison. Miss Dunning seems to think my education lacking . . . perhaps she will receive the details of it more willingly from a third party." His posture was studied relaxation, his expression was maddening self-assurance.

"Me?" Jamison pointed to himself with exaggerated surprise, then waggled his brows and rubbed his hands together eagerly. He turned to Aria and took her hand, fork and all, between his. "Rutland here is the epitome of eddy-ca-tion and breeding . . . especially the breedin' part."

"Jamison—" The earl sat forward an inch.

"A man of letters, he is." Jamison ignored him and took the fork from her, stroking her hand with unabashed reverence. "Most of them from ladies . . ."

"Jamison—" The earl's mouth barely moved; the growl came from deep in his throat.

"Oh, he had the standard earl's schooling and tutelage, never fear." He glanced at the earl with an impetuous grin and returned, now moony-eyed, to Aria. "Knows his share of the love sonnets, I daresay . . . the Bard, Ovid, not to mention the sterner stuff—Aristotle, Homer . . . oh, very fond of Plato. Went off to some school—with the unlikely name of 'Eating' or some suc—"

"Eton," came a very calm correction.

"Whatever." Jamison waved the assistance away. "He speaks enough French and Spanish to get good rates in the best bawd hou—"

"I think she's heard enough, Jamison." The earl sat forward, his face a smooth mask of control.

"No, no." Aria leaned adoringly toward Jamison, wide-eyed with interest in this new game. "I must hear more. It fascinates me." From the corner of her eye she saw the earl sit back and stoke his slow-burning ire. She smiled sweetly into Jamison's reddening face.

"As the eldest son of the old earl, he was given every advantage: schooling, tutors in the arts, a grand tour of the continent . . . where he applied himself to his study of the grand pleasures with monumental vigor . . . and likely picked up a bit of his extravagant polish . . ."

"Oh, that explains why he is so lust-rous . . ." Aria quipped quite seriously.

"No doubt." Jamison was chewing his lips.

"And to think we have such a sage, a luminary, in our poor corner of the world," Aria intoned with straight-faced awe.

"Indeed. I apprenticed myself to his magnificence the moment we met and I can say: it has been an education to be proud of. Three years of sighing and receptive ladies, heavenly exhaustions, classical quotations, supremely satisfying debauch. . . . And freely bestowed amongst all classes—the earl is notoriously egalitarian with his enlightened favors."

"Three years?" She looked at the earl's dark face with genuine surprise. "Three years of his profoundly profligate presence here . . . small wonder the colonies are in revolt!"

"Enough." The quiet intensity of the earl's voice arrested their play.

"But tell me," Aria asked Jamison while still pondering the earl's dangerous mood, "isn't it a bit dangerous for his exalted English personage traveling about in this uncertain political climate? One would think he would hie himself home to England to enjoy his more civilized entertainments and his safe, comfortable estates."

"Uh-h—" Jamison drew back suddenly, loosening his hold on her hand and placing it on the table. His eyes flitted to the earl's closed expression and he smiled unconvincingly. "Rutland . . . makes friends easily. And those he cannot win over are not willing to test his sword arm."

"Three years?" Aria searched the earl visually, ignoring the tingle of interest that trilled along her nerves. "Surely you would have exhausted the charm of our rustic pleasures in so long a time. What keeps you here, in these rebellious and contrary provinces?" She suddenly recalled the gossip Gillie Parnell had purveyed so vividly on the first night at Sir Lowell's party. He was disgraced, barred from court by some debacle over a woman. Against her reason and resolve, the insight washed over her like a warm, seductive wave. With a man like him, a woman would always be involved.

"I am here because the foment of ideas and passions interests me. And I have found the notions and passions here worth continued study . . . especially now." The earl sat forward and let his flinty eyes rake her pointedly. "I have purchased land here . . . deepening my 'interests' in these colonies. And now I have a colonial wench beside me—I am content with things as they are for the present."

"And when you become discontented with things as they are, what then?" she retorted, stung by his emphasis on the "present." "Would it not be simpler to go back to England now and avoid the unpleasantness that lingering here must inevitably cause?"

The earl's head tilted as he absorbed her careful wording and sorted through it. "I am not known to be fickle with my decisions; once decided, I am not easily disenchanted. And there is no way to be proof against unpleasantness either here or in England. I think the northern Carolina will prove both profitable and pleasurable, with you by my side, sweetest."

Aria stiffened and rose slowly, keenly aware of Jamison's gaze upon her. "Under your hand perhaps, but not by your side, sir." She jerked her skirts abruptly, upsetting her stool. Her sea-green eyes were stormy as she whirled to make straight for the stream.

The earl watched her go with a slow, creeping lechery added to his intensive scrutiny. And as he watched her, Jamison watched him with arms folded over his chest and one hand stroking his chin thoughtfully.

"I've seen quite a few betrothed women, Rutland, and some even destined for spinsterhood . . . and every one of them was happier about their future than that wench is about hers. I hope you know what you're doing."

Tynan Rutland leveled a fiercely determined look at his friend. "Keep your bloody opinions to yourself, Jamison. And take a lesson . . . the best part of your worldly 'apprenticeship' is yet to come."

Shortly, the earl rode out with Jamison and two others, not troubling to mention to Aria that he was leaving or where he was bound. Probably off for a bit of other sport, Aria mused

vengefully as she watched them go from the comparative secrecy of the tent. Let him go, without a word, she fumed silently, she'd suffer that much less of his suffocating
possessiveness and lusts. But it served to accentuate his power
over her; she was accountable to him for every second of her
whereabouts, while he answered to no one.

In less than half an hour she had completely renewed her
acquaintance with every square inch of the tent and its furnishings and she meandered outside to relieve her boredom.
Acre was cleaning his metal cooking grate in the sand of the
bank of the stream and she sat down on a nearby stump, hoping
for a bit of conversation, or a tidbit of information.

"Have you been with the earl long . . . hunting?"

"Four month now," came the dead-ended reply.

"Did you know him before?" she tried again.

"Some."

This was getting her nowhere. It is best to be blunt with
those who are blunt, she decided. "Do you like working for
him?"

"I don't work for him." Acre paused, his knuckly hands
pausing over the half-cleaned grill. Then he looked up at her.
"I jus' hunt with 'im."

"Oh." Aria drew back, puzzled. "You don't work for
him . . ."

"I come because I speak some 'o the Injun tongues. Him
an' Jamison, they needed a body to talk for 'em." He returned
to his work, rubbing the grate back and forth in the sand and
tending it carefully with his work-gnarled fingers.

"And you cook . . ." She hoped to elicit more, but realized
how hopeless it was when he responded.

"I cook."

She let it lie for the moment and gazed about her at the
balmy autumn day. The sun was warming the velvet of her
shoulders, relaxing them. "The leaves will be turning soon."
She spotted a tender poplar whose leaves were already rimmed

with bright yellow. "If you hunt in summer, what do you do of a winter?"

"Hunt, trap," came the reply. It did not seem unfriendly, just simple and strangely complete.

"Oh." She was less eager to break the next silence.

When he started back to the center of camp and his waning fire, he paused to look at her. "Coffee, miss?"

"Yes." She looked up, surprised by the gesture. "I'd love some."

She followed him back to the fire and took the cup he handed her. He waved her to a seat on a small keg and sat down on a bit of a log across from her.

"Has the hunting been good?" she asked idly, sipping and hoping to prolong this bit of companionship, onesided though it seemed.

He looked at her keenly, as if trying to decipher something in her question. "Reasonable. I'd rather we kept to the woods an' stayed outta them big houses. Don't like them fancy folk much . . . nor *him* neither, when he's about 'em. He's diffr'nt out here." His grizzled head rolled as he looked about him with eloquence of appreciation. "I'd rather *he* kept to the hills an' trees."

Aria nodded slowly, burying her nose in her tin cup and watching him over its rim. The silence, she realized, need not always be filled. And there they sat, sharing a cup of his strong, flavorful coffee and perhaps a bit more.

By midafternoon, Aria had explored the camp and talked with the remaining hunters as they were drawn to the central fire by the aroma of Acre's coffee. She seemed a bit less lonely, and when Acre started out to collect small twigs for tinder and kindling, she braved his disapproval to accompany him and help.

"Yer . . . dress, miss," he motioned to it as if it embarrassed him to even speak of it. "Ye'll dirty it."

Aria looked down at her fine velvet dress, once one of many such and now her very best. She swallowed hard as her eyes filled betrayingly. "I'll . . . be careful," she tossed out with a false lightness to her tone. What good did it do her to own such a dress? She would never be fit society again, she thought miserably. Better that she soil it in honest labor and see it gone . . . than to be reminded of all she had lost each time she wore it. And she filled her arms with twigs and small branches from the forest floor.

Fourteen

The sun was lowering quickly when the peace of the little glen was invaded by the dull thud of hoofbeats. The earl's return seemed to stir the camp like a wind whipping leaves into whirling eddies. The skin-clad hunters and guides were drawn inescapably toward his presence, joking, questioning, inspecting the great-racked stag that lay across one of the horses. Aria watched it all from the bank of the stream, feeling a queer skip entering the beat of her heart.

The earl's face was flushed, his steel-gray eyes glowing with sparks of excitement that seemed to shower about him and catch in his men's eyes as he looked about him. His sternly carved face was warmed by his obvious pleasure at recounting the bagging of such an impressive animal. He seemed perfectly at ease, perfectly framed for his rustic clothes, perfectly suited to lead this rough band of men and perfectly constituted for conquest. Suddenly she understood Acre's terse observation that the earl would do better to keep to the hills and forests. It seemed he belonged here far more than in the false, mincing atmosphere of elegant drawing rooms.

His broad shoulders rolled, his face smoothed dangerously, then brightened explosively as his arms shot wide, drawing an upswell of admiration and approval from the other hunters. Then his voice lowered past her understanding and she watched as he spoke to each individual man in the party. Jamison spoke, corroborating what the earl had said and adding something Aria could not hear. The skin-clad men watched the earl keenly, and as he turned away toward the evening cook fire, they erupted into a flurry of noise and activity. They hurried to obey his orders as if he were a military commander.

Aria watched him bend over the stocky, grizzled Acre, intent on some matter, and she saw the hunters' expression repeated in the old man's face. Her breath stopped in her throat. He held these hard men enthralled as easily, as effortlessly, as he held the reins of her passions. What chance did she have against him?

She squared her shoulders against the seeping dread that invaded her middle and worked its way up her spine. He already commanded her body better than she did herself. Heaven help her if she ever surrendered more than that to him. He would destroy her utterly when he grew tired of her and put her away from him. And that day, she knew, must inevitably come. Despite his talk, he would someday sail away back to England and choose a real lady-bride to produce heirs upon. And this episode in the colonies would fade into memory as a charming diversion, retold and embroidered for the amusement of his noble cronies.

She gritted her teeth and felt her battered pride rising to full flood. She could not stop him from taking and using her body, but she could and would stop him from taking a whit more. He had made her a whore; she would see that his place as whoremaster was made excruciatingly clear to all. If there was any truth in the myth of nobility, it undoubtedly lay in the uncommon pride they held. And the Earl of Penrith had more than his share of that commodity.

She knelt on the rocks by the creek and lowered the bucket into a deep spot to fill it. She straightened and shifted the heavy bucket to her other hand as she started staunchly back toward the center of the camp.

Tynan turned around to face her when Acre gestured behind him. What he saw darkened his look measurably. He strode toward her, leaving Jamison and Acre staring after him uneasily.

"Just what in hell do you think you're doing?" He planted himself squarely before her, fists set at his waist and his massive shoulders jutting forward angrily.

"Carrying water." She quelled the quiver of warning that ran through her and started around him.

"That's Acre's job," he growled as he grabbed her arm to hold her beside him.

"I just made it mine." She jerked her chin up defiantly and spoke quite clearly. "Since you did not see fit to set down orders for me, I chose duties in keeping with my new station. What do you think? Does a whore overreach herself to aspire to the honest duties of a water bearer?"

His face bronzed with sudden anger and he jerked his head about to find Jamison and Acre staring at them. From the looks on their faces, they had heard her words all too clearly.

"Dammit! Hold your tongue, wench!" he threatened in a loud, rasping whisper. But her emerald-green eyes flashed with pride's undoused flame and she raised her spiteful glare full into his face. Seized with impotent fury, he ripped the bucket from her hand to trounce it savagely on the ground, wetting them both in the process.

She startled back with a cry of protest, but he grabbed her and dipped to clamp his arm around her legs and jerk her up into his arms roughly. Aghast, she pushed at him and flailed her legs from her knees down, ordering him to release her.

"You wretch!" she growled furiously, pushing without effect on his rock-hard shoulders. "Put me down!" He was already near the tent and desperately Aria appealed to their astonished audience of two, "Don't let him do this to me!"

But in seconds she was inside the tent and dumped unceremoniously on the cot. He stood above her with his fists clenched, his chest heaving from the exertion. He was a black tower of displeasure that raked her cruelly with white-hot eyes.

"Don't you touch me," she spat, scrambling up to a crouching position against the tent wall, at the head of the cot.

"I'll do more than touch you, if you ever repeat that little scene again." He lowered his voice to a panted threat.

"You wouldn't dare," she hissed, clamping her jaw tightly to bolster her resolve.

"Wouldn't I? Try me again and find out." His body eased above her, but the intensity of his face remained in warning. "You've developed a strange predilection for the word 'whore.' I'll not hear it again from your lips, nor will anyone else. It ill becomes a lad—"

"Now I am not only forced to bear your bulk in bed, but I am commanded to put a pleasant face on my whoredom and pretend to enjoy it with all wellborn grace!" She blazed at him like a cornered vixen. "Well, I won't. If I must live with the ugly truth of this sin day after day, then I will not lie about it to spare your face before the others. If you despise the truth so much, then send me away—send me back—" She stopped, choked suddenly by the realization that she had no home, no family to return to. Tears welled in her eyes and clung there mysteriously as she dropped her head. Her arms curled about her waist as if corralling her reeling emotions.

"I do command you to bear my 'bulk' at night," he bit out, "but I do not think my weight is entirely loathsome to you. I cannot reach inside your skin and command that you respond to me as you did. That, wench, was your desire, your need for me . . . and it will be again. I want you and you want me. That makes us lovers . . . and someday—"

"No," she ground out, swiping her blurring eyes with the heels of her palms, "I earn my keep with you on my back. And whatever pretty word you choose to put to it, the truth is the same. Mistress, courtesan, lover . . . harlot!" She slipped off the edge of the cot and stood unflinchingly before him. The time had come for truth.

"Aria—" He hadn't counted she would still take her new life with him so hard. He had thought that after last night's loving, some of pride's sting would be gone.

"Why argue! Likely, your cultivated tastes will seek nobler

fare when you learn the truth about me." She drew a hot breath and braced herself. "My mother was not nobly born . . . the Baron of Wrenwythe was not her father. She came from a penniless younger son's marriage to a penniless squire's daughter. After my father's death, I learned that my mother's nobility had been fabricated to appease my father's vanity and make good his boasts. Our home, our lands, my mother's jewels, all were mortgaged to the teeth to maintain the illusion of our status . . . our 'nobility.' I've scarcely a drop of noble blood in me.

"So you see," she managed to lift her head even though her face was burning, "all you have purchased with your tainted coin after all is an unwilling whore, not an unwilling 'lady.' " To her consternation, he stepped back a pace and let harsh laughter boil up from his chest.

"My dear, half the wellborn females of Europe are whores, and yet they retain the title of 'lady.' Your breeding, common though it be, and your manners would put most of those highborn trollops to shame. You seriously underestimate both your charm and the infallible elegance of my tastes." He laughed softly at the shock turning to anger in her crimson face.

He caught her as she tried to duck around him to flee the tent. She struggled with subdued intensity as he dragged her to him.

"And you betray a virgin's naivete in thinking I would find you less desirable for knowing the dark secrets of your origins." He felt her stiffen in his arms at his gentle mockery. "You can never be a true whore while you still harbor such innocence."

"I despise you," she uttered softly. Her heart had dropped into her stomach like a lead ball, leaving a dull, aching chasm where it had been.

"That may be." It was his turn to stiffen. If she spoke the truth, then he was wise to withhold the part about the vows. If she refused to wed him when the time came, who could blame him for a broken oath? "But if you prize honesty so highly, you must admit that you want what I do to you at night, what we do together. That is the only truth that matters now."

Aria slowly turned her head away, standing with silent resignation in the hard circle of his arms. No matter what he said, no matter how harsh or honeyed his words, it was still wrong for him to take her—and wrong for her to let him. And yet she knew he spoke the truth. She responded to him freely, wanted him to touch and caress her. And in that moment, she knew precisely where the battle lines had been drawn.

He recognized her withdrawal and drew his arms from around her. Muscles in his jaw flexed impatiently as he watched her wrap herself in her thoughts, sealing him out. He shifted back onto one leg and felt strangely thwarted. He thrust aside the temptation of taking her into his arms at once and demolishing her sham of indifference. His saner self turned him around and sent him out into the cool, blue twilight.

Jamison was waiting for him near the fire with a cup of strong coffee and a sly, muffled curiosity. They sat, watching Acre's final supper preparations in silence.

"Is . . . she all right?" Jamison managed, looking strictly into the flames.

"She's none of your concern," came the terse reply.

"She's not taken kindly to your starting the honeymoon before the vows are spoken." Jamison summed up his conclusions with a quiet tone that goaded Tynan in an unexpectedly vulnerable spot.

"It's none of your damned business, Jamison, leave it." The implied threat stalled Jamison's response only a moment.

"She's a refined young lady . . . bound to—"

"Dammit, Jamison!" He rose, flinging his remaining coffee into the fire, causing a hiss. "Don't test me. We've been through much together . . ." He stopped abruptly and straightened, pulling his jagged emotions back under control. He gave

Acre orders to bring their food to the tent and left to wash in the stream.

Acre watched the earl's rigid back retreat into the murky dusk and glared disgustedly at Jamison. "Can't ye ever keep a rein on yer tongue an' jus' watch?"

Supper that night was endured through a somber silence worthy of the tombs of the Caesars. Aria would neither speak nor look directly at Tynan. Conversely, he watched her every motion, scrutinized her posture, examined her eating habits, evaluated her dress, her hair, her hands. Through it all she managed a stoic mein, determined to give him as little satisfaction as possible from her company and to even deprive him of her justifiable ire.

But when he reached into his trunk for a pouch of tobacco and a pipe and exited, she wilted with relief. She massaged the back of her neck and kneaded her tight shoulders as best she could. She put hands to the back of her small waist and rubbed them downward over the thick layers of soft fabric to soothe the ache in her lower back. Her legs were pinging and twitching with tension and her head throbbed as if someone were pounding a drum inside it. She hardly knew which part of her body to comfort next. Every part seemed to scream for attention.

She knelt by her leather bags and pulled out her warm nightdress and her brush. Fighting a choking swell of loneliness, she closed them quickly and hurried to deposit her things on the cot. Her hands trembled visibly as she put them to work on the ties at the rear of the tent. She stepped out into the darkness and looked about warily, half expecting to find the earl staring at her with cruel amusement. But all was quiet and she hurried off into the shadowy bushes.

Tynan's evening smoke was nearly as silent as his supper had been. The men were subdued and each tended his own

Betina Krahn

thoughts closely tonight. He rose and asked who was on watch. Tall, swarthy-faced hunter by the name of Carrick answered.

"We felt them today," Tynan said rather flatly. "They're probably watching our fire this very minute. Keep alert and sound out if anything . . . seems amiss. Remember, we want to talk to them, not fight them." He looked from face to weathered face and turned back to his tent, knocking a shower of red sparks from his pipe as he went.

The tent was empty and a spear of anger shot up his spine before he could conquer it and scour the interior. His eyes flew to the cot, where a heavy woolen nightdress lay beside her carved ivory brush. It had a strangely calming effect on him. He moved to the rear flaps and frowned at the limp, hanging ties. He touched them experimentally, turning it over in his mind. Just as his eyes returned to her nightdress, a movement at the rear of the tent caught his eye and he wheeled around.

"Oh," she said, startled, putting her hand to her throat and stopping in the entrance.

"I told you not to leave the tent at night," he declared.

"And I believe we settled this earlier." She moved to the cot without looking at him. "I need not be accompanied for certain 'necessary' functions."

He snatched her arm as she passed and pulled her shoulder back against his chest. "You'll do as I say, wench. This is not some safe little town or cozy settlement. There may be animals . . . or Indians about."

"So," she looked up into his face with all the calm she could muster, "I'm back to 'wench' again, am I? And just when I was learning *your* name. As to safety, the greatest threat to my well-being exists within these walls."

"Hardly—the force of my arms and my pleasures are your security," he growled from low in his throat. But he stopped there and brought a hand up to travel over her hair and her face. His touch was excruciatingly gentle, making her want to curl up around his hand. Some trace of her warring feelings appeared in her eyes and his sensual mouth curled slightly.

"I am nothing to fear, Aria. As I take my pleasures, I am bound to give some back." He laughed sardonically at the mistrust that sprang to her eyes. "And I'll be gentler with your tender flesh, this time."

Wordlessly, he tugged at her laces and ignored her passive resistance. Heat rose under her cheekbones as he pulled her bodice open and she whirled away from him, fearing a repeat of last night's slow seduction.

He watched her finish the unlacing and turn her back to peel the bodice down, leaving her chemise in place. He shrugged and eased himself into the chair, soon enwrapped by her tauntingly slow disrobing. He knew she meant it to defy him and smiled broadly at this further reminder of her innocence. She could not know how thoroughly tantalizing a spectacle she made, reluctantly peeling her garments from her soft, curving body.

Aria felt his gaze touching her everywhere as she shed her petticoats and stood only in her thin lawn chemise. She reached for her nightdress hurriedly and heard a forbidding rumble from his chair.

"You'll not need that. Set it aside."

"I must sleep in something—" She held the heavy nightdress before her like a shield as she turned.

"What a quaint notion," he mocked with glowing eyes. "Purely colonial, I assure you. On the continent, ladies sleep *au naturel,* unless they sleep alone." He saw the riposte rising to her tongue, where it was bitten back. "And how would I know?" he asked it for her. His smile was pure devilment. "I made a deep study of the custom at every opportunity . . . with every available lady." He laughed at her stiffening face. "Isn't that what you expected me to say?"

She glowered and threw the nightdress on the rag carpet floor, grabbing the comforter up and around her instead. Im-

pulsively she made a screwed-up face at him, and instantly
loathed herself for giving in to so childish an impulse.

He laughed sardonically, reading her thoughts in her face,
and rose. Methodically he dealt with his buttons and shed his
belt and shirt. She dropped her eyes and climbed onto the cot,
tucking her feet beneath her and seeing her fate draw closer
with each garment he removed. Overt resistance was futile,
she knew. He was massive and . . . expert. But she did not
have to respond, to increase his pleasure by taking hers.

When he joined her on the bed meant for one, she jumped
skittishly, shrinking from his hand on her shoulder. He encountered the gathered shoulder of her chemise and handled it disapprovingly.

"This must go as well." He measured her response carefully,
knowing the game she was playing and also knowing its futility.

"It wouldn't be decent," she ground out, twisting angrily
from his touch.

"You slept without it last night."

"I was . . . not myself last night. My behavior was disgraceful on all counts. But then, I was not responsible for my harried
state." She looked at him accusingly, her lower lip in a luscious
pout.

"No," he pulled her toward him, easily overcoming her to-
ken resistance. "I'll take credit for your behavior of last
night . . . and tonight's, as well." He covered her pouting
mouth with his own, troubled little by its determined tightness.

His hands turned her about and pushed her back on the
pillow as his kiss warmed. Her lips were closed to him, but
undaunted, he traced their opening with leisurely strokes.
When his hand floated intimately down her chemise, her lips
parted in a gasp of indignation and he captured the sweetness
of her mouth fully.

Above her now, his eyes crinkled knowingly as he tested
her determined lack of response. He swept her hands aside to
raise her chemise and caressed her bare skin with mesmerizing

tenderness. Gradually his touch became more like kneading. He lingered over her shoulders, her abdomen, her arms, driving out the aches and replacing them with treacherous warmth.

She lay still beside and beneath him, shivering as he pulled her chemise up and over her head. Almost instantly, the hard, heavy warmth of his great body covered her, and these shivers had another source. His lips followed her throat and played on the field of her chest, producing such heavenly sensations that it was all she could do to remain still. She sent her hands out to grip the edges of the cot, forbidding them to abandon their post. Her eyes were squeezed tightly against him, as she searched desperately for something to fasten her thoughts on—anything to keep from thinking about what he was doing to her, what she was feeling.

His hot face nuzzled her breasts in lazy, titillating circles, and a soundless moan escaped her lips. She must remember she hated him . . . what else did she despise? Numbers! *One, two, three* . . . inspired by the rhythm of his movements, she began to count mentally, trying not to fall into synchrony with the pattern he had established. *Eleven, twelve . . . seventeen* . . . the count was suspended for a moment by the deep ravishment of his extraordinary kiss. His full, sensual mouth had the power to absorb the essence of her into him, robbing her of will, stealing her very spirit. Her hands released the cot and would have sought him, had he not paused above her, braced on his elbows, to enjoy the sensuous sight of her wrapped in mists of pleasure.

"God, you are sweet . . ." His voice brought her dark-centered eyes open. The sight of his bare chest pressed against her breasts made it hard to breathe and she tried to turn her head away so he couldn't see the panic in her face.

Think! Count! she commanded her waffling reason, feeling her legs being parted, feeling him fitting his hard body intimately against her woman's flesh. Twenty, start at twenty! she thought frantically . . . *twenty-one . . . twenty-two . . .*

Her heart was pounding in her throat as he slipped inside

her slowly and lay still above her. His movements were tantalizingly gentle, thorough. Her woman's flesh was tingling, then burning with the need to press against him and the unfilled need tightened her legs involuntarily against his. She bit her lip savagely, feeling the bitterness of frustration boiling up into her throat—*thirty-five, thirty-six, thirty-seven* . . .

Then, inexplicably, he began to move in perfect harmony with her counting, making it seem that her numbers somehow tallied their mounting pleasures. The voice in her head became hoarse, sporadic, defying sequence to leap to ever larger numbers as she soared helplessly on passion's reckless spiral.

Her arms wound around his shoulders and her palms flowed downward over his rippling back. Against her will, she began to move, to meet his thrusting body. Rising, expanding, she was pushed to higher, brighter realms where feeling and desire joined in a single towering spire that beckoned her upward to some unknown summit.

His voice was hoarse, pained, as he murmured her name over and over through passions fiery crimson. Straining, reaching for the center of her being, the essence of her, his body exploded in white-hot convulsions of pleasure so intense they seemed to sear his very soul.

He collapsed over her at last, exhaustion blurring all but the image of her that passion's brand had burned into his heart. She was warm, soft, perfect beneath him. She fitted his hard, unyielding frame with every curve, every slope of her irresistible body as though she had been fashioned only for him. Wonderment flooded his mind as he felt her wriggle pleasurably beneath him. Concern for her moved him to her side and sent his hands gliding over the warm, damp satin of her body. His eyes were lidded with marvelous exhaustion as he raised his face to hers.

"Are you . . . all right?" he managed thickly. "I didn't want to hurt you, sweetest." His hand came up to push a damp lock of hair back from her cheek and he smiled tiredly into her wide, dark emerald eyes. Something weighted his lids and closed them stubbornly. But against the dark veil of his mind, he still saw her breathtaking eyes. It was his last thought as he drifted off into dark peace.

Tears rolled freely from Aria's eyes, wetting her hair further. She felt like an overwound clock, the tension of nameless, unfilled expectation coiled tightly in her body and loins. She bit her lip to keep from uttering the little sobs that clogged her throat.

She had tried her best to resist her own responses, to suffer his passions with cool detachment. But everything had gone wrong. His expert touchings and caresses had worked too strong a spell within her and she had clung to him as a drowning man does to a plank of wood. And afterward, it was the same, this humiliation, this tightness, this rage that seemed to want to burst inside her to somehow set her free.

Aria felt the choking tide drain gradually from her, and hearing his deep, even breathing, she turned her head to glare resentfully at his sleeping form. This passion that he spent so eagerly on her left him in sleep's restoring arms while it tortured her mercilessly, body and soul. If only she had been able to resist him fully. . . . This raging discontent was cruel punishment for the weakness she bore for him. And yet she hadn't wanted to respond to him, to enjoy and to please him.

In repose, his face was smooth, unlined by arrogance or care. His mouth, those full, curving lips that had the power to obliterate her reason, was soft under her questing fingertips. He stirred briefly and she jerked back, holding her breath. But when he did not rouse further, she continued her secret tactile exploration of his lips, his shell-perfect ear, his strong nose with its blunted tip, the exquisite symmetry of his stubborn, muscular jaws. Only then did she realize how often, in her secretmost heart, she had longed to touch him like this.

A deep, painful emptiness opened in her chest, aching with longing. And tearfully she realized that he was the source of that painful sensation. *Honestly* . . . she wanted him every bit as much as he desired her . . . only the physical contact that seemed to content him so fully did nothing to assuage this relentless need of hers. Horrified by the drift of her thoughts, she turned her face from him and berated herself sternly. Mooning, silly cow . . . you will not think of this again! You will not!

Gritting her teeth, she managed to turn onto her side beneath his heavy arm and his casually draped leg. And it was a long torturous while before she, too, found release in sleep.

We have 4 FREE BOOKS for you as your introduction to KENSINGTON CHOICE! To get your FREE BOOKS, worth up to $23.96, mail the card below.

FREE BOOK CERTIFICATE

Yes! Please send me 4 Kensington Choice (the best of Zebra and Pinnacle Books) Historical Romances without cost or obligation (worth up to $23.96). As a Kensington Choice subscriber, I will then receive 4 brand-new romances to preview each month for 10 days FREE. I can return any books I decide not to keep and owe nothing. The publisher's prices for Kensington Choice romances range from $4.99-$5.99, but as a preferred subscriber I will get these books for only $4.20 per book or $16.80 for all four titles. There is no minimum number of books to buy and I may cancel my subscription at any time. A $1.50 postage and handling charge is added to each shipment. No matter what I decide to do, my first 4 books are mine to keep, absolutely FREE!

Name _____

Address _____ Apt._____

City _____ State_____ Zip_____

Telephone ( ) _____

Signature_____

(If under 18, parent or guardian must sign)

Subscription subject to acceptance. Terms and prices subject to change.

KC1196

4 FREE
Historical
Romances
are waiting
for you to
claim them!

(worth up to
$23.96)

*See details
inside....*

KENSINGTON CHOICE
Zebra Home Subscription Service, Inc.
120 Brighton Road
P.O.Box 5214
Clifton, NJ 07015-5214

Fifteen

Water dripped from the mist-shrouded trees above, plopping coldly on Jamison's forehead and running down the side of his face. The day had been gray and wet and grindingly hard. The exertion of rambling about in the wild had netted little but fatigue. Jamison reined up on the hillside overlooking their campsite and leaned his elbow on the pommel of his saddle. Running a hand back through his thick, sandy hair, he searched for the earl and found him impatiently guiding his mount down the forested hillside. He watched Rutland's rail-straight back and broad, unsloped shoulders and stiffened his own spine.

The man clearly was not human, that was the unvarnished truth of the matter, he grumbled mentally. Up half the night plying his amorous pursuits with his lusciously reluctant bride and by day he still ran the rest of them into the ground. His stamina deserved ranking as the eighth Great Wonder of the World.

Still, he had not seemed quite so pleased when he emerged from his tent early that morning. Perhaps he found his pleasures costly in other ways. Jamison smiled wickedly with his thoughts. It would serve Rutland right to find himself hopelessly ensnared by a fiendishly sweet-faced young beauty with a razor-sharp wit, the body of a living Venus, and a healthy contempt for things noble. And from what little he had been permitted to glimpse of her, Aria Dunning was exactly those things.

Jamison scowled thoughtfully. Never before had he heard

the word "betrothal" fall from his friend's lips and never before had Rutland behaved so possessively with his lady of the moment. Still, old patterns die hard and it was difficult to credit that he actually meant to marry the girl. Jamison sighed sharply and set a course down the track left by the rest of the hunters. She was probably too good for him . . . and too good to him. He snorted with self-derision at the lusty bend of his thoughts. Damn Rutland . . . taking her when they were on a mission like this!

Aria sat primly in the folding chair near the evening cook fire, watching the earl and his men dismount. She rose stiffly and walked slowly toward the tent. She was steeling herself for the confrontation to come and part of her welcomed it. She drew a shuddering breath and planted herself in the center of the tent, facing the doorway.

"Well," the earl paused inside the opening, assessing her calm demeanor and fetching velvet gown, "you seem quite recovered. I was not sure this morning when I left you—"

"I am . . . healthy, if that is what you mean," she uttered tersely, lifting her chin a fraction.

He studied her and frowned. But then he lifted his brows, as if casting his concern aside, and headed for his wooden chest.

"And was your hunt successful?" she managed, growing uneasy about the topic she was to raise, now that his powerful presence filled the tent.

"No game worthy of mention." He pulled out another shirt and compared it to the one he wore, mumbling that it must be time to return to civilization.

Aria watched the easy movement of his heavy muscles wondering again at his agility and the control he exercised so effortlessly over his massive frame. Given his size, he should not have been able to move as he did. She shook her head surreptitiously and tore her gaze away to inspect the scuffed toes of her shoes.

"Did I understand you to say once that you have a penchant for biblical numbers?" she remarked with deceptive naturalness.

He paused with his shirt, soap, and toweling in his hands. "I have been known to say such things upon occasion." His head cocked warily as he studied her. Her aura of infinite calm disturbed him.

"Then the number I give you may not totally displease you. Seven. Seven days, starting now . . . that you may not intrude in my bed."

"What are you saying?" he scowled, trying to ferret out her truthfulness while ignoring her meaning.

"Surely a man of your vast worldly experience requires no further explanation. There are times a woman's body may not be shared . . . or taken." Her terse emphasis on the last two words smacked of raw defiance. But the tension of her soft mouth and the paleness of her face made him consider that it was more than just a gambit to avoid him.

He felt a foreign pang of indecision. Gambit or not, he would have to give her the time . . . and let time itself prove her true or false. If he pressed the issue and she had told the truth, it could wreck the promising future he planned in her bed. He shifted his weight back onto one leg and wandered over her visually.

"Then you'll have your time, Aria." His eyes narrowed, "but not your solitary bed. There is only one place to sleep in this tent and I prize my own comfort enough to command that we share it. You need not fear I'll behave boorishly. I am, despite what you may think, a gentleman and have been known to behave like one, given the occasion."

She opened her mouth to protest, but he swung through the tent opening before she could lodge her objections. Sharing his bed through this discomfort was certainly not what she had in mind. How was she going to manage through this?

That night, after his evening smoke with his men by the fire, the earl entered the tent to find Aria already tucked snugly inside the comforter on the cot. The wick on the oil lamp had been turned down to a reddish glow and she did not move or acknowledge his presence. He shed his boots, shirt, and belt quickly, doused the lamp, then joined her on the cot, still wearing his breeches and stockings.

She lay on her side with her back to him and had tucked the comforter tightly around her. He tried pulling it up to slip under it beside her, but she had wrapped it securely about her, and despite his stealthy tuggings, it remained her exclusive comfort. Heaving a disgusted breath, he sat up and lifted her bodily to unfurl the cover, expecting a battle royal. He squinted suspiciously at her undisturbed face as he laid her back down. Then he slipped beneath the cover and immediately encountered her heavy woolen nightdress.

Undaunted, he slipped an arm about her waist and pulled her back against him, curling about her spoon fashion. Her soft warmth soon penetrated his loins and one questing hand rubbed her breast gently.

Aria lay excruciatingly still, her eyes mere crescents as she forced herself to continue her slow rhythmic breathing. She waited to see what he would do and closed her eyes with relief as his hand relaxed on the cot beside her.

The next night passed in similar fashion; Aria feigned sleep in the comfort of the earl's big body. But the third night Aria's sleep was genuine and the temptation her trusting, curvaceous form posed to the earl's easily roused desire nagged mercilessly at him. Each wriggle, each sigh, each sleepy, snuggling movement raked fire across his belly or poured molten lead into his veins. Pressed inescapably against her sweet bottom on their narrow bed, he felt himself rise ingloriously after her and groaned silently. When she turned restlessly in her sleep and her cheek came to rest against his chest, he shrank from the excruciatingly arousing contact.

He bore the torture for what seemed hours, trying to quell his mutinous rousing, and finally lurched from the bed, staring at her in the dim light as if she had bitten him. He snatched up his shirt, boots, and deerskin jacket and escaped in to the damp, miserable chill of the dead of night. Four more nights of this and he'd be a raving madman.

Aria was roused by the aroma of coffee the next morning and found the earl sitting in the chair watching her, sipping a cup of Acre's strong brew. She drew herself up slowly and pushed her hair back over her shoulder. Her cheek bore the imprint of the wrinkled sleeve of her nightdress and was blushed with the residue of dreaming.

His face tightened involuntarily as he stared at her. She had never seemed more appealing. He shook off the feeling as if it were poison and took another gulp of coffee. Rising, he set the cup on the table and adjusted his brass-buckled belt.

"I am taking several of my men deeper into the hills. The hunting here is not . . . satisfactory. We'll be gone three or four days." He seemed to be talking to the tent pegs, his voice flat and faintly displeased. "Jamison, Acre, Carrick, and MacKean will remain behind with you."

She rose, blinking the sleep from her eyes and wondering what she had done to displease him this time. He was leaving . . . for days.

He paused above her, studying the unhidden concern in her lovely face. Unable to resist, he lifted a hand and traced the side of her cheek with his knuckles. Her skin responded with a charming charge of color while her luminous eyes searched his taut face.

"Give Jamison no cause for worry, Aria." His tone dropped to an intimate rumble. "While we are gone, don't leave the tent unescorted." His head lowered suddenly and he brushed her lips lightly as if stopping her protest. Then he pushed aside the tent flaps and was gone.

Aria wasted no time ridding herself of her nightdress and donned clothes hastily in the damp, bone-seeping chill. In the thick morning air, she could hear horses snorting and men's raised voices echoing through the clearing and sounds of movement. Hands shaking, she pulled her brush through her hair several times and ran her hands over it to be sure it was orderly. She rolled her stockings up and shoved her feet into her shoes and headed for the tent opening.

All attention was focused on the far side of the clearing where the earl stood, his hands propped on his hips, staring at the edge of the trees. Everyone in camp was moving slowly toward him, fixed on whatever absorbed him so completely. Aria grabbed up her skirts and made her way along behind them, unnoticed.

She stopped dead, straightening, her eyes wide. Two Indian warriors clad in skin breeches and breastplates of bone and colored beads approached cautiously. Their long black hair swayed with their rocking gait and Aria could see brown-tipped feathers adorned a braid woven on the side of each warrior's head. Their bronzed shoulders shone as if oiled and their faces bore dark and light streaks of bear grease paint. They stopped, paces away from the earl, studying him and his camp openly. Carrick, in turn, stopped a few paces behind them, his musket leveled at their backs.

Acre moved softly to the earl's side and murmured something to him. Aria watched, fascinated, as Acre then slipped to one side and spoke to the braves in their tongue. From her position, she could not make out what was said, but Acre translated several messages and his face seemed to relax as the exchange went forward. The earl's back was to her, but she saw him lift his hand and lower it. Carrick lowered his gun slowly and moved around them to stand with the other men.

Curiosity spurred her forward. She weaved around the

campfire and slipped between two of the hunters, MacKean and Bosarth. Neither made a move to stop her and she edged forward until she could hear fully what transpired. This was some sort of invitation, from what she could gather. Their chief wanted to speak to the chief of the hunters. And to her amazement, she heard the earl agree without hesitation.

As they spoke, the braves continued to inspect the camp unabashedly, staring around the earl and his men while their words were translated. And now one's eyes fell on Aria and widened with interest. Soon his fellow brave joined him and the earl stiffened, turning about to follow their line of sight.

As he took in her fair skin and the honey-golden blaze of her unhidden hair, his face became a storm cloud and his eyes flashed with menacing lightning. "Aria!" his voice boomed, "get back to the tent and stay there, where you belong!" When she hesitated, stunned by his swift fury, he jerked about to find Jamison. "Jamison, take her to the tent and keep her there! Don't let her out for any reason!"

Aghast, she grabbed up her skirts and jerked her arm away as Jamison tried to take it. She stomped to her canvas prison with her face on fire and her blood beginning to boil. Furiously she slung the pillow on the floor, threw the comforter against the wall, and kicked over the folding chair. And when there was nothing left to vent her wrath upon, she made fists of her trembling hands and vented her most virulent oaths.

When at last she heard them leave, she could only sink to her knees on the floor of the tent and try to fend off the overwhelming urge to cry. She was a possession, a toy, a vessel of pleasure to him, no more. And he treated her without the commonest decency. He was callous, arrogant, infuriating, lecherous, possessive beyond reason. . . . Then why in heaven's name was she crying, feeling . . . hurt? He behaved in perfect accord with his one value . . . his own desire, whatever it happened to involve. Did she honestly expect anything else?

"I'm sure he was only concerned for your safety, Miss Dunning," Jamison ventured when he brought her supper that evening. "We've seen Indian signs about for days. We knew they were watching us. Rutland had just decided to search them out when they came to us. Fortunately, they were friendly."

"He might have told me," she answered desultorily. "I'm not a half-wit or a child."

"Nay." Jamison's boyish smile bloomed and he sat down on the edge of the chair opposite her. "You certainly aren't either. It's just that Rutland is . . . used to making decisions. Sometimes he forgets the niceties with us mere mortals."

Aria smiled in spite of herself. Merrill Jamison probably knew him better than anyone and Tynan was still something of an enigma to him, too. She felt that somehow put them in league just now.

"Does he ever talk about England or mention when he's going home?" Aria picked up her fork and poked at the strange concoction of possibly meat and what appeared to be beans on her plate.

"Uh," Jamison winced as he watched, "Acre went with Rutland, so Carrick's cooking." He couldn't suppress a shudder and Aria nodded agreement, dropping the fork with a wry tilt to one side of her nose.

"England?" she reminded him.

"Ah, yes, the homeland. It's strange. I've heard Rutland discourse on everything from plowing methods to agnosticism to the merits of a certain silk for ladies' stockings. But I don't believe he's ever willingly mentioned his home. He's not over-eager to return, I can say that."

"Because he was barred from court?" Aria's head cocked appealingly and he drew a deep breath of resignation.

"Perhaps. That part at least is true. Everything else, including the reason for it, is conjecture and better left unspoken." He sat forward and patted her hand as it lay on the tabletop then rose abruptly. "He's a hard man to know, Tynan Rutland, but worth the effort." And he left.

* * *

How long had she been sitting here in this miserable, damp forest? Aria counted back over the days and they came to just over a week. Nine days in his possession . . . nine interminably long days. It seemed like a century! She pushed up from the cot where she was resting and looked around her, aware of some subtle, but agreeable changes. It was the light; the sun was finally out.

She hurried from the tent and stood with her hand shading her eyes, looking up at the welcome clearing of the sky. Jamison's familiar voice came over her shoulder.

"Wouldn't you know, he's due back today and the bloody sun comes out to herald his appearance." He joined her and scanned the autumn blue that was deepening above them.

"I don't care why it's out, it's here and I'm going to take advantage of it," she declared, ignoring the way her heart skipped when he mentioned Tynan's return. She turned determinedly back for the tent.

"What are you up to now?" Jamison scowled, following. "I won't let you get me into trouble this late in the day."

"I'm going to the stream to bathe and wash some clothes." She knelt and began pulling clothes from her leather satchels.

"Oh, I'm not sure—" he shook his head dubiously.

"I promise to be a good little prisoner, but I've got to bathe and this may be my only chance." She cast him an irresistible, pleading look and got her way.

Jamison helped her find a suitable spot just downstream and promised to return for her in an hour. As she began to wash her clothes, he scouted the woods immediately around and left. Hanging her petticoats on branches to dry, she removed all her clothes but her chemise and waded into the cold water up to her knees. She shivered and hurried with the soap, realizing that she had missed Acre's hot water almost more than his cooking.

She soaped and rinsed and considered washing her hair. But her hour was fast drawing to a close and she dried off hastily, shivering back into her sober woolen dress. She sat down on a rock and pulled her stockings up and fastened them and slipped her shoes on.

A twig snapping behind her sent her up like a shot with her back to its source.

"I didn't realize an hour could pass so quickly." Sorting and pulling at her laces, she righted them and began to tighten them. "These last three days they've seemed to crawl by like an inchworm." She turned as she put the finishing tugs on the bow at the top and she froze.

Two Indian braves lunged for her at the same time, one pinning her arms to her sides while the other stifled her belated cry with a punishing hand. She wrestled and struggled with everything in her, but their wiry strength seemed only to tighten about her. The hand was soon replaced by a wet cloth shoved in her mouth and bound with a thin leather thong. Her hands were bound with a wetted strip of leather and she was hoisted up onto a lean, hard pair of shoulders like a sack of flour.

She kicked and rocked and wrestled furiously as the breath was pounded out of her by his relentless bouncing gait. She had almost succeeded in tussling off when the other brave doubled back to see what was delaying them. His solution was brutally simple. He drew back a meaty fist and sparks flew across Aria's sight before everything settled into merciful blackness.

"Carrick says from the tracks there were at least two of them." Jamison's ruddy face was lined and miserable under Tynan's burning glare. "Rutland, she wasn't out of the tent more than two hours the entire time you were gone—"

Tynan turned away toward Acre and ordered him to prepare a week's rations. His face seemed paler as he looked at Carrick next. "Show me where it happened."

"You're not going after her alone?" Jamison hurried to keep up with him as he strode down the stream bank.

"No." Tynan paused and raked him with a murderous look. "You're coming with me."

Jamison nodded grimly. "You couldn't keep me back."

The grassy bank was just as they had found it three hours before. The grass was trampled and wet, and a length of damp toweling lay piled on a rock at the stream's edge. Two embroidered petticoats hung over nearby bushes; one drooped almost to the ground, a piece ripped from its hem. Aria's spare chemise hung over a small branch and beside it was a large, wet linen shirt.

Tynan's gaze fastened on his shirt and his bronzed face seemed to pale. He drew a deep, ragged breath and pulled it from the branch, wadding it into his palm. He couldn't take his eyes from it. It was like someone had just hammered him in the gut. He couldn't breathe and he fought savagely for his legendary control. When his head raised, his eyes burned like hot molten steel.

"Let's go," he growled softly.

Aria awoke on the damp ground and opened her burning eyes slowly. Her shoulder was propped against the trunk of a tree and her hands were bound tightly behind her back. Her neck ached and her stomach felt as if it had been pounded with a club. Pains shot up her arms from her wrists, and her mouth and throat were parched, making it nearly impossible to swallow. She tried to shift to ease the pain in her wrists, but found no position that offered relief.

She lay her forehead against the rough bark of the tree trunk and tried to push away from it with her shoulder, but with little success. She moved her legs and sighed jerkily, at least they weren't bound.

She was in the forest . . . somewhere, tied to a craggy oak tree by a thonglike tether. And as she looked around dizzily through the pounding in her head, she saw a makeshift fire and blankets. She knew immediately the full extent of her peril; she had been captured by Indians.

She slumped bonelessly against the tree, closing her eyes and moaning softly. Her voice was cracked and her throat hurt. Dark tales of the fate of Indian captives floated back from her girlhood. Their hapless victims were burned, tortured, made to work like animals until they dropped . . . even sacrificed, some said. Panicky waves of nausea flooded over her, one after another, and she gritted her teeth, trying to control them.

"Are you a-vake?" came a hushed voice from nearby and Aria's head shot up to scour the shadows of the trees around. A brief flash of hope filled her, only to be dashed when her eyes lighted on a figure, slumped on the ground in a position similar to hers. "Ah-h-h . . . I hope I did not schtartle you, miz. I vas vorried. You slept a whole day already."

"Have . . . they got you, too?" Aria felt all the more exhausted for the dashing of her hopes.

"Ja, I been with them five days now. Who are you, miz, and vere from?"

"Aria Dunning, from—" She stopped and tried to wet her lips as she realized she had no real place to be "from" anymore. "I was raised in Virginia. I was with a hunting party . . . when they took me." She wrested her shoulder a bit farther around the tree to see him. He was a younger man, short, she surmised, though it was hard to judge from his slumped position on the ground. His face was broad and fleshy and his middle, beneath a somber black coat and waistcoat, matched it. His face was covered with a patchy set of new whiskers, probably the result of his captivity.

"They von't vant us to talk. And you must do as they say . . . always. I give you a little help. Maybe you can slip through da arms, unter your bottom side and to de knees. Get your arms in front." He wriggled his fingers to show his hands were bound in front of him.

"I don't understand," she rasped.

He held up one finger as if to collect her attention, and

slipped his feet through his arms, over his bound wrists. "Den like this." He pulled his wrists up under his legs on the ground and half squeezed, half bounced his ample bottom over them. Now his bound hands were behind him and he began to reverse the process.

Catching on, Aria worked at bringing her hands to her front and finally succeeded, at the cost of only a strained muscle or two.

She leaned back gratefully on the tree, moving her screaming shoulders gingerly. "Oh, that's heavenly. Thank you."

"You don't be a captive of de heathen for five days and not learn nothing." He leaned back against his tree, obviously weakened by his exertions.

"I'm so thirsty." She swallowed hard and tried not to think about water or anything else but her companion. "Who are you? How did they capture you?"

"I am Frederich Mueller, Miz Dunning, a mizzionary of the Lord in these zavage places."

Aria squinted and tried to make out more of him as he spoke. "A missionary? To the Indians?"

"Them and whoever else vill listen. I vas coming from Chief Mosquer's camp and going home to my vife, before bad veather comes. She is vith child, my sweet Anna, and she needs me."

"What did you do to make them angry?" She frowned, feeling a dart of pain through her cheekbone.

"Nothing . . . jus' ride by. They jus' take captives, dese ren-e-gades. They vere driven off from the chief's people and now raid an' steal to live. Dere has been zickness in their camp an' now they need vomen an' zlaves."

"Renegades? You mean they're outlaws even to their own people?" Aria's head swam dizzily. "Dearest God—"

"Ja," he said, nodding sadly, "ve only put our trust in Him. He vill save us, in de end."

A long depressing silence fell between them. Aria tried to make herself more comfortable between the bare tree roots.

"Where is your wife, Anna?" She finally could not bear her own fears in the silence any longer.

"Nort Carolina . . . Vilkesboro, near de frontier. A little zettlement maybe a veek's ride avay. Ye must be near de border here. Maybe your people look for you and help us, eh?"

It was the final blow in what seemed a round of crushing realizations. How would they know what had happened to her? Would they realize she hadn't run away of her own accord? How would they know where to begin looking for her? Could they track and follow them through these dense woods? And most painful of all, would the earl care enough for . . . his money's worth . . . to come after her? She remembered his rage that last morning when he saw her standing there in the open with the Indians staring at her. Her heart expanded in her chest, making it difficult to breathe.

He had every reason in the world to wash his hands of her and chart a course straight back to civilization. She had openly proclaimed her loathing for him on numerous occasions . . . she resisted him and denounced him as lacking even common decency. But was he really capable of abandoning her to these renegades? Even hardened hunters and trappers had often joined in the hunt for women and children captured by hostile bands of Indians. Could the earl be so callous as to do nothing?

"I . . . don't know if they'll . . . come for me or not." Her voice was small, but the clearing was quiet and his answer let her know he heard her.

"Den ve pray on it."

And she could just make out his face as it lifted to the arching cathedral of trees above them.

The braves returned soon and Aria learned there were only four of them—a stringy, mangy lot, nothing like the braves that had come to their camp a few days previously. Their hair was shaved back on their heads, well above their ears, leaving a broad, matted row of hair down the center of their heads. Their skin breeches were filthy and ragged, and when they approached her, she shrank back from the overwhelming stench of rancid animal grease, sweat, and rotted breath.

They laughed raucously, handling her hair and poking and prodding her body insultingly . . . as if she were a horse or some other animal. One drew his long knife and held it poised above her while he grabbed her hair and jerked it up cruelly. He said something and the others laughed mirthlessly, calling him back to their meager meal of spitted rabbit. She held her breath and winced with the pain of her pulled hair, refusing to cry out. Eventually he decided against cutting her hair or scalping her . . . or whatever he had contemplated doing and ambled back to his accomplices.

They squatted and ate the rabbit half raw, offering nothing to their captives. The air was turning cold and they wrapped up in the skins and blankets as if to settle in for the night by their paltry fire. Frederich Mueller called out to them in his heavy English and again in some Indian tongue, asking for a bit of water for Aria. He received a cruel blow across his mouth for his effort, but in a short while, one of the renegades brought an oiled skin and poured some water into her mouth. He stooped to check her bonds and stayed to inspect their prize thoroughly.

Instinctively, Aria kept her gaze averted, barely breathing as he examined her eyes, touched her breasts, and ran his hand over her hip and leg appraisingly. She fully expected that she would become their night's entertainment . . . all of them, one after the other. She had heard talk of frontier women falling on their own kitchen knives or shooting themselves with their last ball rather than be captured and used so brutally. Bile boiled up in her throat and she stifled a wretch, trembling violently.

But he soon satisfied his curiosity and wrapped another leather strip around her ankles, tying it with an authoritative jerk that secured her for the night.

She spent the night shivering, huddling into her upraised skirt for warmth, and at dawn the same Indian came to her and undid her feet and tether, pulling her to her feet and jerking her along into the bushes. It was a minute before Aria realized what he meant as he pointed at her and the ground. She colored crimson and did as she was bade. And soon she was back at her tree, tied hand and foot once more and given another drink of the distasteful water.

After some time and argument, the renegades left their camp and Aria sighed tightly. Frederich Mueller heard her and asked if she was all right.

"I'm all right. I'm just cold and hungry . . . and scared."

"I don't fear for myself," Frederich uttered, "but I vorry for you and for my sweet Anna. How she vill manage mitout me?"

"What will they do with us?" Aria asked after a while. Her voice seemed weaker than the growling of her stomach.

"Me they vill work like a horse . . . you vill do vhatever their women von't do . . . and 'varm' de braves ven they vant. Ve are not of their people, so ve are not people."

"Like slaves . . ." The horror of it shook through Aria anew.

"*Ja,* ve be zlaves now." The resignation in his voice was awful and added to Aria's misery.

She couldn't accept that it was really happening to her . . . that she would end the painful downward spiral of her short life as a slave to outlaw savages . . . worked like a beast of burden and raped whenever they pleased. How far she had fallen. Just two months before, she had lived in total luxury, oblivious to the harsh struggle for survival that consumed the frontiers people of her own colony. The lives and problems of the rest of her own countrymen had been totally foreign to her. Her only concerns had been *her* marriage, *her* future . . . the continuation of her life of uninterrupted ease and prestige.

Now she had lost her beloved home, her family, her virtue, even her dreams. She had escaped with nothing but her life and the clothes on her back, only to be sold into sanctioned whoredom by her own mother. She choked, thinking of Marian Dunning . . . reliving their time on the harsh trail to Lathrop's house, remembering Marian's gentle determination to survive, feeling again her comforting arms that horrible night Aria was almost raped. Now Aria would never know the truth about her mother; and as long as she breathed, it would haunt her.

That relentless downward spiral of loss had reached its cruel, final twist . . . the ultimate degradation . . . abject slavery.

It was a long time before they spoke again, and as if by some unspoken agreement, they did not speak of the future or their hopeless situation. Aria learned that he was, as she had suspected, German born. He professed the Moravian faith, which, he proudly stated, numbered the famous martyr John Huss among its numbers. His people had once lived a communal life like that of the early church on a count's estates in Germany. They had been persecuted vigorously by the Roman church, but survived and now had taken a more conventional form of life and worship. Aria learned there were important Moravian communities in Pennsylvania and North Carolina and that they often sent missionaries into the frontier to preach and convert the heathen tribes.

When he asked about her life, she swallowed her chagrin and told him of her early life at Royal Oaks and of their misfortunes. But when he asked how she came to be in a hunting party in the wilderness, she stammered betrayingly.

"I am . . . the g-guest of a nobleman that my mother . . . knew."

"Oh," he murmured after a telling pause. "It is good, to have . . . friends in time of need."

Her deliberately vague response should have raised more questions than it answered, but he asked nothing else. Aria sensed that this gentle, good-hearted man was loath to condemn anyone in her dire circumstance, and she was grateful beyond words. Tears sprang to her eyes and another long silence descended upon them.

In the interminable waiting, her thoughts turned inescapably to the earl and their time together. She defied, resented, and resisted him, and yet some part of her was perversely thrilled each time he touched her or let his steel-hard gaze melt over her. He could be so tender at times, but the next minute he was a tyrant, ordering each detail of her life and commanding her to surrender the most intimate parts of her for his enjoyment. He had wanted her to satisfy his arrogance as much as his lusts and had taken advantage of her misfortune to buy her like some waterfront doxy. She had every reason, every right to despise him.

And yet, in her present distress and with her life shattered around her, her thoughts were consumed with him. She relived the way he touched her with his looks from across a room. His raw strength drew even hardened over-the-mountain men to follow him, and the strong, animal-like agility of his big body pulled covert glances of desire from her. She recalled the strangely reassuring persistence of his presence about her on that narrow bed, even when her passion was beyond his reach. And with the poignant clarity of feeling that only hindsight can bring, she wondered what it would be like to love him freely, to perhaps learn to enjoy his company, and to eventually share something of his closely guarded self.

The ache that rose in her middle and the choking in her throat were greater torture than anything these savages might yet do to her. She would never see him again, but she vowed that every night as she closed her eyes, she would give herself to him freely. And this aching would finally end when she could sleep and dream no more.

Sixteen

Tynan's gaze narrowed to an intense point as he searched the far side of the stream bank. It took a moment to recognize Carrick's silent arm movements through the underbrush. It came again; this time it was unmistakable.

"Looks like he had better luck than we did," Tynan rasped lowly, tapping Jamison's arm. "Let's go." He rose quietly and parted the bushes that hid them, stepping out into a cloak of tree shadows. His leg muscles cramped as he stretched; his shoulders burned as he rolled the tension of waiting from them. His bristled jaw was set like granite under shadowed eyes that glowed with inner fire.

Twice in the last two days they had lost the trail and twice the Earl of Penrith felt as if part of his life had been drained from him. He tried not to think about what might be happening to her, to concentrate only on finding her. But glimpses of her delicate face, battered, or her soft body lying crumpled and abused, kept recurring in his mind, spurring him savagely.

Whatever happened to her was his fault. He'd taken her with him, into this wilderness, knowing that he owned her passion and thinking that was enough. Her will would mold to his eventually and she'd give him her tempting body willingly, eagerly. But there were other hours in the day, and places other than his bed. When he took her, he had given no thought to what his life, what her life would be like outside their hours of shared desire.

Worse yet, he had withheld mention of the vows he had

sworn to speak with her, even as he had watched her struggle
with the humiliation of her worldly status. Had he honestly
hoped to avoid those vows through her refusal . . . to put the
keeping of his honor onto her shoulders? They were such delicate shoulders, so soft . . . so in need of protection.

His face was black with double loathing as they slipped
across the creek to join Carrick.

Aria must have dozed briefly in the late afternoon. But her
cold, aching body made both waking and sleeping equally miserable and for a time she drifted fitfully, unable to distinguish
much of her state. The braves returned just before sunset with
a blanket gathered up into a bundle of some sort and a bounty
of two scrawny rabbits. They seemed to be arguing and Aria
lost the capacity to even fear as she watched them devour the
gamy food.

Almost as an afterthought, they tossed a bony, half-eaten
rack of ribs on the ground before each captive and settled
down around their warm fire to drink from a captured jug. It
wasn't long before they were arguing over something again
and one seemed to settle it by jumping up and pulling
Frederich up, untying his tether. He cuffed the missionary mercilessly about the head and Frederich deflected the blows as
best he could. Then the savage barked something in a nasty
tone and jerked Frederich along behind him into the blackening
forest.

The others seemed to think this great sport and howled and
yipped their support. When the two returned, Frederich was
burdened with a huge armload of branches and pieces of logs
that he dared not drop. Aria could see him straining and she
tightened all over, sending him whatever aid her spirit could
offer. The lazy jackals had argued over who would gather wood
for the fire, and in the end, Frederich was forced to begin his
role as a beast of burden.

To her dazed relief, they seemed to have forgotten about

her and, after a while, settled down to sleep in the warmth of the fire. Aria pulled her woolen skirt up around her shoulders, depending on her petticoats to keep her bottom half from freezing. After her long fast, her stomach was queasy from the half-raw scraps of meat.

Again the boundary between wakefulness and sleep was disturbed. Twice her eyes sprang open in response to some nameless sensation. But whether it existed in the darkness about her or in her beleaguered mind, she could not say, and she slumped, unable to release the tension it built in her. The third time she jerked to alertness, she saw a dark, shapeless shadow moving. Frozen, she watched as it crawled stealthily along the ground around the center of camp . . . toward her.

Tynan's sharp blade bit at the corners of his mouth as he moved closer to the sleeping figures on his hands and knees. Four—there were four of them. His burning eyes raised and searched the far side of the clearing for signs of Jamison and Carrick. Their shadows were slowly closing in on the sleeping renegades. Then Tynan stopped dead, staring at the base of a tree not far away. A dark outline lurched into the gray mist, jerking to a frantic halt at the end of a tether.

"No, please, no . . . *please,* no-o-o—" Aria's wail grew from a whisper to an audible cry and a sudden explosion of bodies occurred about the camp, bringing the renegades up snarling.

Aria's scream slowly curdled in her throat and became garbled, panicky cries as she scrambled around the base of the tree where she was tied. Her arms came up to block the grunts and savage thuds from her ears. The coiled tensions of the last three days sprang free, crashing through her battered wall of self-control. The raking, snapping, thudding sounds of conflict receded and her own desperate wails filled her head. She curled into a tight ball, unable to comprehend more than her rampaging fear.

Tynan swung his long knife savagely, again and again, connecting and slashing several times, using his feet Indian-style to unbalance his furious opponent. His dark face burned dull red and his eyes glowed with fires of retribution. His foot snaked out and missed its target, but in dodging, the stringy outlaw stumbled over a half-buried log and fell backward. Tynan pounced on him, driving his blade within an inch of the Indian's throat before force matched force and suspended it.

They grappled, frozen in contest, until the earl snarled a guttural phrase in the outlaw's tongue and the Indian's eyes flared with the impact of the curse. Twisting and jerking, the Indian managed to get part of his lower body from beneath the earl's hard weight and kicked at him desperately. The effort was wasted. The earl's muscles tightened relentlessly, and with one final surge of his powerful arm, he drove the blade home.

The fierce battle ended abruptly and an eerie silence descended on the dank forest again. Twigs snapped beneath feet and Aria's breathless cries had slowed to drained moans; they were all that could be heard. Voices floated, strange and distant, on the thick air and died.

Aria was hauled up and she shrank and tried to scramble away, barely hearing her name for the sound of her heart pounding in her ears. She thrust blindly at whoever held her in that unyielding grip.

"Aria, you're *safe* . . . safe! Look at me!" Tynan struggled with her, trying to untie her hands as she fought to pull away from him, eyes clamped shut. He slit the tight leather that bound her bruised, chafed wrists and picked her thrashing form up in his arms, carrying her toward the center of the wrecked camp.

"Build up the fire," he ordered, furious with reined anxiety, "she's freezing!" He knelt with her, grasping her flailing arms and holding them as he tried to tilt her head and make her look at him. "Aria, look at me! You're all right now. They won't hurt you anymore. . . . I won't let anyone hurt you."

Aria's resistance slowed as exhaustion took its toll, and Tynan pulled her close against his chest, murmuring her name and stroking her hair. Something in that consoling gesture penetrated her jumbled mind, and she pushed away, opening her eyes. Her stricken blend of fear and hope raked across his gut like steel claws.

"You?" she gasped, her chest heaving as she gulped for air. She wrenched a hand free to bring it up to his bristled chin and touch it with disbelief. Her fingers were like gentle brands that left hot marks on his heart. Her beautiful eyes were red-rimmed and full of pain, and one cheek bore a greening bruise just below her eye. And yet she had never seemed quite so beautiful to him.

"Yes, Aria—" His voice was thick.

"It . . . is you," she gasped, reaching for his face with her other hand as her tortured face lit with understanding. "Oh, it is you!" Suddenly she embraced his shoulders, tears spilling down her cheeks as she buried her face in his jacket front and gave way to unchecked sobs. "It . . . is . . . you!"

She clung to him, spending the stored anxiety and torment of the last days in a deluge of hot tears. When at last he tried to pull her away to look at her, she tightened her hold on him fiercely and refused to allow it.

He looked up anxiously from her to find Carrick kneeling to wipe his knife on the grass nearby and Jamison standing above them, nursing a wounded arm and urging the other stumbling captive forward.

"He says there were only four. We got them . . . all . . ." Jamison's words trailed off as he witnessed Aria's panicky sobs. He urged the other captive down beside the fire Carrick was building and said nothing more as he turned away to look for blankets.

The warmth from the fire seemed to soothe her as she lay curled on Tynan's lap. Her crying slowly dissolved into little shudders of fatigue. But even as drained, dreamless sleep overtook her, she would not relax her tight hold on him.

For a long while, there were only the sounds of Carrick's movements about the camp as he disposed of the bodies and scouted the area. Tynan wrapped her protectively in his arms and gently touched the bruise on her face again. Her breathing deepened and slowed to a more peaceful rhythm and he sent Jamison a grave look.

Frederich Mueller intercepted that look and pulled the blanket they had given him a bit tighter. He had watched the powerful man's gruffness and glimpsed underneath his true anxiety for the lovely fellow captive. Frederich sipped gratefully from the small flask of brandy Jamison offered, then sat forward to hold his hands out to the hot, snapping fire before him.

"She was very brave, Miz Dunning," the missionary managed, drawing their guarded interest as he wiped his mouth on his soiled sleeve. "But ist very hard for a young voman."

"You were with her all this time? They . . . didn't—" Tynan stopped and swallowed back the words as he stared at the round-faced man that had shared Aria's captivity. His insides were churning at the thought of her facing that mangy, rabid pack alone.

"She vas tied an' starved like me, but I don' think she vas harmed . . . in that vay. Tanks be to God, they vere too busy with their raiding an' stealing. Another night and—"

"There will never be another night," Tynan bit out tightly, then softened it, "as you said, 'Thanks be to God.' "

"I am grateful to you, zir, for my rescue, my life." Frederich bowed his head in deference and managed a wan smile when he raised it again. "I prayed an' vas comforted that help would come. But I tink Miz Dunning vas not so sure . . . that zomeone would look for her."

Frederich's tone carried a hint of question that struck Tynan as a reproach. His face reddened and stiffened as his eyes lowered briefly to Aria's quiet form, nestled trustingly in his arms and against his body. She seemed so girlish, vulnerable . . . misused.

"Would I not search for my betrothed wife?" Stinging, he raised his chin as if daring any disagreement. A muscle in his square jaw jumped defiantly.

"Betrothed?" Frederich sat back tiredly against a log and

evaluated the tight lines around the earl's mouth with discerning eyes. "Zhe did not mention that. But . . . zuch trials are hard on a young voman."

Jamison was watching the earl openly, and a question formed on his face before finding its way to his tongue.

"Who are you and how did you come to be captured?" Tynan demanded brusquely, blocking any further comments. The firelight reflected on the polished steel of his eyes as he regarded Frederich Mueller's pleasant, fleshy face and somber black clothing.

"Frederich Mueller, sir, missionary to de heathen in these parts. I vas on my way home to my vife in Nort Carolina . . . ren-e-gades they vere. Zome days later they took Miz Dunning." He looked from man to man apologetically. "I could do nothing to help, but ve talked. I tried to comfort her."

Wordlessly, the earl nodded understanding and shifted his delicate burden in his arms. Her arms tightened about him frantically, as if afraid he might yet abandon her. His face clouded like the heavy dawn sky and flicked toward the mist-shrouded forest that seemed eager to close in around them.

"We must move out as soon as it is fully light. Rest while you can."

Tynan hardly allowed Aria to leave his arms during the two days it took to reach the camp. The first day she had slept for long periods as she rode in the comforting strength of his strong arms. And when the horse halted or lurched on uneven ground, she instinctively tightened her arms about his muscular ribs.

"I'm sorry." She colored, chagrined by her impulsive embraces.

"I'm not," he rumbled softly, pulling her back against his chest again. "If you want to stop and rest, just tell me." His hand gave her cheek a tender stroke and then slipped around her, tightening reassuringly.

Aria's chagrin melted into drowsy contentment. And for the first time in weeks, the bleak vista of her future was sealed away from her consciousness. It was enough to be alive and safe, here with him.

That night, Tynan pulled her into his arms to sleep by the fire, sheltering her against his big body. Her red-faced protest was cut off when Frederich took up a place at their feet and Jamison lay down at their head to share the warmth.

The next day, she found her weakened state provided more than adequate cause for his continued support. "It must be true; every cloud has a silver lining," he muttered, as Jamison hefted her up into his arms the second morning. The bow of her mouth turned upward in a little smile he did not see. And strangely, though they both found occasion to speak to Frederich, Jamison, and Carrick, they remained mostly silent with each other. For Aria, the day turned into one long caress, its innocence ensured by its blatant nature. It spoke eloquently of her gratitude and his relief at having her back.

Aria had never seen anything so beautiful as the plume of smoke rising from Acre's fire as they crested the hill above the earl's base camp. The burly men she had once regarded with suspicion seemed familiar and friendly as they crowded around to welcome her and her rescue party. She sat bolt upright, unnerved by all the noise after the quiet of the journey.

In the center of camp, Tynan finally allowed her to be taken from his arms and lifted down gently. Before his boots touched the ground, he was issuing orders to prepare to break camp and head south by next daylight. And as he escorted her firmly to the tent, he ordered hot water and food to be brought for her.

"You'll want to wash and rest before supper." He made it sound like an order and Aria turned to look at him. Again, his back was poker-straight and his eyes were cool and analytical as he scrutinized the tent. Seeing the ties of the back flap undone, he set about tying them securely.

Aria watched his square-tipped fingers work and felt their

actions betraying the softening of her feelings in these last several days. She shook her head and blinked at him disbelievingly. What was happening to him . . . to her? Was it possible that her harrowing experience and his determined rescue had really changed nothing between them at all?

"Do you still think I'll try to escape?" she managed thickly. The warmth that had enveloped them in the past two days was stripped rudely away.

His hands dropped to his sides and his gaze was shrouded as he turned to her. "No, you've learned what awaits a woman alone in the wilderness. This is to ensure privacy." He moved past her to the tent opening, where Acre handed in two buckets of hot water. He pulled some soap and toweling from his oak chest and plopped it on the table beside the metal basin. Then he slid down into the chair, pushing his crossed feet out before him and tucking his arms across his chest.

Aria understood his move for the declaration it was and narrowed her green eyes as she felt herself slipping back into an unbidden pattern of resistance. Everything inside her chilled. "I'd like a bit of that privacy you just ensured."

"Our privacy, sweetest, not yours." His steel-gray eyes blued as they flowed over her. "I don't intend to allow you out of my sight or out of my reach for the next two weeks."

Aria stiffened, guessing what he had in store for her. The instant the danger was passed, he asserted his crass "rights" of ownership again.

"Only two weeks?" Her tone was light, but acrid. "That's a relief. I thought you meant to make my *service* of longer duration."

"A longer term might be arranged." He cocked his head to study her reaction closely. "But two weeks is the time it will take us to travel to Mueller's home in North Carolina."

Aria had picked up the soap and set it down at this bit of news. Surprise softened her face slightly. "You're taking Frederich Mueller home?"

Tynan laughed wryly. "I'm not sure he could make it on

his own. It's along our general route and I would see him repaid for his kindness to—" He stopped abruptly and Aria thought his face might have reddened a shade.

"Your water is cooling, sweetest." He tilted a brow toward the basin.

"So it is." Aria snapped back to her former frame of mind, furious with herself for allowing him to divert her from her irritation so easily.

By the time she had scrubbed her face and unlaced her bodice, her hands were trembling. His eyes warmed her skin as she peeled her bodice down over her arms and she paused before loosening the waist of the skirt and sliding it down over her hips.

"If you were any kind of gentleman—"

"But I'm not." His mouth curled. "I'm a lecherous boor—you said so yourself."

Aria glared at him and shoved the soiled dress from her. She shed her petticoats, then sat on the edge of the cot to remove her stockings. Shivering, she wetted the cloth and slid it over her curving body, beneath her chemise, and down her bare, silky legs. She knew that wherever the cloth went, his heated gaze followed in hungry fascination and it made her hands tremble.

When she finished drying and pulled clean petticoats and her rose velvet dress from her bag, he snagged her arm as she passed and he sat forward, pulling her to him. She clutched her clothes to her thinly clad breasts and tugged away, knowing that eventually he would have his way. He pulled her between his legs, putting his hands at her waist and looking up into her reddened face.

"I worried about you, Aria." The seductive vibrations of his lowered voice set her skin atingle.

Instantly, she recalled her desperate thoughts during her ordeal and that they were filled by him. She had recalled his gentle touch, his sweet, shocking pleasurings, and had bitterly regretted that she would never know what it was to give herself freely, fully to him. But, she chided her weakening knees and disclaimed the puddle of warmth in her middle, that was when she was weak and frightened and sure she would never see him again. Now that she was beside him, she could recall other things as well: his arrogance and opportunism, his relentless lust, and . . . this latest, unexplained transformation that mocked her own womanly warmth.

Her level gaze and thoughtful, dark emerald eyes unnerved him. "Don't ever run from me, Aria." The command invaded her very skin.

"Then you expect me to patiently warm your bed and amuse you until you tire of me and cast me off like some moldy old shoe?" she gritted out with a bit more emotion than she would have wished.

"Would I have hazarded life and limb to reclaim a shoe? Aria, I want you with me and I'll take whatever steps are necessary to keep you by me."

"Indeed?" Her heart seemed to flop over in her chest. "And what would your elegant friends say if they knew you kept your contrary 'harlot' chained to your bed?"

"There are better ways to secure you, sweetest . . . as you will soon see." And as he said it, he admitted to his thoughts what had been working on the borders of his conscience most of the afternoon. During the torturous, sleepless hours they had tracked Aria's captors, he had vowed never to lose her again, whatever it cost him. And he was bound to keep that other vow . . . a vow that seemed more appealing by the minute. Seldom could a man satisfy honor twice in one simple act . . . like marriage. His mind had turned the idea over and over, examining it from all angles and finding it a thoroughly agreeable solution. How strange that providence had made it possible so soon. And the considerable salutary effects of respectability on a woman's reluctant passions were not to be overlooked.

He grinned rakishly and slid his hands up her sides. But to her astonishment, he set her from him and rose, stripping off his shirt. Aria backed to the corner of the tent, hugging her clothes to her fiercely, sure he meant to take her to prove the conquering effect of his mesmerizing loving. But he picked up the basin and raised one edge of the canvas wall, tossing the dirty water out beneath it. Then he poured a fresh basin for his own bathing as if dismissing consideration of her altogether.

Furious with the way her responses refused to ignore him, she dropped her clothes on the cot and began to jerk them on, one by one.

When the tent flap was raised sometime later, Aria had lighted the lamp and sat repairing the big rip in the hem of her petticoat. She didn't bother to look up, assuming it was Acre, come to take away her supper plate. But there was rustling and throat clearing and Aria looked up quickly, pushing her skirts down hastily as Frederich Mueller edged farther into the tent to make room for Jamison and Tynan behind him.

"It will be tight quarters, gentlemen, but it won't take long." Tynan eased between the two men and came to Aria, bidding her rise with an extended hand.

Consternation filled her face as she pointedly ignored his hand and rose, tucking her needle into a fold of the lace adorning her bodice shoulder.

"Well, this is a pleasant surprise . . . I am allowed visitors," she quipped with a pleasantness belying her mistrustful glare.

"Not quite a . . . visit, Miz Aria." Frederich's fleshy face reddened considerably and he frowned quizzically at the earl.

"More in the way of a professional call, I should think," Jamison muttered, clamping his hands behind his back and lowering his chin to regard her doubtfully.

"Oh." Aria stiffened, glancing from Frederich to Jamison and then to Tynan.

"He's here to marry us, Aria, dearest," Tynan explained casually, reaching for her hand and pulling her toward him.

For a moment, he succeeded in drawing her closer, for the proper sense of his words eluded her. When they finally took shape in her mind, she tried unsuccessfully to jerk her arm back.

"What?" she demanded, only half believing what she had heard and sure he would never say it twice.

"Marry us, sweetest . . . join us in wedlock." He pulled harder, feeling her resistance rising to equal his increasing force. The smile on his lips hardened slightly as her eyes widened, then narrowed dangerously.

So this was what he had meant—his way of securing her, binding her to him! The low, disgusting— And by the wary surprise of his face, he had not expected serious opposition.

"In a pig's eye he will." She succeeded in wrenching her wrist from him. She sputtered speechlessly, then swung her foot viciously and smashed his unprotected shin with the hard toe of her shoe.

"*Ow*—dammit!" he yelled, grabbing for his leg, his face scarlet with the wound to his dignity.

"You have a bald lot of nerve—"

Frederich Mueller lurched forward to intervene as Jamison burst into gales of nervous laughter.

"You honestly think you can just march in here . . ." she shrugged off Frederich's tentative hold on her arm and shoved his conciliatory words aside, "and order me into marriage as if I were some sniveling serf?"

"Please, wait outside for us, gentlemen." Tynan tensed, his eyes suddenly white-hot and the muscles in his jaw jumping. "Out!" he thundered at their startled faces.

The flurry for the tent opening would have been comical, but for the impending explosion. Jamison jerked Frederich to a halt outside the tent, taking a deep, sobering breath.

"You see, Herr Pastor . . . theirs is a rather . . . 'delicate' situation," he tried to explain between jerky gulps of air.

Frederich waved the explanation aside with a fleshy hand. "*Ja* . . . I guessed." He paused a minute to listen to the voices coming from the tent. "But I never saw a voman who vill not marry the man zhe loves. It vill come." He smiled cherubically and shoved his hands in his pockets, strolling back toward the comfort of the fire.

Jamison watched the missionary quizzically, then shot a thoroughly puzzled glance back at the tent before joining him.

Aria backed away as Tynan stalked her and in a few steps she found herself pinned against the cot. His dark displeasure was scarcely reined.

"Do you hold me in such contempt . . . to expect me to participate in such a farce without a murmur?" Her green eyes danced with luminous fire even as her voice thickened. "And to mock a good and pious man like Frederich Mueller—you're not worth the effort of despising you!"

He grasped her shoulders and gave her a furious shake. "What's gotten into you, wench? I mock no one and I swear I'll have what I want of you before this night is out—"

"You expect me to believe you'd actually marry me and honor vows spoken in secret before an itinerant preacher?" Her words choked her and she had to swallow a great lump in her throat just to breathe.

"He assures me he is fully ordained," Tynan countered tightly. "The bonds he forges are as real and as permanent as any man's."

"You're an earl, a peer of the realm, a titled nobleman," she bit out incredulously, twisting her shoulders in his iron grip. "You wouldn't honestly marry beneath you even if you wanted to . . . no nobleman would!"

"I had forgot what an expert you are on the nobility," he growled angrily. "I am a man first, Aria, whatever my birth—is that not the popular sentiment here in the colonies? I answer to no one and for no one, save myself. My marriage is not subject to another's approval, if that concerns you." The earl took her averted face in hand and forced it up to meet his burning stare. Aria had never seen his face so dark, so intense. "I have no need to pretend, Aria. I don't need to marry you to have you."

The charge began to drain from Aria's anger, replaced with a deep, painful ache that frightened her more than even his full-blown ire. "You have me as your whore," she flung at him accusingly, jerking her face away as her eyes began to fill. "You have no need to make me your property as well. What would it gain you?"

"I should think that was rather obvious." He relaxed his hold on her.

"I know nothing about you—" she blazed, infuriated by his smugness.

"Don't belittle your powers of observation, sweetest. Like most women, you hide your acuity beneath a show of innocence or modesty when it suits you. What could you need to know that you do not already? You know I have wealth and can give you comfort and pleasure." His hands propped on his narrow waist as if inviting her inspection. "And you cannot truthfully deny that you find my loving pleasurable. What more could you have thought to gain in a marriage?"

He straightened sharply, stung by the earnestness of his persuasion. Why did he find the prospect of marrying her so damnably compelling all of a sudden? His hand returned to her shoulders, though with a softer grip. "I plan to keep you for a long time to come, Aria. Sooner or later you will bear me a child that will need a name and protection. I promised you security and have chosen this route to provide it." The liquid jewels of her eyes lost their angry spark and with it a bit of their life as well. He drew a deep breath and felt his chest annoyingly full as he pressed on with his stubborn logic.

"There is yet another reason for the surety of vows. Those who might spurn a mistress will flatter and cajole a wife. I will not be denied your company and pleasures because of some aged doyen's delicate sensibilities. After our vows, I shall be free to take you anywhere without comment."

It was the final stroke. He would marry her to give him power over her and any children she might bear . . . and to save him the inconvenience of being separated from his pleasures by social censure. Aria lowered her head and stared unseeingly through the haze of her unshed tears. She could never have dreamed he could be so intentionally cruel . . . not after. . . . But perhaps her own need had concocted in her mind the closeness they seemed to share as they returned to camp. He certainly seemed oblivious to it now.

Abruptly, she sat down on the cot behind her and gripped its wooden frame with white fingers. What good would it do to refuse? He would only find some other way of coercing her . . . or tempting her. And she knew that the greatest danger in such a marriage was also its major temptation . . . the hope, the promise of something real, something dear and sweet between them. How could she explain that for her it would be worse to live with the same loveless, married lie her mother endured than to be justly branded and shunned as a harlot?

"You find the prospect of marriage so distasteful?" he demanded, his tone thick with anger, or frustration. When she did not answer, he stared down at her rounded shoulders and gritted his teeth. "You have already experienced the full scope of what will be required of you . . . and I do not think it has proved overly taxing. The eventual benefits may someday outweigh these present impositions."

She raised a pale alabaster oval set with luminous beryls to his stern gaze. "Then nothing is really changed between us, except your legal rights to my bed, and my legal right to use your name. Do I understand you properly?" Her voice was low and steadier than she had thought possible.

His look was guarded, but he nodded.

She rose, commanding her shaky limbs to support her as he stepped back to watch her reaction closely. She clasped her icy hands before her and tried to meet his consuming gaze. "Then know the full truth of your bargain and let there be no pretense between us. I have nothing honorable left to me. I have no dowry, no home, no family, not even a country." Her voice caught on a ragged emotion and she paused, looking down briefly as she freed it. "You have already taken my innocence, but I still have one last virtue to bring to you in this marriage contract . . . honesty. Without complete honesty, this 'arrangement' will be unbearable for me. I will speak my mind openly, and I will expect the same of you. If . . . *when* you tire of me, I must be the first to know. Then you will be free to take . . . someone else."

Confusion welled up inside him as she spoke. The resignation, the raw pain in her flattened voice shocked him, as did her cold tallying of their future. He had not counted that she would take respectability so hard. The absurdity of it rendered him speechless for a moment.

"And my duties are to be as before?" she questioned, looking at him intently with luminous eyes that had conquered their flood. "Your entertainment in bed and . . . conversation?"

"As before." He finally found his tongue, wondering what else he might have lost in this exchange.

Aria lifted her chin suddenly and shook off the lingering outward signs of her troubled heart.

"Then call good Pastor Mueller and make an honest woman of me."

Seventeen

A short while later, Tynan sent Acre to escort Aria from the tent and the grizzled cook related to Aria that the change of location was explained by the earl's comment that such a splendid occasion deserved a wider audience. Though Aria suspected it had more to do with dispelling any hint of secrecy than the celebrating a grand occasion, she held her tongue and accompanied him. He offered her his arm hesitantly and led her out to the center of camp where the earl waited for her in his shirtsleeves, breeches, and boots. And when Acre made to leave her, Aria held his sleeve and asked the wire-whiskered man to stand beside her.

Frederich Mueller's clear, sonorous voice pronounced the vows by the blazing campfire, with the entire camp in attendance. She repeated each vow, line by line, faltering only slightly when she promised to faithfully love, honor, and obey the arrogant and commanding Tynan Rutland. She imagined a certain softening in his bronzed face as he promised to love, honor, and cherish her through all the conditions of their life to come. And she knew it was the treacherous melting of her own heart that she was reading in his face. No vow of honesty, no brutal recitation of his worst qualities, no outraged recount of his calloused maneuverings would stop it now that it had begun. Now by her own vows, she yoked herself to the one man who could command the tender stirrings of her innermost heart . . . and to whom she must never show it.

Despite the crackling fire's heat, her hand was cold when

Tynan took it in his to put his own heavy signet ring on it. His eyes glowed golden with the borrowed warmth of the fire-light and Aria searched them for clues to her future, unaware that they probed hers for the same counsel. When the bene-diction was pronounced, there was an expectant hush in the clearing, measured by the wheezing hum of the burning logs beside them.

"You may kiss de bride now," Frederich leaned closer to suggest, his face cherry-red from the fire's heat and beaming broadly with pleasure.

Tynan leaned down slowly and brushed her lips almost ex-perimentally. Frederich tucked his chin and allowed himself a mischievous grin at Jamison as he cleared his throat.

"Now you can really kis-ss her, man, yer married!"

And a general outcry began that would not abate until he swept her up against him and planted a lusty kiss on the well-warmed bow of her mouth. Caught up in his game, he crushed her to him for a third kiss as the hunters chanted a rhythmic encouragement. And as quickly as he had begun it, he drew back in astonishment.

"Ow! What in the world?!" He pushed her back by the shoulders as if she'd bitten him.

"What's happened?" She seemed just as bewildered at his behavior as he had been at the sharp prick on his chest.

Amid the catcalls and laughter, he rubbed his shirt front, inspecting it. "You pricked me with . . . something," he man-aged somewhat gruffly.

Face aflame, Aria looked down at her fashionably cut bodice disbelievingly. "I assure you, I—"

"Careful, Rutland, your rose has hidden thorns!" Jamison taunted, drawing hoots of relieved laughter from all looking on.

Glowering, Tynan turned her face to the firelight fully and began a thorough manual inspection of the shoulders of her dress, oblivious to her tightly whispered protests.

A silvery glint in the lace on her shoulder betrayed the culprit and he withdrew her silver needle with a flourish, holding it up for all to see before tossing it into the fire. The grin that spread over his fire-bronzed face was dazzling. "Any other hidden weapons, wife?" he murmured with lecherous delight as he pulled her to him.

She shook her head, purple-faced with embarrassment. He kissed her deeply, rousing the noisy, raw approval of the rough congregation. And when he released her, she was fully dazed, breathless, having somewhere lost her embarrassment in the scalding fury of his kiss.

She was whirled about and kissed soundly by Jamison, bussed paternally by Frederich Mueller, then hugged brusquely by Acre. And everything began to whirl again as a small keg of rum was hauled out and toasts were drunk all around to the couple's health and bliss.

Tynan held her blushing form close against his side with a muscular arm and shared his cup with her. The strong rum went immediately to her head and then flowed downward, burning a path into her very loins. She put a hand to her head, feeling dizzy and breathless . . . almost nervous, like a proper bride.

Tynan downed the last bit of his rum, watching her closely in the firelight, feeling her softness melting against his rock-hard body wherever they touched. That troublesome swelling began in his chest again. To combat it, he tossed his cup to Jamison and swooped Aria up into his arms, striding purposefully toward the tent. Tonight he was a man who knew exactly what he wanted and now nothing would stand in his way.

The tent was dimly lit and refreshingly cool when Tynan stood her on her feet in the center of it. She swayed against him, still dizzy from the toasts.

"I'm sorry," she murmured softly with a hand to her temple, "I've never had anything stronger than sherry to drink before . . ."

"And never again," he gazed down on her polished-apple cheeks and sweet cherry mouth, "except in my presence." He traced the luscious curve of her cheek and slid his fingertip over the ripe curve of her lips, as he had wanted to do for the last hour. His touch absorbed the last of her besieged resistance.

It didn't matter that his tone carried a lecherous taunt or that his hand on her face somehow pulled the strength from her legs. Her eyes came up to focus warily on his square handsomeness, and impulsively, she caught his palm between her rosy cheek and her upraised shoulder, brushing it lightly with her skin. When she met his gaze, her often stormy eyes were as calm as a lake on a still summer's day. She made herself stand quietly before him, determined that her honesty with him would begin now, here . . . in this bedding.

He brought her hand up to his lips and traced her palm with the tip of his tongue, touching his heavy ring as it drooped around her slender finger. The action reminded her of its presence. Shivering inexplicably, she pulled her hand back and clasped it, staring at the massive gold ring that bore the crest of the house of Penrith. He watched her closely, feeling oddly drawn to her in a way that did not involve his rousing physical need.

"I shall replace it for you with one more fitting, at the first opportunity. Until then, I ask that you wear it with care, it is my family signet . . . the ring of the earldom." When her other hand closed gently around it as if caressing it, the curious divisions in his need for her no longer contained his vaulting feelings. All overflowed and mingled, becoming focused in a singular pang of desire that registered plainly in his dusky face. He would have reached for her, but at that moment, she turned away.

"I'll treat it with care," she murmured softly, tossing her long, honeyed hair back over her shoulder. And to his surprise, she laid his ring gently on the table and began to loosen her laces.

Watching her slowly remove her garments, he was rooted to the spot, fascinated by her emerging form. Each time he saw her thus, he saw something new in her. Her mood shaped her posture, her movements, and shone through her very skin, making her a different lover each time he had taken her. He glimpsed snatches of the woman inside her, but only jumbled elements that did not always fit easily together in the picture he held of her. Both his puzzlement and his paralysis were swept roughly aside when she turned to him clad only in her chemise and covered by the mantle of her soft hair.

Shivering, she slipped onto the cot beneath the comforter. Her green eyes were raw, expectant emeralds, awaiting the strokes of passion that would free their brilliance. Lying back on the pillow, she lifted her arms to him, stopping her heart for the instant it took him to accept her invitation and fill them.

Tynan sank down atop her, his head swirling strangely. Her lips moved beneath his, seeking, learning from him as she clasped his shoulders and ran her fingers up his corded neck. His hands sought the sleekness of her shoulders, her throat, her cool cheek. When he drew back to look at her, his eyes were dark, burning coals.

Aria looked up into his face with a dazed sort of desperation. How could she have resisted him further, vows or none? She lowered her gaze to fix it on his linen-covered shoulder and hoped he would not see the turmoil of feeling he stirred inside her . . . anything to prevent him from gaining further power over her.

"There is one other thing I forgot to mention . . . nay, demand in our bargain," she murmured, veiling her trepidation with calm tones.

"Demand?" He raised a bit farther above her, frowning. "The echo of vows scarcely dead and already you have demands?" He felt himself tightening all over with a nasty bit of lingering expectation.

"A larger bed," she uttered evenly, seeking his eyes with her own as she felt his tension mounting.

The tempered glow returned to his steel-gray eyes as they searched her disbelievingly. "That's your demand? A larger bed?"

"I hardly think it too much to ask, considering you would share the benefits as well." She sounded surprisingly reasonable for a woman drowning in her own senses.

"A larger bed?" He raised farther above her, growing more incredulous as he sought, guiltily, to hide his relief.

"You see, there's a leather strap here that supports—" She felt for the edge of the cot, arching to one side to produce the offending fastening. His startled laughter vibrated from his heavy chest into hers as he lay across her. He caught her face in his hand and turned it up to meet his unguarded mirth.

"By God, Aria, you'll have it—your larger bed—as soon as it is humanly possible! Anything else, while you've got me warmed and willing to be generous?" His deep, resonant laughter washed under her skin in warm waves. It was like nothing she had ever experienced before . . . the flood of his freely shared humor invading her, lapping seductively about her loins, her heart.

"Well?" he insisted, the planes of his starkly chiseled face lifting into a lush, beguiling grin. How could he seem so much like a charming little boy and so much like a sensual rake with the same expression?

Dazzled, Aria stared at the intriguing curve of his full lips and just managed to shake her head.

"Nothing?" His face tightened knowingly. "You are a curious woman, Aria Dunning . . . Rutland. I daresay, you'll think of a few more things in time." His finger pulled the top of her chemise down over her shoulder and he pressed his lips to her creamy skin.

"No," she managed huskily, "I don't . . . want anything from you." Her eyes closed as he shifted to the cot beside her, stroking her bare arm teasingly.

"Nothing, Aria?" He caught her lips with his and moved over them with perfect tenderness, brushing them with his breath. "You want nothing of mine? Where is this honesty you promised me?"

Her eyes opened into the mesmerizing heat of his and she whispered her helpless truth. "I do want . . . you."

His eyes crinkled with unabashed pleasure as he pulled the comforter from between them. "I think I could come to *honestly* relish your last virtue." He slipped his hand up beneath her chemise, following the splendid curve of her bare hip and waist. "You set my very blood afire, Aria."

His mouth descended upon hers as he pulled her tightly against him. She embraced him with all the hunger she had disowned from the moment she had first seen him staring at her across Sir Lowell's salon. She returned his kiss with all the passion he had built in her since their lips first met. Her body molded itself intimately against his broad, forbidding frame with all the unleashed need of her emerging womanhood. She held nothing back, reserving nothing and seeking everything in a kiss that exploded between them into a maelstrom of raw heat.

Everything was surrendered to him and yet claimed from him—sensation, warmth, will, even breath. And when they finally separated, Aria's eyes could scarcely focus on his dark face as it moved away. He turned down the lamp to a mere orange glow and shed his clothes, his eyes never leaving her. As he approached the bed, she rose to her knees and drew her chemise over her head, casting off the last of her resistance with it.

Stopped by her motion, he watched her shake her hair about her naked shoulders and hold out her arms to him again. Her eyes shone like shore beacons in the dimness, calling him, wanting him. Instantly he was in her embrace and pushing her back and beneath him, covering her like a hot blanket of flesh.

Aria responded to his kisses, his touches, reveling in the

driving weight that pressed deliciously downward on her craving body.

He shifted to one side and stroked her satiny sides as his kisses lowered on her body. His lips seemed to cover every inch of her burning skin, returning frequently to sip the fragrant nectar of her mouth. He tended her limbs, her body, her breasts with caresses that made her writhe wantonly and press against his hands. His tuggings and nuzzlings at her breasts sent a shower of sparks into her loins, teasing and stirring them wildly. Shamelessly, she wriggled her hips against him, somehow understanding that only his flesh completing hers could ease the splintering ache within her.

Reading her need in the sensual undulations of her lithe young body, Tynan molded himself above her, fitting his hard body between her sleek thighs. He felt her arch with an exultant shudder beneath him as he entered her and his last rattled thoughts gave way beneath her supple embrace and breathy moans of mounting pleasure.

She was caught again on that sharp upward spiral of passion's dizzying rise. Pulling her arms tighter about him, raking the powerful muscles of his back with her nails, she clasped him closer to her, burning for the conclusion that he seemed to contain for her within his body.

"Aria . . . Aria—" Her name seemed ripped from his very soul as he arched and plunged into her fiercely, again and again. He crushed her to him convulsively, spending the great eruption of his desire within her womanly frame. Again she witnessed the awesome potential of passion completed and again she felt him spiral off from her into realms of sweetest pleasure that beckoned her to follow, then seemed to elude her.

It was as though they had almost entered paradise. And the "almost" was so splendid that she closed off all wonder at what unthinkable riches of sensation might lay beyond that unattained portal. She panted for breath under his weight and quivered hotly, burying her face in the hollow of his damp neck as he relaxed over her. His pulse jumped against her temple and her head filled with his musky male scent. But she could not fully banish the aching need for him that still coiled inside her. When he slid to the cot beside her and loosened his hold on her, she knew a sense of loss that colored her face with chagrin. He was massive enough to crush the breath from her and still she longed to keep his hard, driving weight upon her.

His stern gray eyes were very dark beneath lazy lids as he watched her lovely face calm. Her profile was exquisite, her hair a tactile treasure, her body a feast of sensory delights. She had met his need fully, opening herself to him freely—without the slightest fear or quailing. She had trusted him with her body, her blossoming passions, her most intimate responses. It touched a cold, shaded part of his being. She mattered to him more than he imagined possible . . . for the wild pleasure she gave and now also because of these strange new feelings she produced in him.

"Are you all right, Aria?" He propped his head lazily on one hand and ran the other up the little valley between her ripe young breasts. She rippled beneath his hand and her eyes closed, bringing his attention to sudden focus through seductive mists of satisfaction.

A bolt of cold trepidation launched itself in his veins. He had meant to hold back, to consider her inexperience on this night of all nights. And as soon as he touched her, he had abandoned himself to passion's unfettered lead. It was not like him to allow his control to lapse so utterly and at so crucial a juncture.

"Are you all right?" His tone was stern to mask his doubt.

"I am . . . fine." Her head was partly turned and her voice was small. He turned her face to him, annoyed by the anxiety that constricted his lungs. When her eyes opened to him, they were misted and luminous with distance.

"Aria—" His mouth was suddenly dry as his concern lurched a notch higher. "You must tell me if I . . . am harsh with you, or hurt you in any way. I would not have you come to loathe me because of the way I take you. I would not be . . . brutish with you."

Aria stared at him, having difficulty comprehending his concern, it contradicted her experience so. But the earnestness of his tone seeped into her sore, hungry heart, sweet succor for her flagging spirits.

"You . . . did not hurt me," she said simply, lowering her chin to rest her forehead against his chest.

It was not enough.

"Aria, I demand that honesty of you, even in matters of our bed."

She lifted her face to him, searching for the concern that made his expression formidable. "I am well used, but . . . unscathed." Her lips tilted tiredly into a fetching bow.

He nodded and clutched her head to his chest, holding her tightly for a moment. And he made to rise.

"Where are you going?" Aria sat up, holding him by the arm.

"You observed, the bed is small—"

She tugged obstinately, pulling him back down on the cot. "If you leave me . . ." She paused to submerge her feelings under recognizable honesty. "I'll be . . . too cold." Her chin raised, daring him to refuse her.

And he allowed himself to be drawn back under their cover, smiling.

"This is all you get for breakfast." Tynan handed her a huge biscuit stuffed with fried salt pork and a cup of Acre's strong coffee the next morning. He had arisen and shaved and fully dressed long ago, only now returning to the tent to waken her. Standing in her chemise and petticoats, she took the food from him and frowned as she listened to the sounds of camp being broken.

"Acre's packing up his gear," he explained as she sat down

on the cot to eat. "We're starting back this morning. I'll need you to pack your things as you want them—" He stopped abruptly and sat down in the folding chair to look at her. Her shoulders were back and her spine was straight as she perched on the edge of the bed. Her eyes rolled with raw pleasure as she took a second bite of biscuit. But his eyes drifted down over the top of her chemise where her pert, well-ripened breasts strained against the soft fabric. He could see the effects of the cool morning air in the little buds outlined at their tips. And the sight twisted something in his loins.

"Did you sleep well last night?" he managed tersely.

She saw him jerk his face away and became acutely aware of her state of undress. But this time the blood that rushed to her cheeks was not from embarrassment. A confusion of curiosity and pride prevented her from drawing the cover about her. She knew instinctively what darkened his face and mood a shade.

"I slept soundly," she mused, nibbling the biscuit and recalling inescapably all that was said and done on their wedding night. "And I was warm." Her voice softened in spite of her.

"That you were, sweetest . . . hot, in fact." He ventured a sidelong glance at her as if testing the safety of it. Then he turned to her with a slow spreading smile that took a lecherous turn. "Never let it be said I'd leave a wife cold in my bed."

A brief frown flitted over Aria's brow and she dropped her gaze in confusion. She remembered those events with tenderness, while he apparently thought of them as proof of conquest! The warmth of her mood vaporized instantly and she was back to the wary edge of her nerves, as if preparing for combat.

He reached for her cup of coffee and held it up flamboyantly. "To the successful start of our marriage . . ." He drank deeply and offered the cup to her, as if he expected her to do the same.

The rakehell— She tossed her food on the table and stood abruptly, furious with herself for the waffling of her resolve. Already he taunted her with the emptiness of their vows! She blazed at him visually, then snatched up her dress and pointedly turned her back on him to pull it over her head.

But he was already on his feet and he jerked it back over her head, pulling it from her as his arm circled her small waist. She turned, sputtering angrily, to push at his hard body.

"Let go! I have to dress."

"Now, now." He mocked her efforts, pulling her fully against him to prove the futility of her resistance. "I only meant to salute you . . . and your honesty. Let me have a bit more of it, sweetest . . ." And his lips captured hers relentlessly, pouring his heat into her anew. Just as he had intended, the strange power he asserted through her senses punctured her swelling pride and charmed her into response.

"That," he breathed jerkily, "was honest." His hand drifted down over her buttocks and caressed them boldly, causing her to stiffen. He laughed huskily and straightened his deerskin jacket, settling back into his chair.

Aria watched him, stunned by the swift response of her desires when he summoned them. She knew he did it to prove his complete dominion over her, but somehow that mattered less than the shattering eagerness of her passion. Were all women like this? Did all women experience such torture in their own bodies? Was this her unique punishment . . . or was it his unearthly power?

He watched the kaleidoscope of feelings in her face and felt an unwelcome pang of uncertainty. He had expected her to blaze at him, or perhaps freeze with icy disdain until he thawed her tonight in their traveling bed. But she was so openly confused . . . distraught.

She stooped to retrieve her dress, her eyes unseeing as she clasped it to her vulnerable breasts. Her eyes were wide as she turned to him. "Am I . . ." Her voice came out a whisper and so she started again. "Am I . . . supposed to do what you do?"

Thoroughly taken aback at her unexpected manner, he stared at her girlish mingle of passion and desperation. "Do what I do? When?" He shook his head, unable to comprehend what was happening between them.

"When you . . . take me." She colored to the roots of her honey-silk hair, but she did not flinch from his incredulous scrutiny. He had commanded her honesty in matters of the bed . . . now she must have his or be tortured evermore. "Surely you must know . . . you've had so many other women. Do the others—"

"So many others? I—" He rose and spread his legs solidly, locking his knees. "I have known other women, Aria, I would not deny it." His face was gruff with his attempt to ferret out her meaning, knowing it must be dire indeed for her to risk asking about what passed between them in bed.

She took a step toward him and stopped, her face surging with crimson. "Then—" she swallowed, "—am I doing what I should? Am I supposed to do . . . what you do . . . that gives you such pleasure?" Aghast at her words, she clamped a hand over her mouth and turned away in horror. What had possessed her to say such a thing . . . to him, of all people?

"It's nothing—" she muttered, fumbling furiously with her dress. "Forget I spoke."

"Aria?" He watched her embarrassment grow as her ineptness with her simple dress increased. She was trembling violently. A slow bud of understanding began to open in his mind, and even before he fully comprehended her question, he knew he had to take her into his arms to put her strange misery to an end.

"No, please." She strained away, still obsessed with trying to right her contrary apparel. But he dragged her into his embrace and forced her crimson face up to his. Her eyes were bright prisms of moisture and her lips trembled temptingly. He did what came most naturally; he covered them with his own.

Somewhere in their kiss, as he plundered the sweet riches

of her yielding mouth, he knew what she meant. And when he drew away, the glazed look of newly wakened passion in her emerald eyes confirmed it. She leaned against him weakly, humiliated by the unfathomable maze of her own desires.

"I never thought . . ." He laughed hoarsely at himself, running a hand back through his dark, shoulder-length hair. "I thought to go slowly with you." He made her look at him. "But I hadn't counted on such eager heat, sweetest."

Jerking her face down, she pulled away and tried to bolt around him. He caught her with ludicrous ease and ignored her resistance as he reeled her to him. She raised a face scarlet with defiance to meet his lecherous taunt. And she read in his face what he intended.

"My love, if you can ask about it, you're certainly ready to experience it." His dark head lowered toward her.

"Are you mad? They've broken camp already . . ." She scarcely evaded his lips, all too aware of his muscular arms wrapping ever closer about her body. "This is no time to pursue your disgusting pleasures."

"It's not my pleasures we'll pursue, my hot little wife, it's yours." He proved the superiority of his power by holding her wriggling form perfectly still against him. "And for that they will most certainly wait."

This time his mouth found hers unerringly and he plied his wanton magic over it, coaxing her into compliance. Her defenses were weakened by his earlier kisses and now crumbled utterly beneath the double assault of his persistence and her own traitorous desire. Slowly her arms wound about him and she rose onto her toes to meet his ardor. But when his hand reached for the top of her chemise, she stayed it.

"Take it off," he commanded, "or I will."

Dark-eyed, she fumbled hurriedly with her petticoats and was startled by a rumble that sounded suspiciously like laughter. She looked up at him with dazed puzzlement.

"There's no rush, Aria." He brushed her trembling hands aside. "Let me." And he proceeded to peel her garments from her slowly, one by one. And each bit of skin he bared was made to glow with the heat of his appreciation. He pushed her down on the cot and covered her delectably shivering form, then removed his clothes as slowly as he had hers. And by the time he filled her arms, her heart was pounding in her throat and she ached all over with that strange hunger he awakened in her.

He ignored the guidance of her hands and pursued with maddening leisure the stimulation of her every nerve. His hands kneaded and pressed and tickled and probed, taking her breath time and again. She began to wriggle under his expert touch and the burning in her breasts and empty woman's hollow became unbearable before he obeyed her behest and lavished his full attention on her most intimate areas.

She gasped and arched against him in invitation and later in demand. He filled her by what seemed torturous increments and his movements were mercilessly languid and uncannily effective. He rode between her thighs gently, then, responding to her throaty, urgent cries, pressed his full weight tightly against her as his rough strokes sought to burst that unknown barrier that separated her from paradise.

Aria clasped him to her savagely, writhing and meeting his thrusts wildly. That coil inside her loins wound tighter and glowed hotter with each stroke and suddenly the updraft ended, shooting out in all directions, expanding into an infinite plane of unbelievable brightness. Her body seemed to explode, releasing in one blinding snap all of passion's hot potential—flinging white-hot bolts of lightning through her in successive waves. She heaved and shuddered and felt Tynan's convulsive release as though it had occurred inside her own hot skin.

Together, they soared and clung and floated in brightness, in undreamt-of pleasure. She was with him, holding him, in a place of their own making, a place fashioned of their dreams, their joy, their love.

How long it took for her to return from that wondrous, far world, she would never know. But when she settled on earth once more, it was in Tynan's arms that she nestled. Everything was lovely in shades of rose and purple—all but him. Her eyelids kept falling shut, despite her efforts to look at him. She sent her hand to stroke his face wonderingly and felt a hum of pleasure from him. She couldn't remember ever feeling this peaceful, this completely at rest . . . satisfied.

He held her for what seemed a long time, allowing her to doze sweetly in his arms. And he marveled at the translucent allure of her sleepy smile of satisfaction. Things were stirring inside him that he did not fully understand. But with his customary arrogance, he determined firmly that the only thing that mattered was the joy she brought him, in bed and out. And all the rest would work itself out to his eventual satisfaction. He would not let it occur otherwise.

Outside, Jamison sat on a half-rotted stump by the little stream, his face in his hands and his elbows propped on his knees. Frederich Mueller strolled over to him with hands clasped behind his broad back and a faintly sympathetic look on his fleshy face.

"Oh, God," Jamison said without lifting his head, "I can't take much more of this. First them, then you and your Anna, and now them again . . . always them." He raised his head and looked at the other men, lounging about on the ground, whittling, killing time by tossing a knife at a tree-knot target, or just sitting with dead patience. He turned a furious glare on the tent.

"What on earth are they— We were supposed to leave just after daybreak—Rutland said so."

"Jamison—" Frederich looked at him from beneath his bushy brows as if Jamison were a petulant child. "You must learn patience. *Ist* their wedding night . . . a very critical time in a marriage."

Jamison jumped up and raised an accusing finger to the sky, where the sun was rising ever higher.

"It's near to noon, not night. And it's not decent!"

"As you zaid," Frederich raised a knowledgable finger, "theirs is deli-cate zituation. They just vork it out."

Jamison's arms flew out, palms up in mute supplication, then they dropped heavily. "I'm going for a swim," he growled, "come get me when they've finally got it *worked out*." He tromped off down the creek with Frederich's sympathetic laughter trailing.

When Aria woke again, the sun was bright through the tent walls and the morning sounds of birds close by and camp movement had given way to the sunny quiet of midday. Tynan still held her, his gray eyes closed in rest that ended abruptly with her first movement.

"It, is still morning?" She pushed up on her elbow, half fearing to look at him after what she had just experienced.

"It may be. What does it matter?"

She looked at him and felt something in her middle melting into a warm puddle again. His face was softer, his eyes heavy, and his hair was tousled sensually. Just now he seemed so human, so . . . lovable.

"Did you learn what you wanted to know?" He pushed her hair back from her face gently.

She lowered her eyes and nodded, bombarded suddenly with a million new questions. She allowed one to escape. "Is it always like that?"

He laughed from deep in his chest and hugged her to him. He turned her chin up to catch her gaze. "My experience has been that it's a little different every time."

"Even with the same woman?" Her eyes were wide and irresistible.

"Especially with you, sweet thing. That's why I wouldn't let you get away from me, no matter how hard you tried . . . to the point of even marrying you." He kissed the tip of her nose and brushed her lips with his before rising.

All she could see were the bold muscles of his chest and shoulder rippling before her eyes as he left the cot.

Eighteen

Aria sat on a mossy log near the circle of firestones, holding a tin cup of coffee in both hands. She rolled it back and forth in her slender palms, using it to warm her hands as much as to drink. The day had grown old and tired as they wound their way through untouched forests, and clouds had gathered to block the sun's modest comfort. Every sound in their temporary camp seemed close in the heavy air. Aria listened mostly and said little, feeling herself to blame for their late start and meager progress.

More than once during the long afternoon, she had turned or glanced aside to find a pair of eyes fixed on her in speculation and she lowered her gaze, feeling her stomach sliding into her knees. Merrill Jamison had hardly looked at her much less spoken, and the tight silence of his usually cheery mien pronounced his disdain unmistakably. When Tynan delayed them further, insisting that a packhorse be unburdened to provide her with a mount, she caught Acre's look of disgust at Tynan and counted it an indictment of her presence . . . and purpose. But she was completely at a loss to explain why they had accepted her so freely as his harlot, but now spurned her as his wife.

Again she felt totally alone, unnecessary and unwelcome, serving only Tynan's whims for pleasure . . . otherwise abandoned. And worse, his grand lordship was totally oblivious to their guarded looks and tacit disapproval. He rode before her, his back rail-straight and his proud shoulders impossibly square. Each time she looked at him, she was reminded of another recent journey, when she rode in the circle of his arms, instead of at his heels. But she was his property now, "secured" under his hand and bearing his name.

A small branch nearby snapped underfoot, sounding like a shot and startled Aria into upsetting her coffee. She turned to find Frederich Mueller stepping over the log and then settling his stout frame on it beside her.

"*Ja,* vell—" He looked up at the darkening gray of the sky above and then clasped his hands together, resting his elbows on his knees. "*Ist* most miserable veather. I vill be glad to be at home once more, vith my Anna. Ve have a big stone fireplace that is zo cozy and varm."

"Tell me about Anna." Aria was grateful for the mercy of his company. He of all people had right and reason to condemn her, but of all people he seemed the most understanding . . . forgiving. It was an example she would remember. "What is she like? And your home, what is it like?"

Frederich looked at her with a boyish smile of delight while his perceptive brown eyes read the strain and loneliness in her face. "Ah . . . she is a lovely girl with hair like rusty cornzilk and fair-like-milk zkin. Her heart is tender as a babe's. And her voice is zoft like the vind through the villows. I vorry for her as her time comes. I vill stay vith her now for a long time . . . an' zee to the little flocks in the zettlements nearby. Zhe needs me, my Anna. It vas the hardest thing on my mind vhen de Indians captured me."

Aria watched an otherworldly glow creep into his fleshy face as he joined his little wife once again in his thoughts. A sharp pang of envy pierced her, turning quickly to guilt. Just knowing such devotion existed between man and wife made her situation all the more difficult to bear.

"You must . . . care for her deeply Frederich," she murmured, managing a wan smile as she set her now cooled cup on the ground by her feet.

"I care for my sweet Anna wit all the love de Almighty can

put in a man's heart. From de beginning, such vas meant, for a man to cling to his vife." He smiled broadly and took her hand between his hard, fleshy paws. "You vill zee, in time."

"I . . . don't think it is always so, dear Frederich." She might have said more, at honesty's goading, but her throat began to tighten with humiliation. "We . . . aren't . . ."

"*Ja*, I see." He patted her hand. "I tie the knot goodt for you. It vill come."

"But we . . . w-were" she stammered, blushing scarlet with unspoken confession. How could she contradict his simple assumptions without seeming to disparage his practice of his calling? She would not trouble his gentle, faithful soul.

"Aria. Married is married. The Almighty don't care how it come about . . . if the vorkmanship is goodt." He had seemed to read her mind. "No one is perfect . . . without zin. Ve all must try hard . . . an' harder." He stroked her hand and dipped his head to peer into her lowered eyes. "You vill see."

Aria raised her head and managed a tight smile, wishing she could believe him. But how could he know the bitterness of the cold transaction she had entered into? She was commanded to warm a man's bed, not to share his life. And each passing hour threatened to erode her ability to protect herself against the desire for those tender but forbidden realms of marriage.

Her face flushed as she thought of the inner conflict her "husband" wrought within her. She wanted him physically, just as he wanted her . . . but she abhorred his arrogance, his disregard for others, his overt manipulation of people and events for his own benefit or pleasure. He could be so tender and yet so callous, so achingly handsome and yet so loathsome. He would demand everything of her, even her innermost heart, as if it were his due . . . and then dismiss any demands made upon him with a wave of his lordly hand. If Frederich Mueller had not just provided proof otherwise, she would be tempted to believe that the vows themselves were only a dream, or some cruel spell he had caused to linger in her mind.

Why would Tynan Rutland, the wealthy and worldly Earl of Penrith, stoop to forcing marriage on a friendless, penniless colonial girl? It baffled her anew.

A series of water drops fell on her shoulders and she looked up at the gray sky, which seemed to weep with the tears she would not allow. Frederich pulled her to her feet and jerked her cloak hood up, pushing her toward the tent Tynan had ordered set up for her. She glanced around at the rest of the men, huddled under trees, wrapping themselves in oilskins, and her heart sank. Aria tried to grasp Frederich's arm and pull him inside with her, out of the wet, but he was already out of reach, running through the pelting rain for the tree where Jamison had taken shelter.

Soon Tynan appeared in the tent opening and lowered the flap behind him. He brushed the water from his jacket and hair and reached into a pocket for his handkerchief to dry his face. And as quickly as his eyes adjusted, he searched for Aria and found her seated on one end of the cot.

"This is the part I hate . . . no permanent camp. This," he spread his arms apologetically, "is the best we can do for—"

"It's not right." She bounded up and pulled her cloak tighter around her.

"I make apologies for the accommodations—" He stiffened gruffly.

"I mean, it's not right that your men sleep in the elements while you install me in this." She swept the tent with a cold hand.

He straightened as far as the tent would allow. "And what would you have me do? Invite them in to watch our honeymoon?"

"What can they be thinking? The real reason you put them to all this trouble is perfectly clear. They know what—" She stopped and tried not to cower under his withering stare.

"Someone spoke amiss? Who was it and what did he say?" Tynan's eyes sparked dangerously in the semidark.

Aria pulled back, surprised at his conclusion. "No one said

anything . . . but they must know what you're . . . what we're . . . doing. It's not right."

After a moment, his rigid posture eased and his mouth tilted wryly. "Of course, every man jack of them knows what we're doing. It's what all newly married couples do on their honeymoon . . . acquaint themselves with the pleasures of married life. Who cares what they think, as long as they confine it to thinking only." He laughed shortly. "If it helps your feverish conscience, think of it as helping them stay warm at night."

Aria gasped and sputtered. "You are . . . unspeakable."

"Then don't speak." He took her into his arms, overcoming her protest easily. "Kiss me instead, wife." And he captured her lips, holding them against the ransom of her will.

His hands slipped inside her cloak, up and over her shoulders. Defiantly, she began to count in her head to block awareness of what he was doing to her. But her white fists against his chest slowly began to uncurl and finally spread over the muscles of his ribs. Her arms made their way around his waist as his made their way about hers. His warmth was lush and dizzying, banishing every trace of her shame and anger and turning her counting into a sensual cadence. When he untied her cloak and placed her on the cot, she was powerless to resist. And as he sank down beside her, spreading her cloak over them both, her arms opened to him.

Tantalized, Aria felt him loosen her clothes and send his sinewy hands to explore her body beneath them. She would have removed her dress, but he halted her, whispering against her bee-stung lips: "No, sweetest, I would not risk baring you to this inhospitable weather more than necessary. You needn't worry clothes will impede our pleasures. Indeed, they may enhance some aspects agreeably."

And to her surprise, he was right. With his deft hands and incredibly rousing mouth, he seemed to leave no part of her untouched, proving her clothing was no barrier to sensual enjoyment. Never again would she think herself secure against his rapacious need when merely clothed. And when he completed her, she reached that same bright plane of ecstasy that he had opened for her only hours before. They slept in each other's arms, sharing passion's recklessly squandered warmth, wrapped in her lady's cloak.

The next several days ground by in similar fashion, gray and wet and thoroughly uncomfortable. And each night the routine was set that after a sometimes cold supper, they would sit about the fire and hear one of Frederich's seemingly countless stories. Sometimes MacLean or Acre would volunteer a tale of hunting or trapping lore, and sometimes they just shared the fire's smoky warmth in silence. But then the time always came when Tynan pulled her to her feet and ushered her into the tent to their bed and she would feel their eyes upon her as she lowered her gaze and obeyed the summons.

Frederich looked around him at the sober, thoughtful faces of these rough men and knew their common doubt. Thus when Jamison finally spoke his impotent irritation, Frederich already knew the frustrations that prompted it.

"He'd best take care," Jamison grumbled, "or he'll wear her out."

"I think zhe's made of zterner ztuff." Frederich grinned indulgently.

Jamison's brow lifted as he glanced across the fire toward the tent. "You haven't seen him work, Pastor. I've seen him wear out three of Madam—" He clamped his jaw shut and lowered his gaze.

"Zhe is his vife now." Frederich sat down on the cold ground beside him and pulled out the pipe Tynan had given him. "He takes care vith her vhen he takes her to his heart. A man does zo with his vife."

Jamison looked at the soft-spoken German as if he were witless and shook his head. "Your head must already be stuck in heaven, Pastor. First, Rutland has no heart to take her to, and second, no mere vows in heaven or earth have the power to tame the beast in his nature. You've seen her face each night when he drags her off . . . she's miserable. It's not right, Mueller."

Frederich looked thoughtfully at the dimly lit tent and pursed one side of his mouth. Then he shrugged and spoke through jaws clenched around the stump of his cold pipe. "Marriage is not just vords, Jamison. Maybe zomeday you marry andt you understand. I think now you just vish for a varm vife tonight, too, eh?"

"God!" Jamison jerked up from the log and glared at Frederich's cherubic grin and mirth-shaken shoulders. "I can't take much more of this!"

Night after night Tynan's hands on her skin, his lips against her soft flesh, made her forget Jamison's choleric mood and the odd, furtive looks from the other hunters. As she surrendered her desires, her bed joy, her womanly delights, she fought desperately to hold back all else. Honesty, she reminded herself, was her salvation. She must never pretend there was or could be anything more to this sham of a marriage than existed right now. She must cling to that at any cost.

Increasingly, Tynan reined aside and dropped back to ride beside her. Frederich often joined them, talking increasingly of his longing for his home and little wife. Occasionally even Jamison deigned to endure their company. Aria made herself smile and parry Jamison's double-edged retorts with grace, feeling some of her tension abate as he thawed and gradually regained most of his former humor. And as they neared civilization and her spirits began to lift, the mood of their nightly camps seemed to lift as well.

One afternoon, they paused on a ridge overlooking a river valley and Tynan maneuvered his mount close against hers. "Look at it." He swept the panorama. His face was animated and his eyes seemed filled with light in the warm afternoon sun. "As far as the eye can see—timber, land . . . possibilities.

And in autumn, she puts on her fanciest dress . . . so we won't be tempted to forget her in the gray winter ahead."

Aria heard his poetry with surprise. "You sound as though you actually like this land."

"A man would be a fool not to." He shifted his seat to look at her. "There's a vastness, a freedom here . . ."

"And hardship."

"That, too." His smile was subdued. "But more people will come and the frontier will be pushed westward. And every year it will grow a bit easier."

"Not if the king has anything to do with it."

"But he has nothing to do with it, nor will he again. His chances have run out in these colonies. We now follow a separate destiny."

"We?" She frowned. "Not me, surely. I have no part in this land, now. The mob that burned my home made that all too clear. And you, an English noble, can have no stake in this mad revolt."

His brow cocked with tantalizing question. Before she could say more, he reined off, leaving her curiosity totally frustrated.

He was bound to deny her access to even the most basic of his thoughts. Later, she was bound to try again.

"Tynan—" Aria still spoke his Christian name mostly in their bed and so blushed each time she needed to call his attention to her. "Where are we bound?" She watched him rock back in his saddle and saw how the light of the bright afternoon sun danced playfully around the leaves, eager to touch his smooth, taut skin. Strange that the question of their destination hadn't occurred to her until now.

"To Mueller's house, of course," he answered offhandedly, watching the soft glow of her face from the corner of his eye. Her hood was sliding back and the thick honey-colored braid of her hair rested casually against the slim column of her neck and on her soft shoulder. He took a deep breath, forcing his eyes ahead.

"No," she persisted, "after that. You once said it was on our way . . . where are we going?"

"I suppose you have a right to know," he answered without looking at her, making her feel as though he had just magnanimously granted it. "I have a house and some land in the northern Carolina. I thought to spend some time there . . ."

"Before you go back to England," she finished for him when he paused. That infuriating air of noble superiority had slid firmly back into place on his face, making it seem a cool, dispassionate sculpture. It was times like this that she could manage a hearty distaste for him.

His face tightened and he fixed her with a cool, appraising look. "No. Before going on to Philadelphia." He looked away, as if declaring the subject closed.

"You have business in Philadelphia?" She clipped her words neatly, rearranging her grip on the horse's reins.

"It might be more accurate to say he has 'friends' there." Jamison's voice broke in as he urged his horse up beside hers. "In fact we have many friends in common there—Lily, Amelia, Polly, Margareth . . ." He laughed at the cold warning on Tynan's face, enjoying this bit of sport keenly. "But come to think of it, they could be called business acquaintances as well—"

Tynan watched Aria's lashes flutter down to veil her eyes as her cheeks flooded with crimson. "Have you become as reckless with your life as you have with your tongue, Jamison?" His voice carried a low rail of steel.

Jamison sobered and stared at Tynan's imperial ire, surprised by its genuine depth. And Frederich's sage words came back to him? "Zhe is his vife now . . ."

"I hope I have not offended you, Miss Aria. Perhaps my references to your husband's colorful past were a bit indelicate. My apologies, madam." He bowed his head extravagantly.

"She is Lady Rutland now." Tynan's level pronouncement jerked Aria's face up toward him. His eyes glinted dangerously at his friend. "You would do well to remember it."

Jamison reined off tightly and rode ahead, his back ramrod straight and his heels digging in.

"That was unnecessary." Aria tore her eyes away from the way his dark glare followed his friend.

"He overstepped his bounds and he knew it."

"I took no offense." She felt herself tightening inside.

"Perhaps you should have." He seemed to redden a shade.

"And overstep *my* bounds, your lordship? I know my place too well," she declared with a bitter edge she could not withhold. In the silence, she felt his displeasure crowding her, but she held her shoulders erect and rode on. She would not let him cloak her status in pretense to salve his highly selective conscience.

"Cover your hair," he ordered curtly, kicking his mount into action and riding ahead quickly.

Aria sagged in her saddle. He allowed her no hope.

"Anna!" Frederich ran toward the house with his black coat flapping behind his broad back. "Anna—it's me!" He pushed open the front door to the neat, two-story frame house and burst inside. "Vere are you, Anna?!" His voice faded as he moved deeper into the house, and in only seconds, he emerged, his face scarlet.

"Zhe's not in here . . . maybe de barn . . ."

Aria could see him trembling with eagerness as he hurried off the little side porch and headed into the yard beside. She widened her eyes and looked at Tynan, who raised his brows and shrugged.

"Someone must be about, there's smoke from the rear stack," Jamison volunteered, having intercepted their exchange.

"I hope nothing's happened," Aria breathed, clasping her hands before her nervously.

"Nothing would dare interfere with their reunion," Tynan rolled dryly and rocked back onto one leg with hands set at his waist. "We are all too eager to meet this paragon of femininity."

"If I had to go another day hearing 'lovely Anna' this and 'sweet Anna' that—" Jamison stopped, making a murderous face that brought a guilty giggle to Aria's lips.

Suddenly Tynan cocked his head, listening, and was in motion around the house to the side yard before Aria, Jamison, and the others understood what he was about. From the distance, there came a growling racket of squawking birds, shouting, growling, squeals, and snorts. Dropping their reins, Aria and Jamison ran after him, slowing to a dead halt beside him in the midst of the dusty side yard.

In a flurry of dust and straw and flapping, scrambling chickens, several children squealed and chased a strange unwieldy beast that snarled and thrashed in and out of the barn door as if being rent asunder from inside. Over the screaming and snarling and caterwauling came a female voice booming furiously. A banshee in woman's clothes came through the barn door, wielding a pole viciously and spouting bone-chilling threats.

"Get outta here, ye scabby, sneakin' son of a maggot-blown old bitch! Let *go!*" She whapped at the bizarre, bedeviled creature with the pole and there was a whine-grunt and the children screeched feverishly. "Scurvy son of everlastin' perdition! Ragin' pox on ye!" She swung mightily again and the skittering billow of dust proved her deadly aim.

"Ye nearly 'ad 'im, Mam!" a rangy boy of twelve screamed, his eyes wild as he dodged and scrambled to keep up with the squealing, snarling beast. "Get 'im off, Mam!" the others hollered and jumped and screamed in concert, like a chorus of frenzied camp meeting goers.

"Spiteful, stinkin' wretch—ye'll roast in hell's fire by time I get through with ye!" She drew back and struck again, partially stunning the creature. The dust began to settle and several pairs of incredulous eyes made out not one beast, but two: a rangy, wolflike dog with his teeth sunk tenaciously into the ear of a fat, healthy suckling pig.

"Anna!" Frederich ran yelling across the yard from the back of the house, skirting the fracas by a wide berth. He stopped and fairly danced back and forth with anxiety. "Anna, be careful!"

"Frederich?" With her pole raised for another strike, she straightened with astonishment. For a second, the frenzied scene seemed to freeze. Then her wicked pole struck home on the mongrel's head and he relinquished his hold with a yowl and rolled head over tail, scrambling away. The older boy hurled stones and clods and heated epithets at it as it laid its ears back and ran for its worthless life.

"Get the pig!" she ordered, and the herd of urchins dived for the grunting animal in a flurry of dusty triumph. The air filled with porcine protests and a rowdy clamor of activity as they dragged the pig back into the barn. And through the commotion, sweet Anna flew to her Frederich, engulfing him like a happy typhoon.

Aria stared, dumbfounded at the sight. Frederich hugged his wife joyously and showered urgent kisses on her flushed face as she grasped him tightly. They swung around and around like delirious children, and from what Aria could see, it was Frederich's feet that sometimes dangled above the ground.

Aria managed a look at Tynan and found one of his brows raised and his mouth tilted with wry disbelief. He turned to her and shook his head helplessly as his astonishment melted into amusement.

The reunited couple finally broke apart and Anna examined him from stem to stern while he hugged her repeatedly and patted her burgeoning middle. They both blushed as they exchanged assurances in intimate tones. There was no doubt that this was indeed the "dear Anna" he had pined for these last two weeks. It took a moment for Frederich to regain his senses and recall his benefactor and companions.

"Come, Anna." He pulled her along after him, beaming.

"You must meet my friends—and rescuers." Anna hurriedly dusted and smoothed the apron over her bulging figure and checked her linen day cap with a fluttery hand. They halted midyard, just in front of Tynan and Aria. "Dis is my vife, Anna." Frederich glowed with unbounded pride. "Anna, this is the English earl who zaved me from de renegades . . . and his new vife."

It was impossible to say whose surprise was greater: Anna's at meeting an English nobleman, who had rescued her husband, in her own yard after a fight with a dog over a pig—or Aria's and Tynan's upon finding the much-lauded Anna to be a sturdy, buxom young woman, several inches taller than Frederich, with the tongue of a fishwife.

Anna sputtered and flushed to match the burnished cast of her hair, whisking her skirts out at the sides, in an awkward half-bow. Aria was paralyzed, scarcely able to manage a nod and a brief smile.

"Delighted to meet you at last, Mistress Mueller." Tynan stepped forward into the awkwardness, reaching for her work-reddened hand and bending gracefully over it to spend the courtliest kiss Aria had ever witnessed. His dark face was utterly serious and devastatingly charming.

Anna flushed wildly and looked at Frederich. "What do I . . . call him?"

"Rutland will do nicely." Tynan straightened, drawing her surprised gaze upward. He was smiling enchantingly and Aria was astonished by his smooth, gentlemanly air, after what they had just witnessed.

"Lord Rutland . . ." she breathed, "an' Lady Rutland." She started another awkward bob, and Aria reached for her hands to prevent it.

"Not Lady Rutland. Aria, please." She saw Tynan's look darken a shade and she explained, "Frederich and I were fellow captives and it seems silly to stand on pretense when we have weathered so much together."

"God!" Anna's eyes grew wider, "be praised!" she added,

with a quick glance at Frederich. "Ye must come in!" She jerked as if stuck. "I had pies abakin' afore that mangy, flea-bit son-of—"

"Anna . . ." Frederich lowered his chin and his voice.

"Afore that beast commenced to steal our winter bacon," she corrected, drawing a muffled cough from Jamison, who was forthwith introduced and bowed to.

" 'Twas Frederich's fault." Anna harked back to the spectacle they had stumbled upon: "He was always bringin' home some stray or slippin' out my slop scraps for some worthless critter. An' this mangy . . . dog . . . repays him by stealin' the food from our mouths. Too tenderhearted . . . my Frederich." But the strange softening in her eyes belied her reproach and she shoved her arm through her husband's, smiling with resignation at his reckless charity. "You best come inside." She craned her head around the small party to glimpse the rough-clad hunters behind them. "All of ye."

They filed through the back door of the house and found themselves in an enormous kitchen that was dominated by a massive stone fireplace, complete with heavy oak mantle and brick warming ovens. There were two buffets displaying blue willow china and a massive plank table flanked by heavy benches that ran the length of the room. A settle and a rocker nestled just to one side of the hearth on a hand-braided rug. Dried dill, wild onions, and various dried roots hung in bunches from the open rafters above them, lending a strange blend of spice to the fragrance of sweet stuffs coming from the hot ovens.

Anna hurriedly pulled the thick, golden-crusted pies from the ovens and set them on the sideboard to cool before an open window, then ordered everyone to the table and set out coffee and golden shortbread and pale, creamy butter. Then she sat down by them to demand every detail of her husband's rescue.

Jamison began the tale, which was embroidered by Acre and finished with authority by Tynan. Aria watched her noble mate rise twice to assist sturdy Anna with a pot and a platter, and his actions nettled her thoroughly. She applied herself to watching closer to determine the motive for his exaggerated deference to Frederich's unexpected wife. It was not like him to observe such dignities without some promise of benefit for himself.

Shortly, they were inundated with the brood of urchins from the farmyard. Each launched him or herself at Frederich and hugged or wrestled until the amiable cleric was fully frazzled and Anna intervened.

At her resounding order, they gathered in a line of five: uneven in heights and looks, but all amply clad in the same simple linsey-woolsey. She bade them say their names and glared sternly at the littlest when he clamped his jaw shut and buried his head in the side of the girl next to him.

"I thought this was your first child." Aria's brow knitted briefly.

"Oh," Anna's hand went to her expanded middle, "it is, milady."

"Then who are these children?" Aria sat forward, puzzled.

"Strays." Anna shrugged. "Frederich is always fetchin' home strays . . . an' I take 'em in. They be ours now, his an' mine, same as this one." She touched her belly gently and Aria saw Frederich's hand steal over to squeeze her other one beneath the table. Aria's chest felt hollow.

"However do you manage," Aria asked hesitantly, "when he is gone so much?"

"Oh," Anna answered brightly with a fine broad smile on her strong features, "I'm used to it. Had several brothers an' no ma. This is my home place." She looked around her. "I lived here since I's small. My pa made good here, it be fine land. And these little'uns are all extra hands." Her crooked smile brought toothy grins to their faces and she reached for the dwindling platter of shortbread, holding it out to them. They snatched pieces eagerly and fled out the back door when she jerked her head that direction. The littlest one paused long

enough to give her a hug. Aria felt her stomach slipping downward and she tried to smile the sinking feeling away.

Everything seemed to grate on Aria's nerves that evening—
Frederich's jocular mood, Jamison's unabashed teasing, Anna's
covert sighs whenever she looked at her rotund husband, and
especially Tynan's restrained gentlemanliness. There had been
only one short lapse in Tynan's new demeanor . . . a brief glare
of displeasure when Aria insisted on helping Anna with the
supper. But even that was quickly supplanted when it became
clear that Anna's advanced state of motherhood made certain
hearth tasks difficult. By the time the food was stored and the
dishes were cleared and wiped, Aria's suspicions were sufficiently thwarted to make her peckish with him.

"So my Frederich married ye out in the woods?" Anna
asked as she sat by the fire, brushing hair and helping replace
the children's shirts and smock with nightshirts.

Aria reached for a nightshirt to help her. "Yes . . . the very
evening we returned."

Tynan cleared his throat in his place on the settle, evidence
that he attended their conversation. He drew from his pipe and
settled his gaze upon her intently.

"I would 'ave figured a lord an' lady to be married in a
fancy kirk." Anna seemed impressed. "Belike, his lordship
wanted things proper on the long trip back . . . seeing you
was already bespoke. So glad to have ye back, he'd take no
chance you'd get away again."

Aria stared at Anna's blunt assumptions and was goaded to
brash honesty. "The earl is loath to lose anything he considers
his own. But the haste had more to do with his desire to get
started on the honey—"

"Aria," Tynan interrupted, rising to stretch his heavy limbs
extravagantly, "come and walk in the fresh air with me before
bed." His tone made it seem a command and she knew her
frank disclosures had angered him. She rose reluctantly and

walked to the pegs by the door for her cloak. Instantly he was beside her, taking the garment from her hands and settling it on her shoulders firmly.

Outside in the cool air, Aria threaded her arms through her cloak and clasped them about her waist, acutely aware of his masculine presence and his displeasure.

"A little honesty is charming, too much is vulgar." He spoke casually, but Aria knew there was more beneath his tightly controlled exterior.

"No more vulgar than dishonest charm." She flashed a furious glare at him from the corner of her eye. She saw him pause a moment then push ahead.

"I will not have the details of my marriage paraded about and subjected to speculation . . . just to please some vengeful whim of yours."

"Your marriage happens to be mine as well," she faced him with an upraised chin, "and I will not pretend it is more than was agreed, simply to spare you embarrassment. I am not your 'wife,' I am your 'mate.' "

His hands closed on her shoulders and he glared down into her face. "You agreed to our arrangement."

"I agreed to abide by it, not to honor it."

"They are one and the same." The moon reflected on the stony resolve in his light eyes.

"No, sir, they are not!" she declared, letting out all the day's frustrations and doubts.

"Like it or not, you are bound to me," he growled. "And if you can find no other reason to give me a husband's respect, do it to acknowledge the honesty of what passes between us in the bed. You wanted me to take you . . . you want to be my 'mate.' "

"I . . . don't deny it." She felt her mouth going dry and her voice growing strangely smaller. "But pleasure does not make a marriage. Otherwise, according to Jamison, you would have hundreds of wives."

He wanted to shake her, but the fringe of her downcast eyes

and the moon-gold streaks of her girlish plait of hair punctured his inflated ire. That irksome aching began in the center of his chest again and he found himself relentlessly drawn to her. Why did she resist him so? What was it that made her seem so sad and stirred in him this unaccustomed need to know of it? He lifted her chin and captured her unhappy gaze in his.

"I never vowed to honor and protect any woman but you. I've never offered luxury and comfort to any other." The huskiness of his voice lifted hope briefly in her heart, but knowing its loss would be devastating, she tried desperately to quell it.

"I do not seek luxury or comfort . . ." she murmured, losing herself among the wild torrents of longing that battered her heart.

"What do you seek, Aria?" His soft, insistent query vibrated through her entire body, setting her on fire.

Aria gazed into the luminous gray slates of his eyes. There she read the frightening sum of her needs, her desires. There was only one truthful answer and she yielded it up to him in the tortured longing in her face. Him, she wanted him . . . all of him. She wanted to hold him inside her always, in her heart. She wanted to cherish this maddening, intoxicating man who had taken her to wife and to have the full measure of her heart returned. She wanted him to care for her, to need her as she had come to need his sensual, demanding presence. She wanted to share his life, not just his bed. She wanted to be a woman to his man, a helpmate, a partner, a person. She wanted to say all these things to him and know he would welcome them. She wanted his love.

The realization was shattering. Icy shards of destroyed resolve rained down through her chilling limbs. She had no more defense against him. He had claimed her innermost heart without mounting a campaign . . . and without valuing the prize, once taken.

Tynan watched the wonder, the longing, the fear that mingled in her lovely face and hoped that he had some part in their making. He wanted her to think of him constantly, to want him, to surrender him that sweetness that he sometimes glimpsed inside her. He wanted to dwell in the center of her, even as she had seemed to carve a place for herself in the very center of him. This overwhelming desire for her confounded him; it was unexplored and yet familiar, as if it had always lain within him.

He took her fully into his arms and her head turned to reach for his kiss as she allowed herself to be fitted against his solid frame. She slipped her arms about his waist, claiming both him and the passion he stirred within her. He was warm and hard in the cold night air, and she sought to capture that warmth to hold inside her for as long as she might.

When he straightened, he scooped Aria up against him and carried her toward the front door of the house. Inside, he found the small bedchamber they had been given and pushed the door open with his broad shoulder. Setting her on her feet, he closed the door and latched it, sealing out all that could intrude between them.

Their kisses deepened and their clothes were shed. And when Tynan took her to their bed, she embraced him with all the joy and despair of her longing. This much, she thought despairingly, this much is honest—he does want this from me.

Nineteen

Aria slipped from the kitchen, where the hearth was already ablaze and the smells of cooking rose in tantalizing spirals. In the narrow hallway she shifted the hot crockery mug to her other hand and smoothed the quilted bodice of her moss-green woolen dress. At the end of the hallway, a small ripple-paned window admitted the gray light of new morning and she heard the faint cock's crow. Her hand traced the long, honey-gold plait on her shoulder, and when she was reassured of its presentability, she lifted the latch and slipped into the chamber.

The room was gray and chilled like the morning, but it was the sight on the bed that caused the shiver through her shoulders. Tynan's heavy chest and muscular arms lay bare to the cool air and one leg was thrust carelessly atop the hand-tied quilt. His black hair was tousled about his face and his features seemed more smooth than hard. Aria tiptoed to the bed and set the steaming cup on the floor beside it. She lowered her weight gently to the edge of the feather ticking and watched his untroubled face. A full minute passed and she reached out a hand and lifted a lock of his hair back from the side of his jaw. Unable to resist, she let her fingertips trace the lean plane of his cheek and float tenderly over his full, sensual lips.

Suddenly, her wrist was caught in an ironlike grip and clouded gray eyes opened upon her, only to clear with recognition. Langor replaced the tension so quickly that Aria wondered if she had only imagined it.

"The sun is well up. I . . . brought you coffee," she managed, only now wondering why she had brought it. Likely he would mistake it as acceptance of her servile status. "Breakfast is nearly ready."

He pulled her to him slowly, seeking her gaze. "A wifely gesture, Aria." He seemed to look for something in her response and she lowered her face to prevent him from finding it.

"A civil gesture," she corrected him. "I would do the same for Jamison or Frederich . . ."

His mouth curled tauntingly. "Not if you wanted them to see the next sunrise. Come, bestow a bit of your 'civil' nature upon me." Instantly, his hand forced her head down to his waiting mouth and he released her arm to encircle her waist and pull her chest over against his.

When his hand began to search her bodice lacings, she tugged her lips away and breathed. "Not now . . . they'll be waiting for us!"

"Let them wait," he rasped determinedly, pulling sharply on the top lacings and feeling them give. He pulled her lips back to his as his big hand slipped inside her bodice to the cool satin of her well-rounded breasts. And in mere seconds, Aria forgot coffee, food . . . the rest of the world.

The thundering in her head seemed to go on forever. Tynan had risen and was half dressed, and she could still scarcely move. She watched him pick up the cooling coffee and drink deeply from it. Try as she might, she could not keep the hunger from her face as she watched him. She would never tire of seeing him, studying him. It was her own secret and personal torture.

He raised a sated grin above the edge of the mug. "Did you want something else, wife?" Lying on the bed, her stockinged leg upraised and bared to the hip, her green eyes lidded with a blend of contentment and lingering need, she was sensuality personified. He held his breath as something lurched in the center of his chest.

"No. Nothing else," she murmured huskily.

He tugged on his tall boots, then sat down beside her. "I'll make it my business to procure you a maid quickly." He began to relace and tighten her bodice with sure, practiced movements. "If I have to do this every morning, we'll never see the other side of the door till midday."

Later that afternoon, Aria stepped outside the kitchen door, wrapped in one of Anna's shawls. Tynan and Frederich had ridden out to the farm's rich bottomland fields to check the results of the donated harvest labor. They were gone most of the afternoon, and she and Anna had spent time in some household tasks and small talk. It was a relief to speak unguardedly, to listen and laugh, even work, without his constant scrutiny. She had not realized the toll he was taking on her nerves.

Pulling the shawl tighter, she looked at the parting clouds and sighed. It would be good to see the sun again. She slowed, gazing up, as she turned the corner of the house.

"I don't like it, Rutland," Jamison's voice sounded clearly through the straggly laurel bushes beside her. She looked through the woody, green-tipped branches to find Tynan staring determinedly at the tight expression of his Bostonian friend.

"You can make the report." Tynan's voice was low and calm. "It is not imperative that I return with you; it is only necessary that the report be made soon."

"Look," Jamison was reddening and set his hands to his waist, echoing Tynan's frequent posture, "this whole expedition was your bloody idea. Now you're washing your hands of it?"

"Not at all, Jamison . . . my friend." Tynan's tone was decidedly unfriendly. "The cause is dearer to me now than ever, but I have acquired other responsibilities of late . . . ones that for now take precedence—"

"Good God!" Jamison lifted his arms and dropped them in exasperation. "All you've thought about for the last month is plying your damn pleasures. When are you going to get your fill and remember what we forayed into this godforsaken wilderness for in the first place?"

Tynan's jaw muscles worked visibly as his gaze narrowed into a lethal glare. "Damn you, Jamison, I've forborne much from you. But that is the last reference you will make to my marriage or my 'pleasures.' I'll appear to make my report when it pleases me . . . and it does not please me just now."

Jamison blanched under Tynan's murderous heat and looked away. "Look, Rutland, they'll not take a report from anyone but you seriously—"

"What report?" Aria stepped around the bushes, her puzzlement matched by theirs when she appeared.

Tynan straightened with a disdainful glance at Jamison and brushed it aside. "Nothing to concern you. Some business Jamison and I will soon conclude."

"Then you weren't just 'hunting' when you came across Lathrop's trading post. What were you doing?" She stepped closer, clasping the edges of the shawl tighter and feeling her heart beginning to drum.

"Looking for you, of course," Jamison said truthfully, turning Tynan's displeasure upon himself again.

"Hardly," she scoffed. "What report would you need make on me . . . and to whom?" Her sea-green eyes had the lucidity of cut sapphires as she dismissed Jamison's offering and pressed for an answer.

"It does not concern you, Aria." Tynan's face had the imperious noble look she had disliked so much at their very first meeting. "It is a matter . . . between men. Nothing you need to know, I assure you."

Jamison saw her tighten and he bowed slightly, withdrawing as graciously as haste permitted.

"I need know nothing outside your bed, is that what you mean?" she demanded frostily, turning to Tynan and knitting up her raveled pride.

"I might have put it differently . . ." he drawled, eyeing her

tauntingly. "But you have such a way with words." One side
of his mouth curled at his display of wit.

"Then enjoy these, your lordship—" She stepped closer and
her voice dropped to a raw, angry whisper. "I have been slow
to learn a whore's place, but be assured, I will certainly be
slow to forget it." She turned on her heel and strode furiously
back to the kitchen door.

Tynan watched her and gradually allowed the perverse grin
on his face to fade.

The rest of the day, Aria busied herself helping Anna stitch
small garments for her coming babe. She did not look at Tynan,
nor attend his pleasantries as he answered Anna's questions
about the splendors of London, Paris, and court life. When
she was a young girl, she would have hung upon every word,
she mused vengefully, but now she found it all empty and
vainglorious. Again she was reminded of the painful spectacle
of her father's boasting and his truckling and maneuvering
around "people of quality." All the while, her father was cruelly hiding the secret of his wife's common background and
forcing her to live a bitter lie. Half-truth and pretense, she
despised them even more in her present circumstance . . . having the earl parade her about as his lady-wife while taunting
her with her base status at every turn.

She pricked her finger savagely with the needle and winced,
sticking its tip in her mouth to salve it. She looked up to find
Tynan opening the door for Anna and lending her a gallant
arm. He was carrying in a basket of string-dried beans and
potatoes from the springhouse and responded quite genially as
she thanked him. He was nauseatingly charming. It set Aria's
teeth on edge . . . the duplicity of the rogue!

She fled straight to her borrowed room. She sat down on
the straight, cane-bottom chair and folded cold fists in her lap.
What horrible thing had she done in her short life to deserve
such punishment?

The door opened and she snatched up a bit of toweling from
the wash stand beside her, folding it with assiduous care. She

didn't look up as Tynan's boots planted themselves before her knees.

"You make poor company this afternoon," he ventured, testing her mood.

"You make company enough for both of us," she retorted, still absorbed in the ever-decreasing folds of linen. "Such gallantry."

"You dislike my courtesy?" His tone was carefully neutral.

"If I recall correctly, you only kiss the hands of kitchen maids and farm wives when you have something else in mind." She raised her head briefly and looked at him without really seeing him. "What can you hope to gain from our hostess?"

"Jealous, wife?" The old taunt had crept back into his voice, now with a bit of an edge to it.

"Jealous?" That brought Aria's face up, slack with disbelief at the perpetually carnal trends of his mind. "Nay," she snapped, "it is quite clear where Anna's affections rest."

Tynan, stung by her implication, sneered, "Ah, yes . . . virtuous Anna. I would have little hope there . . ."

"You are crass and low-minded. Everything you do serves your vaunted self-importance in some way, even carrying a peck of beans. The rest of us rate only as pathetic thralls or adoring minions to serve you. You bandy about your fancy words and grand manners while you mock us colonial bumpkins behind your hand." She jerked up from her seat to glare into his tightening face without flinching. Her voice thickened with hurt she failed miserably to hide. "Well, these people are too good to be made to suffer your sly abuse. Go back to being your surly, arrogant self and allow us the dignity of honest disdain."

The vehemence of her denouncement broke through his consummate self-assurance, surprising him. "What has turned this morning's honey into this evening's vinegar?" He stepped back, studying her with genuine puzzlement, and combing through the day's events for clues to her state of mind. "What makes your tongue so waspish, wife?"

She turned on him with eyes dark-centered and snapping sparks. "I'm not your wife!"

"Don't be absur—" He grabbed her arm just as she gained the door and raised the iron latch. She was stiff with fury as he dragged her back to him.

"Come—tell me what I've done to displease you so." His voice was silky and cajoling as he captured her jutting chin in his hand and lifted it. He waited for his touch to work its magic and when sufficient time had passed, he pressed her tight lips with his.

But her mouth was drawn firm with rejection. He lifted his head and was astonished to see a glint that hinted at contempt in her steady gaze. Slowly he released her motionless form and she lowered her eyes, making straight for the door.

Tynan stood in the small bedchamber, staring sightlessly at the heavy planks and worked iron hinges of the door. And after some undefinable period, a chill coursed through his powerful frame. The look in her lovely eyes, the stony resistance of her pleasurable mouth filled his sight, his mind. He had never admitted it as a real possibility before now. Did she truly despise him?

It was unthinkable . . . but his mind kept coming back to it all the same . . . over and over. Could a woman make love with such deep and tender passion and respond to a man so completely in bed if she actually hated him?

He half stumbled back to the bed and sat down heavily. Resting his elbows on his knees, he rubbed his face with his hands. Had their exchange in the yard worked so profound a change in her? Or had the anger, the sting of pride, always been there . . . overlooked and festering until it threatened to consume whatever good had happened between them? Her and her damnable "honesty." Why had he never taken her seriously?

Her words pounded through him again: "I'm not your wife!" He had thought her defiant denouncement of her role as degrading whoredom was little more than a maiden's

ploy . . . expected of a well-born and genteel young woman.
He had watched the enchanting blossoming of her passions
and felt her reluctant warming as he introduced her to pleasures she had never dreamed existed. And in his overconfident
way, he assumed that vows and the persuasion of persistent
pleasure would soon overcome any lingering resistance.

An ache began in the middle of his gut and spread upward
into his broad chest. He expected that she would eventually
soften toward him and yield him what he wanted—needed—
from her.

And what was it he expected, needed, from her?

His ragged breath settled his shoulders into tense knots of
muscle. He wanted her to please him willingly, to talk to him,
laugh with him, to be proud to bear his name and eventually
his children. He wanted her to be his wife.

Marian Dunning's words flashed back to him: "You want
her to wife you, whether you know it or not." The woman had
been right. He shook his head slowly, astonished by the near-
sightedness of his desires. He had wanted only her passion
and had abandoned all else to gain it. Now he wanted her
willingly at his side, supporting and upholding him as he pro-
tected and provided for her. He wanted her to need him, to be
the center of his home and the hub of his turbulent and unsettled world. He wanted her to look at him with caring as
well as passion. He wanted all of her . . . everything there
was.

And how did a man make a woman a wife?

A very sober Earl of Penrith pushed up from the bed and
shook resolution into his staunch frame. There must be a way.

Twenty

A week later, on the third of November, they left the Mueller's house and began to wend their way east. Aria learned of their destination thirdhand; Tynan told Frederich, who told Anna, who mentioned it to Aria.

"Raleigh?" She felt herself shrinking under Anna's too perceptive gaze. "I didn't—it's just that . . ."

"You didn't know." Anna had put down the knife she was using to pare potatoes for the dinner meal.

"He . . . doesn't tell me much." Then she looked at the concern in her friend's face and felt a reckless urge to confide. "You must know by now . . . ours is not a usual marriage . . ."

"Yea, but it will come, Aria." Anna's sturdy face softened. "My Frederich has the damnedest way of seein' clean in the hearts of folks. A strange thing, it is . . . gives me gooseflesh." She shivered and ran her hand up her arm. "He says ye and his lordship were fated and ye'll know it, too, in time. I never known Frederich to come up wrong in matters o' the heart."

"But we're not like you. You and Frederich have a marriage, Anna." Aria lowered her gaze to the pan of apples on her lap. "T—his lordship and I . . . just live together."

"But your marriage'll never be like ours. Each one's differ'nt; s'posed to be . . . as differ'nt as folks are. You'll settle in . . . you'll see."

Aria managed a wan expression that approximated hope, and Anna patted her hand with a reassuring smile. Aria knew she meant well, but the last thing she needed just now was false hope of having real happiness in her marriage.

Adamantly refusing to ask Tynan anything, she determined to serve only her nightly function with him and to speak only when spoken to. He deserved no more than he had bought with his convenient vows and she would see that he got not a whit more. But when they finally threaded their way out the gate and down the rutted lane in front of the Mueller's house, the misery in her heart overwhelmed her better sense. Her eyes were laden with crystal prisms. She sought Tynan's face and found unexpected consolation for her pain at yet another parting. He leaned over to touch her hand, but the contact was so brief, she had not time to react before he was riding briskly ahead, leaving her to trail at his heels again.

Oddly, Tynan's pleasant, courtly manner had remained in place for the rest of their stay with Frederich and Anna and it lingered as they began the trek eastward, into real civilization. Whenever a twinge of guilt made Aria wonder if perhaps she misjudged his motives, she would glimpse the arrogance that frosted the edges of his light eyes and her conviction remained firm. The man who had assaulted her on that first night at Sir Lowell's was indeed the man who had forced her to vows and now denied her the meager respect of answering her simplest questions.

Travel was easier as they stopped in towns and found real lodgings in inns or with farmers. They hurried through the larger towns and it did not take long for Aria to realize that it was for some purpose, though she was at a loss to explain just what it might be.

The hunting party dwindled as they neared Raleigh. Some, like MacKean, departed for their homes, and some, like Carrick, felt crowded by the encroaching wave of people and headed west again, into the hills. Aria felt her heart sink a bit with each departure. MacKean, Carrick, Gray, Bosarth . . .

each of them had come to mean something to her. And when they doffed their hats and took her hand, their respect had a curiously tender quality that touched her deeply. It was all changing, she realized—they were emerging slowly into the sometimes comforting, sometimes cruel world of civilized men. And in this world, her status might prove more untenable than in the deep woods.

Finally, only Jamison and Acre remained to accompany them through the streets of Raleigh to the grand brick home that Aria eventually learned belonged to Sir Ansom Jaggers. Tynan lifted her down from her mount and turned to the massive front door without noticing the question framed on her lips.

She stood dumbly, watching Jamison rap the heavy brass knocker on the stout door. When she ventured a look at Acre, she saw that he wore a long-suffering expression and she had to squelch a contrary grin. They could read one another's thoughts quite well. And Aria's spirits were lifted to know she was not the only one who dreaded what might befall them on the other side of this fancy entrance.

A slender, apron-clad serving woman answered the door and admitted them the moment Jamison mentioned Tynan's name. She eyed the men's rough clothes and Aria's mud-spattered cloak and hurried off, leaving them standing in a spacious center hall that smelled of bee's wax and turpentine.

Moments later, a stocky brown-haired matron in severe gray appeared and greeted Tynan warmly. "Your lordship," she said, then curtsied and yielded one hand self-consciously to Tynan as she looked over the balance of the party. "Such an honor to have you return to us again. My brother will be overjoyed. He often speaks of battles you and he waged last year over the chessboard."

Tynan bowed from the waist and smiled with blatant charm. "Miss Elizabeth, you are a splendid sight, as always." He touched her visually and Aria saw that the woman responded. It annoyed her.

"May I present my wife, Lady Aria Rutland." He put his

hand out to Aria to draw her forward, and when she withhel
it, he put his arm around her and pulled her against his side
"Aria, my dear, this is Miss Elizabeth Jaggers, sister of m
friend Sir Ansom Jaggers, and mistress of this bountiful house
hold." He beamed beatifically between them as Aria nodde
and plastered a semblance of pleasure on her face. "And d
you remember Merrill Jamison? I believe he visited me whe
I stayed with you before."

"Ah, yes," Miss Elizabeth managed to recall and then man
aged a dram of manners when confronted with Acre's grizzle
mistrust. "Please, do come in and refresh yourselves. You'
stay with us, of course," she presumed breathily on the wa
to the parlor. "Ansom will be devastated if you cannot . .
you and your wife." A wave of her hand sent the servin
woman forward to collect Aria's cloak and the men's hats
Acre's resentful scowl set her off without his, which remaine
firmly in place on his head.

To Aria's ears, there was a bit of question in the way Mis
Elizabeth said "wife." But her wariness was soon submerge
beneath an avalanche of wonder at the magnificence of th
Jaggerses' parlor. Rightly, it should have been named some
thing grander. It was a masterpiece of the dyer's trade: ever
possible shade of green, deepest forest to faintest spring
adorning walls and windows and extravagantly carved furni
ture. The windows were beautifully hung with heavy brocades
and richly carved gilt moldings capped the walls and sur
rounded the huge fireplace and mantle. Grand portraits an
glittering mirrored sconces hung about the huge room, an
thick Persian rugs of deep claret-red cushioned their step abov
the polished maple floor.

Aria lagged behind, gazing about her at the kind of luxur
she had never thought even to see again, much less be wel
comed into. Tynan stepped back to grasp her hand and h
pulled it through the crook of his arm, trapping it there wit
his other hand on it. He sauntered forward with her unde
Elizabeth's scrutiny.

"What brings you to Raleigh, your lordship?"

"We have just ended a magnificent hunting expedition on the frontier—in the mountains." Tynan's tone made it sound so totally grand and important that Aria looked at him with something akin to disbelief. "Fascinating country . . . savages, game . . . we were enthralled." He deposited Aria on a settee attentively, capturing her in a rare, dazzling smile. "Aria and I were only recently married and are now making our way south to Oberon, where we shall reside."

"Felicitations then on your recent marriage, your lordship, Lady Aria." Elizabeth seemed somewhat reassured. Aria took a breath and opened her mouth to rebut the title yet again, but Tynan gave her no opportunity.

"Actually, I was hoping you'd assist us with the name of the best dressmaker in Raleigh. You see, Aria's luggage suffered horribly—"

"It was left behind," Aria managed to wedge in.

"In the wilderness? How awful." Elizabeth's hand went to her fleshy cheek.

"No, it was left behind when my mother and I escaped with our lives. Our home was burned—"

"Burned? Gracious! How appalling!" Elizabeth pulled a lacy handkerchief from her waist and pressed it to her cheeks and forehead as if growing faint with distress at such news.

"Aria's family is from Virginia, the Dunnings of Royal Oaks," Tynan put in, narrowing his gaze ever so slightly in warning to Aria.

"Royal . . . ? Oh, that Dunning!" Elizabeth Jaggers forgot her delicate sensibilities at such a revelation. "Such a horrible incident. My dear you have our profound sympathies. We were all so agog with it—"

Aria lowered her head and toyed with the worn kid gloves in her lap. She hadn't imagined that news of her family might have carried so far beyond the bounds of her home county. And for the moment she was speechless.

Tynan's hand settled on her shoulder. "It is still difficult for her at times. But now, about this dressmaker . . . I am eager to see her gowned properly once more."

"Ah." Elizabeth settled a look of understanding on her matronly face and smiled benevolently at Aria. "I know just the one." Her hands painted some vivid scene known only to her, "the finest of everything . . . with goods just in from the Continent."

"Your lordship, the brandy is in the same place as always. Come with me, my dear." Elizabeth rose and pulled Aria up with her and to the door. "You must be exhausted!"

Later, Aria soaked in a tub of gloriously hot water that covered her up to her neck. She gazed languidly at the elegance of the bedchamber around her. It was done chiefly in golden tones, which were reflected in the polished, dark mahogany of the new Chippendale-style furniture. The generous fire wheezed and crackled with maturity in the hearth beside her. And in the room's drowsy warmth, the chambermaid had dozed on her stool by the door.

The rose-scented vapors of the delicious tub filled Aria's head and she dropped it back against the edge of the tall, beaten-copper vessel. Her lids fluttered closed as she slowly released her tensions to the soothing water. She could not recall feeling such physical delight upon merely bathing before. But since Tynan had taken her to him, so many things in her life seemed to acquire a bold sensuality. She sighed and ran the precious rose-scented soap down the curve of her side, over her abdomen, and down her silky leg. Her nerves sprang to life under the soap and she found her breath quickening as her mind turned to Tynan.

"That will be all, girl." Tynan's voice seemed to float from nearby as if in response to her rising desires.

"But, sir—" The startled little maid sprang up. "I'm ordered—"

"Nay, girl, I'll maid her." He winked lecherously as he

shoved the girl out the door and bolted it firmly. He turned and set his hands at his waist, surveying the languorous scene of his tempting wife's bathing.

Aria had sat up quickly, her green eyes luminous with drowsy satisfaction. Her skin was a palette of becoming peaches and pinks and the water covered her just above the rosebud tips of her breasts. His eyes were drawn to the sinuous line where breasts and water met and his licentious smirk faded into a hungry stare.

"You really shouldn't be here," Aria said huskily. "What will Miss Elizabeth think?" But as she straightened and her taut nipples escaped the water, she made no move to cover herself.

"I think she secretly loves being scandalized," he answered as though his mind were elsewhere. He crossed to the tub and took her by the shoulders, pulling her straight up, out of the water.

"What . . . are you doing?" She found the heat had melted her resistance with her tension.

His hands drifted down her wet arms as his eyes feasted hungrily on her bare body. "I want to see you . . . and I don't care who it scandalizes." Rivulets of water streamed through the valley between her breasts and his finger followed. His palms cupped her breasts and then flowed down over her bare waist and hips.

Aria stood quietly before him, feeling a strange expansiveness, almost like pride, at the way he looked at her, the way he wanted her. She looked up into his darkening face and was lost to everything but the need that was between them.

He shed his jacket and boots, then pulled her wet, chilling form against him and sent heat searing through her with a scalding kiss. Lifting her from the tub, he cradled her against him and carried her to the heavily draped bed.

"But . . . I'm wet," she murmured without conviction.

"So am I, sweetest . . . now." Tynan stood her on her knees

on the bed, facing him, and went over every inch of her damp, rose-fresh skin with his big hands.

Her arms threaded around his neck and she sought his lips hungrily, pulling him back onto the feather-soft bedclothes with her. As his body covered hers, they both gave passion its lead.

Together they mounted rapture's highest plane, joined and turning slowly on pleasure's bright wheel. And when they were restored to earth, Aria's eyes were unexplainably wet, though the rest of her was long dried.

"What was that you said?" Later, Tynan turned on his side, his head propped on his hand to look at her. He traced her face lightly with one finger. "At pleasure's fullest tide, I could have sworn you said *'one hundred seventeen.'* "

Aria colored slightly and pulled his head down to brush his lips with hers. "You hear things. Did I hear you say 'Oberon'?"

"In our loving?" he puzzled.

"No . . . today in the parlor. What is Oberon . . . ?"

"A mythical king of fairies and sprites—" he answered, grinning.

"Not the Bard's Oberon." She gave him a playful shove, reveling in the intimacy that lingered between them. "The Oberon we're going to. Is it a town, a house . . . what?"

"It's your new home, a plantation in need of a strong hand and a glut of coin. Decent sized, but once overworked, it's beginning to come back. You'll have a lot to do, keeping up with it."

"I'll have a lot to do?" She drew back a bit, realizing that twice he had said "you," not "we."

"Running a plantation in North Carolina can't be all that much different from running one in Virginia. I'll do what I can, while I'm there, and you'll have plenty of help." He was smiling guardedly, running his hand up and down her arm.

"While you're there?" Aria echoed blankly.

"I have other responsibilities that will take me away at times."

Seeing the shock settling on her face, he pressed on, "First there's the house . . . I've ordered new furnishings already and most of the repair work should be complete by now. There are gardens that need redoing . . . my stablemaster assured me the barns will need work. You'll have plenty to keep you busy in my absence; you'll scarcely miss me." He pulled her onto her side, facing him, and planted a lusty kiss on her mouth. "Come!" He gave her a smart whack on her bare buttocks, eliciting a squeal of protest. "We've wasted the daylight completely and outraged Miss Elizabeth enough for one afternoon."

He bounded from the bed with a dazzling display of rugged muscles that Aria almost found it in herself to despise as she sat up in the fading light. He began to pull on his clothes, his mood buoyant and his movements brisk. She watched him, and shook her head with disbelief.

Never had she considered he might abandon her on some godforsaken patch of worn-out land . . . marry her only to enjoy her for a time, then hide her away from society's notice while he pursued . . . whatever it was he pursued. Her heart began sliding into her stomach. He might even mean to leave her there while he returned to England, where no one would know of his obscure colonial marriage. His words drummed in her mind: *"Your* home . . . your home . . . your home."

Somehow she slipped from the bed and endured his embrace and the touch of his hands. And when he was gone, she seized her brush and pulled it through her still damp hair with mechanical precision. The little chambermaid reappeared and helped her into her freshly pressed rose-colored velvet. When the girl set about lifting her hair into a ladylike coif, Aria stared sightlessly into the mirror glass on the vanity and welcomed the numbness that enveloped her.

Sir Ansom Jaggers was a smallish, graying man of delicate manners and dry wit. Beside him, Tynan, still dressed in his rugged clothes, looked like a great hungry bear. Aria found the comparison apt in all ways and turned a decidedly cool shoulder to his overt attentiveness.

Calling on her most genteel demeanor, she tried her best to assuage Miss Elizabeth's slightly ruffled sensibilities and was eventually rewarded by the return of the good woman's humor. Through supper, Jamison provided welcome entertainment and Ansom riposted Tynan's increasingly petulant barbs without a hint of irritation.

"So you've been snagged by one of our colonial beauties, Tynan." Ansom swirled his goblet and savored the fine claret that ended his meal.

"So it would seem, though it is sometimes difficult to say who 'snags' whom." Tynan flicked a casual eye toward his frosty bride, emphasizing his double meaning.

"As it should be in a good marriage." Ansom regarded their side of the table a bit more keenly. Then he shook a genial finger at Aria. "He's been a sly one . . . ranging free a long time amongst the cowslips. Don't let him wriggle out of a single syllable of those vows."

Aria colored sweetly and replied, "Oh, I've already learned how adept he is at wriggling."

Jamison exploded into laughter and Ansom hooted with delight at her unintentional double entendre. Tynan's granite shoulders were even moved to tremble as Aria looked around in wide-eyed horror. Elizabeth bit her quivering lips and dabbed at her forehead with a handkerchief. Colored scarlet to the roots of her hair, Aria simmered in agonized heat until Elizabeth rose and suggested she and Aria retire to the upstairs parlor for coffee and sherry. In that moment, Miss Elizabeth Jaggers earned Aria's undying gratitude.

That night, when Aria slipped alone between the soft, luxurious sheets in the gracefully draped bed, she thought helplessly of the traitorous joy she had shared with Tynan there. She tossed and turned, trying to find a comfortable position, but it was no good. The bed was too soft and her thoughts were too hard. She had lowered her guard with him, and again she experienced the callous dismissal he practiced on those closest to him. He'd not find her so vulnerable again.

Finally curling into a tight ball, she resolved to have nothing whatsoever to do with this ramshackle farm he seemed bent on abandoning her to. He'd not make her a convenient drudge to improve and oversee his holdings while he gadabouted and played the elegant rake half a world away. He had bargained only for a bit of flesh . . . and she would see he never got more from her than he had bargained for.

Much later, in the darkest hour of the night, Tynan stood, watching her face that frowned even in her sleep. What had come over her since their wild, enchanting loving in the afternoon? He heaved a deep, disgruntled breath and wove around the bed to the other side, sitting down gingerly on it. This was their first night in truly civilized surroundings and for the first time since their vows, they did not go to sleep in each other's arms. His head was throbbing from the brandy; this was no time to think about anything so important.

Twenty-one

"Nothing but the best, madam. Be perfectly clear in that." Tynan sat back imperiously in the heavy, carved chair, his gloved hands resting nonchalantly on the silver head of his walking stick.

"But of course, your lordship." The tightly laced and over-powdered dressmaker nodded with exaggerated deference. The glow of gold could be seen lighting her eyes as she gazed at Aria's fairness. "Leave the matter in my hands and we shall see her ladyship exquisitely gowned."

"I am not *your* ladyship, nor indeed anyone's." Aria found her voice and lifted her chin, knowing Tynan's teeth would be clenching and that one muscle in his jaw would be jumping.

"W-well, yes . . . of course . . ." the dressmaker stammered uncomfortably. She could have sworn the earl had called her his wife . . . but perhaps it was his way of avoiding indelicacy.

" 'Madam' will do." Aria's disdain was fully as regal as her husband's.

"Of course. Then let us begin." The dressmaker waved a hand to the double doorway leading to the rear part of the shop and led the way.

Tynan rose and picked an imaginary bit of lint from his elegant blue velvet sleeve and followed. At the doorway, the dressmaker seemed flustered by his intent to follow.

"You will much prefer the comfort of the front of the shop, your lordship," she suggested twiningly.

"And deprive myself of the spectacle of my coin being lavished about. Never, madam. I shall see my wife is clothed to my taste and station . . . and to my pleasure." His gray eyes chilled her further protest and of habit he ducked his head as he passed through the doorway. Straightening beyond, he smiled tauntingly into Aria's anger-blushed face and followed them into the fitting room.

The fitting and working rooms of the dressmaker's shop were well lit but strictly functional, lacking the comfort of the showy front of the establishment. Bolts and swatches of cloth, pattern pieces and sketches littered the edges of the floor and the small worktable. The dressmaker and her two young seamstresses scurried to make a place for Tynan on a bench and to erect a dressing screen that was folded out of the way against one wall.

"Here, madam." The dressmaker sighed tightly, leading Aria toward the screen. "You must disrobe so that we may take your measurements."

"That won't be necessary, madam," Tynan rumbled. "I am well acquainted with what lies beneath her clothes; it is not in the least offensive. You may do your work here." He indicated the floor between his knees, and the dressmaker smiled tightly, acquiescing.

Aria's glare was hot enough to ignite the lint dust that floated in the beams of sunlight coming through the high window. She stomped to the center of the square little room and stood rigidly as the dressmaker's assistants peeled her velvet gown from her. The proprietor deftly plied her tape and called out Aria's measurements of interest. The room grew steadily warmer with tension and Tynan contented himself with watching the proceedings and adjusting the fine lace of his ruffled cuffs and jabot.

"And now the corset, 'Lissa, quickly. We would not tire the lady," the dressmaker snapped, venting her tension in the only way open to her. Quickly the lace-decked garment was produced and Aria was laced snugly in it.

"One moment, madam." Tynan sat forward and reached out

a hand to stroke the stiffness of Aria's waist experimentally. "It won't do." He sat back, resting his hands on his walking stick again.

"But your lordship, I assure you—"

"They are a must for properly dressed ladies of quality," Aria snapped, turning to the dressmaker. "Continue."

"I cannot feel the warmth of her skin." Tynan engaged Aria's eyes coolly. "It will be a waste of coin, since she will not wear it."

The subject was closed and the dressmaker pulled her disapproval under control and nodded. She produced sketches for Aria, who perused them halfheartedly and handed them back.

"I think something simple . . . unpanniered . . . in serviceable calamanco and good damask," she declared flatly.

Tynan rose and took the sketches from the dressmaker, gazing at them critically. Two he tossed on the floor with the comment that they were outmoded on the Continent already and four he selected, handing them to the nervous dressmaker.

"These styles please me. Vary the sleeves, necklines, and trim. Let us see your fabrics."

The flurry of dressmaker and assistants stirred a haze of lint into the light. Soon a veritable mountain of bolts and swatches and rolls began to grow around him. He sat watching Aria's tightly laced waist and ran his gaze up over the creamy mounds that seemed to want to escape confinement in the corset.

"Choose, Aria." He waved a hand about him, expecting the mesmerizing avalanche of color and texture to storm her icy walls, "as many as you like."

She saw the expectant gleam in his silvering eyes and knew his game. "I have no preference." She maintained a level tone and looked away. "You decreed the style, you must also dictate the goods. It is of little importance to me what I wear." Her arms crossed just below her breasts, accenting their unconscious allure.

Tynan took the hit like a gentleman, spurred to even greater craftiness. "Very well." He sat forward, searching through the riot of color engulfing him. His hands lingered caressingly over several pieces as he held the others' attention riveted on his every movement. He appraised a piece of shimmering icy green brocade and smiled sardonically.

"This one. It is like the color she wore the first night I saw her . . . dancing like a cool sea wave amidst a glut of gawdy scows." The bolt was yanked up immediately by a wide-eyed seamstress and carried to the worktable.

Again his hand stroked and rubbed the luxurious goods. A second bit found favor with him. "And this velvet, like the blush of a ripened peach. It is very like her lips, do you not think so?" He pulled it out and handed it over to the dress-maker, who nodded eager agreement. Still another caught his eye, a stiff, gold-embroidered satin. "And this is like her hair in the afternoon sun, though not as soft to the touch." The bolt was whisked away.

He glimpsed the surprise and uncertainty in Aria's face and cocked his head to study her. "She has a fondness for greens, I believe. Like drawn to like, I suppose. Emeralds in her eyes and now in the swing of her skirts." He raised a deep emerald velvet embroidered with ecru rosebuds for her to see. Her eyes widened a few pleasurable degrees, betraying the dour line of her lips.

A teal blue, gauze-like silk wrapped itself around his hand and molded over the points of his knuckles. "Um-m-m. It flows like the blue waters she once called me from to follow her." A russet taffeta brocade was next, paired with a creamy taffeta moire. "The color of the leaf bed on the floor of a grove of regal oaks . . . where . . ." His voice trailed off se-ductively. He swallowed hard, seeing her posture soften and telltale little bumps arise on her upper arms.

He returned to the task with a heavy breath. An ashlike rose damascene became the blush of her skin when she was de-lighted and a lush chocolate brown velvet recalled the whorl of her lashes. A bright golden buttercup became the color of the sparks that showered from her eyes when she was angry.

Aria felt his seemingly casual assault striking at the very heart of her. In his outrageous manner, he forced her to review the details of their unique history and to contemplate the bond of need it had built between them. And in recounting it, he announced to her and the world just how thoroughly he recalled each event, each exchange that had brought them this far. Each addition to the growing stack of bolts on the table added fuel to the fire in her heart that was melting the beleaguered resolve in her head.

"She is fond of riding. . . . Her father's great roan stallion was just this color," she heard him saying and straightened with renewed surprise. "Make it up into suitable riding clothes. How many have we now?"

The dressmaker glanced anxiously at the groaning table. "A score at least, your lordship."

"Will a score do, my love?" His tone had absorbed the softness of the velvets. The casual endearment brought Aria's confused gaze up from the swirling floor.

"More than well," she managed quietly, unable to take her eyes from him even when he looked away from her.

"Suitable undergarments, petticoats and such . . . nightclothes to hold a man's interest. You know the kind?" When the dressmaker reddened and nodded curtly, his generous mouth tilted and his eyes glided over her appraisingly. "I thought you might."

"Have you gloves in her size?' He received an affirmation and ordered, "Bring them, let us see them." When the young assistant returned with a dozen pairs of fine kidskin gloves and spread them on the bolts for his inspection, he looked at Aria. "Choose and we will take them with us. We have yet other stops to make."

Reluctantly, Aria approached and touched them. She selected a pair of long white ones and a shorter pair of dark brown ones for riding. "These, then." Her slender fingers stroked the buttery-soft leather tenderly.

Tynan looked at the dressmaker. "A dozen in each style." He ignored Aria's indrawn breath and let his warming gaze fast on the bounty of her breasts, now temptingly within reach. "Perhaps I shall relent. There is something to be said for this bit of invention after all." He ran his hand up Aria's side, along the corset. She pulled back immediately and he laughed, a low, luscious vibration. "We'll have whatever number is usual in such a wardrobe. And your finest Cathay silk stockings, a goodly number. I leave the rest to you, madam."

He rose and stretched his shoulders sinuously, basking in the fascination he inspired, before nodding politely and making his way from the room. Aria watched him go and observed the undisguised adoration in the three faces about her. The handsome swine . . . he certainly knew how to put on a spectacle!

The rest of the afternoon she was whisked from carriage to shop and treated to whatever her eyes lingered on more than a moment. The last stop seemed little more than the modest parlor of a merchant's house. But the wiry little proprietor produced a tray of gemstones that took Aria's breath. Her finger was measured and Tynan gave terse instructions that elicited a succinct nod of approval.

Once in the carriage, rolling over the brick and cobble streets, Aria sank into the luxurious seats with a quiet sigh of fatigue. Tynan's hand closed over hers and drew it over onto his thigh. She looked at him and found him staring out the window, his thoughts seemingly elsewhere. He could not know that the answer he sought was to be found in the tender expression of the face that watched him that very minute.

The next day and on each succeeding day, packages arrived from the dressmaker. Only three days had passed when Aria was bade come for a fitting of the gowns. She was astonished at the speed with which the woman and her minions worked. Within the week, several gowns and day dresses arrived, finished.

She hurried to their bedroom and called the little chambermaid to assist her. Laced into the elegant creation of embroidered emerald velvet, she stared at herself in the long mirror glass and whirled with unabashed delight, enjoying the flow and wrap of the skirts and the elegant sway of the selfed panniers.

The sound of applause startled her and she jerked abruptly toward the door. Tynan stood with one shoulder leaned against the door frame, watching her excitement with a pleased grin.

"You look superb." He pushed off from the door and strolled closer, pausing by the postered bed. "You like it, don't you?"

"I don't deny . . . I find it pleasing." Aria tried to tighten her grip on herself.

He laughed sardonically at the reluctance of her honesty.

"Good God!" He rolled his eyes. "At these prices be ecstatic—" he collected each word from the ceiling, "be delirious, be intoxicated, be enraptured!" The teasing in his smile faded to a more earnest admiration. "But most of all, be . . . grateful."

The silence slowly lengthened and charged about them. The chambermaid read the tilt of his head and hurried to the door and out. The closing of the portal seemed to jolt Aria back to consciousness.

"I am not ungrateful. But it seems to me that your purchases were meant more to please yourself." As soon as it left her lips, she wished to recall it.

Clearly nettled, he straightened and walked to the small settee near the fire, sitting down stiffly. "Just how am I served by your wardrobe? You are as capricious as the wind before a spring storm."

"Then you are the thunder and lightning," she blurted out.

He looked at her with surprise and snorted a self-deprecating laugh. "Then we are admirably matched, are we not? We are like the two sides of a coin, joined inseparably and yet forever facing away from each other." All trace of amusement left him. And yet no arrogance, or anger, or condescension replaced it.

"Frederich did not think so." Aria's voice was softer than she thought wise.

"Yes," an unusual variation on his smile appeared, "the good pastor sees everything in terms of possibilities."

"And are there no possibilities for us?" She scarcely heard her own whisper.

Tynan's concentration deepened as he gazed at her, trying to read what was behind her question. "Who can say what is possible and not between a man and a woman?"

"Perhaps it is found out only in the living," she offered, careful to match his neutrality.

"Perhaps . . . or in the sharing."

Aria knew it was senseless to feel for her heartbeat; it was stopped totally. But she did. And when it quivered and lurched back to duty, she flushed with the shock. Could it be that he wanted more, needed more, from their marriage than he had so boldly declared?

"I don't know you very well," she ventured aloud.

"You've seen me at my best . . . and worst, Aria—what more is there to know?" His eyes grew dark and expectant as he eased his shoulders forward.

"I don't know . . . what foods you favor, or who taught you to command a horse so well, or even where those clothes came from. You refuse to answer my questions, dismiss them as if I am a nosy and troublesome child. You scheme and bully to get me, then you reject those parts of me that make me what I am." Her voice was calm but tinged with a certain bewilderment.

"You despise my honesty by day and relish its fruits at night in our bed. You treat me like a tiresome doxy and torment me with the title 'wife,' while you insist others bow and scrape before me as if I were your true lady. I find nothing flattering in that hypocrisy."

"You make me out a hopeless rogue indeed." He clipped his words closely and rose, feeling his muscles coiling defensively.

She stepped closer before she could halt herself.

"I can't make you out at all." It was more honest than she had meant to be.

His mouth pursed at one corner and she saw his hands ball into fists at his sides. His face drained as he seemed to wrestle with something inside him and Aria fought the urge to reach out to him.

"I favor roast duckling, beef, cheeses, and fruits; I am overfond of chocolate and honey-nut tarts . . . and I had my clothes shipped here two months ago, knowing I would be coming this way."

Then he turned with leaden steps and left her there, holding her heart together with her hands.

Twenty-two

"Last year at this very time, Lord Rutland was our guest and attended the Linden's ball with us." Elizabeth Jaggers's round face was flushed like a young girl's in the soft light of the upper hall of her home. She preened the bright riot of brocade tapestry that covered panniers at her ample sides. "He was quite the success of Maureen Linden's evening, as you might imagine . . ." she confided in Aria, ". . . had all the ladies aflutter . . ."

"Tiptoed through quite a few cowslips that night, I imagine," Aria said quite soberly, folding her gloved hands around her silk fan.

"Oh . . . well . . ." Elizabeth caught the twinkle in her eye and tittered uncharacteristically. "I suppose a wise woman will always know her own husband. Tonight may not be as grand as one of Maureen Linden's do's, but I know with your appearance, it will be no less exciting."

Aria managed to look flattered and allowed her hostess to take her hand and pull her downstairs to the burgeoning party. She was wondering which was more trying, having Elizabeth's disapproval or having her confidence. In the fortnight since their arrival she had been feted at the infamous North Carolina "tealess" teas, exhibited at interminable dinners, scrutinized, flattered, and grilled.

Through it all, Tynan managed to stay as distant from the proceedings as possible. His amused detachment irritated Aria and lent weight to her growing suspicions about his purposes for her. It was only in their bed that his possessive pride and attentiveness seemed to soften into something more. Hungrily she absorbed as much of him as she could in their loving, knowing that in the morning she would breakfast again with the Earl of Penrith.

Fortified with a deep breath and a last pat to the narrow waist of her lush, peach velvet gown, she plunged into the round of introductions with all the grace and charm of another era in her life. It was easy, she realized, to slip back into the familiar pattern of impressions, coquetry, and empty civility, but it was not altogether agreeable. She was no longer an innocent and self-absorbed young girl, and the exaggerations of mannerism and speech common to polite society sometimes seemed to border on the bizarre.

She had seen him earlier, as he finished dressing, but the sight of her husband bearing down on her from across the parlor made her knees wobble. He was glorious. His dark hair was powdered, creating a frame of light around his finely chiseled features. His broad, woodsmanlike frame was cloaked intriguingly in a grand coat of royal blue velvet and camouflaged beneath tiers of Belgian lace down his shirt front and clustered about his large, sinuous hands. His short, white waistcoat was lavishly embroidered in a blue that matched his coat, and his breeches were a soft white velvet that snugly announced his masculinity. Tonight there was no other man present for her. And she wondered how the other women could bear to look at him and not touch him.

He smiled full pleasure at her appearance and kissed her lingeringly on the cheek. She felt the heat from his hands on her shoulders through her garments and was temporarily robbed of wits. He offered her his arm and led her to a group of men that included Sir Ansom, introducing her as his wife.

"Gentlemen, my husband is titled," she demured sweetly, "but I am Virginia born and bred. Respect him, certainly, but I entreat you to reserve a warmer regard for me." It was a noticeable variation of her usual denial of "ladyship." The gentlemen were utterly charmed. And when Sir Ansom took her from her husband to claim a dance with her, she looked up at Tynan and was relieved by the amused confidence in his face.

Aria's first dance was with her host; the second and third were the exclusive province of her mesmerizing husband. And as he later drew her through the gaiety to find refreshment, she was twice thrust against him, her sweetly arched breasts against his dapper chest. Each time she witnessed his face darkening a shade and she smiled a secretive little smile. Why should he be spared a share of her torture?

Before collecting her a cup of punch, he deposited her in a chair just around an arching doorway of Sir Ansom's library and she gratefully plied her fan over her damp, rosy skin.

Something in a tone, an inflection, perhaps a familiar name, drew her slowly settling thoughts into a conversation that seemed to be growing closer to her.

"I don't care. He's an English earl. He shouldn't be allowed to freely galavant the countryside collecting valuable information for his master."

There was only one English nobleman present to discuss and the emphasis of disgust on the word "master" left little doubt in Aria's mind who was meant there. She sat stock still, her fan suspended. A whirl of images, of nagging little perceptions and half-caught meanings, suddenly clunked into place in her mind like the tumblers of a lock that had guarded a secret from her.

"Look here, there are nobles both on this side of the water and in London that support and lobby our cause."

"Not him." The terse reference dripped spite. "He's done nothing but swagger and posture and rut his way through all thirteen colonies."

"Exactly," returned the voice of reason. "If he were up to something, we'd have had wind of it by now. Good Lord, Winslow, you're beginning to see lobsterback spies behind every bloody bush. He's too busy with his little Virginia flower . . . and I heard he's bought a place south of here . . ."

Unconsciously Aria lent the calmer voice her hope as their muffled tones faded once more. Her fan clicked shut mechanically and dropped to her lap.

A report. Jamison had said they had to report on something . . . had urged Tynan to get on with it—not to forget their "cause." She recalled every word as though it were only this afternoon. And when she questioned him, he had dismissed it and her in the same breath. A chill passed through her burning skin.

Then she recalled other things, statements about the land, the frontier, about people like Lathrop and Frederich and Anna. Confusion buzzed in her ears. Surely he didn't sympathize with the arrogant king who had bounced him from court . . . unless . . . he hoped to win back George's favor by helping tame those obstreperous colonies. But was proud Tynan Rutland a man to stoop to such deceit in order to redeem his position? Oh, why did she know so little about the man to whom she had given everything?

"Here." A crystal cup of punch appeared before her eyes and she took it, looking up into her husband's warming smile. He lowered himself into the chair beside hers and slipped his arm behind her shoulders. As his eyes flowed over her hair, the bare skin of her breasts, they began to glow. "Have I told you how completely ravishing you are tonight, wife." His voice was husky as he leaned his chest into her shoulder and brought his lips against her ear.

"No." She shivered as his breath flowed like warm honey down her neck and across her breast.

"Well, you are, my love." His words vibrated through her. "I could have you for supper." Giving in to impulse, his head dipped and his hot mouth pressed the cool satin of her throat lustily. Then he straightened and tried to pull his desire back under strict rein, sipping from his cup.

Aria looked at him helplessly. The minute he appeared, he had again captured her body and heart completely. Only her beleaguered mind held out weakly against him. Why should it matter to her if he garnered information for the king? She had no stake in this treasonous struggle . . . did she?

"Good God!" Tynan moaned softly, drawing her mind back to him. "I knew I should have forbade those damnable corsets. I only have to look at you to embarrass myself in these breeches."

Aria's hand fluttered over her lusciously displayed breasts and she lowered her lashes, looking wildly about to see how much of a spectacle they were making. But no one seemed to take special note of their secluded presence or activity.

"Perhaps I should remove the source of your discomfiture." She spread her fan and made to rise, but was not really surprised when his grip on her arm pulled her back down. She turned to find a teasing curl on his sensual lips.

"What . . . and deprive yourself of enjoying my torment? That's not like you."

Aria laughed at his all too apt remark. When she sobered, she began to study him. "Tynan . . . what are you doing here, in the colonies?" Then she held her breath.

He frowned thoughtfully and straightened, considering his reply. "I've been living a shamelessly hedonistic existence until of late . . ." He grinned again. ". . . When I've bought a farm and married a ripe peach of a wench who seems to be slowly reforming me."

"Reforming you? You exaggerate my capacities. It would take more than mortal might to accomplish that feat," she grumbled teasingly.

"Scoffer—" He took her chin in his hand. "Then why are there no other women here tonight? Not a single one, but you. Do you have some secret spell that compels such terrifying fidelity?"

"I have no spells." She was suddenly lost in the soft gray of his eyes. "All I have is a woman's heart."

"Then it is even worse than I feared," he groaned, caught in the sweet web of her womanly melting. "Come wife—" He took her cup from her hand and put it on the floor, pulling her up. "I would have you meet more of these people amongst whom you will make your new home."

Aria rose and slipped her hand through the crook of his arm. Her query had failed, but at least he had not dismissed it out of hand. Then she realized he had said *her* new home again. It stabbed like a needle somewhere near her heart. Screwing up her courage, she forced herself to seem pleased with Tynan's introductions and the range of his acquaintance, but the joy of her evening was shadowed now by a chance conversation and by his unwitting reminder of her distrust of him.

"We were through Durham not long ago, on our way here," Aria mentioned to one lean, august-looking gentleman whom Tynan introduced as hailing from there.

"Then you should have stayed with us, your lordship—or at the very least, called! My Barbara will be devastated that you did not honor us with your bride."

"We had pressing engagements in Raleigh and did not linger," Tynan explained. "Be assured, on our next visit, you shall find yourself saddled with guests."

"If he's your friend, why didn't we stay with him in Durham?" Aria asked after they had turned away. She was wondering what possible "engagements" he might have meant . . . what "reports" he might have needed to make.

He was thoughtful a moment, then stopped and looked down into her upturned face. "He's more—an acquaintance. I thought it best that you not meet these people while disadvantaged by travel in a band of men and by lack of wardrobe. I knew Ansom and Elizabeth well enough to trust they would extend friendship to you immediately."

Aria's shoulders slumped slightly as she looked up into the genuine concern of his gaze. Heaven help her, she believed him . . . mostly because she wanted to so badly.

And as he drew her hand about his arm, she felt the strange tenor of his voice set her stomach fluttering. And somehow the rest of the exhausting evening was more bearable.

Twenty-three

The air was cool along the road, but the sun was bright and unseasonably warm for late November. Aria scowled against the sun as she watched the road ahead. But she would have scowled even if it had been overcast. For the tenth time in the last two hours, she reined back beside the wagon and questioned Acre.

"How much farther now, do you think?"

Acre didn't bother to look at her this time, but stared straight ahead, over the backs of the plodding horses, and fingered the reins. "Same as last time . . . we'll get there when we do."

Aria huffed irritably and looked back at the mountain of trunks and cases and crates in the wagon behind him. Here she was, with the rest of the baggage, trailing his imperial lordship to the aging pile of wormy lumber she was supposed to call home. Her green eyes narrowed sharply. Her mind was firm about her course and she took a determined breath and squared her shoulders. She would have nothing to do with *his* house.

The journey had gotten off to a bad start; Tynan abruptly announcing they were leaving the next day after the party and Aria steaming that she was not consulted or considered in making arrangements. When she finally swallowed her pride to approach him about taking the efficient little parlor maid with her, he waved the request aside perfunctorily, declaring a maid already awaited her at Oberon. And Aria realized that the slow melt of relations between them during the last two weeks had seduced her self-protective sense. It took a long, miserable afternoon in her room to repair the damage to her resolve; she would not let it be breached again.

Then as they rode, the baggage wagon had slowed them considerably in their three days of travel. Tynan had said it would take a journey of a day and a half to Oberon, but it had stretched well beyond that now. He had been exceptionally testy at the inn that morning, and as soon as they had made the last major turn, he declared he was riding ahead and gave his horse the spur.

Aria had gritted her teeth and fumed silently. And now her irritation had solidified into one great, heavy lump, like a stone, in the middle of her.

"I think *I'll* ride ahead as well. We must be close," she insisted.

Slapping the reins on the horse's neck, she tightened her knees against her lady's saddle as they bounded forward. The wind tore at her hair and stung her cheeks, but she bent to her uncoiled mount and reveled in the sense of freedom the speed gave her. Down the rutted road, between fields, and around gentle hills she raced, her pulse pounding like the animal's hooves.

Cresting a gentle rise, she finally slowed and let them both catch their wind. And there it was, Oberon. It was a large, whitish structure with a dark roof, half hidden in a cluster of gracious old trees. And on the far side were barns and outbuildings that looked almost like a small town from her far vantage point.

She reined up and closed her eyes. This was it, the place she would live. It was nothing like she had imagined, not even from a distance. There couldn't be trees . . . oaks especially . . . and it was much too large. She looked again, wondering what to do next. Should she wait for Acre or proceed and discover whether she had taken the wrong way and was somewhere other than her husband's dilapidated farm?

Wresting about in the saddle, she looked back over her

shoulders. It could take another hour for Acre to catch up. "Let's go," she said, and set the horse in motion again.

It was a longer way to the main house than she had expected and she felt her hands growing cold inside her gloves. The trees had lost some of their leaves, but they still shaded much of the road that wound toward the house, and in their shadows Aria grew even colder.

Sooner than she had wished, she emerged from the trees into bright sunlight again and stopped stock still, facing a huge brick and stucco house that seemed to bristle with rows of bare lumber. It was scaffolding. Huge cylindrical blocks of stone lay tossed about on the ground like a child's jacks. A massive stone column stood in place at each end of the big house and Aria quickly surmised that there was enough stone to complete several more.

She sat watching the slow progress of the carpenters, then threaded her way among the construction materials that littered the unkempt lawn and saw a set of rough wooden steps leading up to a grand pair of front doors, well above the ground.

"Dammit!" came a harsh but familiar voice as one of those doors opened and a man in gentlemanly dress, clutching a ledger, hurried out without looking back. "I don't care what you have to do! You agreed to have it done——" Tynan appeared in the doorway, his face blustery red—"and by God you'll have it done within the month or I'll have your hide nailed to the wall, Prentice!"

"Yes, your lordship." The man turned at the bottom of the steps to look back at him and make an excuse of a bow. "I'll do whatever is humanly possible——"

"——or *im*possible!" Tynan thundered, jerking himself out onto the top of the wooden steps. His white shirt was silhouetted against the darker interior of the house and he seemed a massive specter of fury. Prentice jerked his clenched jaw around and scurried toward his horse, which was tethered on the nearby scaffolding. Tynan watched him, oblivious to Aria's presence. Two workmen who were pounding pilings for the base of a new stone column had stopped to stare at the spectacle of the nobleman's rage, and Tynan stomped down another step, snarling.

"Don't just stand there gaping! Get back to work!"

They returned to work sullenly and Tynan's sizzling glare turned to the unfinished work about him. It was another full minute before he saw Aria, sitting calmly on her horse, looking at him and the jumbled mess he had meant to give her as a gift. Her whipped-honey hair was like a halo of light in the sun, and the soft velvet of her riding clothes accentuated the womanliness of her frame and posture. He took the steps two and three at a time and made straight for her, trying to curb his ragged display. This was not the welcome he had planned for her here.

But as he reached her, he realized she was alone, and his first words to her were, "Where is Acre with the wagon?"

Aria straightened and explained in a constrained voice, "He's coming. I rode ahead."

"Well, he shouldn't have let you. Something could have happened . . ." He stopped and lifted her stiff body down from the saddle, noticing she touched him no longer than necessary and pulled away from his hands immediately.

"This is Oberon?" She stood looking up at the towering three-story structure.

"Yes." He took a heavy breath as they walked toward the porch and he tied the horse to the scaffolding. Then he ushered her up the wooden steps and inside. She stopped just inside the door to stare at the chaos. Crates, barrels, trunks, and odd pieces of furniture sat stacked in the main hall, some draped with canvas. Ladders bearing workmen lined one half-papered wall, and sawhorses, buckets, brushes, boards, and tools littered the canvas-colored floor.

Aria watched in silence a minute then commented quietly. "It seems we weren't expected yet."

"This—" he waved a furious hand around them—"was to have been done a month ago . . . and the portico, two months ago. The sniveling weasel," he referenced Prentice. "He thought an absentee owner would make easy pickings. He hadn't even begun construction when my letter arrived—Mrs. Bonduell informed me. But I'll have it done within the month or I'll wring his puny neck.

"Do you want to see it?" he demanded more irritably than he meant.

Stung by the coldness of his welcome, Aria looked around her and began to remove her gloves from her cold, trembling hands. "If it doesn't trouble you. There will also be time later, I assume."

He looked at the stiffness of her chin, and his shoulders sagged measurably. Only now he realized he had not given her even a word of greeting. "Perhaps you are tired . . . need to rest . . ."

"I am not fatigued. I am quite used to riding long distances in a day." She would not look at him. "Is this the parlor?" she indicated with her hand, and stepped toward the left archway, in the direction of the least confusion.

"Yes." He was soon beside her, taking her hand and drawing her into the room. It was a massive salon with banks of tall, shuttered windows on two sides and matching marble fireplaces on either end. The walls were newly papered with an intricate red and blue Jacobean pattern against a white background. The moldings and window frames were freshly painted and the polished maple floors were newly waxed, giving off the telltale smells of a beeswax and turpentine mixture. The decorative walls were bare but in the center of the room was another huge pile of crates, barrels, stacked wooden boxes, and cloth-draped furniture.

"This room at least is finished. It still must be put to rights. Most of the furnishings are new . . . some exceptional Chippendale pieces in good cherry and dark mahogany. When you're through, it should prove quite a pleasing effect."

"When *I'm* through?" Aria paused in her circuit of the grand room and looked at him.

"I had hoped to have the workmen out of your way . . ."

"Oh——" she sailed toward the door. "They won't be in *my* way in the least." Out in the hallway, she found the staircase and began to mount it, evaluating the cool mahogany of the ornate railings and balusters under her fingertips.

Tynan caught up with her by taking two steps at a time and his expression was anything but pleasant. "The bedrooms and nursery are upstairs and there's an upper parlor near the master suite."

"How interesting," Aria said blandly. "Please show me *my* rooms."

"*Our* rooms are this way," he stated curtly, taking her wrist and pulling her along after him. She had to snatch her skirts up out of the way with one hand and run to keep up with him. He hurried along the hallway to a pair of carved doors and pushed one of them open, dragging her through behind him.

Aria stared at the bright, sunlit room with its long, French-paned windows and doors that opened out onto a balcony and she was momentarily speechless. The carved marble fireplace was flanked by wooden paneling and gilded carvings. The walls were a lacy, papered garden of intricate golden designs on a white field, and the other moldings and windows were freshly painted white, trimmed in gold-colored accents. The room was completely bare and her footsteps echoed hollowly as she walked farther in. A second set of doors stood ajar and she approached them slowly, pausing before venturing into the other room.

In a room decorated with the same use of white and gold stood another large pile of crates and draped tables, chairs, and chests. But what captured her attention was the mammoth postered, mahogany bed that dominated the room. She had never seen anything like it. Undraped and bare of mattresses, it stood like the bare bones of a noble giant, waiting to be awakened.

She felt Tynan's eyes on her as she walked around it and ran her fingers up the massive corner posts and over the ornate, shell-carved footboard. All she could think was that it was this bed she would share with him . . . and perhaps this was where her babes would be born . . . if she ever had babes. Her hand went to the front of her waist and her face softened with a secret pain. For how long would he stay with her . . . how long would she continue to fascinate him in their bed? How long would it be before he was off to tend his other "concerns"?

"I promised you a larger bed. Will this one do?" His voice was calmer and lacked both the taunt and command she had expected.

She turned and dropped her hands to her sides. "It is a fine bed, though perhaps you meant to share it with more than just me—it is so huge."

Her feeble jest made him uncomfortable, but he managed a tight smile. "You have work to do if we're to sleep there tonight. I'll call Mrs. Bonduell and you can meet her. She's the housekeeper . . . came with the house. And I suppose you'll want to see your maid . . . she's here somewhere."

Biting her tongue, Aria looked about her with counterfeit calm. When he left, she wandered about the great bedchamber, peering out the tall windows and touching the textured surfaces almost sadly.

"This is Mrs. Bonduell." Tynan interrupted her reverie minutes later, ushering the stout, florid-faced woman into the room. "She's had charge of the house for over fifteen years. And this is my wife." He introduced Aria to the housekeeper without mentioning her name.

"Welcome . . . Lady Rutland." Mrs. Bonduell's yellow-tinged eyes narrowed beneath her starched day cap and she bobbed her head from atop a rigid spine. Her dark look scrutinized Aria's elegant riding clothes and ripe young figure boldly, evaluating her new mistress. "We all be purely mortified at the current state of the house, ma'am." Her mouth pursed in a disagreeable expression that mocked a smile and her hands lapped limply over themselves at her ample waist.

"I am certain you'll do your best, Mrs. Bonduell. We'll need the bed assembled and the furniture put in place in this room right away."

"I'll see to it presently, madam." The housekeeper jerked a nod and then squinted thoughtfully. "I'll have to bring up a table an' chairs and a settee from downstairs for the sittin' room . . ." Her plump face lifted in question, "Be that all right?"

"Whatever you think best, Mrs. Bonduell." Aria smiled disinterestedly. "The house is totally up to you."

"And in good hands, ma'am." The housekeeper's eyes glowed with satisfaction as she turned and waddled out.

Tynan's face was as dark as his mood. "What was that about? What's gotten into you?"

"Gotten into me?" She set her gloves on the footboard of the bed and began to remove her trim velvet hat.

"With Mrs. Bonduell," he supplied, roundly irritated at her abdication of responsibilities.

"Why, I would not presume on your housekeeper's position . . . good ones are always in such short supply. I imagine well-groomed harlots are far easier to replace."

"Dammit!" He pounded one fist into the other and stomped over to her. "I've had enough of your little game, Aria."

"And what 'game' is that, *husband?* Do I not honestly fulfill my duties as agreed before our vows? I pleasure you willingly and give you conversation when you bid me speak. I make no other demands upon you. Do you say otherwise?" Something clutched at her throat, but she shook it off.

"You're my wife, Aria, and by God, you'll act like one!" He shook an angry finger at her. "Including seeing to my household and setting it to rights . . . and behaving as befits a woman of your station."

"You—" she pounded a hostile finger against his chest— "have station. I have a whore's duty and nothing else."

"You—" he grabbed her shoulders and gave her a shake of

frustration——"have whatever you want! And it never seems enough for you."

Aria stared up into his livid countenance and spoke in an angry whisper that might have been uttered only in her thoughts. "The only thing I have asked of you, you are unwilling to give me."

"What?!" he thundered. "What have I denied you, wench?! I've spoken the vows with you. I kept near a dozen men waiting all day while I introduced you to the pleasures of your body. . . . I've dressed you like a queen and put my household at your disposal—"

"Your honesty . . ." She felt his hands tighten on her shoulders briefly and she blinked to release the tears that had collected to blur her vision. She meant to say more, to ask him about those things which were coming to mean more to her each day: his dreams, his loyalties.

"Honesty? You harbor more than enough of that perversity for us both . . . and wield it like a bludgeon." He jerked his hands from her as if she had scalded them. "I feel no compulsion to copy your 'virtuous' example."

Aria watched him go, feeling each of his footfalls tromping on her heart. Everything he had said was true . . . he had given her the outward symbols of respectability, of husbandly generosity. And he had tutored her tenderly, almost lovingly, in the delights of their bed. Dare she seek more like some greedy harlot?

She unbuttoned her soft, roan-colored riding jacket, removing it numbly and laying it over the end of the bed. Then she stood looking around her without seeing.

Since the night of the Jaggerses' party, Aria had looked at Tynan with new eyes, seeing him as a man, a force, in a larger world of men and ideas . . . and conflicts. Combing her memory, she tried to make sense of his enigmatic statements and observations, his strange reticence on the explosive issues of the widening war of revolution. He was a strong, clever man who led other men with an innate ease and for whom the exercise of power was as natural as breathing. How could he resist involvement in a struggle based largely on ideals . . . the "foment of nations" that he claimed fascinated him so? But when she tried to ask him, she glimpsed the stranger inside him and her own fears turned her away.

She had learned from her pretentious father's fate that a man's politics were an extension of his beliefs his person, his soul. And if Tynan would share none of his loyalties, his thoughts, his beliefs, with her, then she could never share his life, his being—only his bed.

She desperately wanted access to the tender, loving man she glimpsed inside him as he made love to her physically. What would it take to dispel the pride and secrecy that seemed entrenched between them? Until he cared enough for her to give her his honesty, they would never have a true marriage. And Mrs. Bonduell could see to his bloody house!

"Miz?"

A voice jerked her back to the present and she whirled, finding herself staring at a strapping young woman standing just inside the bedchamber, wearing worn homespun and a wary blush. Slowly Aria's eyes widened.

"It's just me, miz. Do ye remember me?"

"Levina?" Aria stared at the servant girl as if seeing the past through present eyes. "I can't believe it," she whispered.

"I'm to be yer maid, miz." Levina winced at the surprise on Aria's face. "I'm purely sorry, miz." Her round face stiffened with disappointment and she turned to go.

"Wait!" Aria jolted back to reality and rushed to grab the girl's hand and halt her. *"You?* You're my maid?!"

"I told him, Miz Aria . . . said right off I didn't know anythin' about maidin' a lady. But he jus' said—"

"That rough creature has no business out of the kitchen, your ladyship," came Mrs. Bonduell's strident tones. And the woman herself instantly appeared in the doorway, her fleshy face red with distemper. "She's been nothin' but a kitchen scull since she come here. She's ignorant and unused to civi-

lized folk . . . and hog-stubborn. Totally unsuited, your lady-ship. I'll find someone far more presentable—"

Aria straightened, barely restraining the rush of ire inside her. The house had been Mrs. Bonduell's exclusive province for fifteen long years, and clearly she intended to see her reign continue. Moments ago, Aria was more than happy to let her have her way. But she was certainly not about to allow the irksome woman to dictate her personal maid.

"Levina," Aria turned to her, "how did you come to be here at Oberon?"

"His lordship hired me on . . . after Master Parnell give us our last wages. I been here near three month, Miz Aria. This mornin' the master rode in and sent for me and said I was to maid ye."

"There you have it, Mrs. Bonduell." Aria's chin lifted regally and she fixed the woman with a cool, civil smile. "You see, Levina was with my family in my former home. No doubt his lordship thought a familiar face would make me feel . . . more at home here. I am aware of Levina's considerable deficits, but I will not insult my husband's gesture. She will maid me after all. . . . I shall instruct her myself."

Mrs. Bonduell's temples throbbed visibly as she spoke through tight lips. "As you say, madam. I could not have known . . ."

"And her first duty will be to assist you in setting our rooms aright."

The housekeeper nodded testily with a warning glare at Levina, wheeled, and exited.

Aria sighed heavily. What made her say such things? If Ty-nan's overweening arrogance demanded that he arrange even the details of her life so completely, why would she defend it? Was it the unpleasant housekeeper's assuming manner . . . or a simple desire to preserve some association with her past? She looked up and found Levina grinning at her expectantly.

"I'll learn good, Miz Aria, I promise." She beamed, her

ruddy cheeks flushed with eagerness as she rocked up and
down on her toes.

"Well, Levina, you'll learn *well*. And stop that—ladies and
their maids never bobble."

Late afternoon, Aria paced the sitting room of her new
chambers, viewing the fruit of Mrs. Bonduell's labors from
every possible angle. The damask chairs, the silk-covered settee, the glossy mahogany parlor table, the heavy carpets . . .
everything beckoned to her fingers and she gave in to the
impulse to give each piece of the sumptuous furnishings a pat
or an adjustment. She stooped and recurled the stubborn corner
of the thick Persian carpet, watching its obedience with undi-
luted satisfaction. Now if only husbands would prove so pli-
able.

Hearing Mrs. Bonduell apply the lash of her wickedly
barbed tongue to the servants, Aria had to grit her teeth, reminding herself that it was *his* house . . . and it was no concern of hers that a soured old witch of a housekeeper turned
the servants surly and uncooperative.

But soon, the new golden brocades were pressed and hung
at the windows and on the bed. The thick feather mattresses
were laid out and the elegant linens were admired and fondled
as the great bed took shape. The dark golden carpets were
unrolled and the graceful wardrobes and high boys were polished to a high sheen.

It was beautiful . . . grander than anything she had expected
to have . . . even grander than Royal Oaks. But Royal Oaks
had been her true home, and the one faithful, genuine aspect
of her earlier life. Though it existed only in memory now, she
would always love it. She sighed her tension, leaning her head
against the open door. She didn't want to like this place, but
her determination to have nothing to do with this "ramshackled farm" was already dealt a series of serious blows. Every-

thing here, with the exception of Mrs. Bonduell, was too likable, too tempting.

She turned on her heel and left the master suite to wander about the second floor, peering into bedchambers, a parlor, and a group of smaller, but no less elegant, rooms that were interconnected . . . like a nursery. In every room there were stacks of crates, piles of draped furnishings, the smell of fresh paint and floor wax. Not a single room was ready for occupancy and every one beckoned her to investigate its varied textures and still-crated furnishings.

She reminded herself bitterly that he expected her to spend her time laboring to improve his holdings while he dashed about the countryside pursuing . . . his other concerns—those involvements he guarded so jealously from her. And for assistance, he gave a viperous old crone of a housekeeper and a lady's maid who knew more about milking and scouring than about coiffure and clothing.

Late that night, when the fire was built up and Levina withdrew, Aria sat with her feet tucked under her in one of the great stuffed wing chairs positioned beside the hearth. She wore a filmy rose-colored nightdress that revealed more of her lush young body than it concealed. It was the first time she had worn one of the shameless garments Tynan had ordered made for her. When she walked, the translucent folds of cloth slid over her bare skin, making her feel strangely more exposed, more wanton than when she was naked in his bed.

Her eyes flew to the stately bed with its soft mattresses and smooth, inviting linens. She wanted nothing more than to climb into the middle of it and . . . But the growing tension of the late and solitary hour had wound itself inside her like a clock spring that refused to release.

The doorlatch rattled and clicked and Tynan slipped through the door as though it extruded him into the room. He leaned heavily against the wooden panel, seeming surprised when it closed under his weight. He sauntered jerkily into the room, his eyes fixed on the bed, where he stopped and tucked his thumbs into his waistcoat. Aria could have sworn he was weaving.

"Wife!" he bellowed, his voice strangely husky. And when she rose from the chair by the fire, he seemed to have difficulty adjusting his position to face here. "Wife—come to me."

Aria tucked her chin dubiously, eyeing his inebriated state and disheveled appearance. She had never seen him like this. He never had more than a drink or two to her knowledge. Approaching him with caution, she curled her nose at the slurry of rum and stable smells that assailed her.

"Where have you been?" she asked, wincing.

"I've been doing a man's job—putting my stable to rights, wife," he declared boldly trying to take in more of her appealing form. "And I've tilted a few with Acre an' him . . . that other fellow—"

When he weaved abruptly forward, Aria caught him and propped him up, steering him toward one side of the great bed. He plopped down unceremoniously and wrapped both arms around her.

"Let me get your boots off." She pried his muscular arms loose and escaped them to tug his filthy footgear from him. Then she peeled his straw-littered coat from him, and started on his waistcoat and shirt.

Tynan sat on the edge of the bed watching her, submitting to her wifely ministrations. Then, as if something stung him, he grabbed back his waistcoat and fished clumsily for something in its pockets before allowing her to take it away.

"Lie down," Aria pushed his broad shoulders back and pulled the top covers from beneath him. But his arms grabbed her tightly and she was drawn up onto the bed, across him. Then he rolled and in a flash, she was trapped beneath him. It was so smooth a move, Aria was instantly sure it must have been rehearsed many times . . . and in just such a state of intoxication.

"Aria, my love . . . you're so beautiful," he mumbled against the skin of her chest, kissing her ardently, though with haphazard aim.

"You're drunk, Tynan," she said quietly.

"Not too drunk," he uttered, making his way up her jawline to her lips. And Aria learned that drunk or sober, his kisses still had the power to intoxicate her senses. His hands slid up her sides, exploring the tantalizing feel of her skin beneath the gauzy fabric. Soon his lips drifted downward to her half-revealed breasts and tantalized them. He nuzzled the valley between her breasts and raked a stubbly cheek over her taut nipples, jolting her onto the first plane of arousal.

"No," she whispered desperately, "not too drunk."

He mumbled something and Aria took his hot face between her cool hands to bring it up even with hers.

"What did you say?" Her heart was thumping queerly at the unguarded warmth in his poorly focused eyes.

"Why do I need you so badly?" he scowled. "I feel like I have to be with you . . . touching you . . . loving you all the time. Feels strange," he tapped his chest with an unsteady finger, "in here."

Aria's heart stopped, then lurched.

"Here . . ." he propped himself on his elbows and fumbled for her left hand. He blinked and pressed a sweet, off-center kiss on her palm, then squinted and pushed something on her third finger.

Aria had to blink to believe her eyes. It was a ring set with a large emerald surrounded by a ring of fiery diamonds. It must have been the ring he ordered made for her in Raleigh. She gazed at it through a haze of moisture.

"Meant to give this-s to you our first night in our own bed. I promis-sed you a big bed, did-n't I?"

"You did," she blinked to force the tears to fall so she could see him.

His eyelids drooped in spite of his determined efforts to keep them open. "Be my wife, Aria. Say you'll be . . . my wife . . ." She felt him relaxing about her and pushed him to one side, slipping from beneath him as he rolled onto his back.

But he grabbed her to him in a frantic return to consciousness. "Be my real wife, sweet Aria . . . and . . . love me."

"I'll . . . love you, Tynan," she bit her lip as she saw the peace that invaded his drink-reddened eyes, "I do love you." His tense grip faded instantly and his eyes closed for a final time.

"Thas-s good," he mumbled, then was gone.

Aria sat up on her knees in the middle of the bed, staring at her besotted husband and at the ring on her hand through a deluge of hot tears. He had finally asked her to be his wife, he had finally entreated her love. And she had told him she loved him. And tomorrow he would recall none of it.

Mechanically, she left the bed and doused the candles. When she slipped between the soft sheets of the great bed, she moved as far from him as the bed would allow and curled into a miserable little knot, sobbing herself to sleep.

Twenty-four

Aria worked the handle of the dusty door on the little-used third floor and was surprised when it opened. She peered around the solid door into a modest room with walls that slanted between the dormers of the roof. It was piled with a jumble of old furnishings, candle stands, picture frames, and half-spilt barrels. The light of two dusty windows permitted her to see it all clearly and she edged into the room, curiosity overcoming her.

Here were probably some of the original furnishings of Oberon. She weaved around the lidded crates and barrels of old curtains and fabrics, peering high and low. She picked up a book from a dusty stack, but its deteriorated condition barely permitted her to turn a page without destroying it and she put it down. Sighing heavily, she looked around her, wondering if someday a young wife would discover her things in a musty old room under the eaves and feel sad for her.

It was a dismal flow of thought on such a bright wintery day and she shoved it from her mind, turning to go. But as she left, a picture propped high upon some crates stacked in a corner caught her eyes and she stepped back to study it. It seemed to be a portrait, done in dark tones, in an ornate, gilt frame.

The only way to reach it seemed over that stack of trunks and barrels. She pulled up her skirts and began the climb, testing her footholds and working her way ever higher. It was an unsteady, precarious climb to the pinnacle of the room. She had her hand on it, chewing her lip in concentration on her task.

"What in damnation are you doing?!" a verbal volley exploded in the tomblike quiet of the room.

She screamed as she flailed and scrambled, and slid down the hazardous trail, snatched up at the last minute in Tynan's strong arms. She sputtered and waved at the cloud of dust stirred into the air by her wild descent.

"You scared me out of my wits!" Her heart was pounding and her face flushed angrily. She pushed hard against him and he dragged her from the pile of crates and stood her on her feet before him.

"What were you doing up there?" he demanded, pointing imperiously toward the high corner. "You could have been hurt—"

"Thanks to you!" She brushed furiously at the dust covering her golden calamanco skirt and puffed, lace-covered sleeves. "Why do you have to bellow at everyone?"

"I don't bellow at everyone." He glared down into the angry blush of her dirt-streaked face. "I was con—"

"Only at me, I suppose. A singular honor—" She brushed a hasty hand over her upswept hair.

He grabbed her hand tightly and stared at the glowing emerald ring on her finger. She looked up into his face and saw the tiny lines and lingering redness of his eyes that spoke of his night of excess. He was clean-shaven and impeccably dressed in his customary dark blue and gray, but Aria knew he must still suffer inwardly. The faint circles under his eyes seemed to deepen.

"You're wearing it," he mused aloud. Aria paused, watching some strong, nameless feeling flicker across his strong features as he struggled to read in the fiery gem on her finger the events of the bygone night.

"You gave it to me last evening." She tugged on her hand, but he would not relinquish it, and she added, ". . . before you collapsed dead away from drink." Combined with her blazing eyes and tightening chin, it was enough to loosen his grip.

"Damn," he swore softly, clenching his teeth. He had meant to give it to her in their new bed . . . to savor her pleasure and to sample her gratitude. What an irredeemable ass he was . . . drunk as a coot on what should have been the sweetest night between them yet.

Aria straightened, struck cruelly by his displeasure at seeing the ring on her finger. The searing, indescribable ache of the long night wound through her afresh.

"You want it back—" she bit out, trying to wrest it from her finger.

"Don't be absurd," he growled, grabbing her hands and squeezing hard to still them. "You must know it was made for you." His tone of disgust was not meant for her, but he saw it register on her face. His frustration deepened as he realized everything he said and did seemed to her a criticism or a condemnation. She saw his every action through a screen of mistrust and shame . . . perhaps even loathing.

"Keep it," he managed limply, releasing her bloodless hands.

Unable to bear the ache in her chest that his dark mood aroused, she turned away, looking for the painting. Sweeping aside a cobweb that extended from her hair to her shoulder, she stretched across the cloth-draped crates to retrieve her hard-won prize and drag it to her gently.

"Is this what you were doing up there?" he demanded flatly, nettled that she should shun his fashionable offerings for another's moldy leavings. "Leave this dross to the dry rot. You've more than enough things downstairs to occupy you." He made to take the picture from her, but she cradled its unwieldy bulk against her chest as if daring him to touch it.

"I liked it," she snapped, feeling the backs of her eyes pricking with warning. "I thought a family portrait—even a nameless one—might make this place feel more like a *home*. But I see now how wrong I was. I had no idea I was forbidden to even roam *your* house." She forbade the flood of tears that threatened to overwhelm her.

"Don't be absurd, Aria," he glowered, grasping the picture in pure frustration. "Leave this thing to Mrs. Bonduell and the servants and go back downstairs where you belong."

She stiffened, utterly betrayed by her own womanly weakening. "Gladly," she bit out in a choked voice. "I wouldn't dream of tampering with your precious house again or Mrs. Bonduell's valuable responsibilities. I know my place too well to need reminding!"

Abruptly, she abandoned the picture to his unsuspecting hands and stalked out.

"Aria!" he growled, fumbling to keep from dropping it. But by the time he reached the hallway, she was already on the stairs, ignoring his calls.

Irritably, he jerked up the small portrait and glared at it as if he could set it alight. But he was still carrying it as he strode to the narrow stairs and hurried down them. A door slammed savagely, somewhere in the vicinity of the master suite, and he stood in the hallway, listening, thinking.

He walked determinedly toward the main staircase, his eyes narrowing with his thoughts. He scarcely saw the housekeeper when she planted herself before him.

"Take this—" he handed her the dusty portrait, "and see it is cleaned and hung in the parlor."

"Yes, your lordship, of course." Mrs. Bonduell's smile was syrupy and the fleshy bulges of her cheeks made her eyes disappear temporarily into fat half-moons. The tightness of her mouth hid yellowed and decayed teeth that became visible when she spoke again. "We got the parlor straightened around, just in time, sir. There's two neighboring gentlemen awaiting you downstairs. I put 'em in the parlor, your lordship."

"Gentlemen?" Tynan scowled as the gears of his mind suddenly seemed to mesh. "You've put the new furnishings in place?"

"Yes, your lordship. And the effect is quite pleasin', if I do say so. Your lordship does have an eye for the elegant," she said, beaming.

A cool smile spread across his aristocratic features. His direct approach was a dismal failure, but there was more than one way to tame a wife. "I shall see it when I see our callers. Then you will put it back, exactly as it was until Lady Rutland herself directs the placement of each piece. And the bulk of the house, the same, Mrs. Bonduell . . . not a stick is turned unless by her order and in her presence. Do I make myself clear?"

Mrs. Bonduell blanched as if slapped in the face, then reddened abruptly. "W-well, sir . . . I–I . . . As you say, your lordship."

Aria fumed and paced her lacy golden sitting room under Levina's perplexed eyes. She stopped long enough to ask again, "He had his coffee—"

"—with chocolate, jus' like you ordered it," Levina finished, fidgeting and putting down the needle she was trying to learn to thread. "An' he asked after ye . . . where you was—"

"Were."

". . . where you *were* . . . if'n you took a horse. I said you was—*were* somewheres in the house. An' he didn't seem peevish when I left."

"Well, he was a full boil by the time I saw him. Something sparked his tinder." She paced again, pausing to brush at the same dusty spot on her skirt she had just brushed a moment earlier. The movement drew her eyes to a flash of green fire on her hand and she brought the ring up, fingering it gingerly. Her head spun crazily with the pull of conflicting forces. She felt the uncontainable tide rushing to her surface.

"I can't take any more of this!" She lifted her skirts and sailed out the door.

* * *

"Welcome, gentlemen," she heard Tynan's voice say from the open door of the parlor as she hurried down the sweeping staircase. She slowed and stopped on the steps. Someone was with him—visitors? Near the bottom of the stairs she was surprised to see Tynan appear and pull the great doors to the parlor shut. His eyes lighted on her briefly but he closed the doors with an authoritative thud that Aria felt was aimed directly at her. Stopping in her tracks, she sputtered and glanced angrily about at the main hallway. Workmen were quietly putting final touches on the molding and trim in the elegant entry hall. There was no distraction here to warrant his sealing them out.

She marched to the parlor doors with the intention of pulling them open, but what she heard stayed her hand on the doorhandles.

". . . unfortunately my wife is indisposed at the moment," Tynan was saying in his most lordly tone. "Please forgive my greeting you in the midst of such disarray. I fear we arrived earlier than expected."

"Oh, quite all right, your lordship, we understand fully," came a male voice. "We do not wish to inconvenience you, merely to introduce ourselves as neighbors and bid you . . . welcome."

"And bid you come to supper with us at Greenwood," came another, more genial, male voice.

"Most kind of you, Mister Halifax. Perhaps when my wife is more recovered. May I offer you refreshment, gentlemen? I have questions you may be able to answer—"

It was like being hit by a pail of icy water. Aria turned on her heel and heard no more. She was through the front door and down the wooden steps before she had any thought of a destination. She wove her way sightlessly through the scaffolding and out to the gardens she had glimpsed from the window of their bedchamber.

Treading the grass-choked brick paths, she looked at the overgrowth of wild rose brambles and the seedy beds of with-

ered plants and broken, shapeless shrubs. Coldness and neglect
had driven the life from them, leaving them shriveled and mis-
shapen. How long would it be before the same elements took
their toll on her heart as well? She sat down numbly on a low
garden wall and clasped her arms about her cold shoulders.

"Recovered" indeed! What was he afraid of—that she would
commit some horrible social gaff at her very first meeting
with them? That she might make some embarrassing reference
to their empty marriage? He had been seen publicly with her
in Raleigh and she had done nothing to compromise his precious reputation. In truth, nothing a wife could possibly do
could blacken his reputation any more than his own profligate
pleasures had done. Still, he now hid her from their neighbors.
What more proof did she need that he planned to make this
place a luxurious prison for her?

Well, she was not some weak, milk and water maid, to be
bullied and closeted away . . . like her mother! She picked up
her skirts and started for the one place she had always found
solace for her troubles—the stable.

Her last thought rumbled like approaching thunder in her
head: *like her mother!* The realization burst on her mind like
a bright bolt of lightning, stopping her dead in her tracks. It
was happening all over again! A marriage of convenience,
based on pretense . . . a life of comfort made a prison to separate her from the outside world. . . . He had chosen her
clothes . . . even dictated her maid—to have control of every
minute detail of her life! It was history repeating itself—bringing the sins of the past to bear cruelly on the next generation.
Tynan was her father made over and he was trying to make
her into the image of her mother!

She saw nothing else until she was in front of the long,
stone and timber building. She was trembling with the dreaded
insight. She had to get away—to think . . .

Ever-grizzled Acre was sitting in a beam of warm sunshine
on an overturned barrel just inside the open door.

"Can you help me get a horse ready?" She hurried past him into the main alley of the huge stable.

"In a bit of a hurry, ma'am?" He ambled along after her, clutching his pipe in a gnarled hand. "Where be ye bound, without a cloak or ridin' gear?"

"Just . . . out." She turned to him, with a silent plea for understanding in her face.

"Well, ye've a right to get out alone, I guess." He scowled with concern. "Feel like that meself sometimes. Come on, let's find one of these fancy four-leggers for ye. We'd best hurry. The stableman's pure finicky about his animals."

A minute later, Aria stood by the big box stalls at the far end of the stable, speechless, There, in the most princely of equine accommodations, stood her father's prize roan stallion, Rondelay. And behind her was the famous Black Warrior and beside them was her favorite mare, Pirouette. She was stunned at first, then ran to the bars above the wooden walls of Pirouette's stall and called to the proud animal as if she were a lap dog. The horse's ears picked up and she came to nuzzle Aria's eager hands through the bars.

"You know these animals, ma'am?" Acre pushed his flat beaver hat back and scratched his wiry head in disbelief.

"Of course she knows 'em, man. She was raised right alongside 'em," came a voice Aria never thought to hear again.

"Franklin!" She wheeled and rushed headlong into the barrel-chested stablemaster's somewhat flustered embrace. She squeezed him tightly, needing comfort, any comfort, just now. Seeing him was like having a bit of her home restored to her.

"What are you doing here?" The tears she had suppressed now vaulted down her face.

"Why, I'd never let these pets outta my sight, miss." He pushed her back a bit to look at her with a beet-red grin. "You know that. When the earl bought 'em, he took me right along with 'em. Been here more than three month now."

"I had no idea . . ." Aria realized the extent of his embarrassment and released him, stepping back. "I can't tell you how good it is to see you . . . and them."

"Sort of back in the family, miss. Or ma'am, now." Franklin rested his hands on his ample waist. "His lordship's a fair man, though I admit I had my reservations at first."

An awkward silence grew as she struggled to master her unruly emotions. The last thing she needed to hear was praise of her treacherous husband.

Acre finally spoke up. "She wanted a mount, Mr. Franklin. I told her the stableman was particular with his charges."

"Oh, I am, sir, most particular." He caught Aria's wet gaze and recognized the needs it hid. "But this young lady . . . she can have any mount that suits her fancy . . . anytime at all."

"Excellent tea. I've had none since our North Carolina ladies purged our houses of the herb more than a year ago." John Halifax breathed in the beautiful brown vapors of it, then quaffed the rest. "I confess, I have suffered terribly in the drought." He sat forward in his chair, placing his empty cup and saucer on the parlor table at his side. His plain, sturdy face was pleasantly embodied and his brown eyes encompassed the nobleman and his elegant home admiringly.

"Indeed." Tynan's hands rested casually on the arms of the royal-blue wing chair in the main parlor. His features were a bland and civil mask that effectively countered the glint of calculation in his cool gray eyes. He assessed these men objectively, noting the quality weave of their good broadcloth coats, their starched linen shirtfronts, and their fine polished riding boots. This was the vanguard of local society, come to investigate what an English noble could be doing taking up residence among them. Their intelligence must have been thorough indeed for them to come the very day after his arrival. His chin rose as he considered how well his movements might be noised about.

"How fortunate we are to have you amongst us, Lord Rutland . . . reminding us of . . . British ways." Sallow, long-faced Stewart Morgan set his untouched cup aside and leaned forward irritably, eyeing John Halifax.

Tynan's smile lost a few degrees of warmth and he turned his head languidly to observe Halifax. He had obviously been chosen spokesman for the pair.

"I . . . understand we have friends in common, Lord Rutland. In Raleigh . . . and perhaps Philadelphia," Halifax ventured genially, ignoring Morgan's testiness.

"And who might that be . . . in Raleigh, Mister Halifax?"

"Sir Ansom Jaggers and his delightful sister, Miss Elizabeth."

Tynan felt his muscles contracting slowly as his attention narrowed ruthlessly behind an undisturbed expression. "Then you say right, sir, for Ansom Jaggers is a good friend of mine. A fine man, lettered and cultured, though a bit overburdened with conscience."

Halifax shot a conspiratorial glance at the dour-faced Morgan, then continued. "I was last in Raleigh a month ago and he mentioned to me your purchase of Oberon, asking me to welcome you properly . . . and see you introduced to those in the county of like mind."

"And what mind is that, Mister Halifax?" Tynan's posture seemed to drape even more casually over the chair, causing Morgan's spine to straighten as if by a screw.

"The right mind, sir." Halifax's genial expression dimmed, but was not extinguished.

"The mind set on liberty, sir," Morgan blurted out.

Tynan studied the lean, intense colonial as be stroked his chin with one finger and let expectant silence stretch between them.

"Do you mean this craze for independence from England . . . that 'liberty'?" His gaze shifted from Morgan to Halifax and back.

"Don't cross words with us, sir." Morgan reddened. "You know very well what we mean and that we would not be here in a nobleman's house, speaking such, if we had not been assured you would be receptive."

Tynan leaned forward abruptly and smiled in a way that did not quite warm his eyes. "I do not know you, gentlemen. Anyone might learn a name to claim as a credential."

"I told you it was no good." Morgan jumped to his feet and glared at Halifax while he addressed Tynan. "We have been mistaken, sir, and will not trouble you again." The tension collected and crackled on the air between them.

Halifax frowned and studied Tynan's handsome, beguiling face and made his reluctant decision. He leaned back and threaded his fingers together across his chest as he propped his elbows on the arms of the chair.

"May I have another cup of that fine tea, Lord Rutland?" Halifax forced an expertly gauged smile. "You must forgive Stewart, here. Of late, his politics dictate his diet . . . and his taste often runs to the sour."

This time Tynan's smile made it into his eyes as he reached for the bell. "Then he will have to meet my sweet wife," he quipped. "She certainly cured me of my taste for the tart."

Halifax erupted into relieved laughter and Tynan allowed himself a chuckle at his own unintentional jest. Morgan stood there, clenching his fists, confused and roundly irritated by this unexpected burst of humor that purged the atmosphere of the room.

"Be seated, Mister Morgan—" Tynan's face was again composed, "and tell me what it is you have come for."

Morgan straightened, offended, but after a long moment, edged warily back to the settee and settled on it. He looked dubiously at Halifax's red-faced nod, and as soon as Mrs. Bonduell had brought a silver pot of fresh tea, he began.

"We came to apprise you of the state of the counties around and to . . . enlist your aid. Feeling here runs deeply divided, that is not secret," he explained tersely, still not convinced of the wisdom of this revelation. "These hardheaded Scots have taken a vow of loyalty to George and their Royal Governor

Tryon. There's bad blood in every county between farmers and planters, Scots and Englishmen, royalists and sons of liberty. There's hardly a field fence anywhere that doesn't mark a line of resentment."

"Worse yet," Halifax took it up, "the royalists have been recruiting men and laying in stores. They've set up a network of correspondence and couriers . . . and have contacted Howe pledging their support. They hope for a British force to land and help them secure North Carolina for the king."

Tynan sat straighter, all trace of taunt gone from his striking features. "And you? You cannot have been idle through these preparations."

"We," Halifax glanced uncomfortably at a still skeptical Morgan, "have made our own provisions. We, too, are linked by a committee of correspondence and have men pledged to fight . . . when it becomes necessary."

"And what is it you want from me?" Tynan's gray eyes silvered.

"At this moment, your sympathies are known only to Jaggers and the two of us, Lord Rutland. To the rest of the county you are a tantalizing mystery . . . an English nobleman of certain . . . reputation . . . come to live in our volatile society. The air is rife with speculation on where your resources, your support, might be thrown. Some doubt that you could be other than loyal to your king; some swear you have reason to despise him. Such confusion is understandable, Lord Rutland, since you have been scrupulous to avoid display of your true leanings."

Tynan rose and paced to the mantle then turned, resting a muscular arm on the blue-veined marble. "Such confusion is intentional, Mister Halifax."

"So we see." Morgan assessed his host's elegant frame critically and leaned forward, propping his elbow on his bony knee. "You move with easy neutrality through all circles . . . wherever money flows." His tone was almost envious. "A valuable

ability . . . one which would be of great benefit to us right
now."

Tynan said nothing, but watched the rangy Morgan intently.

"We have difficulty getting dispatches to our representatives
in Philadelphia. Of late, two couriers have been lost—"

"Dead?" Tynan's easy posture did not change as he demanded the clarification.

"Yes. Highwaymen, it was said." Morgan lowered his eyes
to control the bitterness that threatened him. "We know they
watch our homes. Whoever visits is suspect of carrying com-
muniques. We need to let our people in Philadelphia know
what is happening here at home . . . and to get word of the
growing loyalist militia and the location of their military stores
to General Washington."

"The general's ragtag army is too far removed to do you
much good, gentlemen, and occupied with more direct conflicts." Tynan dropped his arm to his side and strolled toward
them. "Are you not prepared for more immediate action?"

"We have plans to harass the loyalists and steal or destroy
their stores . . . until it comes to a real fight. But we are afraid
the redcoats may agree to land troops along our shore . . .
counting on the strong loyalist support of these stubborn
Scots . . ." Morgan's voice trailed off as if daunted by the unthinkable consequences.

Tynan strolled to the window with his hands clasped behind
his back and looked out upon the dried and shriveled gardens
below. His land, his home, everything he wanted to build here
might well hang in the balance. What had begun as a convenient vehicle for reprisal against his ponderous and overweening
monarch had grown into full treason. In the last three years,
these raw and boisterous colonies had become far more than
a diversion or self-inflicted exile. They had wooed and
charmed him like a shameless hussy . . . beguiling him with
things he had never known he lacked until the need was
met . . . friendship, a cause, a woman to claim his very heart.

Aria's words to him on their wedding night had returned to

him more than once. "I have . . . no home, no family, not even a country." She had not guessed that she spoke for them both. Nor could she know the strange, aching sense of oneness with her that her poignant admission had produced in him. He had no family to claim him, no home except the one he might make with her here, no country but these coarse, lusty colonies so fraught with promise and hazard.

Some undefinable place and moment, he had crossed the frontier of commitment to this rebel cause, just as he had crossed that same boundary with Aria. She was his woman, his mate . . . in a way no other could ever be. Somehow she and this rebel cause were bound together in his mind . . . challenging him to help make this the home, the land, the country that neither had.

"Gentlemen—" Tynan turned abruptly, his eyes silver with light collected from the late morning sun. "I must leave for Philadelphia myself, quite soon. How soon can your dispatches be ready?"

Twenty-five

Aria pulled her borrowed jacket closer around her and looked out over the sluggish stream wending tortuously through the brownish fields of harvest stubble. A speck in the distance, moving, growing, caught her eye and she watched it develop into a fiercely driven mount and familiar rider, bearing down on her.

She plopped down on a freshly cut stump near the water's edge and braced herself for the tempest of her husband's fury. Anticipation prickled up and down her neck. Let him rage and demand she cease riding his valuable breeding stock . . . or command that she remain inside Oberon's walls . . . she had fury of her own to vent.

She was prepared for almost anything except the strangely pent-up expression that was turned on her after he jerked his big mount to a harsh stop and bolted from it. It was not like him to trouble himself about his temper, especially with her.

"I see you have found one of my favorite spots." He shoved his big hands in his coat pockets and strode toward the stream stiffly, as if straining for some semblance of calm.

"It seemed peaceful to me," she managed, still expecting an explosion and unnerved that it did not seem imminent.

"And are you in need of peace?" He turned to seek her gaze with his.

"It is a scarce commodity—"

"—in *my* house?" he provided, seeming to tighten the rein on whatever he constrained within him.

Aria looked down at her oversized, borrowed gloves and stubbornly let her silence answer him.

"Well, perhaps you will find more enjoyment in it when I am gone," he ventured tightly, watching her reaction keenly.

"Gone?" Her eyes seemed like tidal pools as they came up. "You're leaving?"

"I believe I had mentioned going on to Philadelphia. I am preparing to leave this afternoon . . ."

Aria rose and whirled away. The news stunned her ire and her heart began to rise into her throat. He was leaving her . . . going away . . . perhaps home, to England, without a second thought of her. It began to make horrible sense: He had created her opulent prison to see she did not interfere in his life when he decided to leave her.

"I could wait until tomorrow." He cocked his head, studying her for clues to the state of her mind.

"Why delay?" Her voice was bitter. "The weather is dry . . . good for travel." Her shoulders rounded slightly as her heart sank.

It was the signal he needed. He turned her around to face him and had to force her chin up. Those impossible liquid prisms that always seemed to defy nature clung there in her eyes. His heart swelled painfully in his chest.

"Do you not want me to go?"

"I should have known." She spoke mostly to herself, unable to focus her eyes on more than the hazy outline of his features. She pushed back from him and turned to one side.

"You'll have much to keep you busy." He frowned, unable to decipher her mood. "The house, the gardens. . . . You'll scarcely know I'm gone, except perhaps in bed at night. I insist you pine for me there, wife."

"You vile, insufferable bastard!" She turned on him with a vengeance. "How dare you stand there and taunt me with your abandonment. *Pine* for you?!" She choked on her pain and rage, unable to speak, then grabbed up her skirts and kicked his silk-clad shin savagely.

He hobbled after her, furious from the pain in his shin, and caught her as she made to mount her mare. "Good God, Aria!" he thundered, giving her a shake. "What's gotten into you?"

"I should have seen it earlier," she ground out bitterly. "You're exactly like my father—pretentious, opportunistic, callous. You don't care whom you use, whom you hurt as long as you have everything your way!"

"Aria—"

"Well, I'm not meek little Marian Dunning and I'll not suffer as she did. You hold me a prisoner in a palace and mock me for the queen—" Her voice failed in a miserable rasp and she struggled afresh against his harsh grip.

The exploding white heat of her rage stunned him. His mind reeled trying to take it in, to make sense of her virulent charges.

"Well *go!* Go back to your precious family, your noble England! You'll have no trouble putting this little episode in the colonies behind you. And the annoying little matter of a marriage . . . easily disavowed at your pleasure or annulled before a sympathetic British magistrate! Leave . . . leave this minute, you miserable, unfeeling wretch!"

Angry confusion momentarily slackened his grip and she struggled desperately, almost succeeding in freeing her shoulders.

"Aria! Aria, listen to me . . ."

She stopped her ears with her hands against the calling of her name, and channeled the pain in her heart into her straining limbs to spur them on. He had difficulty constraining her without hurting her arms and was slowly dragged by her thrashings up the grassy bank toward her horse. And as his own ire bested him, he used the slope to his advantage, sweeping her feet from beneath her with one leg while pushing her down into the dried grasses. Instantly, he covered her with his hard weight, pinning her on her back on the weedy slope and imprisoning her wrists beside her crimson face.

"Just go . . . and leave me . . . alone! The sooner . . . the better," she gritted out in ragged spurts from between clenched teeth.

"Now you listen to me, wench," he spat dangerously, "I'm not your damn father and I'll not be scourged for his sins. He was a stupid, pretentious fool who thought himself wronged because he wasn't born to a title. He wasted his life, blind to his real fortune and bitterest toward those he should have cherished. But I don't have to pretend. . . . I *am* a nobleman. I have all the wealth and the power I need."

"Then your abuse, your cruelty is all the more heinous!" She thrashed angrily beneath him. "You use people like playthings, and when you tire of them, you just toss them off, abandon them!"

"What *is* this madness about England . . . abandoning you?" he thundered, wanting to shake some sense into her.

"Don't bother denying it." She managed to turn her head to glare at him, but his face was too near. His breath flowed over her lips in a cruel torrent and she jerked away again. "Allow me at least that bit of honesty."

He released one wrist to turn her face back to his and she pushed breathlessly at his massive shoulders.

"Get off me, you oaf!"

"No," he growled, slowly losing the battle with his own anger. "I have you exactly where I want you and you're going to tell me what in the blazing hell you're screaming about!"

"Then get off me . . . I can't breathe."

He obliged by parting her legs further and sliding a bit lower on her to fit himself intimately against her inner curves. And he watched as she gasped and colored with rage to the roots of her hair.

"Better?" he growled nastily.

"I despise you—"

"Tell me!" he demanded. "Or I may seek a more diverting pastime." His angry gray eyes glinted as they traced the inviting line of her corsetted breasts where the jacket had fallen open. And to enforce his ultimatum, he began to kiss those creamy mounds ardently. He felt Aria shudder beneath him and raised his head to find her green eyes blazing with emerald fire. She knew he was fully capable of taking her, there and then, despite her struggles.

"You brought me here to see me installed as *caretaker* of your colonial holdings," she charged, rolling her eyes away angrily as she defied the burning in their corners. "You conveniently dispose of a cumbersome harlot-turned-wife and gain a drudge in the process. Now you're free to go back to your family, your precious home—where none will know of your marriage and you'll be free to pursue your 'civilized' vices. Expecting that a 'wife' would tend a husband's holdings with more care, you spoke the vows with me to bind me to the task." Her voice became bitterly even. "Then at your leisure, you may dispose of both the property and the 'wife,' clearing a tidy profit. How clever you are . . . how perfectly heartless . . ."

"Damnation!" he thundered, his face dark with frustrated rage. "You honestly believe that! You believe I'm leaving Oberon to be shed of you . . . that I married you to make you slave your fingers to the bone enlarging my fortunes!" He could hardly say it, much less credit it. But the furious conviction of her declarations convinced him she spoke them earnestly.

"Why else do you constantly remind me of the work you require of me in your precious house? You cannot deny it!"

"Deny it?" he growled, sending a low vibration through her body beneath him. "How can you say I married you to salve my carnal conscience when you have so often proclaimed I have none? Would I stoop to speaking vows of marriage just to tidy a balance on a clerk's ledger sheet?" His muscular fingers threaded into her hair and forced her face closer to his molten silver eyes.

"Disgraceful as those possibilities are, my love, my motives for marrying you were baser yet. From the minute I saw you, my life has been dictated by a burning, half-mad desire for your delectable young flesh. Some jaded fate saw high irony in my situation and supplanted fleshly satisfaction with even hotter need. The more I had of you, the more I wanted of you. I spent hellish weeks thrashing about in the wilderness looking for you. Then when *you* found *me,* I thought to sate myself and save myself from the peculiar misery of wanting you. Instead, I found myself drowning in a sea of your treacherous pleasures."

Aghast at his complaints, she struggled afresh, only to have him capture her open lips with his. And soon she struggled against him and against her own waning ire. When his mouth drew away, she felt a humiliating burning in her loins where he lay fitted against her.

"Let me up," she bit out, "I don't need to hear any more!"

"You'll hear more, all right," he declared over hot, jagged breaths. He stopped short—why had he never spoken these things to her before? Was it because she might. not have accepted a future with him if she learned the truth? Despite her professed disdain for things "noble," he knew women too well to believe his title had no effect on her.

"I bought this house and land well before I ever saw you, planning to make it my home . . . my only home. I am not bound for England when I leave here . . . nor will I ever be." A desperate intensity filled his face and his words came in forceful blasts. "I'm not going back to England, ever. I have nothing to return to there. I was banished from court, and to prevent reprisals against my family, I signed the estates over to my brother and left the country."

Something in Aria's heart vibrated strongly in response. This was the honesty she had so often sought from him. And until this very moment, she had not considered that it might have consequences.

"It's true, then. You were banished because—"

"I killed a man." He waited for disgust to register in her face, for her to recoil or berate him. But instead, she searched him with a gemlike brilliance in her depthless eyes and seemed to wait for more.

"I'd do it again." His voice dropped to uncover his raw, steely core. "He deserved to die."

"What did he do to you?" Aria whispered. The grave tightening of his face and the hollowing of his eyes unnerved her. Suddenly she wanted to touch his face, to somehow prevent him from recalling it. But she must know it all if they were to put it behind them.

"He abducted and raped my youngest sister after I refused his suit of marriage with her. He wanted her dowry and thought we could not refuse him if he planted his seed. The bastard brutalized her, nearly drove her mad. When she died birthing his spawn, I called him out and killed him. She was barely sixteen when she died—a child.

"The king was outraged that I refused to give her to the swine to quell the scandal. When I killed him, our sovereign George tried to call it murder. But it was too well witnessed a fight and he had to settle for less obvious, crueler punishments. I was his target, and when I left England, he abandoned his crusade against the house of Penrith. As long as I stay away, they are safe. I'll never return to England . . . and after me, my brother and his sons will bear the title."

When his eyes focused on her face again, he saw his own pain reflected there. And not recognizing it as his own, he read it as the horror and rejection he expected.

"So you see, my dearest sweet—" the bitterness in his tone turned caustic, "I am free to wander all the earth, except my native land, and to make my home wherever I please. I chose here . . . and I chose you to share it. You'd best reconcile yourself to it, *Lady Rutland!*"

Before Aria could respond, his weight lifted above her and he pushed up to his knees, then stood astride her. He was a strange colossus: strong but capable of hurting, ruthless and yet tender to a fault, generous but miserly with things of real value to her. He was a labyrinth of strange twists and turns, unfathomable and compelling. Aria couldn't move or even swallow under his dark scrutiny.

He stood over her, looking at her misted eyes, her quivering lips, her vulnerable, desirable form, and something raked steely fingers through his belly. He had to leave, to put distance between them—to know he could still live, breathe, without her. Jerking his waistcoat down and adjusting his ruffled cuffs, he stepped over her prone body and walked to his mount.

Jolted up, scrambling to her knees, she was stunned by the turn of this confrontation and by his adamant withdrawal. She turned in the tall grass to see him pause as he lifted the reins. He spoke with his back to her, not trusting himself to see her.

"You're not to ride alone again." His tone was curt and faintly disdainful. "There may be those in the county that resent my coming and you may find them as unpleasant . . . as your last neighbors."

Aria heard the scorn in his tone but somehow it mattered less than the reason he would not look at her.

"When . . . will you return?"

"When I can stay away no longer." He swung easily onto the back of his big bay stallion and reined about sharply, managing to avoid all but the merest glimpse of her, sitting, tousled, in the old summer's dried grasses with glass-rimmed eyes. He spurred his horse hard and it shot into frantic motion.

Tynan was already gone when Aria reached the house, nearly an hour later. Aria found Mrs. Bonduell in the center hall, supervising the rehanging of the great crystal chandelier.

"He left no message? No—" She halted under the woman's ill-disguised sneer.

"Spoke not a word to me, madam."

Aria could see the pleasure it gave the woman to say her no and inquired no further. She straightened her back and mounted the stairs to the refuge of her rooms. Sinking exhaustedly onto the settee, she felt utterly empty. Tynan was gone.

"Look miz . . . I finished!" Levina hurried into the darkened sitting room some hours later, waving a half-stitched bodice. She lurched to a stop and frowned at the darkness both in the room and in her mistress's mood. Puckering one corner of her mouth discerningly, she perched one hand on her cocked hip.

"There be no shortage o' candles in the house, miz." Gaining no response, she set her needlework on the table and snatched a taper from the candelabra to fetch a light from the sconce in the hallway.

The golden light revealed the strain on Aria's face and the puffiness about her eyes. She rose stiffly from her seat and colored under Levina's unabashed scrutiny.

"There are things a lady's maid is privy to, Levina, that must remain in confidence."

"Confi-dense?" Levina frowned.

"Secret." Aria sighed. "About . . . intimate, personal details and . . . opinions and things you might overhear."

"And like when you an' the lord don't get on?" Levina cocked her head insightfully.

Aria stared at Levina's strong, broad-featured face and was jolted by the perception she read there. She smoothed the front of her skirt and turned away, loath to speak of this to anyone, yet desperate for sharing.

"Yes, as when the lord and I . . . disagree. You see, Levina, Tynan—Lord Rutland is a very strong man . . . used to having his way."

"Oh, I seen that, miz. He can even put the fear o' God in old Bonduell. He'd be a hard man t'wife, I reckon . . . alwus wantin' his way with ye. Men is like that—"

"*Are* like that—" Aria corrected, her color deepening.

"—are like that," Levina finished earnestly. "That first time when he come to Royal Oaks, I knew he was smit wi'ye. An' he's not a man to take no, I reckon."

"I reckon," Aria echoed, watching her own fidgeting hands. "That's not to say he has no good qualities . . . it's just that . . . he's so . . ."

"Men likes to toss a bit o' muscle about," Levina offered sagely.

"Oh, it's not that—he'd never . . . he *has* never struck me. He just insists everything be done his way . . . in his time. And he seldom lets me into what he's thinking. We've been married nearly two months and I still feel like we're . . . strangers." Her candid admission surprised her.

"Belike there ain't no harm in that." Levina's sage expression became almost saintly. "Cain't let a man know everything . . . 'specially when he's so much bigger'n you."

Aria stared at her quizzically.

"Y'see—" Levina stepped closer and lowered her voice conspiratorially, "my ol' pappy was a big'un too . . . alwus struttin' and hollerin' an' thrashin'. My ma was alwus hoppin' to please him. Oncest she said yes, she never had much say agin. I 'spect you didn't have much say in it either—with his lordship wantin' ye. But me . . . I got a say." She jerked a sly thumb toward her ample bosom and lowered her head and voice again. "I'm gonna get me a *short* man . . . one smaller'n me. Then he'll have to reckon wi' *me*."

A bubble of surprise burst upward from Aria's middle, escaping in an astonished giggle that grew into sweet cleansing laughter. The tension of the day and the gloom of the late autumn evening were banished in the bright release of unexpected mirth. They laughed together, each igniting the other's humor afresh when reason threatened to overtake them again.

Side aching, eyes wet, Aria sank onto the settee, gulping breath weakly. Her gaze finally righted on Mrs. Bonduell, standing in the doorway wearing a black look of suspicion.

"Oh, Mrs. Bonduell." Aria managed to conquer her humor for a more ladylike mein. "With his lordship gone, I'll have supper here on a tray . . . and bring for Levina as well. I think it's time her manners lessons begin in earnest."

In the long night that followed, Aria tossed fitfully in her huge, empty bed, aching physically, longing for Tynan's strong arms about her, wanting his big, warm body to cover and comfort her. Tortured by the memory of his deep, unfathomable passion for her, she wakened over and over in the darkness, burning for his touch. She could only pray he felt this agony of longing, too, and that it would be enough to bring him home to her. And perhaps it might soften his heart enough for him to care for her as more than a trapping in his privileged life . . . or a conquest.

Each day she added a bit more polish to her rough gem of a maid, teaching her proper grammar and etiquette and sharpening her coarse skills at sewing and coiffure. She sent Levina to the library for a big book, then required her to walk while balancing it on her head to correct her galumping gait. Beneath that unrefined exterior, Aria found a quick and willing pupil. To her chagrin, Tynan's judgment was thoroughly vindicated.

Desperate to fill the empty hours from morning to evening toilette, she determined to scour the estate, learning all she could and meeting everyone who called Oberon their home. The overseer, William Skeen, was new to the plantation himself. He seemed a knowledgeable man, straight-talking and unafraid of the hard work ahead in restoring Oberon's considerable resources. He showed Aria the extent of their lands, the condition of their neglected barns, the site of the kitchen gardens, and the abandoned mill on the stream. Quickly, she grasped the scope of the work to be done and insisted on meeting with him daily to review and plan their progress.

It was only when Mr. Skeen showed her the slave quarters that Aria saw a darker side to the bewitching Oberon. Her husband's holdings included three Negro slave families and several individual blacks, purchased as part of the inventory from the former owners. They worked primarily in the fields and their ramshackled quarters were well hidden from sight, near the river bottom. She walked among them, hearing their names—Toby, Meribah, Lottie, Jeroboam, Liza—and felt a cold, depressing chill settling on her shoulders. The warmth and awe of their greetings struck a melancholy chord deep within her.

All that evening, thoughts of them oppressed her, gnawing at her conscience. During the long, sleepless night, she kept recalling how narrowly she had escaped slavery herself. If Tynan had not cared enough to come for her . . .

The thought lodged sideways in her mind, refusing to settle into place until examined from all sides. In those early days in the wilderness, Tynan had cared enough to risk his life in rescuing her . . . even then, when she had fought and defied him. Even then, he would not abandon her. No mere lust, not even manly pride, could fully account for his efforts to get her back and for the tenderness he showed in those first days afterward. Then vowing not to lose her again, he had demanded she speak the vows with him, there in the wilderness, not waiting for a single night to pass. He was determined to keep her by him.

Now in her miserable, wakeful bed, she wrestled with regret. She had accused him of using her, then abandoning her. At the time it had seemed so clear, so undeniable. The strangely coincidental flow of events had forged in her mind a link between her father and him, between her mother's fate and hers. History had seemed to be repeating itself in the very next generation. As she had watched it overtake them, she had felt powerless to halt it.

Perhaps if she had asked those questions that had burned upon her tongue, if she had demanded or entreated access to his closely guarded self, his thoughts . . . perhaps if she had been more honest . . .

Honest! She was horrified by her own weepy conclusion.

When had she ever been anything *but* honest with him?! She had never pretended their vows were more than a convenience that served his pleasures. She had honestly demanded nothing of him and had taken what he gave with candid reluctance. And she had admitted her passion for him and yielded her body to him freely, even eagerly. When had she ever spoken or done anything that was not scrupulously forthright . . . excruciatingly truthful?

She groaned to admit it, but he was right. She had wielded her unflinching brand of truth like a bludgeon.

But had there not been deception in her heart also? She was careful to hold back the tenderness she felt for him, to restrain the urges of her melting heart, to keep from him the devastating knowledge that she was coming to love him.

Perversely, it was exactly that kind of honesty that she wanted from him most . . . honesty of feeling. But she knew that in such honesty, there was terrible risk as well. What if he cared for her only as a possession, as she had often charged? What if he had no real love for her? Could she be happier knowing that?

In her dark, chilled bed, she wrapped the down comforter closer about her and ached with emptiness inside. Honesty was her last virtue, her comfort, her one real value in a world where things and even people could be wrenched from her life at a moment's notice. Her mother's face crept into her mind, sending a wave of troubled longing through her. No, honesty was not enough. She wanted more.

She realized there was something greater, more valuable to her human heart than even truth. She wanted love. Tynan's love. What would she have to do, to be, to gain it?

Reluctantly, Aria surrendered to Oberon's earthy spell. It was a solid but genteel place with a faded graciousness that tempted her hand to restore it. Everywhere she looked she began to see possibilities, beautiful and haunting possibilities. Tynan's true motives for bringing her here mattered less each day. She could make this place her home, she decided, watching the sway of half-bare oak limbs out her bedroom window. And perhaps someday, when he returned, he'd make it his home, too.

Twenty-six

Since the field work was past, Aria collected several slaves and set about clearing the debris of decay and neglect from the once glorious gardens. In the process, she discovered that the tall, soft-spoken Toby was reputed to be a wizard with plants, able to coax the most bashful or obstinate greenery into lush display. After three strenuous days of clearing and resetting the brick pathways, grubbing out the weedy thickets, and studying various aspects of the views, she drafted a plan for the gardens and turned it over to Toby for implementation.

She moved on to the repair of the fences and the patching and rebuilding of the roofs of the tobacco barns and outbuildings, authorizing the purchase of materials and inspecting the work firsthand. Then she determined to make a corrected inventory of tools, implements, livestock, and buildings. Mr. Skeen proved as pleasant as he was knowledgeable and Aria took pains to compliment his evenhanded management. To her grateful surprise, he did not seem resentful about taking orders from a woman. Franklin grumbled good-naturedly when his stables fell under her quill in the inventory, but he assisted willingly whenever her familiar figure appeared in the stable doorway, leather-bound ledger, quills, and inkpot in hand. Gradually they were drawn together by the labor of putting Oberon to rights, each learning to respect the work and contribution of the others. With each passing day, it felt more like home.

The work on the porticos had stopped two days after Tynan

left; silence reigned over the bony understructure of Oberon's new face. After a week, Aria questioned Mrs. Bonduell on what had happened to them and the surly housekeeper disavowed all knowledge with a malicious glint in her bilious eyes.

"Then send for Mr. Prentice right away . . . today . . . now!" she ordered. "And let him know it is *Lady* Rutland that summons him."

Astonishingly, the man appeared the very next morning and Aria greeted him in a well-warmed, though unfurnished, parlor. They stood, cups in hand, by the crackling fireplace as though it were the most commonplace manner of entertaining. Aria smiled her most charming smile.

"I was surprised to see the workmen have not returned in more than a week, Mr. Prentice."

"Well, my lady," he stuffed the rest of a pecan tart into his mouth and wiped his fingers hastily on his breeches, "I . . . do have other commitments. To schedule these workmen is fraught with difficulty."

"I hope you are not anxious over your payment . . . in Lord Rutland's absence."

"Oh, no—" an oily smile appeared. "I have already been paid . . . and little is owing to the suppliers."

"Already paid. How fortunate . . . for you." Aria was surprised, mostly by her husband's careless business practices. Small wonder the man was reluctant to finish—Tynan had taken his incentive completely away. And how fortunate for her free-spending husband that he had married George Dunning's daughter. A lush smile bent her lips into an appealing bow.

Prentice found himself staring at those lips and licked the sugar from his own. He grinned his most ingratiating and foolish smile.

"Then I see no impediment to the workmen returning and finishing—beginning at first light tomorrow. I shall expect to see them here, Mr. Prentice."

"But that is quite impossible, Lady Rutland." Prentice jerked his chin back, confused. "They are in the far end of the county—"

"Tomorrow morning, Mr. Prentice." Her smile chilled and the hapless builder raised his eyes to find cold resolve in the brilliant beryls that searched him. "You are not dealing with *Lord* Rutland, Mr. Prentice. You deal now with the Countess of Penrith. And I can assure you that, when roused, his wrath is paltry compared with mine. What was that he promised you? Something about your neck I believe?" She tapped her chin with one fingertip as if recalling.

Prentice's face reddened and his beakish nose flared with indignation. "Lady Rutland . . . Countess . . . I really must protest!"

"I wish no unpleasantness, Mr. Prentice. I have only money, a terrifyingly inventive nature . . . and a keen desire to see my house finished within the fortnight. I leave it to your own productive mind to imagine the myriad ways in which a man in your position is unexpectedly vulnerable." She sipped her coffee sweetly and continued.

"On the other hand, I can be a generous patron, sir. Your work could be exhibited and extolled to the finest families in North Carolina."

Prentice was speechless as he hastily altered his assessment of the Lady of Oberon. Now he saw the strength, the purpose, the cleverness behind the soft feminine exterior.

"Will I see workmen at daybreak?" she urged.

"Yes, Lady Rutland," he barked gruffly, gouged at being had so completely by a young slip of a woman, even a countess. His cup went down on the table with a clatter and he pivoted, striding out.

"Mr. Prentice?" She halted him with his name, and when he turned back, she had warmed into that irresistible woman again. "You will not regret it, sir."

The next morning the workmen did appear, grumbling from their long night's ride—but present all the same. Aria welcomed them personally—with ewers of coffee and sweet buns. By the time they clambered up the scaffolding to work, their attitudes were much improved. And the porticos, steps, and brickwork were completed in only nine days.

As much attention and energy as Aria lavished on the rest of Oberon, she scrupulously avoided the interior of the great house itself. It was clearly Mrs. Bonduell's territory and Aria was determined to have nothing to do with it, however great her curiosity about the furnishings and contents. Tynan had never asked her to take it in hand—only ordered her as if she were a simpleminded scullery maid, then chided her when she set a hand to it. And in the face of conflicting orders, Aria felt no obligation to assume any responsibility for the redoubtable house.

But it had now been more than three weeks since Tynan's abrupt departure and still ugly stacks of draped furnishings and raw crates and barrels were lumped in the middle of every room in the main house, except the master suite. The paint work and papering and scant interior repairs were all completed within the first week after Tynan's departure, and the slow work outside had not obstructed the settlement of the inside. Silently, Aria watched Mrs. Bonduell oversee the incessant cleaning and polishing but never raise a hand to touch a stick of furniture or to set the place aright. When she could bear it no more, she called the surly housekeeper to her sitting room and broached the subject.

"When will you begin to set the rooms in order, Mrs. Bonduell?" Aria tried to maintain an even disposition, though it was increasingly difficult around the woman.

"I have my orders, madam," the housekeeper snapped. "I go by 'em to the letter, madam."

"And just what are those orders, Mrs. Bonduell?" Aria bit back.

"I'm not to touch or move nothing, madam . . . his lordship said it was for you to do." The housekeeper's face was drawn up in a pugnacious scowl and her chins lifted.

"He told you not to touch the rooms?!" Aria hadn't even imagined that possibility. It was just like him . . . forbid the servants to do their jobs and force her to do it instead. She was roundly irritated that the housekeeper seemed to lay the blame for inaction at her feet. "Why didn't you say something before?,"

"You been too busy—" Mrs. Bonduell's head jerked nastily toward the door, "out there, *madam.*"

It took everything in Aria's will to keep from launching herself at the woman. How dare the old witch challenge Aria on the way she spent her time and energies! Aria rose from the settee, putting her lap desk aside, and faced her foe.

"Then I amend your orders, immediately. You will take the matter in hand starting today, Mrs. Bonduell, and put an end to this foolishness. Set the furnishings aright, starting now."

The housekeeper drew herself up even straighter, puffing up like a purple turnip, and glared nastily. She left without a word of acknowledgment. And Aria sent wide-eyed Levina for her cloak and headed for the sanity of the stables.

Later that same afternoon, Aria found Mrs. Bonduell in the kitchens, browbeating the kitchen staff furiously. The woman barely ceased when Aria appeared.

"Is there some problem, Mrs. Bonduell?" Aria demanded, irritated at the woman's ever-present viciousness.

"Nothin' I can't handle, madam." She shot a warning glare at the hapless cook and chore girls, who shifted uncomfortably and slunk back to their duties.

"So I see," Aria mused tersely. "I brought you some assistance for your work with the furnishings." She stepped to the door and motioned inside two shivering black women, Lottie and Meribah, who hung back near the door, pulling their thin shawls closer about them. "You're to direct them and teach them the proper care of good furnishings . . . as you set the rooms aright."

"Negroes . . . in the house?" For the first time Aria felt she had really unnerved the ill-tempered old crone. "Well . . . I never . . . it ain't fittin'!"

"It is fitting if I say it is." Aria stepped forward, eyes blazing emerald fire. Her voice lowered an angry octave."And I say it is."

Mrs. Bonduell sputtered again, paling, then flushing. And Aria lifted her skirts and sailed out of the kitchens in triumph.

The triumph was qualified. For the next two days, Aria stayed close to the house, copying records and going over the costs of needed improvements to fences, outbuildings, and slave quarters with Mr. Skeen. Under her watchful eye, Mrs. Bonduell lashed Lottie and Meribah verbally, but restrained her more physical urges. But Aria eventually learned, through Levina's vigilance, that the old harridan only stored up her vengeance to loose it each evening down in the slave quarters. Small wonder Lottie and Meribah wore perpetually cowed and wary expressions.

Determined to see for herself, she roused Mr. Skeen and Acre and Franklin to accompany her down to the riverbank well after dark, following a trail blazed quite visibly by the vengeful housekeeper. They found her in a poleshed, lash in hand, administering what had become a daily venting of frustrated cruelty. Lottie's glistening back was stripped bare, revealing abuse not yet healed and her hands were bound and held by one of the stable hands. She sobbed and pleaded incoherently for mercy from her impervious abuser.

"Dearest God," Aria breathed in horror. They stood just outside the circle of ugly yellow lantern light, riveted by the unleashed hatred of the vicious crone. "Stop her . . . for God's sake, stop her!"

In a wild flurry of bodies, Mrs. Bonduell was wrestled to the ground and the conspiring stable hand was sent sprawling in the dirt and held there by Franklin's heavy boot on his neck. When she was dragged to her feet, the housekeeper's eyes were wild and her lips were flecked with foam.

"She deserved it, the uppity black bitch! I said not to bring them scum into *my* house. And I made 'em pay for it . . . every night they paid for it!" Then she broke into a fiendish laughter that seemed to roil from the madness of hell itself.

"You depraved, evil old witch!" Aria growled, trembling violently as she worked Lottie's bonds and pulled clothing together about the slave's quaking shoulders. "If I find you're in the county one day hence, I'll see you have a taste of your own cruelty! Mr. Skeen, take that revolting piece of trash back to the house, put her things in a flour sack, and get her off my land . . . now!"

As Skeen and Acre pulled the thrashing, screaming form of the maddened housekeeper away, Aria put her arm around Lottie and started toward Lottie's meager shanty.

"What about him, Miz Aria?" Franklin glowered down at his captive.

Aria paused and said tightly, "What would you do to him if he were abusing your horses, Franklin?"

Franklin's eyes leapt with fierce flame. "Leave it to me," he snarled.

The next day, Aria met with Mr. Skeen, Franklin, and Acre in the library and handed the overseer a stack of documents. She dipped a freshly sharpened quill in the inkpot and offered it to him for his signature. When Skeen read the first lines of the first document, his eyes widened with disbelief that faded into true horror as he skimmed the rest of Aria's fluid script.

"Ye can't be serious, ma'am. This be some kind of a jest, don't it?"

"Not in the least." She leveled a calm, determined gaze on him from across the library desk, where she had labored strenuously all morning. She had risen early and dressed, then sequestered herself in the library. She had dragged the writing table from beneath a stack of draped chairs, procured pen, ink, and parchment from Tynan's personal things, and set to work.

As she worked, her determination to see it through overpowered consideration of the risks it might involve.

"Seven year's work, then freedom?!" Skeen's face was slack with disbelief and he lowered the documents to the table, looking to Franklin and Acre for support.

"What's that?" Franklin snatched the papers away and scanned them, reddening. "No," he raised a disgusted face to her stubborn gaze, "ye can't be doing this, Miz Aria."

"Well, I am. They'll work seven years, then have their freedom. It's the Sabbath Year and on Oberon it will be a year of Jubilee." They all stared at her as if she had lost her senses. "Even in the Old Testament scriptures a slave was to be freed in the seventh year. If they work well, and they will, they will have purchased their freedom. It is no different from an indenture, Mr. Skeen."

"But it is different, Miz . . . they be blacks and they never had freedom. I know ye mean well . . . especially after last night, but this won't change what happened. If you turn them out, who'll work the place . . . and where'll they go?! This is their place, miz . . . same as ours. It's not decent—"

"After seven years, if they wish, they'll stay with us for wages. If they want to leave, they'll be free to do so—"

"Miz Aria," Franklin interrupted, glowering, "yer father had peculiar notions about slaves and wouldn't have none . . . said they showed a man didn't have enough to pay good hands to work for him. But he was wrong, Miz Aria. You done a man's work in the days just passed and know a lot about runnin' a place, but you don't know the first thing about working slaves. And this country here's different from Virginia. Here you need more hands in the fields . . ."

"Then we'll have them, Franklin, but not as slaves." She planted her hands on her waist and glared at her old friend. "This is *my* home, and it is *my* responsibility."

"Well, Miz Aria, I'd do much for ye, but I'll not do this. Not until his lordship comes back." Skeen dropped the papers on the desk and turned on his heel, stalking out.

Aria rounded the desk quickly, stopping short at the flush of ire on Franklin's face. "His *lordship* won't return for a very long time and he's left me to see to Oberon," she gritted out and picked up the papers to hold them to him. "Will you sign as witness?"

"Old George coulda whalloped ye now and again. It mighta done you good." And Franklin copied Skeen's irritable exit.

Aria's shoulders slumped a bit as she turned to Acre. The furious color was draining from her lovely features and her green eyes seemed luminous with frustration. She hadn't counted on such opposition to such a reasonable-seeming plan . . . from these men she had grown to respect and count on. With belated insight, she realized that Skeen and even her own Franklin saw her first as a female whose main importance stemmed from the fact that she was attached, however tenuously, to the wealthy, powerful Lord Rutland.

Acre's weathered face broke into a toothy, yellowed grin as he leaned against a stack of draped furniture. "I'd sign it for ye . . . only I cain't write."

His chuckle and the glint in his eye goaded her even more than the others' righteous indignation. And it was Aria who fled the room next.

Twenty-seven

The pounding of the dry, packed dirt of the road matched the pounding in Tynan's head as he neared the last rise before Oberon. Gripped by a powerful sense of urgency, he had dug his heels into his tired mount and left Jamison in a walk. For the last week he had wrestled with this unreasonable desire for Aria and his home, usually subduing it with an iron will and a caustic mental dialogue. But the closer they got to the object of his painful longing, the more uncontrollable it became—and the more volatile was his lordly temperament. Poor Jamison had given up trying to engage him in companionable conversation and for the last day had just dared to look at him at all. He was a man possessed.

Jerking his heaving mount to a halt atop the last ridge, he forced himself to settle back on the saddle and breathe deeply of the cold, crisp air. He had ridden for ten grueling days, intent on this moment, and he was not going to have it go awry like their last greeting at Oberon. He had stomped and thundered and carried on like a royal fool, instead of taking her into his arms and bed and loving her until he melted an opening into her heart. This time, he thought as he ran a brawny hand over his stubbled chin, it would be different. He would declare how good it was to see her and to be home. He would compliment her work in the house and show her the gifts he had brought her from Philadelphia . . . watching her green eyes grow brilliant with pleasure. They would have a quiet dinner in their chambers and then he would have the pleasure, the paradise, that would begin their new life together here.

Philadelphia had lost some of its sparkle as the seriousness of the conflict with England deepened and the first flush of patriotic exuberance was translated into the structure of committees and congress and documents. The challenges and dangers of forging a country had taken on a new urgency for him and he was impatient with the city's frequent diversions from the tasks at hand. The philosophy and pleasures that had so charmed him were now diminished by constant comparison with all he had left behind. The women had been as available as ever, but none was as deliciously tempting as his fiery little wife. The discussions were as deep and lively as ever, but none challenged the very core of him the way Aria did.

He had sought to put time and distance between them and discovered, to his angry chagrin, it was an impossibility. He carried her in his heart, in his mind. She was always with him and yet his longing for her was unbearable. He recalled his arrogant assumption that marriage changed little for a man of means, and wagged his head in disbelief at how pathetic it seemed. Everything seemed changed, especially himself. And Aria was the cause. He could only hope she had suffered similar miseries in his absence.

Jamison's horse thudded to a halt beside him, and still absorbed in expectation, he waved a hand before him without looking at his friend. "There it is . . . my home."

"What are you waiting for?" Jamison panted irritably between gulped breaths as he saw Rutland's pensive mood. "You've nearly killed two good animals and hazarded my health and sanity to get back here—and here you sit on a cold, godforsaken hill, just looking at it!"

Tynan grinned wryly at Jamison's insightful complaint. "Let's go." He urged his horse ahead, knowing Jamison had reason for his disgusted glare.

Riding down the sloping road, they picked up their pace as they spotted a crew of men at the brick and iron-work pillars that announced the entrance to Oberon. Tynan's back was rail-straight as he halted before the overseer and dismounted.

William Skeen wiped his cold hands on his breeches and extended a surprised greeting to his employer. "You're home, your lordship! Welcome back, sir."

Tynan gave him a hand in return and gazed over the man's shoulder at the fence work in progress. "Good to be home, Mr. Skeen. What's that you're doing here?"

"Just a bit of repair on the fences, sir, some was needin' it badly. And we thought to spruce up the old gate here in the boodle."

"Good." Tynan nodded approvingly. "And how have things gone in my absence, Mr. Skeen? Have you made progress?"

"Oh, indeed, sir," copper-haired Skeen smiled. "I think ye'll be pleased when you see."

Tynan hesitated, but thought it best to be prepared for whatever lay ahead, and he asked, "And Lady Rutland . . . has she . . . fared well?" Skeen's pleasantry seemed to fade and Tynan felt himself bracing in the brief silence.

"Her ladyship's been a busy one, sir. Always somethin' a doin'. Just this week alone she sacked old Bonduell and freed the slaves—"

"What?!" Tynan blurted out, incredulous and feeling betrayed by his recent admission of need. "She did what?!" he thundered again.

Skeen's chin drew back, startled by the eruption of his employer's ire. "I said, this week she—"

"Fired the housekeeper and freed my damn slaves!" he finished for the overseer. "Yet—" his hand shot toward Jeroboam in the work party behind Skeen, "I see one in your crew, Mr. Skeen."

"Well, it's a story, sir." Skeen stepped back a pace, shaking his head slightly, realizing he had put it badly. "There was a nasty bit of trouble with old Bonduell, and Lady Rutland, she felt horrible and wrote up the papers and asked me to sign 'em. But I said I'd wait 'til you come home—"

"Dam-nation!" Tynan roared, not waiting for another word as he jerked around and swung up furiously onto his horse. He spurred the tired animal and raced down the treelined road for the house.

"Rutland! Wait—" Jamison shot a dark look at the sputtering Skeen and took off in Tynan's turbulent wake. He couldn't quite overtake Tynan and slammed to the ground beside his horse just as Tynan was stalking grimly toward the new front steps of the main house. One glance at that unyielding back and Jamison was seized with an overpowering urge to thrash him within an inch of his imperious life.

"Rutland!" Rushing, Jamison grabbed his arm and wrenched him back a step. "You fool, don't you see what you're doing? You're charging in like a rampaging bull to accuse her of God-knows-what! She deserves a chance to explain—to be treated like a human being instead of just your doxy!"

"Shut up, Jamison! She's *my* wife—and what passes between us is none of your concern!" Tynan turned on him with a vengeance, his visage carved of glowering granite.

"You don't deserve a wife, Rutland . . . let alone a woman like Aria!" Jamison's face was crimson with seething outrage; he was beyond the recall of reason. "You slave her and maul her—"

"Shut your filthy mouth!" Tynan thundered, grabbing Jamison's jacket in twitching fists. He lifted furiously, straining to bring his reckless tormentor nose to nose with impending disaster. "If you value life, *never* speak to me of my marriage again! You think I can't see why you champion her: I've seen you pawing and rutting at the flick of her skirts. Stay away from her, Jamison, or be prepared to pay for it!"

"Stupid bastard!" Jamison spat dangerously. "As if she'd look at me! You had to force her, humiliate her, to take her! And—God help me—I went along—"

A bone-cracking blow landed square in Tynan's eye, jarring his head back and ending his savage hold on Jamison. But before Jamison's lowered shoulder plowed into his midsection, Tynan recovered enough to meet his thrust and force him upright. Dazed and hurting, Tynan poured his pain into his steelcorded arm and landed a savage blow up under Jamison's jaw, sending him sprawling back in the dirt and gravel of the drive.

Aria was standing near the window of one of the front-facing bedrooms, straightening the newly hung brocades, as Tynan rode toward the house. A glow of approval settled rosy in her fair cheeks and she turned to appreciate their morning's hard work, breathing deeply of the strange mingling of freshly dyed fabrics and newly waxed furnishings. But something outside had caught her attention and she turned back to the window to search for it again. A rider was barreling down the main road, headed straight for the front of the house. And as she watched, her heart slowed to a stop. It looked like . . .

It was Tynan! She jumped physically at the recognition. Tynan was home! A shaft of joy pushed upward through her and exploded in her senses. She whirled and ran to the middle of the room, stammering excitedly.

"He's . . . he's home! Oh-h-h—he's home!" She shook her hands anxiously, trying to remember everything she'd thought of doing at his homecoming . . . someday. And now he was home after only a month!

Levina ran to the window and excitedly announced to the others what Aria seemed incapable of uttering . . . Lord Rutland was coming home.

"Lottie!" Aria finally seized hold of her wits. "Go to the kitchen—get hot water ready for Lord Rutland's bath and tell cook to lay on a special supper . . . especially her cherry duckling and . . . chestnut dressing, and . . . yam pie. Levina—" She grabbed her maid's hands, primarily to still the trembling of her own. "Run to our rooms and lay out fresh clothing for Lord Rutland. Then . . . put fresh linen on our bed."

"Yes miz!" Levina's eyes glowed excitedly and she hurried out.

"Meribah, take the others into the far wing and see the last two bedrooms are arranged the same as this one. Then begin work in the main dining room below."

Then Aria ran down the hallway toward her rooms. She had meant to make it to her mirror and straighten her hair but had to settle for jerking off her linen day cap and running a hand up over her simple coif. For at that very moment, Tynan's voice came rumbling, reverberating through the main hall.

"Aria! . . . Aria!"

She stopped at the top of the graceful staircase, her face flushed and eyes sparkling with excitement, and saw him outlined in the front doorway by the bright afternoon light. Her heart tumbled to her knees at the sight of his powerful form framed in light, the striking outline of his dark hair, his stubborn jaw. She ran down the stairs as quickly as possible, intent on keeping aright on her own wobbly knees. And it was only when she reached the bottom and hurried toward him that the strange nuances of his posture and the curt tone of his voice seeped through to her. Too late, she recognized the signs of ire and jerked to a halt scarcely five feet away from him.

"Tynan—I . . . we didn't expect you . . ." She clasped her hands before her uncertainly, feeling her face beginning to burn with confusion.

"So I gathered," he bit out nastily. "But it appears I have returned just in time to foil your little game, Aria."

Dread dried her mouth, while beneath her astonishment, anger suddenly blossomed. This was all wrong!

"What game? I saw you from the upstairs window and . . . came as quickly as I could . . ." She ground to a halt under his hot glare and took a step backward. How could he still be so furious with her after an entire month?

"You thought to take your petty revenge on my property in my absence—to spite me for *abandoning* you here. Only you didn't reckon that I'd return so soon. Your game is finished, *wife!"*

"Revenge?" Frustration boiled up inside her, clogging her throat briefly. She swallowed hard, forced her chin up, and took a step closer to his glowering wrath. "I don't know what you're talking about, but I won't stand here and suffer your abuse a minute longer!" Scarlet-faced, she snatched up her skirts and started quickly for the stairs, only to be yanked to a dead stop and then corralled by his arms in a merciless grasp.

"Let me go, Tynan! What's got into you? . . . Are you mad?"

As they struggled, Tynan became dimly aware of several pairs of astonished eyes turned on them from the top of the stairs. He began to drag her, twisting and protesting, toward the main parlor.

"You and I have business, wife, and you're not going anywhere until it's settled!" He shoved her forcibly through the large doorway and pulled the doors securely shut behind them.

Aria stumbled, but righted herself quickly and hurriedly put the room's still-stacked furnishings between them. When Tynan turned to confront her, the flame in his eyes was stoked even hotter by the sight of the untouched pile of furnishings in the center of the room. He caught Aria's fiery gaze above the wretched pile and her angry defiance seemed all the confirmation he needed. More the fool, he, for underestimating her. He stalked her until her tense, woolen-clad frame came fully into view. His face was a mask of contempt.

"You fired Mrs. Bonduell, is that not true?" he demanded, eyes narrowing onimously.

"Yes, I sent the old harridan packing," Aria snapped, trembling with pent-up hurt and anger. But the question made her think. "How did you hear of that?"

"And you tried to divest me of my rightful property!"

"I did no such thing!" She jerked around so that her side faced him, as if making herself a smaller target. How could he just charge in like a bull with its horns down—after being away a full month? How dare he accuse her of so ridiculous a—"That's not true"

"You deny you freed my slaves?!" He raked her with a contemptuous look and took menacing steps closer.

"That I won't deny—" She lifted her chin to quell its trembling. "I made out papers that—"

"Then you did dispose of my property, wife, for those blacks do belong rightfully to me!"

"Only if it is possible for any human to 'own' another. You, *husband,* left Oberon in my charge, or have you forgotten?"

"I left the *house* in your charge, *wife* . . ." His arm struck out toward the miserable lump of unused goods. "And apparently it wasn't enough for you to set my house in turmoil. You took it upon yourself to disrupt the fields and stables as well. Did you honestly think you'd get away with it? What convenient lie had you planned for when I did return?"

The outward push of her anger was almost bested by the inward crushing force of hurt and disbelief. But he called her a liar—saw only deceit and mean-heartedness in her, when she had given him nothing but honesty and loyalty . . . and even love. Over and over she had proved her honesty toward him— giving him her passion, her tenderness, without reserve. She had swallowed her pride to tend his precious Oberon as if it were her own . . . hoping that it might become a bridge between them and, someday, the home neither had. She had waited for him, pined for him in her bed . . . as if in obedience to his arrogant order. And he cared nothing for any of it . . . or for her!

Flame leaped suddenly into her luminous beryl eyes, dimming his implacable image and burning out the last traces of the sweet submission she had planned. Gone was Marian Dunning's vulnerable child, supplanted by George Dunning's willful daughter . . . primed for battle.

"You insufferable *ass!*" she shouted, startling even herself with her sheer volume, "You dare accuse me . . . *me* of plotting and lying to you?! Pull the mote from your own eyes, *husband!* You called this *my* home, ordered me to see to it, restore it . . . care for it in your absence. Do you now deny it?"

"But you clearly chose not to raise one dainty hand about the place," he sneered, jerking his head toward the mute testimony of the furnishings. "You chose instead to spite me by interfering—"

"Interfering?" Aria's fists clenched at her sides as she stepped closer. "So I was interfering when I stopped that evil witch of a housekeeper from stripping the flesh from the backs of your slaves? I was truly interfering when I got Prentice to return and finish his work after you foolishly paid him in advance. And I suppose I was also interfering when I ordered the slaves quarters repaired so the cold night air wouldn't seep in and sicken *your* workers!"

Intent on the shifting shadows in his angry eyes, she had stalked even closer. Now she bashed a foolhardy finger against his rocklike chest. "Well, *husband,* you can easily see my interference undone! Just rip the roofs from the barns! Grub out the fence posts! Pull down the porticos . . . beat your slaves and let the grounds go to seed—and all will be just as it was before!" She ended furiously, and running out of words, she jerked up her skirts and gave his knee a savage and totally unexpected slam with the sharp toe of her shoe.

Tynan howled and grabbed instinctively for her and his knee both at once. But Aria had already fled an arm's length and his clutching fingers just brushed her slim waist.

"Dammit, Aria!" he roared, recovering to charge after her.

Horror bloomed in Aria's flushed face as she realized the depth of Tynan's rage and the sheer audacity of her counterattack. Panicking, she ran to put the cloth-covered mound between them, thinking desperately how she might make it past him to the door. He now stalked her, his face seeming swollen with anger and impending retribution. His eyes were hot, silvery discs and his coiled muscles made his shoulders seem like mountains.

The fear that flickered over her features was quickly replaced with taut defiance. Her face was flushed, her honey-colored hair was slightly mussed, and her eyes sparkled with provocative emotion. Her breasts rose and fell deeply with her panting breaths and Tynan's skin began to contract all over his body. A trickle of strange sensation ran over his broad back. Had he judged her motives too hastily? Or did he suddenly want to believe her because she exerted so powerful a spell over his senses?

"It will be easy to test your honesty, sweetest." His eyes became lidded and unreadable.

"It matters little to me what you think. I won't be here to witness my vindication." She pulled a fluted china vase from the things stacked near her and continued to back away from his circular chase. "Do your worst while you can, I'll not stay here a moment longer!"

He lunged for her and she threw the heavy vase with un-erring aim, smacking him in the shoulder as he dodged belatedly. The crashing sound as it shattered on the floor jolted Aria's pulse into a frantic rhythm. His sidestep gave her time to put the furnishings between them again, except that now, they also blocked part of her view. Her heart beat in her throat. He now had the advantage; she wouldn't see him coming until it was too late.

Deciding quickly, she gambled and dashed for the door around the side she could see best. Tynan bolted after her but his foot slipped on a piece of broken porcelain and he went down, grabbing her skirts and crashing down on one shoulder.

"No! Let go!" Aria pulled frantically for the door, feeling his fingers close about her ankle like steel bands.

Stretched and precariously balanced, she was slowly being pulled back toward his straining form. The sound of stitches ripping at her waist could have been coming from her stretched nerves as she reached desperately for something, anything to hold. Her hand struck the cast-iron brackets beside the marble hearth, but what she grabbed came with her as he pulled her inexorably closer.

Tynan yanked her foot and skirt and succeeded in hauling her a significant bit closer. Then to his surprise, her resistance ceased abruptly and she straightened above him. His eyes followed the billow of her skirts upward to her curving waist and there they stopped and widened. She held a heavy iron poker in both hands, poised like a club.

His face smoothed and tightened, as he sought her gaze. Her eyes were flashing emerald fire and her ripe lips were tight with disdain for his now diluted threat. He made to rise, but Aria's foot was instantly planted in the center of his chest, forcing him back down. His hands came up, open in surrender, but she left it there all the same.

His head dropped back to rest on the floor, his eyes lidded to veil their calculation. "Well, at least you finally deigned to touch *something* in this room.

"You're more to blame for the state of the house than I," she charged. "Your foul-tempered housekeeper refused to touch the place, despite my orders, and only this week I discovered the reason for her obstinacy. She said you had ordered her not to touch a thing!"

"I . . . believe I said she wasn't to touch a thing until you personally directed its placement."

"A distinction that was apparently lost on her," Aria declared, fingering the poker determinedly.

This was a unique and somewhat dangerous view of his wife . . . from her feet up . . . with one slim foot, one shapely calf, planted squarely in the middle of him. His ire drained almost instantly and other, equally heated, feelings flooded in to replace it. He began to relax his muscles, but not his guard.

His dark face tilted as he studied her, and his light eyes darkened a shade even in the strong light. For once the truth seemed as reckless a gambit as the boldest lie.

"I thought you'd grow curious about the place . . . or at

least tired of staring at the mess . . . and begin to act like the lady of the house . . ."

"Instead of the whore?" she sneered, surprised and irritated by his candid admission.

"I have heard that word from no lips but yours, Aria, since I took you with me. Everyone considers you my wife . . . except you. I thought once you saw Oberon, put some of yourself into it . . . you might begin to feel like a wife." Tynan's frankness surprised him no less than her.

"Feel like your wife?" She laughed shortly, feeling a trickle of bitterness in her throat. "Was that your aim when you came blowing through the doors, accusing me of all manner of low, mean acts against you? To cosset my 'wifely' feelings?" She glared at him through a growing mist she had to blink away. She had to stay angry, she had to tell him what she thought of his arrogant, little-minded ways. Her hold on the heavy poker became deathly.

"Before we spoke the vows, you made my status quite clear. I was to be your legal harlot . . . to entertain you, both in bed and out. I have never pretended otherwise . . . nor have I asked anything of you, except an occasional scrap of honesty. I told you this 'arrangement' would be intolerable for me without truthfulness. It was all I had left to bring you, and today you've shown how little you have valued what I had to give." Her voice faltered at the end and she stopped, struggling to maintain the control that seemed to be deserting her.

"Aria—" Unnoticed, his hand slid around her ankle and she jumped skittishly at the contact.

"Stop that!" She tried to pull her foot away, but he held it fast and she glared at him as ominously as she could.

"What bothers you most, Tynan . . . that I managed well while you were away or that I ignored your wifely little gambit?" And for the first time in all these days and nights together she knew she lied. In the end, she had succumbed to Oberon and thus to Tynan, just as he knew she would.

The glint in his eye should have warned her. He jerked her

foot suddenly out to his far side and set it on the floor beside his muscular chest. For an instant she was off-balance, frantic with indecision.

Was she capable of using the iron in her hand? And when her foot hit the floor, her face colored, but not from rage. He had just proven he was capable of overtaking her anytime he pleased.

She stood astride him, now as acutely aware of his sprawling frame as she was of her false bravado. Pride's angry spur stung her and she sat down abruptly on his chest, still wielding her fire iron.

"I may not have another such chance," she snapped, pushing her skirts down in front as he groaned with the impact and stared at her with true surprise. "You're my father made over—used to having everything your way, proclaiming your desire the only possible virtue. You took me despite my protest, probably because I was the only thing you were unable to buy or to charm. You've treated me like a shameless slattern, a mindless child, an obstinate toy, a half-witted drudge, and now a lying schemer. And here's just how low and untrustworthy I am: If you'd stayed away just one more day, your wretched house would have been finished! As I speak, the last rooms are being completed upstairs. I've worked the servants till they're near revolt, and Mr. Skeen and my own Franklin can hardly bear to see me coming. I've worked my fingers to the bone on your precious Oberon—" Her compulsive flood of words had betrayed more than she wanted; they began to tell of her hurt. "You've had your use of me—and more. And I won't stay in this house a minute longer."

She tried to push from him but found her skirt held fast. Her face colored crimson as she gritted her teeth and tried again. "Let me go!" She brandished the fire iron menacingly and felt the pull on her skirts ease. She paused, looking down into his handsome, unreadable face, then shook off the wave of despair that threatened to overwhelm her and made to rise again.

Tynan's hands slipped boldly up Aria's silky stockings and quickly gripped the bare skin of her thighs, preventing her upward movement. Shock widened her eyes and brought an angry, wordless sputter to her lips. He held her to him beneath her own skirts . . . ignoring her professed loathing to boldly invade her private-most places!

"You're not through with me yet, are you?" he taunted, letting his hands glide higher on her silky thighs even as he held her. "Don't you want to know why I came home earlier than either of us expected?"

"I don't give a fig why! Let me go!" Aria clutched the poker as if she could squeeze some sanity from it. Her responses were shivering under his startling sensual assault on her body. His heat radiated into her bare bottom, sending dangerous tinglings up along her nerves to emphasize the intimacy of her position against him. Aghast at her body's stubborn awakening, she tried to look menacing.

"I said I'd stay away until I couldn't any longer. I missed you too much to stay away a minute more . . . much less a day." His voice grew husky as he explored the svelte curves of her thighs as they fitted tightly against his chest.

"You don't have to lie, *husband*. You have nothing to gain." She clenched her teeth and tried again to wrest away from his marauding fingers.

"True, not a thing to gain." His chest rumbled at her convenient logic. "Then I must be speaking the truth. Isn't that what you wanted, sweetest? Honesty?" His hand reached the satiny ripeness of her buttock and she flinched trying to contain her rioting sensations.

"I don't want anything from you . . . except release."

"That's unfortunate—" His hands began to work their way toward her belly and she grabbed them through the layers of her petticoats, attempting to stay their venial probing. "Because I want something from you, wife."

"Surely some Sarah or Polly or Amelia supplied you well

enough while you were gone to see you through the coming drought."

"Honestly," he captured her gaze in his and his generous lips tilted, *"that* was second on my list. But since you inquired, I hardly looked at a woman while in Philadelphia. I kept thinking of you . . . imagining you here, warm and willing in our big, soft bed. Ask Jamison, he'll verify my celibate sojourn."

"I don't want to verify anything—I want up!" she snapped, her guard slipping dangerously.

"I thought you wanted my honesty." He set his course and wondered why it had never occurred to him before to give her a full dose of what she claimed to want.

"It's too late for mere honesty," she declared, grappling with his rapacious hands again. "I no longer believe you're capable of it. You certainly don't recognize it when you hear it."

"I do recognize that you . . . meant well with what you've done here, Aria. I was forty kinds of a fool to erupt like that . . . without hearing what you had to say." His face was serious. This "honesty" was not as easy as it had first seemed. It felt strange to say the things that had moments before been secrets in his mind.

Aria's jaw slackened as she stubbornly agreed. "You were a fool. But that certainly is not news and it changes nothing. You wanted convenient pleasures—bullied and bargained for them. Well, you've had them and more—"

"How much more, Aria?" His light eyes glowed with the intensity of his question. "What have you given me that wasn't agreed in our vows?"

"Vows?" She colored hotly, feeling her strength of will melting into those treacherous little puddles in her middle. She didn't like this turn a bit.

"I was a fool to settle for what I could master of you in bed." His deepening voice rumbled up through her loins to set her heart vibrating strangely. "I want more, Aria. I've said I wanted you for my wife . . . and you thought I wanted a servant, a housekeeper, a proper face on my life. What I really wanted was what you promised me at our vows . . . your caring, your faith, your trust. I want you, Aria, as a woman . . . beside me in my life as well as in my bed."

Aria covered her ears with her hands, as the poker fell to the floor with a resounding clang. "I don't want to hear any more," she moaned, shutting her eyes tightly and trying to calm the wild pace of her throbbing pulse. After what he had thought . . . accused her of, she would be mad to surrender her love to him. And yet her unstoppable longing was to do just that.

"Aria . . ." His persistent hands withdrew from her skirts, peeling her hands from her ears and capturing them. "Love me, Aria." The powerful thudding of his heart was suspended until her eyes slowly opened to reveal their crystal prisms of tears.

"I . . . do, Tynan." She spoke as if the admission was killing.

Jolting to life, Tynan's face nearly split with joy. He rolled to one side, dumping her half-bare bottom on the floor beside him and he pulled her against him, into the circle of his strong arms. "Oh, my sweetest . . . wife!" He overwhelmed her protest of surprise by half covering her body with his. Holding her head between his hands, he probed deep into her tear-glazed eyes, trembling with constrained exuberance. "You *do* love me?"

"Heaven help me . . . I do love you, Tynan," she choked, unable to see his reaction clearly for the wash of her tears. But his lips on hers relayed his joy, his total release, at her throaty confession. His kiss plunged deep into the core of her aching heart, and his hands, gentle upon her face, her hair, wove a healing charm.

Her hands came up to embrace him, to feel the familiar strength of his back, the reassuring hardness of his shoulders, and the sleek curve of his neck. She arched as his arms slipped beneath her, and she gave herself up to her feelings, trusting them, trusting him. It was too late to turn back.

Tynan's big hands cradled her head and he spent his passion upon her ripe lips, her shell-like ear, her alabaster throat, her silken breast. He wanted to devour her, to take her inside him, to hold her there forever.

His intensity fairly bruised Aria's lips, his weight above her made it difficult to breathe. But inside, she was soaring, lifted, freed. She loved this man, wanted him more than life itself, more than reason, more than breath. And whatever the consequences, she had given him the one last thing of value she had to give.

Hoarsely, she whispered the longing that came straight from her heart. "Love me, Tynan. Please love me as I love you."

The pressure eased above her, bringing her dazed eyes open. Tynan's eyes glowed silver as his sensual mouth formed the words, "I do, my love."

The parlor door jerked open and slammed back just at that moment, but Aria wouldn't have noticed if the trumpets of judgment had sounded. She clasped Tynan's dark head with her arms and poured the raw power of her exploding joy into her rapturous kiss. Though he felt he had explored and understood the depths of her uncommon passion, Tynan was stunned by the wild exuberance of her responses. Nothing pierced his consciousness but the overpowering love of the woman he had finally made his own.

Jamison stood in the doorway, flanked by gawking servants, Acre, and Levina. His shocked eyes flew over the entwined figures on the floor as Aria delivered that last, blistering kiss. Tynan covered her body except for one leg, which was propped, knee up and mostly bare, along his side. The state of their roused passions was all too clear in their wild, heedless kissing.

"Good God!" Jamison uttered, completely appalled.

Acre swayed past the Bostonian's paralyzed form and swung the doors shut with a red face and a bang. "It appears she don't need assistance after all, Jamison. She be doin' just fine."

Levina came to her senses and grinned delightedly, shooing

all but Jamison and Acre from the hall as she headed for the kitchens.

"But, he—she—they—" Jamison stammered and sputtered, feeling like the world's greatest fool. His shoulders slumped and he stalked to the foot of the great stairs, plopping down to hold his pounding head in his hands. Acre's wry chuckle was like the screech of fingernails on slate. "Damn his lucky hide. I hate him."

Acre's raspy laugh became a thigh-thumping guffaw, which pealed noisily about the elegant hall. Some echo of it penetrated the luxurious haze about Aria's senses and she breathed against Tynan's moist lips, "The floor is hard. I have a grand, soft bed upstairs." To his pleasure-glazed eyes she spoke like a promise, "My husband gave it to me."

Moments later, Tynan's boot kicked open the door of the parlor and he strode into the hall, bearing Aria in his arms. He stopped halfway to the stairs looking at the two figures slouched on the bottom steps.

"Merrill Jamison!" Aria's face colored furiously, but she couldn't help smiling with pleasure at seeing her friend again. She turned to Tynan, whose grin was catlike. "You didn't say he'd come back with you."

"You didn't give me a chance."

"Merrill, what's happened to your mouth? It's cut and swollen!" Aria squirmed slightly in Tynan's arms, but he ignored her hint to let her down.

"I . . . ah . . . banged it—on a board . . . in the stable." Jamison fingered his abused lip and jaw and didn't meet Tynan's gaze.

"Then I must talk to Franklin, first thing." She smiled warmly. "We can't have our dearest friends injured on account of our carelessness. You must be exhausted." She took in his dusty, disheveled state.

"I know I am," Tynan said pointedly, shifting her slightly in his arms.

"Then put me down, Tynan, I have a guest to see to." She colored more and self-consciously straightened her bodice.

"You have a husband to see to," Tynan reminded her audaciously, moving toward the steps.

"Stop!" She laughed, embarrassed by his flagrant intentions. Helplessly she looked at Acre over Tynan's shoulder as they mounted the stairs. "See Levina puts him in the front bedroom and heats water for his bath!"

Twenty-eight

Aria watched Tynan's heavily muscled body disappear inch by inch into the steaming tub of water and she snuggled back on the huge, draped bed, sighing with lush contentment. Every movement of his frame held her with unashamed fascination. The light glinted on his damp shoulders, played lovingly over his squarely chiseled features, and was absorbed in the loosened raven hair that framed his face. She wanted to absorb the very essence of him into her.

Satisfaction pulsed through her veins, counterpoint to the hum of expectation that would not still within her. Her hand drifted lazily down over her loosened laces and half-revealed breasts, her raised skirts, bare hip, and stocking-clad leg, reading in their hopeless state the details of Tynan's explosive need for her . . . and hers for him. Pausing only to lock the doors, he had taken her to their bed and covered her with his massive warmth, unlocking her deepest passions as he wove his special magic beneath and through her very clothing. There was no time for restraint, no need for it. Together they joyously sought release of the yearning they bore for each other, writhing, pressing, touching—consumed and surrendering.

Aria's lips curled at the ends, madonnalike, as her eyes glazed again with fresh memory. Over and over he had said it: "I love you, Aria . . . my love, Aria . . . my beautiful, lovable Aria . . ." It had become a litany of caring, a nurturing, healing balm for her sore heart. He loved her. She knew it now with every fiber of her being, exploring it and exulting in it. She wriggled amid the soft linens, feeling deliciously loved and wanted.

When she finally dragged herself from the bed, Tynan watched her sway toward him wantonly, her hair tousled, her bodice open, and her plain woolen skirts rumpled and raised nearly to her waist at one side. She paused before him, near the fire, her eyes smoky and flirtatious. She was like a golden gypsy in the gilded afternoon light. He felt himself warming to her again and grinned with lusty wonderment. He'd never seen her quite like this, openly and frankly seductive.

"I don't know when a tub has ever felt quite so good," he managed thickly, unable to take his eyes from her. "I've ridden almost straight for a week. Jamison was ready to wring my neck, trying to keep pace."

"Tynan?" She hurried abruptly to the side of the tub and knelt by it, clutching its rolled edge. "Your face, your eye. What happened to you?" Her fingertips caressed the blue-green swelling about part of his left eye, and he winced, pulling them away and kissing each one ardently as he shrugged.

"Nothing really . . . that board . . . in the stable. I found it, too. Treacherous things, boards." His eyes glinted mischievously and Aria jerked her hand away to swat him and the surface of the water simultaneously, splattering him.

"Strange that you and poor Merrill should suffer the same mishap." She eyed him suspiciously. "Do you think that wicked board is apt to do further damage?"

"I doubt it. I think we'll both avoid it in the future." Tynan reached a wet hand out to run a finger across her collarbone. Water from it trickled in glassy ribbons down her bare chest and into the valley between the soft mounds of her revealed breasts.

She shivered as the water cooled, and her concern was instantly replaced by warmer considerations. Tynan saw the darkening throb of the centers of her emerald eyes and it nearly took his breath. He reached for her but she was already moving away, a capricious tilt to her lips.

She turned to her wardrobe and drew a filmy garment from it, laying it on one of the stuffed chairs near the fire. She began slowly and quite consciously to shed her already loosened dress and petticoats. Each garment seemed to leave her skin reluctantly as she fastened her entrancing gaze on Tynan. It was the most natural and alluring seduction, disrobing before her husband's fascinated eyes. And it worked its spell on them both.

Knees weakening, Aria sat on the chair, clad only in her chemise, to roll her silk stockings down and remove them. When she finally pulled her chemise over her head, Tynan's breath stopped in his throat. She stood and pulled the thin glaze of the nightdress over her curving form and tied the lacy bodice with trembling hands. As she walked to the vanity table to get her brush, the sleek fabric brushed her bare skin, caressing it.

"Where did you get that?" Tynan groaned as he stared hungrily at the translucent gown. His face grew dusky and his throat tightened.

"You had it made for me in Raleigh." She sank onto the chair and her brush paused midstroke.

"I did? A fit of madness. No sane man would inflict such torture on himself willingly." His hot admiration feasted on the lush lines of her half-revealed body.

"It doesn't have to be torture." Aria felt her stomach slide into her knees with anticipation. It was an invitation she knew he would not refuse.

Hastily he finished soaping and ducked into the water to rinse. Then he rose like Poseidon, rivulets of water caressing his powerful, hard frame as they slithered like sea minions back toward their realm. He stood watching her eyes as they drank in his male beauty, then he stepped out onto the thick rug.

Aria rose and picked up his toweling, but instead of handing it to him, she stepped close and opened the thirsty cloth, running it slowly, gently over his chest, his arms, his hips. When he stayed her hands, she looked up into his glowing eyes and smiled lovingly.

"You've maided me before. Let me do this for you."

Feeling a little awed, a little foolish, he allowed her to dry him. When she finished, he pulled her into his arms and unashamedly displayed his wonder for her to see. "Not three hours ago, you would have accused me of treating you like a lowly servant for that."

"But you didn't order me; you didn't even ask. If I serve you now, it is because I want to, not because you proclaim it your right. Perhaps I resisted you for so long because you always tried to take . . . you didn't let me *give* anything."

"Except your honesty . . . and the delights of your beautiful body." His hand flew over the silky dressing that enticed him so. "You were very generous with your passions, sweetest. It made me crave even more of you."

"That part of me was always your staunch ally and a traitor in my camp. Perhaps I wouldn't have been so stubbornly set against you if you hadn't been so stingy with your honesty."

"You must realize, sweetest . . . honesty with a woman is a novel idea for a man of my position."

"But honesty with *this* woman is required before you assume any position with me."

"Any position?"

"Any position." She giggled.

"Then *honestly,* Aria . . . I cannot wait another minute for you!" He scooped her up in his arms and carried her to their bed, plopping her in the center of it and covering her sweetly molded form with his unyielding hardness.

Aria breathed him into her with his kiss, luxuriating in his weight, the intimate press of him over every square inch of her. She held his hot face between her cool hands and licked and teased his lips until they twitched with need. Then she plunged joyously into his hungry, demanding kiss.

He shifted slightly to one side and set his hands to cover her instead as his lips enjoyed the familiar curve of her throat, the creamy valley between her breasts, then the taut buds of her tingling nipples. His touch was like burning embers, making her arch and shudder with shafts of searing pleasure. And when it was withdrawn, her shimmering eyes flew open.

"Here, love," he rolled onto his back beside her and effortlessly pulled her up above him. "I don't want to crush you."

Aria opened her mouth to protest, but a wayward thought struck her and she kissed him with all the tantalizing promise she could muster. Then she moved up to sit astride his chest, shaking her tumbled fall of honey-colored hair about her. Her eyes were dark, tempting emeralds with fire at their centers. Her creamy shoulders were bare and her filmy rose-colored gown had slipped down them, now held in place only by the ripe swell of her eager breasts. She wriggled seductively on her warm seat.

"I have you just where I want you, Tynan Rutland," she whispered huskily, stroking his square shoulders.

"And where is that?" He recognized this play as what they had begun on the floor of the parlor and his most lecherous grin appeared. "In your bed? Between your thighs? At your mercy?"

"All of those," she murmured breathlessly, feeling his hands creeping up her legs under her nightdress as they had beneath her skirts. Only this time, her eyes closed and she made no move to check his amorous explorations. Soon his stroking palms, his questing fingers made her writhe atop him. Knowing he watched her sensual undulations somehow heightened her desires and she sought his burning gaze with hers.

One hand quested higher, above her waist, sliding beneath the translucent gown to capture her breast and mold it. It was exquisite torture, arousal so keen, so total that it approached pain. Slowly she was being lifted toward that plane of pleasure where only Tynan could take her. Sliding down his body, she felt his rippling shudders of desire and leaned forward to embrace and kiss him. He pushed her farther down and Aria felt him entering her, throbbing with each pulse of his need.

Instinctively, she began to move on him, imitating his strong sure thrusts that so often took her into broad realms of uncharted pleasure. Then she sat partway up, watching his face, the convulsive tightening of his awesome muscles as he met her movements. He held her bottom tightly to him, reaching farther, higher inside her, filling, expanding her. He ground against her, arching and groaning her name as she rasped his.

And as reality was obscured in a blinding bright haze, she felt the core of her bursting into a million white-hot splinters that shot through her nerves, her muscles, her being. She gasped and arched and plunged, shuddering again and again. And she and Tynan were one, mingling, drifting together— knowing each other and known to each other without words, without caution, without pretense.

Aria's eyes were wet, her heart was full as Tynan rolled to his side, resting next to her gently on the bed. She saw nothing but his beloved face and the fulfillment he found in her.

"Oh, Tynan—" She stroked the hot planes of his face and smiled sadly. "Why did it have to take so long? Why couldn't you have loved me right away?"

"Perhaps I did, Aria, if some part of this passion I bear for you may pass for love. I knew I wanted you from that first night. . . . I just didn't realize how much of you it would take to satisfy me. I want all of you, sweet Aria, even your anger when it is necessary."

He captured her tired hand in his and spent soft little kisses on it, pausing to finger the emerald ring he had given her. His frown recalled the circumstances of its being there. "I have regrets with you, Aria—"

Her fingers touched his lips, forbidding him. "Then mine with you will cancel them. Our past does not matter, except that it brought us to today. Be as honest with me as you are loving, Tynan, and I'll want for little."

He drew her fully into his arms and she snuggled tiredly against him. "I love you, Aria." He turned her chin up so that he could see her eyes. "You do understand that our children will have no title . . . no part of what I left behind in England? I would not have you think otherwise, and someday begin to resent—"

"Tynan—" her eyes were lidded with pleasant exhaustion, "I don't want what you've left behind you. I know it must hurt you to know you'll never see your home and family again. I have . . . lost things dear to me as well. But we can make our own family, our own home, here on Oberon. And in time, it may not hurt as much."

Strange dampness misted his eyes briefly and he blinked it away, hugging her with crushing thoroughness. "You fill my heart, Aria and I have no room for pain anymore."

She smiled dreamily and kissed his square, stubborn chin. The arch of her foot rubbed the raspy curve of his powerful leg and she nuzzled against his chest. "I love you, Tynan."

When he blinked that stubborn moisture away once more, he raised his head to look at her. Her eyes were closed, and her breathing was a whisper of satisfaction. Contentment seeped through his exhausted body and he gave his swirling thoughts over to sleep.

Hours later, Tynan awoke to voices, muffled, but faintly familiar in the gloom of his darkened bedchamber. The bed about him was empty, but he heard Aria's voice and relaxed immediately.

She was dressed in a fetching emerald velvet gown that was not yet laced at her back and her hair was gathered over her shoulder into a heavy, twisted rope. Admitting a young serving woman with a tray, she felt his gaze on her back and turned. Her eyes glowed adoringly as they lighted on his sleepy, rising form.

"Wake up, husband." She poured from the pots on the tray and carried the cup to him, extracting a kiss before she put it in his hands. "Supper will be served soon, and I thought you might like something to waken you." She settled on the side of the bed to watch him draw from the cup.

"I'm starved." He smiled, savoring the delicious vapors of the creamed and sweetened coffee, laced with chocolate. "How did you know I like my coffee with a bit of chocolate?"

"I made it my business to learn." Aria smiled and ran an impudent finger up his sheet-covered leg.

"Indeed you have," he grinned knowingly and glanced at her inquisitive hand.

"I meant to have dinner here, in our rooms, but then there's Merrill. I'd not want him to feel unwelcome . . . intruding."

"Even when he is," Tynan quipped, burying his nose in the cup again.

"Even when he is," she echoed, smiling. "We've ignored him disgracefully all afternoon. I can imagine what he must be thinking."

"Yes," Tynan grinned wickedly, "so can I." He pulled her toward him and nuzzled that sweet spot at the base of her throat.

Across the room a throat cleared and Aria blushed and pulled away. "Behave yourself."

"Who's that?" Tynan squinted past her and frowned as she turned back to her dressing table.

"My maid, the one you gave me," Aria answered, feeling his surprised scrutiny as Levina pulled her laces and tied them. "Levina. Surely you remember." Levina dropped a proper, straight-backed curtsy in his direction and led her mistress to a seat before the vanity table.

"I don't remember her like this." Tynan cocked his head, studying the tall, buxom girl dressed in soft woolens, a lace-rimmed mob cap, and a long, pristine apron. Her garments, her movements, her manners, seemed changed—refined. "What's happened about here in my absence?"

"You'll see. There have been many improvements here in the last month." Aria turned on her bench and grinned at

Levina, who smiled smugly and took a brush to her hair. "And not all of them were to fences and barn roofs"

At supper that night, Jamison watched their covert glances, their secretive touches beneath the grand dining table, and felt like a fifth wheel on a wagon, a very foolish fifth wheel. How could he have been so wrong about something so obvious as what was between them?

"Really, Rutland, you should have stayed away longer. I swear, Aria has this place half in shape already. You wouldn't know the gardens . . . and even the barns are neat as a pin."

"I know." Tynan smiled his most adoring smile at his wife.

"Dammit all, how could you? You haven't been out of the house since we got here—" Jamison's irritation flamed briefly before he reddened and pulled himself back under control.

"You just told me." Tynan managed to look surprised at his outburst. "And I know Aria has a way of getting things done. Look at the house." He waved a generous hand about them. "I could have sworn there were piles of household stuff everywhere when I arrived. But it's all been set to rights now. I don't know how she managed it when she . . . had so little time this afternoon." His grin was pure lechery.

Aria colored hotly and opened her mouth to protest, but shut it immediately. If anyone understood Tynan's rakish humor, surely it would be Jamison. Flushed and trying to avoid Tynan's too thorough gaze, she buried her interest in her food.

"Then I take it, you've settled the matter of the slaves, along with everything else." Jamison glanced from Tynan to Aria, whose rosy face came up in surprise.

"Truthfully, we have not spoken about it." Aria put down her fork and knife and looked squarely at Jamison, trying to discern his motive for broaching that sticky subject now. "But Tynan is a reasonable and just man. I know he will hear what I have to say and see the wisdom of it. He trusts my judgement, you see, as I have faith in his. That is the way of things in a true marriage."

Tynan watched Aria's calm declaration and found himself drawn inescapably to her adroit logic. If he had thought of dismissing her explanations, he could not now. In her own sweet, wifely way, Aria had just challenged him to live up to her glowing summation of him and he would not disappoint her. After all, that was what a good marriage was about, wasn't it? And if he wanted anything in this life, he wanted this marriage with Aria.

The next morning, Tynan found the household aflurry and Aria in the kitchens before breakfast, ordering the polishing of the silver and laying plans with the cook for a celebration.

"Up at the crack of dawn and already cracking the whip," he said from the kitchen doorway he filled, standing with his fists propped at his waist, watching the bustling about his wife.

"Good morning!" Aria beamed, hurrying to his side and lifting her face for his lips to brush. "I thought to let you sleep yet awhile." She turned him about and, with a final word to the cook, hurried him into the hall toward the dining room. "I meant to bring you coffee later, to . . . wake you myself."

"I think the cold bed woke me." He pulled her into his arms, glancing about, and kissed her with exhilarating thoroughness. "I thought after yesterday *and* last night's romp, you'd need more time to recover," he murmured against her pliant mouth.

"Your loving doesn't exhaust me, Tynan." She blushed prettily. "Sometimes it invigorates me . . . leaves me humming inside and makes me want to get up and do things!"

His strange smile and the twinkle in his eye as he squeezed her let her know he understood.

"Besides—I have a raft of things to do. Do you know what day this is?" she asked, strolling beside him through the arched doorway into the dining room. "December twenty-third. Two days until Christmas! With you gone . . . I made no special plans. But now you're home." She smiled up into his quizzical face, "and I think I feel more like celebrating. And I must have your help."

"*My* help?' He laughed, seating her at the large, linen- and silver-decked table and taking his seat at its end, beside her. "What can a mere husband do?"

She picked up the silver coffee pot to pour, but put it down again, softening visibly. "Tynan, I want to hear about your home . . . and the customs you practiced at Christmas. I thought it would be good to institute some here, but I have no idea where to start. In some ways we're still strangers to each other."

He watched her love rising into her eyes and he covered her hand with his, becoming pensive.

"What if you discover things about me you don't like?"

Aria met his question fairly, knowing there were questions yet unspoken that craved answers. And with only a slight twinge of conscience for avoiding them yet again, she answered truthfully. "Then we shall deal with them honestly . . . and I will still love you."

Tynan nodded thoughtfully and a slow smile crept over his face. "Christmas . . . at home? That was a long time ago."

"We decorated the whole house with pine boughs and went to church in the morning." She urged him with her own memories. "The Parnells and other friends always called in the afternoon, and of an evening my mother would play the pianoforte and sing—" The rest caught in her throat and she quickly poured the coffee to mask her sudden discomfort. Tynan watched her inner struggle with the past.

"We had a Yule log and gifts," he declared, pushing his chair back to rise. "We always exchanged gifts . . . then stuffed ourselves on the finest goose and plum pudding and the richest nut tarts and chocolates. We were shameful little gluttons . . ." He grabbed her hand and pulled her up and along after him. "Where are my things . . . that I brought back from Philadelphia?"

"In our sitting room . . . I think." She kicked her skirts aside as she hurried in his wake. "What's happened? What are you doing?"

"I'm just tutoring you in the customs of my family," he said over his shoulder as he pulled her up the main staircase. "Isn't that what you wanted?"

"Good morning." Jamison paused at the top of the steps to wait for them, puzzlement replacing his smile.

"Don't wait breakfast for us," Tynan informed him without a pause, pulling Aria after him toward their rooms. She just managed an apologetic, scarlet-faced look at their guest before Tynan closed the door behind them.

He knelt over a pile of leather bags and bundles, sorting through them until he found a long cylinder wrapped in soft chamois leather. He seated her on the settee and squeezed down beside her, putting the object in her hands.

"What is this?" She colored with confusion.

"Your first Christmas present from me." He raised an arm along the back of the settee and trickled one finger up the slim column of her neck. "I went to some difficulty to get it . . . it's one of a kind, I'm quite sure."

Staring at him, she began to fumble with the string and eventually succeeded in untying it. Peeling back the soft leather covering, she found a roll of stiff canvas and sent him a puzzled look.

"Open it . . . but gently. It's old," he urged.

Slowly Aria unrolled the generous canvas to reveal familiar strokes and background colors. Then came a familiar wig and sharp, wizened features, set with piercing gray eyes that only now seemed very like those that watched her unroll the portrait.

"My grandfather!" she whispered, robbed of volume by astonishment. "Where on earth? *How* did you . . ."

"I rode through Chesterfield County on the way back. It was just a stroke of luck that this was not sold off."

Looking from her stem progenitor to the puzzle of her husband's handsome face, she felt her heart swelling inside her, blocking all words. Tears gathered to make bright prisms of her eyes.

"I thought to make you feel more at home here with some things from your Royal Oaks . . . a family portrait from your *own* family, a stableman, a maid—even an ill-trained one. I wanted this to be your home, Aria . . . our home."

"It will be," she murmured huskily, setting the rolled canvas gently on the floor beside her and throwing her arms about his strong neck. "No . . . it already is." Her lips fitted perfectly in the contours of his as her form melted in the closing circle of his arms. Their kisses grew salty from her tears and deepened with growing joy.

"But I have no gift for you," Aria murmured breathlessly, pulling back to look into his loving face. Satisfaction pulsed in his eyes.

"You have already given me all I could want or need, sweetest. Except perhaps . . . one thing."

"Yes?" Her heart stopped for a brief moment as the heat of his face flowed into hers and his need sharpened.

"Give me a child."

"Yes . . ." She melted against his big body, stirring with hunger for him and for his heart's desire, ". . . oh, *yes!*" Her kiss was ecstasy distilled and it was an act of prodigious self-control for him to leave her lips long enough to speak.

"I think perhaps I can wait until after breakfast."

Twenty-nine

"Are you sure I look all right?" Aria sat back in the dimming glow of the carriage window and opened her warm cloak to straighten the lace and piping that rimmed her snug, seafoam-green bodice. Tynan turned on the seat beside her and captured her fidgeting hand in his.

"You look positively delicious." Tynan's deep tones were intimate and teasing all at once.

"I don't want to look delicious." She seemed truly scandalized. "I want to look . . . gracious and well gowned and . . . *proper.*" She glared meaningfully at him and he laughed, leaning back and laying her captive hand on his hard, velvet-covered thigh and covering it determinedly with his own.

"This is the very same woman who has climbed to the top of my tobacco barn roofs, has worn callouses on her hands rearranging furniture, and grubs brambles out of her flower gardens with her own hands." He managed an exaggerated, long-suffering-husband look at Jamison, who was grinning at him from the seat across. "But give her a party and she's adrift on a sea of frippery, scuttled by doubts and indecision."

Aria was glad the dimming light in the glassed carriage hid her heightened color as Jamison joined Tynan in hearty laughter . . . at her expense. "Laugh all you will, Tynan Rutland." She lifted her chin, pouting. "But this is more than just a party for the new year. This is our first chance to meet the people among whom we'll make our lives, and I want everything to go well. I want them to like us."

"Curious notion, liking one's neighbors, don't you think, Jamison?" Tynan winced and brought an elegantly cuffed hand up to stroke his square chin.

"Purely colonial," Jamison muttered pompously, breaking into a grin. "I just hope some of your neighbors have daughters that don't take all their meals from a trough."

"Oh, I knew we shouldn't have brought him!" Aria wailed in good-natured horror. "Tomorrow morning we'll have a score of outraged fathers on our doorstep demanding retribution."

Tynan laughed and slipped his arm about Aria's velvet-cloaked waist, drawing her closer. He watched the sparkle of excitement in her eyes and the rosy sheen of her lips and fell in love all over again. She was everything a man could possibly want . . . a wildly sensual and responsive mate, a fair-but-demanding manager of his household, a spur to his higher impulses, a balm for his disappointments, and a source of unconditional love . . . and forgiveness. In the last week they had talked and loved and worked—even argued—and through her, the doors of life's limitless possibilities had seemed to open for him. Instead of narrowing his views, restricting his freedom, curtailing his pleasures, he found his marriage a vehicle for expanding them all. And it was only Aria's specialness that made it possible . . .

Aria relented and took advantage of Jamison's discreetly averted gaze to press closer against Tynan's side and gaze lovingly into his light-filled eyes. Her heart skipped a beat with the heady effect of his square, sensual features. Her anxiousness melted in the warmth of his consummate self-assurance. In the last week, the man she now owned as husband had blossomed forth all around her. Sharing the intimacies of their light-filled days and long, sensuous nights, he revealed to her the man she had longed for, dreamed of touching. He was strong, fair-minded, and capable of incredible tenderness. Despite his stubborn will, he listened to her, sought her opinions, lent her aid or authority where needed. He was a man who was sure enough of himself to enjoy a woman's strengths and to encourage them.

She sighed, betraying her anxiety as they neared John Halifax's plantation. Tynan was not a man to mince and measure his words for the sake of appearances. She recalled his warning by the stream that day he left for Philadelphia. Indeed, it had never been far from her mind. There would be people hereabouts who resented the intrusion of a wealthy English nobleman into local society . . . some might be present tonight. She could only be on her guard and pray that Tynan exercised restraint in greeting their new neighbors.

The light of banks of costly beeswax tapers flooded them as they entered the center hallway of John Halifax's elegant Georgian home. Guests decked in rich color and texture flowed through the hallway, moving from parlor to salon, pausing to scrutinize the latest arrivals. Low strains of familiar music pulsed on the air, and laughter tinkled above the recognizable swish of silks and brocades. Aria ran a surreptitious hand down the side of her panniered satin moire skirts. She checked her ivory fan at her wrist, smoothed her long, white kid gloves, and took a deep, bodice-filled breath. A low rumble of amusement brought her rose-stained face up to Tynan's wry smile. His eyes flew purposefully over her honey-golden hair and her breasts which nestled appealingly in a bed of elegant laces. The immediate silvering of his eyes was all the mirror she needed.

"Your lordship!" The genial John Halifax greeted them enthusiastically. "Welcome to Greenwood. And Lady Rutland—how perfectly ravishing you are this evening." His dark eyes glowed with pleasure as he took Aria's gloved hand and brushed it reverently with his lips. "Of a certain, you'll reveal how paltry are my powers of description, my lady. Everyone is agog with expectation of your arrival."

"You are too kind, Mr. Halifax," Aria demured, catching the gleam of proprietary pride in Tynan's eye.

But it was as John Halifax had forewarned. People stared unabashedly at the handsome English earl who had chosen to take up residence among them in the midst of the colonial revolt. The commanding air of the dark master of Oberon and the fair beauty of his colonial-bred wife were an awesome spectacle.

Some stiffened and reddened irritably when Tynan and Aria were introduced, some melted and gushed and fawned. But whatever their reactions, their attentions were soon riveted upon the earl's stunning young wife, whose sparkling green eyes and musical voice testified to the grace and charm underlying her rare blond beauty. The rigid formalities they observed in Tynan's formidable presence were moderated by Aria's radiant good will and naturally gracious manner.

Deborah Halifax proved to be a slender, brown-haired woman, as engaging as her amiable husband. As soon as possible, she drew Aria away from Tynan's side and into an eager group of ladies, who plied her with questions about the rumored renovation of the once magnificent Oberon. Aria explained as best she could and found herself inviting them to call for tea in the afternoon. An awkward silence fell and Deborah leaned a bit closer to make an explanation while the others watched expectantly.

"You see, we've all purged our houses of that herb . . . vowing to have none of it until we're freed from British tyr—" She stopped abruptly, seeing the heightened color of Aria's face.

"Until the conflict is over," Aria graciously supplied.

"Yes." Deborah sighed silent relief, though the air was strained.

"I believe the North Carolina ladies are quite famous for their tealess 'teas.' I confess, I cannot always persuade my husband from it, but my preference is always for coffee or chocolate." There was a general easing about the circle and

Aria managed a smile, understanding that this was but her first test of the evening.

"Lady Rutland—" A short, dowdy matron in blue called her attention. "I understand you are Virginia-born. Who are your family?"

"My family . . . is gone now." She felt a surprising wave of loss and her pulse began to throb irregularly. How much could she safely reveal to these women? "My father was George Dunning of Royal Oaks."

"George Dunning?!" the woman echoed, drawing a murmur from the others. "Of course we've . . . heard . . . of what happened."

Aria's heart tumbled into her stomach. If they'd heard of George Dunning, then they also knew why he was killed and his home was burned. And they were not likely to welcome his daughter into their "tealess" midst, whatever her own sympathies.

"Deplorable . . . especially to us who truly support . . . the cause . . . of liberty," Deborah declared upon the strained silence, drawing Aria's quizzical look.

"My niece, who is staying with us, is from Chesterfield County, Virginia." A pleasant-faced older woman beside Deborah took up the unraveling exchange with sympathetic skill.

"Oh?" Aria felt her throat tightening, "That was my home as well."

"You don't say!" The woman seemed to light from within and craned her neck to stare about the room. "Now where is that girl? I came ahead to help Deborah and she was to come with my Henry—I'll find her." She rose and bustled off, somehow signaling the end of the conclave and freeing the chilled conversation.

Tynan stood in the group of gentlemen nearby, and as by some natural evolution, the groups merged just then at their border. Tynan's tall, broad-shouldered frame was the masterful focus of the questioning under way.

"And what do you plan to do at Oberon your lordship?"

"I plan to breed, sir." Tynan's deep voice sallied forth above the ladies' chatter. His roguish face caught Aria's widening gaze with a wry smirk. ". . . *horses and heirs.*"

A titter of shock ran through the ladies, and the men coughed or buried their surprise in their drink. A few dared laugh aloud and received one of Tynan's dazzlingly rakish grins for their courage.

Aria's face drained; she knew well that every move, every word they uttered, was scrutinized in light of Tynan's noble rank. Bold, rakish remarks could hardly endear them to this suspicious crowd of colonial patriots.

"Well, you know what is said—" She turned slightly to the ladies, who were staring at her. " 'The cock does the crowing, but it's the hen that delivers the goods,' " she quipped.

A gale of feminine laughter rolled forth and Tynan frowned suspiciously, letting her know he had not heard her riposte, but recognized its success.

"Here she is, Lady Rutland." The proud aunt returned just then with her niece in tow. "My niece, Gillian Parnell."

Aria whirled about on her chair, grasping its back for support of her waffling senses. Behind her chair stood her best girlhood friend, Gillie Parnell.

"Gillie?" She sprang to her feet, her face bright with the joyful shock.

"Aria . . . ? You're the lady?" Gillie's eyes flew wide and for a moment she was paralyzed. Then she grabbed Aria's hands and fought to contain her eager astonishment.

"Yes!" Aria found her tongue and squeezed Gillie's hands with tightly compressed happiness. "Oh, Gillie—how *good* to see you again!" Instantly she was aware of the score of faces, etched with curiosity, that watched them. She turned a brightly flushed face on Gillie's aunt and explained: "Gillian and I have been friends nearly all our lives. When I left my home, I thought never to see her again. You must please excuse us," she nodded to the circle of ladies, "we have so much to talk about."

"Oh, yes, please," Gillie echoed, starting to pull her along toward the nearest door.

A murmur of stunned agreement ran through the group, and Aria's face lit with delight as she glimpsed Tynan's wry smile. Gillie pulled her into the main hall and, finding it crowded, headed for the main stairs and whatever rooms above were set aside for the ladies.

"Oh, Aria," Gillie squeaked, giving way to her emotions and hugging Aria tightly as soon as they were away from curious eyes in the upper hallway. "I can't believe it's you . . . and a real *lady!* How grand! And how wonderfully elegant you look."

"And you, too, Gillie!" Aria's voice clogged with emotion. "I can't even see a single freckle! Can you know even a small bit of how I've missed my home . . . and you?"

"I do know." Gillie paused, her eyes luminous with a border of sudden tears. "For I miss my home the same. So much has happened, Aria, and so little of it good . . ."

"Then come, we'll find a place to talk and you must tell me everything."

They found an empty bedchamber and settled on the side of the draped bed, each reluctant to release the other's hand for fear she might vanish.

"Two months ago Papa sent me to stay with Aunt Mattie . . . he sent us to a different relative, young Howard, Lizzie, and me. These are hard times for him. His practice has gone down and our land cannot support us all by farming. And the county has changed, Aria. There's a madness in the air; the war is like a fever . . . stirring tempers and passions to suspicion and resentment on every hand. A lot of families aren't speaking and old ties are broken in bitterness. Suddenly it wasn't enough to remain neutral, to try to maintain some semblance of reason. However you spoke someone was offended . . ."

"Oh, Gillie, I'm so sorry." Aria felt a shiver of unwelcome remembrance. The pain, the anxieties of her last days in Chesterfield County, washed over her afresh. And the war of revolt she had distanced herself from seemed no longer remote, but a force to be faced . . . here in her new home as well. The thought sent a chill over her bare shoulders and she shrugged physically to rid herself of its oppressive influence.

"I thought by now you'd be well on your way into Robert Burdette's household," she tried a pleasanter topic.

Gillie flushed violently and lowered her eyes to hide her discomfort at the mention of her former beau's name.

"Mr. Burdette ceased to call. I have not seen him for months."

"That, too? Oh, Gillie—" Aria's heart went out to her.

"It seems Robert's family had other thoughts after Rounder Sizemore's trial and hanging. Papa was furious in his prosecuting arguments. And I guess they found his politics and our falling prospects unsuitable."

Aria blinked.

"Rounder Sizemore's trial?!" she squeezed Gillie's hands tightly. The image of Lemuel Robertson's bullying, swaggering foreman burst on her beleaguered mind. Her breath stopped in her throat. "He was put on trial? Hanged? What for?"

"For barn burning, Aria . . . and killing." Gillie's young face shared Aria's pain. "I guess you couldn't have known. Sheriff Gilbert finally caught him and his rabble of cutthroats burning the barns of some small farmers. Shot and killed one of the farmers in plain daylight. He had joined up the militia not a fortnight before and was made a sergeant straightaway. So when he came for trial, it was quite a brouhaha. Some seemed to think since he was a militiaman, he should be let off with no more than a good flogging. But Papa told them what for—shouted the injustice of it, called them hypocrites, the lot of them. And before Rounder was led to rope, he bragged before the magistrate himself about killing your papa, too."

Aria was paralyzed by the news. Her father's killer had been caught and punished after all. Though the memories this news conjured in her were painful, she welcomed it. It was one more bit of her past laid to rest.

"Then justice was truly done," she whispered tightly, "except to your dear father."

"Papa tried to get credit when the crops were poor, but it was in suspiciously short supply. I listened while Mama and Papa argued." To Aria's unconscious frown, she defended herself. "I had to . . . If I didn't, I'd never know anything that was going on. It's how I knew the earl wanted to find you . . . I listened the day he came to Papa to inquire after you."

"He . . . came to your father? Looking for me?" Aria was surprised.

"And it was I who told him you had headed west. Papa would have been furious. But I was so overwhelmed when he told me about the proposal—"

"Proposal?" Aria straightened, unable to believe her ears. "He told you—"

"That he had proposed and that he wouldn't rest until he found you. He's so handsome, and so wealthy—I couldn't imagine why you didn't accept him and marry him right off, Aria. But now I see how hard a master pride can be. Losing your father and Royal Oaks together . . . now I think I see how you must have felt." Her eyes misted once more.

"But he found you and married you—that's all that matters. And to think I had a hand in it! Lady Rutland . . ." she looked a little sad and dream-eyed, "Countess."

Aria read Gillie's fertile imaginings in her expression and allowed the tension to drain from her shoulders. She'd not disrupt Gillie's romantic view of her "courtship" and marriage, for as Gillie said, she *was* truly married now and that was all that mattered.

"Your mother must be very pleased . . . is she with you now?"

"*No* . . ." It came out a bit too forcefully and a lump deposited itself in Aria's throat, resistant to her attempts to swallow it. That was one part of her past she had yet to come to terms with.

"Well, you must tell me all about it, Aria! Every delicious detail!" Gillie's face flamed with eagerness once more.

"Gillie—" Aria glanced toward the door, where voices were raised in the hallway, and shook oft the somber mood that had settled over her. "You must come to Oberon and stay with me—" She warmed to the idea even as she spoke. "You'll love it and I could certainly use the company. Tynan and Merrill have sport of me all too often. I could use an ally to even the score a bit."

"Merrill?"

"Merrill Jamison, Tynan's good friend, from Boston. I don't think you've met him." Aria rose and pulled Gillie up with her.

"Oh . . . but I have." Gillie's eyes danced with surprise.

They descended the stairs together and Aria paused in the doorway of the main parlor to search for Tynan's tall, distinctive form. He was nowhere to be seen and she clamped a hand on Gillie's arm, dragging her along as she began to search. Though she chatted with several new acquaintances, Tynan's absence from the parlor and the dining room settled a vague sense of uneasiness on her, progressively dampening her conversation and countenance. Her discomfort heightened as she noted that Jamison, their host, and several other prominent guests were also absent.

"Where can he be?" she muttered.

"You know how men are." Gillie sought to allay her concern. "They're off somewhere smoking those horrible cigars and arguing about something . . . like . . . politics . . . "She ground to a halt, seeing Aria's face drain of color.

"Come on—" Aria pulled her toward the main hallway and began to search for that inevitable conclave of male interest. And suddenly she knew the source of the dread that dried her mouth and chilled her hands. At the beginning of a short hallway leading toward the rear of the house, they were stopped by a clamor of male voices. Standing there, she imagined Howard Parnell, nervously fidgeting with his cuffs as he awaited her. Again, she heard her father's strident voice and felt that choking fear. She rushed down the hallway, oblivious to Gillie's urgent questioning . . . fighting the convulsive beating of her heart against her ribs.

She couldn't let it happen again . . . she couldn't! Tynan's deep voice wafted clearly above the others', halting her heart as it stopped her feet.

"—no reason I should proclaim my political sentiments to appease the feverish zeal of those who claim to represent the muse of 'freedom.' My views are my concern, no other's. It was my understanding that such coercion was the root of the current conflict with England." Tynan's words were heavy with disdain, and into Aria's mind's eye came a vision of his face as it must appear; his insolent posture, his imperious displeasure. It would reveal his loyalist sympathies the same as if he shouted them.

"Straddle your high an' mighty fence whilst you can, *your lordship*," came a hostile rejoinder. "When the time comes, you and your house will show yourselves for what you truly are—"

Aria jolted forward and quickly he was in view.

"When the time comes," Tynan bit out dangerously, his powerful frame coiled for response as his eyes showered silver sparks, "my house will be found on the side of right!"

"Gentlemen—" Aria breezed through the doorway and halted, cracking the tension of the room with a bolt of surprise. She forced a dazzling smile as her gaze slid over the assembly—past Jamison's tight expression to John Halifax's uncomfortable stare, and on to Tynan's dusky glower.

"Forgive my intrusion, good sirs, but you devastate the merriment of Mistress Halifax's lovely evening by withdrawing yourselves from our feminine company. And since I am foremost among the ranks of the forlorn, I have come to fetch you back." Her slender fan came up to flutter flirtatiously. She turned to Tynan and filtered a sultry sweetness through her long whorl of lashes as she slid gracefully to his side.

"Aria—" he growled, his face tight with constraint.

"And shame on you, husband—abandoning me just when my feet itch for dancing." Aria could see the muscle in his jaw flicking furiously. She knew just how dangerously thin a line she trod. He had never stinted in censuring her because of an audience before.

"Oh—be peevish with me later, Tynan," she entreated with coquetry carefully calibrated for their elegant audience. "You'll have years ahead to argue these deep and serious matters with your new friends. But you'll only have a new bride for a short while." Playing her role expertly, she took advantage of his taut silence and slipped her arm neatly through his, adding her silken touch to the coaxing of his senses. His broad shoulders slowly eased and the sharp angles of his square face softened a few degrees.

"A bride must be indulged, gentlemen, like an investment that must be carefully tended in order to realize its profits." Tynan's deep voice was perfectly controlled and perfectly impossible to read.

Claiming her narrow victory with a convincing lilt to her sigh, she extended her other hand to John Halifax as they started for the door. "And you, Mister Halifax, must promise me the next turn on the floor."

That dance was very like the last one of her maidenhood, stiff and silent in Tynan's masterful arms. He was an annoyingly graceful and attentive partner and the hollow exactness of every step, each too-perfect movement, warned of the turbulence brewing behind his controlled and genial facade. She managed a gracious mien through it, feeling her nerves being stretched by expectation. She was little relieved when Tynan relinquished her to John Halifax with a promissory glint in his cool gray eyes. Her gaze covertly trailed him about the grand salon while she pretended to enjoy the lively reel and her host's incisive wit.

"I daresay, he won't stray too far, Lady Rutland," Halifax

quipped with an amused light in his face as they whirled, hand to waist.

"Oh—" Aria flushed when caught and jerked her thoughts back to the steps. "I only . . ."

"Make no apologies, good lady. Your devotion to your husband is an inspiration to us all."

But before Aria could sort out the strange current of meaning in his remark, they were separated by the allemande and she was forced to concentrate on her steps again. By the end of the dance, she was besieged with invitations and declined them all, pleading exhaustion and thirst and plying her fan vigorously.

Peach-blushed with exertion, she chatted breathlessly with the ladies about her on her way toward refreshments in the dining room. But her beryl-green gaze scoured the room surreptitiously for Tynan's distinctive form. Just as she saw Merrill Jamison across the room, bending gallantly over Gillie's hand, Tynan's broad, dark-clad form loomed up to block the sight. Wary instinct raised under his too casual scrutiny and she stepped back, feeling his hand close on her wrist with steely persuasion.

"You seem overwarmed, wife." His voice was too level. "Let's find a cooler, less crowded place." He turned her firmly and thrust her along through the crowd toward the main hall. When she tried to resist by slowing in front of him, he pressed her forward forcibly with his big, muscular body and smiled at those they passed. Once in the main hallway, Aria's latent dread turned to true panic when Tynan ordered the manservant to fetch her cloak.

"I don't need a cloak to fetch a dram of punch." She lifted her head and started back for the dining room. But Tynan's ironlike grip on her arm jerked her back and she was spun around.

"What I have in mind may prove just as chilling," he declared, pulling her against him with an iron-thewed arm. She looked desperately around the hall and found it dismayingly empty.

When her cloak was settled on her shoulders, he pushed her toward the front doors, her elbow captive in his grasp. He half pulled, half pushed her along the portico and down the steps toward the cold, silent gardens. When they were a safe distance from the house, he released her arm and confronted her, his face dark with night shadows.

"Don't interfere in things which do not concern you, Aria." His voice lost some of its control.

"D-don't interfere?!" she sputtered. "Don't interfere when I see my family hurtling into the jaws of disaster again? You couldn't have proclaimed your Tory loyalties broader if you had shouted them from the rooftop!"

"My Tory loyalties?" he scowled, towering dark and forbidding above her.

"Your title, your manners, your arrogance—even your wretched tea—everything you are and do touts your royalist sympathies." Angry frustration boiled up inside her and her voice raised steadily. "Do you honestly think they don't know of your work for the redcoats?"

"The redcoats? What makes *you* think I work for the British?"

"I'm not an idiot, Tynan, contrary to your fond illusions. I know you were scouting or mapping or doing something for the British while pretending to 'hunt.' Why else would you need to make reports—and why else would you need to hide them from your colonial-bred wife? And I've overheard things—talk about what you're doing here in the colonies . . . enough to tell me what I hadn't already ferreted out of your motives." Her fists clenched at her sides as she fought the urge to throttle him—anything to make an impact on that stubborn, aristocratic head.

"That's why you charged into the library . . . to save them from witnessing the spectacle of my arrogant royalism?"

"To save you from setting yourself—us—against the entire

county! For all your denials, you're just as pigheaded, as arrogant, as my father . . . and just as royalist." Her voice choked with humiliating tears, and as they rose into her eyes, she grasped the lapels of his lordly coat in her fists and pounded them against his chest. "And I don't want to end by wearing your blood on my skirts like my mother did my father's!"

"Listen to me, Aria—" He grabbed her wrists and held them tightly, his eyes pale with ire as he shook her. "I'm *not* your damn father and I *don't* need your protection! Don't ever do that to me again."

"Have I offended your precious male pride, Tynan?" she blurted between gasps. "Surely no more than the king has—and yet you would see your adopted countrymen suffer again under his evil hand!"

"I *do not* work for George's henchmen," he growled furiously. "I told you what he did to my family. Did I lie? Or do you honestly think I'd betray the people I've chosen to live among into his vile control? Good God—I'd have to be a monster—" He ceased and straightened sharply as the full impact of her suspicions unfolded upon him. By withholding his involvement in the rebellion, he had put at risk the fragile trust that had finally flowered between them. In this reckless confrontation, it seemed to be shattering around them.

"Then what reports did you make in Philadelphia—if not to George's agents?" Her heart was twisting inside her, dreading the revelations to come and yet craving this last bit of honesty. Tynan shifted so that the moonlight fell across his features. She could see he struggled with something inside him, and her legs began to weaken beneath her.

"I reported to the continental delegates on alliances with the native tribes in the west." He spoke tightly, searching her reaction as his fingers tightened on her arms.

"The continental congress? *You* reported to the continental congress . . . on alliances with the Indians?" The turmoil of her heart swirled through her face in the dim light.

"Who better to make such a survey than a high-living English nobleman with a reputation for pursuing only his own pleasures?" he snorted a bitter laugh. "You and you alone know of my reasons for hating the king. And after what you experienced in our elegant camp life, can you imagine I would have thrashed about in the wilderness for five long months because I enjoyed the manly privations of the glorious hunt? My work for the congress is secretive because it must be so—and for a while yet. My rank admits me to loyalist society and my arrogant neutrality ensures I am not suspect of revolutionary activity. I move freely where others may not venture . . . including Philadelphia"

"You . . . *spy* for the colonies?!" She shook free of his hands and backed away, her pride stoked to full boil. "And you plotted . . . and kept all this from me . . . depositing me at Oberon like so much baggage while you trounced off to Philadelphia to ply your secret intrigues. And all without a word of counsel or explanation to your *wife*. How dare you!"

"*Aria*—I'll not answer to you for my convictions—"

"But you must on the matter of our marriage! You *lied* to me—"

"I *never* lied to you about my politics. . . . I never said anything about it at all!"

"Then it's the same as lying!"

Tynan lunged at her and grabbed her shoulders, pinning her to him with judiciously measured strength. She wrestled in his locked embrace, trying to raise her arms to stop her ears as he thundered just above her.

"Aria, I know you have reason to hate the colonial cause—because of it your home and your father were destroyed! What would telling you have done, except bring one more thing between us?"

"Hate the patriots' cause?" Aria stilled in his arms, astounded by the turn of his reasoning. "I don't hate the struggle for liberty. If you had been honest with me instead of plying your slippery charm to evade my questions, you'd have known that! I never shared my father's fanatical love of nobility—or the king. Unlike him, I had no illusions of my birthright. And I certainly had no desire to ensconce myself in some dreary English nobleman's household. My father's prideful delusions were what truly set our neighbors against us and cost us everything!"

Tynan stared down into her face and wondered at his own foolish conceits. His frantic hold on her eased.

"True . . . every word of it." He searched the angry luminescence of her face, and the squeezing about his heart suddenly abated. "But then, you always tell the truth."

"When given the chance!"

"If you're not angry that I work for the colonies, why are you so angry?" His treacherous hand came up to brush the smoothness of her temple and hair gently. Aria pulled back as far as his arms would allow and scowled fiercely.

"You honestly haven't a clue, have you? You deliberately kept it from me!"

"That I did." To Aria's surprise, he sounded none too pleased with himself for it. It was the closest thing to contrition she had ever witnessed in him. "But I did say there were things you did not know of me . . . things you might not like. Do you recall your response?"

"I . . . I said, I'd love you still." In the silence her heart slid down toward her knees.

"And do you?"

"Yes."

It was so soft, so wavery, that he had to convince himself he hadn't imagined it. But her glass-rimmed eyes lifted to his, pouring out the helpless truth of her love for him, love he now realized he had neither earned, nor deserved. He touched the shimmering ribbons on her cheeks and, for the first time in years, knew the aching awe of humility.

"I do love you, Aria." His words were strangely husky.

Her chin quivered and she stiffened, grabbing the lapels of his jacket and crushing them inside tight fists. She tried desperately to throttle him as he had sometimes done to her when she was obstinate.

"Oh-h-h!" she groaned in frustration when he scarcely bobbled. "Don't you ever do this to me again!" He thrust her a full arm's length away.

"You're not going to kick, are you?" He seemed genuinely worried.

"You deserve it!" she declared, using her hold on his lapels to pull him back to her. But as he let himself be drawn back, she rose onto her toes and slid her arms up about his neck. And her wild kiss was full of relief.

Minutes later, Tynan swept Aria into his arms and started for the line of carriages in the field nearest the house.

"What are you doing?" she protested, thrashing precariously.

"I'm taking you home, where we can do whatever it was that made you say *two hundred fifty-seven* last night." His heavy breath was evidence of his roused passions.

"You can't do that!" Aria had to summon her last grain of sanity against that tempting possibility. "Our host—we haven't taken leave—it's too early! And Merrill?"

"Hang Merrill," Tynan tossed off wickedly. "Let him find his own way home."

"Tynan!" Aria's protest was now punctuated with a small fist on his chest. *"No!"*

He stopped, holding her snugly against him, feeling her curves pressing strategically against him. "You really don't want to?"

"I know we shouldn't—it's the same result." Her adamant look melted into acceptance. "We'll have time later . . . lots of time . . ." she promised. "We'll have forever."

He sighed heavily and put her down, straightening her cloak and brushing at his much-abused coat front. "You show signs of becoming dangerously *proper* in years to come, wife. I tell you, it bodes ill. We'd best take the cool air for a few minutes before we go in."

Aria giggled agreement as her eyes scanned his manly form.

He glanced at her in surprise, and a rake's grin spread over his features.

"But then, maybe not *too* proper."

Thirty

The usual slow plodding of winter became a satisfying languor at Oberon in the weeks that followed. The evolving relationship between Aria and Tynan set an easy, restorative pace for the winter household, a comfortable mood extended into the stables, the workhouses, and the barns. The pair were never very far from each other—consulting, discussing, arguing, laughing. Their open fascination with each other drew many a fond wag of a head; it was such a stark contrast to the earlier days in their new home.

Oberon itself blossomed under the care they lavished upon it, growing more enchanting, more involving, with each passing week. Together they saw the first Oberon foal born, planned to rebuild the small mill on the stream, and repaired and refurbished the women's workhouse, the soaphouse, the spring house, and the kitchen. Hand in hand they walked through the cold winter gardens, seeing the bounty of possible beauty as though it were already realized. All around them and within them, they were realizing the "possibilities" that good Frederich Mueller had vowed were there.

Tynan consulted Aria frequently as he met with Franklin and Mr. Skeen to plan for the spring crops and to select sires for his mares. He never ceased to wonder at her thorough knowledge of horses and the vagaries of their care and temperament. With each new day, he appreciated more deeply his true fortune in having Aria. She smoothed and ordered the workings of the great house as if born to the task. And her even pleasantness of temper gentled the extremes of his own, improving the efficiency of his leadership over the entire plantation.

Day by day, Aria's passion for her strong, aristocratic husband broadened with admiration. Few men had Tynan's strength of will, or the deeply engrained sense of confidence that allowed him to acknowledge other men's—and women's—accomplishments freely. And increasingly, his strength seemed to have focus, direction, meaning. Instinctively, and perhaps unwittingly, he shared that strength with her and with all on Oberon.

Jamison stayed on with Tynan and Aria longer than he had planned, enticed by the arrival of Gillie Parnell for a visit. Copying Tynan's former style with regrettable authenticity, he had arrogantly flattered then affronted Gillie at the Halifax's New Year's party. And Aria and Tynan had reentered the merriment that night to find Gillie fuming and Jamison wearing the unmistakable outline of a feminine hand on his ruddy cheek. Aria and Tynan had exchanged looks of wonderment and had sagely shaken their heads at the follies of youthful passions gone awry.

Aria persuaded Gillie to come to Oberon only after assuring her Jamison was leaving before her arrival. Then, perversely, Merrill changed his mind about leaving, the very day before Gillie was to arrive. No sooner had her trunk been wrestled up the main stairs than Merrill appeared and Gillie turned to Tynan, demanding the use of his carriage back to her aunt's.

Merrill's stinging pride resulted in an unfortunate description of Gillie's aunt and Gillie naturally took offense at the terms "moldy" and "gorgon."

It took Aria half a bottle of good sherry to soothe her friend's ruffled nerves And the special supper Aria had planned for that night was an utter disaster. Then Cook was miffed at the untouched food, Tynan irritably dragged Jamison to the stables to prevent further confrontation, and Aria spent the shank of the evening moving Gillie's things into the far wing of the house since Gillie had declared she "couldn't close an eye, knowing *that beast* lurks nearby."

Aria settled, exhausted, into Tynan's arms that night and was surprised to feel the rumble of his chest beneath her head. To her inquiry, he tucked his chin and smiled mischievously down at her.

"I was just remembering Jamison this afternoon. I never knew him to be so perfectly obnoxious in his banter."

"Maybe Gillie brings out the best of the worst in him." She sighed, unable to keep her lips from turning upward at the ends "It happens like that sometimes . . . I ought to know."

"What happens like that?" His gray eyes lit with amusement.

"Love."

She nestled cozily on his shoulder and he soon forgot her teasing insight.

The tension continued unabated for the next week: Gillie exiting breakfast at the sight of Jamison, Jamison boycotting dinner in retaliation, both withdrawing from company of an evening—Gillie to her bedchamber and Jamison to the stables, where Tynan found him sharping poor Franklin, Acre, and Skeen at cards.

Aria began to despair of ever having peace in her house again. And out of desperation, she began to watch and to plot. Gillie's mannerisms provided a wealth of clues. She blushed and lowered her eyes when she encountered Jamison on the stairs or hurried past him to the table during the few meals they could not help but share. Her gaze fluttered inescapably in his direction even as she pretended to ignore his scandalous talk. And her vehement condemnations of him had a suspiciously familiar ring to Aria's ears.

Her deductions firmed to resolve when Tynan revealed similar observations of his much-altered friend. She determined that the direct approach to the problem was by far the best and enlisted Tynan's dubious support.

"What if you're wrong, Aria?" He was truly appalled by the temptation to indulge in something as low and nefarious as matchmaking. "Suppose they really do hate each other?"

"Then the worst that can happen is they'll have a long walk, be furious with us, leave immediately . . . and let us return to a bit of peace and tranquillity." She sat down on the arm of his chair and his arm curled warmly about her waist. "But *we're* not wrong."

"Either way, we stand to benefit . . ." he mused, gazing hungrily at her playfully parted lips.

"Either way," she affirmed.

The next morning Gillie and Aria set off on a leisurely ride and by a crafty twist of fate arrived at a secluded spring on Oberon's farthest corner just as Tynan and Jamison approached it. Aria greeted them warmly, noting with dismay that Gillie hung back and that Jamison refused to venture closer. Tynan dismounted and shot a convincingly no-nonsense look at Jamison.

"If you're going to ride *my* nags hell-bent for leather, the least you can do is give them water."

Jamison stiffened and urged his mount forward into the shallow water as Tynan splashed determinedly through it to give Gillie assistance down from her horse. When Tynan turned, Jamison was standing insolently on the opposite bank, hands on hips, raking Gillie with an insultingly thorough glare.

"Perhaps you have it backward, Rutland. I'm of the opinion, if a nag wants good treatment, she should give a good ride."

"Then spare us your opinions, if they are no more instructive than that," Gillie snapped, her eyes blazing. "The stream itself babbles more meaningfully."

Tynan looked at Aria, whose eyes rolled helplessly. The chances of a favorable outcome seemed dimmer with each passing moment.

Tynan swung quickly into his saddle and, unnoticed, reached

down for the lead of Jamison's mount. On the opposite bank, Aria reached for Gillie's, and in a flurry that knocked Jamison to one side and sent Gillie lurching out of the way with an indignant squeal, they kicked their mounts into motion. Aria managed a backward glance as they mounted the far rise and saw Gillie waving furiously and Jamison standing ankle-deep in the stream, hands braced angrily on hips.

Some distance later, they reined up and Aria shaded her eyes against the bright winter sun to search Tynan.

"What do you think?"

"I think," he pronounced judiciously, "that we shall be fortunate indeed if we're not garroted in our sleep."

Aria winced and he laughed with a clear, enchanting ring, putting out a hand to stroke her sun-blushed cheek.

They were home well before dinner and did not expect to see their feuding guests until midafternoon. But as the afternoon shadows grew long and melted into evening, Aria's worry deepened and she sought Tynan's advice.

"Another hour—" he gauged the sun's filtered strength through his library window—"and it will be dark. I'll take Franklin and Acre out to search for them if they're not back by then." And he gave Aria's knitted brow a husbandly kiss.

A search party was not required. Aria was first to see them, walking up the field road very slowly. They walked side by side, Gillie's skirts brushing Merrill's boots and Merrill's gaze touching Gillie's coppery, wind-ruffled locks. The day's tensions drained from Aria and she stood, smiling fondly as the pair approached the house, oblivious to the growing scrutiny about them.

Gillie finally greeted her, with mannerly absence of attention; and Merrill nodded, terse with preoccupation. Aria had to force herself not to follow. The tone of their light supper that evening was subdued, but lacked the crackling tensions of the previous week. And for the first time since Gillie had arrived, both guests spent the evening in the parlor with Aria and Tynan.

Just as they made to retire, John Halifax arrived to pay a late call and Aria seized the opportunity to have Gillie alone for a few moments. But her slyest inquiries went unsatisfied and she had to be content with the knowledge that she had done their friendship no irreparable damage by her little intrigue.

The next morning, Tynan and Jamison set off for Philadelphia, and in their absence Aria was grateful to have Gillie's presence and support. They rode, talked, stitched, and had the local ladies in for afternoon coffee. Gillie's effervescence and wit were entertaining and usually managed to divert Aria's worries about Tynan's safety for a while.

The long evenings were the most difficult, since they were the times that Aria had come to relish the sweet intimacy of Tynan's company and their growing friendship. In the time since Christmas, they had become closer, finding that familiarity somehow deepened the wonder of love between them. Their passions had ripened into lush flower—sometimes wild and uninhibited, other times achingly sweet and languid. And even in their occasional disagreements, their caring and respect for each other were evident; neither fled or quailed and neither kept a score of hurts and triumphs.

As the third week of their absence ended, Aria was often seen standing in the parlor, staring at the road on the distant hill, her longings and worries plain on her face. Gillie came to stand by her and take her hand reassuringly.

"They'll be fine, Aria. Men like Tynan . . . and Merrill . . . are more likely to *be* a danger, than to be *in* danger."

"So it's *Merrill,* is it?" Aria scrutinized Gillie with amused suspicion and Gillie flamed to match her burnished hair.

"Mister Jamison has asked me to address him so." Her gaze fluttered away uncomfortably.

"Um-m-m," Aria mused, seizing both the moment and Gillie's hand, drawing her to the sofa. "Just what else has he asked you, Gillie?"

She learned only bits and sketches of what had happened

between them that fateful day. But it was clear that Gillie's regard for the boyishly dashing Jamison was more than warmed by the encounter. The thoughts intrigued Aria's imaginings feverishly. And perversely, the Gillie who had never been able to keep a secret in her life chose this time to develop the virtue of close confidence.

Tynan returned alone on a blustery March day, sweeping Aria into his arms and covering her face with kisses of pure joy. He presented both Aria and Gillie with gifts he had purchased in Philadelphia and watched Gillie struggle through her disappointment to seem delighted.

"Jamison had . . . other obligations to attend. And I was instructed this was to be conveyed into your hands, Miss Parnell." He produced a small package, tied with string. "With Mr. Jamison's sincere compliments."

"For me?" Gillie paused to stare at the little parcel, and her pale fingers trembled as she traced the rough cord. With true, ladylike restraint, she tugged the cord away and unwrapped a layer of paper, then another of softest velvet. Inside was a small gold locket made in the shape of a heart. "But I—I . . ." she sputtered, avoiding Aria's knowing smile. And she gathered the wrappings and fled the parlor.

"I thought she'd never leave." Tynan slid onto the seat Gillie vacated beside Aria and pulled his irresistible wife into his arms. He covered her parted lips with his and drank thirstily of her velvety offering. Aria melted eagerly against him, oblivious to time and place—to all but the sheer joy of his return to her arms.

"I'm so glad you're home," she murmured against the heated plane of his cheek. "I was so worr—"

He stopped her with a demanding kiss that drew the last vestiges of anxiety from her. "You worried about a callous, arrogant bastard that degraded and forced you, spoke vows to bind you to his pleasures, and accused you of all manner of

Betina Krahn

low, spiteful behavior?" He drew back to watch the slow glazing of her eyes and the sensual reddening of her lips, and she nodded, her face glowing with dreamy sensuality.

"Good," he declared hoarsely, pushing up and sweeping her up from the sofa into his thick, corded arms.

Much later, as Aria lay curled like a contented kitten in their luxurious bed, she watched Tynan stride to his highboy and pull out a clean shirt. His motions were fluid, seemingly untroubled by his grueling, several-day's ride. The broad fascinating expanse of his bare back and the intriguing narrowness of his waist brought fresh tightness to her throat.

"I missed you terribly, Tynan," she managed huskily.

"I could tell." He turned a lascivious grin on her, then held up a shirt and scowled at its rumpled state briefly before shrugging into it.

"You're really terrible," she chided seductively.

"Scarcely moments ago you said I was marvelous." He strolled toward her, neglecting the buttons. "Perhaps you mean I am terribly marvelous." The bed dipped as he planted one knee on it and then spread his heavy frame gently over her warmed, enticing curves.

"Or marvelously terrible." She laughed impishly, losing herself in the pale splendor of his loving gaze.

"This was my last trip to Philadelphia," he said softly, urgently. "Come next week, the militia will have a new . . . somewhat overcredentialed officer."

"Tynan!" She breathed in shakily. "Are you sure?"

"Things have been moving quickly at the congress. Washington is having difficulty keeping his ragtag troops together; money is in critical supply; Howe is poised in Nova Scotia to strike anywhere along the coast . . . at any time. The time is come, Aria. If, as some think, the redcoats plan a southern landing into open royalist arms, it could mean a swift and nasty end to our growing call for independence. We have to see the colonies aren't split by such a maneuver. Halifax's militia needs equipping . . . and experience. I can supply some of both."

"Tynan—" She choked on the rest and his handsome face shimmered in the liquid that filled her darkened eyes. His fingers stroked back a wisp of honey-colored silk from her face.

"You know, if I hadn't been on that 'hunting' expedition," he mused tenderly, looking at her eyes, "I'd have missed Sir Lowell's little bash and I might never have known what living emeralds are like."

But before she could respond fully to his adulation, he pulled up the crumpled lace of his once immaculate shirt front and grinned ruefully.

"And as you love me, please don't let Levina get hold of my shirts again."

Even John Halifax's chin dropped when Tynan rode into the secluded pasture where the local colonial militia trained that next week. There were a few grumblings of disbelief and not a few distrustful glares, but no one dared challenge openly Tynan's right to be there.

He stripped off his elegant coat in the bright, early spring sun and astonished everyone by taking a place in the ranks. But by nightfall, he was issuing orders . . . that were obeyed.

The spring unfolded with new grace at Oberon. The land itself recognized the efforts made in its behalf and responded. The fields were ready for planting earlier than anyone could remember, the magnolias drooped with blossoms, the garden paths were lined with early flowers, and no sooner were the kitchen gardens cleaned and sewn than green began to sprout.

But intruding on the joy of early summer tasks was the sober preparation for a time of conflict. In the soaphouse, the iron kettles were pressed to use as smelters for the making of lead balls. Stacks of muskets, powder, blankets, and provisions were stored in the women's workhouse. The smokehouse gradually filled with dried meats, the cellar with dried fruits, flour, and meal. Each time John Halifax arrived with more stores to cache, Aria stood and watched with a shiver of dread.

In early May, Tynan took Aria to Charleston for the horse auctions and the attendant merriment. When she was introduced to his former acquaintances, they eagerly accepted her into their astonished midst, vowing privately he had the devil's own luck with horses and women. And they noticed changes in the Earl of Penrith as he squired his beautiful young wife about the city, into the finest homes and through the finest shops.

Aria was awed by the depth and breadth of his acquaintance—and his financial involvements. Expertly, he tutored her in the fine art of investing and in how handsomely a gamble could pay, now and then.

He asked only one thing of her while they were in Charleston . . . to help him find a proper valet. They sat in the parlor of their rented suite of rooms, interviewing likely candidates, and after each, they discussed briefly the merits and deficits of each.

"I don't know." Aria paused over a letter of introduction for the lean, older man who had just exited and made a wry face. "Everything seems in order, but he's so stiff—I'm not sure I'd like having him in and out of my privatemost . . ."

Tynan sighed disgustedly and looked at her from beneath heavily lidded eyes. "He'd be no worse than Levina is for me. That girl near ruined every shirt I own. And she's always rearranging or misplacing my things. I'm having to hire a valet in sheer self-defense."

"Now," she smiled tauntingly, "I'll not have you disparage my husband's gift to me."

He stared at the womanly twinkle in her sea-green eyes and his mood softened. "Umm-m-m. It's true, I'm partly responsible. Sometimes I don't show the best judgment, where you're concerned. Let's see the next one."

A short man of uncertain but younger years appeared next. James Broadrick's speech was educated, his brown eyes lively, and his letter of reference was complimentary, though his prior work had been more of a "house" nature. His clothing was of good quality, somber in color but perfectly immaculate. Tynan spoke to him about Oberon's present operation and staff and about his most recent post. When Aria mentioned that he would share the anteroom and wardrobe area with her maid, Broadrick stiffened slightly and said it would prove no difficulty, so long as the girl stayed out of his way. When he was dismissed, Aria turned to Tynan with a smile of pure relief on her face.

"Well, I'm certainly glad that's over."

"Over?" Tynan scowled.

"Hire him." She nodded at the door. "He's perfect."

"Perfect?" Tynan's scowl deepened. "You heard him. Can you imagine him telling Levina to stay out of his way?"

"Yes." Aria grinned impishly, rubbing her hands together. "I certainly can. It'll be fascinating."

"Aria, I have no desire to see my home made a battleground of the sexes again," he declared firmly, sitting forward to let his broad shoulders reinforce his point.

"Oh, I don't think it will last long. Besides he has a bit of stuff in him you like. . . . I could see it when you spoke to him. Trust me on this, Tynan. It will work out perfectly. He's short."

"What does *short* have to do with anything?" He was becoming exasperated.

"Lots." Aria rose and stretched her arms out wide. "I'm off to take a nap. . . . I can't seem to get enough sleep these days. Are you interested?"

"In your nap?" He sat back sharply, slinging one arm over the back of his chair and glaring at her halfheartedly. "Aria, what's gotten into you?"

She sighed patiently and let her petticoats swish the floor seductively as she swayed over to him. She stood beside him with a sleepy, bedlike look in her eyes and a tempting curl to her lips.

"Believe me, Tynan, this fellow Broadrick will do splendidly. He and Levina will work things out very quickly. You'll see. I was right about Gillie and Merrill, wasn't I?"

"My God, you're matchmaking again!" He paused, truly horrified.

"No—" She tilted her head and her bottom lip began to pout lusciously. "I'm only ensuring peace and tranquillity in our house. Isn't that what you wanted?" When he frowned quizzically at her behavior, she took it for agreement. "Now, my nap." He caught her hand as she bent to bestow a kiss on his forehead.

"Are you all right?" His body came to life suddenly as he scrutinized every detail of her intensely.

"I'm fine. Never better." Her secretive smile might have annoyed him, but she reached for his hand and set it at the waist of her dress, covering it with her own. "I'm working on your Christmas present."

A frown flickered over his face briefly, then he caught the sense of it and jumped up from the chair, nearly bowling her over in the process. "Aria!" He grabbed her shoulders then gentled his grip and rubbed them gingerly. "Are you saying you're . . ."

"Going to have your child . . . probably just in time for Christmas." She smiled brightly, slipping her arms up around his neck and melting against his stunned body. "It never ceases to amaze me how you always get exactly what you want."

"Aria!" He picked her up into his arms and swung her around in a delirious circle. His laughter boomed with delight and his eyes glowed like hot silver. "A babe—a son!" He stopped abruptly. "You *are* all right, aren't you?"

"I'm fine, Tynan. I just need a bit more rest than usual." Her fingers fluttered down the side of his face as he gazed at her with all the love in his expanding heart. "I'm finally going to have a family again . . . a real, whole family."

"Having a family means a lot to you, doesn't it?" He reached into her soft gaze, wanting to feel whatever she felt, needing to be at one with her.

"A lot," she admitted with shining eyes. "When we began to lose everything . . . our wealth, our position, our home . . . I thought I couldn't bear it, it was so hard. But the hardest part was losing . . . my family. I thought the only thing left that mattered was truth—knowing what was real and honest. But there's something even more important than honesty.

"Tynan, I want to pour my love for you into this babe, and into our home. I want us to make a family to share our love."

"You'll have your family, Aria." Tynan's eyes shone strangely. "Babes . . . and more, I promise." At that minute, he'd have moved all of heaven and earth to see her loving heart satisfied.

A wistful dent appeared in his brow as he realized how far a journey it was from mere pleasure to real joy.

Aria pulled his head down and smoothed that bemused frown from his face with a light kiss. Her eyes twinkled.

"Now are you interested in my nap?"

Tynan's grin nearly split his face as he scooped her up and carried her into the shady bedchamber. He deposited her with exaggerated gentleness on the bed. But when her arms refused to leave him, he was forced to stay.

Thirty-one

Aria sighed contentedly and turned her head on the pillow to better appreciate Tynan's well-muscled form as it emerged from the civil restraint of his clothes. His shoulders moved with animal grace and his arms flexed with casual power as they raised his hands to rub the back of his neck.

"Come and I'll rub it for you." She rose onto one elbow and patted the bed beside her. He turned to her and smiled at the sleepiness that turned her into an alluring kitten.

"It'll be fine." He strode to the bed and bent to collect a kiss from her. "Just too many idle hours in a cramped carriage. And you need rest . . . not romancing." He pushed her shoulders down gently to the bed and braced himself above her, gazing at the enchanting picture she made with her hair spread on the pillows in a golden cloud.

"I am tired," she demured, "and so glad to be home again. I think I missed my own bed. Are you sure you aren't ready for sleep, too?" She stroked the hard plane of his cheek with the back of her hand.

"I couldn't sleep yet." His expression was rueful eloquence, "and if I came to bed, you wouldn't rest either. I think I'll walk—out to the stables. And then there's Jamison. I want a word or two with him when he finally deigns to show his face at my home tonight."

"Poor Merrill," Aria laughed huskily. "I feared he'd burst before we finished those last miles from Charleston."

"Like a pent-up stallion at the starting line," Tynan snorted with distaste. "Randy as a goat. It's positively indecent."

"No," Aria teased laughing, *"our* courtship was indecent. Theirs is simply . . . urgent. I wish I could have seen Gillie's face when Merrill came barreling in with the news that he's bought the old Stimson place and is about to become our neighbor."

"If she had any sense at all, she'd have nothing to do with him."

"Tynan Rutland." Aria was scandalized. "You sound like a proper old curmudgeon. After all, who taught Merrill everything he knows about ladies—and how to 'enjoy' them?"

Tynan scowled darkly, but under her warm, teasing look, he melted into resignation.

"And I'm not sure it would harm Gillie to be 'enjoyed' a bit." Aria's eyes twinkled and it was Tynan's turn to act shocked.

"Hoyden," he charged amicably, dropping a kiss on her sweetly bowed lips. "Shameless jade."

"Um-m-m," she affirmed, closing her eyes to drink in the essence of his adoration. "You taught me everything I know, too."

"That I did," he murmured. "But I notice of late, you've added your own unique variations upon my tutoring."

"That I have." She turned her face to accept the butterflylike kisses he rained over it. He straightened abruptly and drew a deep, ragged breath.

"To the stables."

The exact hour was difficult to tell, for the bright moon imitated the early dawn uncannily. Shadows shrouded familiar shapes and clung to the corners of the great bedchamber. Some subtle change about her brought Aria up in the midst of her bed, senses alive and searching the darkness. She heard Tynan's head moving on the pillow beside her and jerked about, finding his eyes open.

"What is it?" he whispered in the darkness, then fell silent as both strained to understand what had awakened them. A muffled rumble sounded in the distance—thunder of perhaps horses' hooves.

They stayed like stoneworks for what seemed an eternity, intent on that mysterious alarm that the wind brought through their half-shuttered windows. The sound stopped abruptly, replaced by more recognizable ones.

"Someone's at the door!" Tynan threw back the light cover and bounded from the bed, reaching for his breeches.

"Tynan—at this hour—" Aria gripped the covers with chilling hands. "Is it Merrill?"

"It must be near morning . . . he was home hours ago," Tynan uttered, shoving his feet into shoes and pulling a shirt up over his shoulders as he made for the door.

"Wait!" Aria swung her legs over the side of the bed and ran to ward him. "Tynan—don't go down there! Let Broadrick see to it!" She grabbed and held his arm as he stood in the doorway to the sitting room.

"Whoever it is, they haven't come for Broadrick, Aria." He stared at her as he hastily worked the buttons at his waist. Her face was ghostly pale in the dim light.

"No, they've come for—" The words caught in Aria's throat as the fierce banging on the front doors floated up to them, now punctuated with unintelligible voices. "Dear God, Tynan, they've come for you!"

"Aria—" He grabbed her shoulders too hard, betraying his own tension. "You must stay here. Don't leave this room until I come for you . . . do you understand?"

"Tynan," she cried as full panic seized her and she gripped his sleeves, "don't go down there—"

"I have to, Aria—now—get dressed." He planted a hard kiss on her forehead, then pulled her icy hands from his sleeves and disappeared into the darkness of the unlit hallway.

Aria could scarcely breathe. A cyclone of emotion swept her into its violent center. The past surged terrifyingly into the present . . . reclaiming the darkness, reawakening terrors long buried. She stood trembling, feeling the past breaking over her, engulfing her in great, cruel waves. Again there was distant shouting, rustling in the hallway . . . faint wisps of acrid smoke on the air. The bright moonlight began to flicker like the ugly yellow of the flame dance that had once shadowed her bedroom walls, casting a spell of destruction on them. Horses screamed over the dull roar of flames . . . compelling her to move.

She dragged her dressing robe up over her arms, neglecting its ties as she hurried stiffly to Tynan's highboy. Her ears rang with the growing rage of the fire's destruction. Her heart pounded in her head, her throat. Her limbs piloted themselves, directing her fingers to the hanging pulls of the bottommost drawer . . . then sliding them through the murky woven depths until they struck the polished wood. She pulled the long, flat case from the drawer and carried it to the table, moving the catch without conscious will. Encased in a numbed hollow, she moved like a self within a self. The smooth, cold steel of the pistol barrels were strangely comforting. She picked one up, with no thought beyond mild surprise at the weight of it in her hand.

She moved through the gloom of the sitting room into the blackness of the hall, the heavy pistol dangling at her side. A slice of light from the main hall spread weakly on the wall at the end of the hallway and she glided into it unseeing, her eyes searching for, then intent on, the sight far below. The image was scarred into her mind and now she moved along the balcony, feeling afresh its heat and pain.

The heavy double doors of the main hall were thrown back, silhouetting a lone figure in the garish light of torches from outside. The noise in her head blocked the nervous sounds of the horses and the harsh voices that would come from beyond that fearsome glow. She glided down the grand stairs on bare, silent feet, her eyes fixed on the halo of light about that beloved, endangered form. There were others in the hall—faceless, silent figures that made no move to stop her.

Time was convoluted, cast back on itself; events were running parallel, then fully merged—time inside time. Nothing would stand in her way. This time, she would not watch, powerless, while one she loved and her world were destroyed . . .

She stopped in the doorway, behind Tynan and slightly to one side. Her shoulders were erect and her face was calm, at peace with her purpose. A man stood just before Tynan, near the steps of the portico. His words were lost in the silent haze that engulfed Aria, but his face was florid, his gestures agitated.

"No!" Aria raised both arms and pulled back the ornate hammer of the heavy dueling pistol. She aimed it squarely at the intruder and began to squeeze the trigger when Tynan jerked around and leaped for her, knocking the weapon down and banging her back against the doorpost.

"Good God, Aria!" Tynan thundered, grappling with her unreasoning fury as he tried to gather her against him. "Stop this—what in the devil has got into you?!"

"Aria . . . Aria . . . Aria . . ." It echoed about in her head, reaching through her struggle to recall her to sensibility, to the present. As the pistol was wrenched from her hand, she came to life, pushing and wrestling against Tynan's overwhelming strength.

"Let me go—don't you see?" she ground out in heated gasps. "I can't let them do it again—"

"Aria—what in God's name do you think you're doing! You've almost shot Stewart Morgan!" His ire was jolted rudely by the haunted dread in her pale face. "Aria—" Concern vaulted over the turmoil inside him and he swept Aria up against him, carrying her squirming form into the small parlor, issuing Broadrick and Levina orders over his shoulder.

The doors closed on them and he deposited Aria on the divan, holding her rebelling form there with hard-won restraint.

"Aria! . . . Aria!" he barked hoarsely, giving her a shake

and feeling her resistance rise anew. Instinctively he countered with the opposite, grabbing her up against his chest and holding her to him in a crushing embrace as he uttered her name softly, over and over. Bewilderment settled over him as she slowly responded to his rough comfort.

"Oh, Tynan—" She clutched his shirt and her tortured words were muffled against his chest. "You're all right!"

"Of course I'm all right." He began to see the glimmer of reason behind her rash action. She had thought she was protecting him.

"I can't let them take you from me, too. I couldn't bear it."

"Aria, they've come for me—I have to go," he murmured, scowling as he struggled to understand what had unhinged her so.

"No, Tynan!" She pushed away, her face strained and frightened.

"I'm a militia officer, Aria. I have to go—the royalists are making their move to the coast. We have to leave tonight—now."

"Militia?" Aria's clouded gaze swirled.

"That's Stewart Morgan and some of the militiamen from the county. Colonel Moore's sent word. They're forming up. . . . I've got to go with them."

"They're not . . . royalists. They're militia . . . and Stewart Morgan." The words on her own lips seemed to penetrate her fears and wilt her resistance. She collapsed into his arms, tears of relief burning her cheeks.

Tynan held her quaking shoulders close against him.

"I thought it was . . ." Her voice was choked. "It was the same as before. It was just like the night my father was killed. I saw it all . . . I had to stand by helplessly and watch while they killed him on our front steps. Oh, Tynan—"

For the first time, Tynan glimpsed the full horror of what she had endured that night. His chest squeezed about his heart as he held her, wishing with all his soul he might take some of her pain upon himself. That part of him that had never fully resolved another senseless, unjust death was roused in oneness of feeling. When he spoke again, after her sobs quieted, he spoke to himself as much as to her.

"The horrors of the past are past, Aria. We cannot live in their shadows, always expecting their pain to be revisited on us."

Aria's head moved against his damp shirt front and he glanced down to see that she was nodding. He lifted her damp face to his and brushed her lips with aching tenderness.

"Aria, the past has no power over us that we do not give it. I'm not your father . . . you're not your mother. We must learn from their mistakes . . . and ours . . . and go on with our lives."

"I know." Her voice was small but the glow of dying pain in her eyes let him know his words had found fertile ground in her heart.

"I have to go, Aria." He touched her face gently. "Will you be all right while I'm gone?"

"Tynan—" But she could never ask him not to go . . . to forsake his duty of conscience. They had spoken of this day before and of the cause of liberty that would take him away from her someday. They had agreed how it was to be. And too much was at stake to go back now. The words spoken in the warm comfort of day must be honored in the gloom of the heart's night.

"Come home to me." Her eyes glistened, but her voice was surprisingly steady. "Come home to us." Her hand placed his on her belly.

Almost an hour later, Jamison brought Tynan's horse around in the still light of first dawn. Aria had dressed fully and now walked slowly with Tynan down the steps of the front portico. She held his hand tightly, absorbing all of him she could in that contact.

"Send word when you can," she said tightly, searching his strong features to hold them in her heart.

"I will." He paused, touching her face with his fingertips, tracing, memorizing, the curve of her cheek. "Aria, there is something I must ask of you." His tongue seemed thick as he spoke the words he had rehearsed in his mind this last half-hour. He pressed his signet ring into her hand and curled her reluctant fingers around it. "If I don't return, you must send this to my brother, Hayden. By it, he will know that I am gone and he is earl."

His light eyes searched her and he found in her composed face a strength that lifted a weight from his heart.

"I will have no need of these instructions, Tynan," she said firmly, clasping the ring with whitened fingers. "When you return, you will only put it on again."

"Probably." He smiled crookedly at the stubborn set of her jaw and gave in to the urge to crush her to him in one last kiss of longing.

Aria clung to his coat, drinking in his vitality and the strength of his presence. She poured all past and the promise of all future joy into her response . . . leaving it to work a charm that would bring him home to her swiftly.

"I love you, Aria."

The words were hoarse as he withdrew abruptly and mounted beside Jamison. Aria watched them ride down the lane to join the troop waiting at Oberon's gate. The lump in her throat threatened her breath and she finally conquered it enough to turn back to the house. Levina stood watching her mistress with uncharacteristically quaking shoulders and red, teary eyes. Reluctantly, she accepted a handkerchief from a stiff, scowling Broadrick.

"Levina," Aria said quietly, once inside, "I want to send for Miss Parnell. I'll need someone to ferry a message." Before the weepy maid could respond, Broadrick spoke up smartly.

"I'll see to it, my lady." And he turned on his heel, leaving Levina staring after him.

An acceptance of Aria's invitation returned with her messenger and Gillie herself arrived two days later. Quickly, they settled into a somber, sultry time of waiting. Each day seemed like two, each week like four. Hardly a day passed that a messenger was not dispatched to or from one of the other waiting houses, seeking word of the troops. There were rumors and frights that resulted in watches being posted atop the main house. But little of substance was known of the militia's whereabouts, and Acre and Franklin vowed that was a good sign. They were keeping scarce until they knew the enemy's route and could meet the royalist force on favorable ground.

Aria went about her daily duties with an even, determined air, speaking purposefully of wanting things fit and proper when Tynan returned. But Gillie, Franklin, Acre—the whole household—marked the absence of her lilting laughter, her tart wit, the sparkle in her eyes. She worried silently for her strong, capable husband, and all of Oberon waited and worried with her.

As the hot, steamy days progressed in orderly fashion, she slowly succumbed to the inconvenience of her advancing pregnancy and allowed herself to be trundled off to bed for a rest each afternoon. Gillie sometimes sat with Aria as she rested or removed her own day dress and joined Aria for a nap in the shady master bedchamber. In the afternoon, they stitched small clothes for the coming babe or let out Aria's gowns to accommodate her more comfortably. And as always, they talked.

"I think Levina and Broadrick are starting to get used to each other," Gillie observed one blessedly rainy afternoon as they sat in the small parlor stitching.

"Um-m-m. They're down to mere snarling." Aria concentrated on her tiny silken embroidery, but smiled absently. "I told Tynan it would work out eventually."

Gillie stared at her speculatively. "It's no wonder you get on so well, you and Tynan. You're exactly alike."

"Alike?" Aria's head came up, frowning. "We're no such thing."

"Oh, yes you are," Gillie persisted. "You both always get exactly what you want . . . and everything always works out the way you plan it. Your marriage, Oberon . . . Levina and Broadrick. Even Merrill and me—and there's no use denying it." Her eyes dropped to the embroidery hoop in her hand and color rose slightly in her cheeks.

"What an exorbitant notion, Gillie Parnell." Aria rearranged her feet on the stool before her and tried to dismiss the comment. "We've had our share of—"

"Extraordinarily marvelous luck," Gillie finished for her. "I think you're both charmed. . . . That's what I think. For instance, imagine you married to Thomas Branscombe." She made a terrible face that brought a bubble of laughter from Aria. Then she pointed her nose up and sucked in her cheeks. "Imagine those long, dreary afternoons with Grandma Prudence Branscombe . . . and the long, dreary night with long, dreary Thomas! Ugh."

"Gillie!" Aria laughed, diluting her proper indignation. "I haven't thought of Thomas in . . . ages."

"Neither, I'll wager has anyone else . . . except possibly Janette. She's spending him blind, I hear. Indecently quick nuptials, too."

"Gillie," Aria warned good-naturedly.

"You got shed of him easy enough. You saw the earl, set your cap for him, and had the good sense to get him to fall madly in love with you at once . . ."

"I'm so exceedingly clever," Aria retorted dryly. "Gillie, you have a fertile imagination . . . and very few of the facts. You don't know half of what went on—" Aria clamped her mouth shut and returned to her needlework.

"Set me straight, then." Gillie slid to the edge of her chair, her eyes expectant and round as saucers. "Tell me exactly what happened . . . everything."

"Never," Aria tossed coolly.

"Then it's as I said." Gillie sat back disgustedly. "You're peas in a pod . . . who have the unreasonable good luck of always getting exactly what you want."

Aria sighed, lowering her hoop and letting her mind drift back over the tumultuous events of the last year. She and Tynan had traveled so precarious a path to find the love, the union, they now shared. She scarcely realized she spoke aloud.

"I pray it was not mere luck that brought us together . . . for luck may change . . ." A squeezing sensation near her heart made her draw a sharp breath. She jolted up and fled to the solitude of her bedchamber.

Three days later, John Halifax's eldest son rode straight in with word of the county regiment. Aria pulled the winded lad inside, and half the house and stables gathered in the main parlor to hear the news.

"Colonel Moore—he took a stand down by the Cape Fear River—built up an earthworks . . . square in their path and them knowing it. Itching for the fight, those hardheaded Scots. It was fast and furious for a while—then it was just over . . . quick and over! About fifty tories down—near a thousand taken prisoner. We only lost a handful . . . but there was plenty of wounded. We took the general himself—old Donald MacDonald . . ."

"And Lord Rutland? What of his troop?"

"He'd 'ave been right in the thick of it, I'd imagine," young Halifax answered, beaming.

"But you've had no word on who the casualties were?" Aria persisted.

Reluctantly, he shook his head and admitted he had no news of just who that brave, unlucky "handful" were who had given up their lives in freedom's cause. Relieved only slightly, Aria fed the lad well and sent him on his way. And as the meager details were mulled and retold, the waiting began again.

Another week passed, with occasional bits of news filtering through the county; the prisoners would be detained in encampments, some militia units would be sent home soon . . .

some would stay active, on guard against a still possible British landing. There was speculation about reprisals against the Tory strongholds, but mercifully, there seemed little enthusiasm for it. Being kept away from their farms and towns and plantations would prove hard enough punishment for the royalist men, come the fall and winter.

Aria strode the topmost floor of Oberon, where Broadrick and Levina contested to direct the house staff in the cleaning and refurbishing of the modest rooms. Time and again, she was drawn to the small windows overlooking the road, staring down at it and willing Tynan's familiar form to appear and end this agonizing wait.

Why hadn't he sent word in these last five weeks? Was he lying wounded somewhere, balancing on a meager thread between life and death? Every frightening possibility played and replayed itself in her head and roiled about in her stomach.

Her hands finally curled into fists that pressed her temples as if trying to contain her anxiety. If anything happened to him—

"Your ladyship—" Broadrick's customary coolness was at a precarious tilt as he appealed to her, "this hot loft is no fit place for you. And the work will proceed faster apace if you take *that wench* downstairs with ye."

Aria turned, scowling at this test of wills renewed between Tynan's man and Levina. With Tynan gone, Broadrick's tasks had gradually expanded to include household responsibilities, at which he proved adept. But for every task he assumed, Levina carved out a corresponding bit of authority for herself, and open conflict erupted whenever their venues crossed.

"Broadrick," Aria managed tightly, "I shall heed your advice. Except, I leave you Levina for assistance and order the others below with me. You may have at one another with fang and claw, for all I care—but see these rooms settled ere I set eyes on the two of you again!"

She swept the others from the upstairs and descended to the breezy relief of the upstairs portico. Collapsing onto a cushioned, woven-birch settee, she dabbed at her moist face with a handkerchief and straightened her back to accommodate both her breathing and her burgeoning middle.

Some detail of the front lawn or road arrested her eye and brought her concentration to full alert. She scanned the far crest of the hill, beyond Oberon's long drive, where the road rose out of the valley. A plume of dust rose in the gentle breeze and Aria's heart slowed, then lurched in dreadful anticipation. She could not admit the avalanche of possibilities that poured over her; she simply had to act.

She bolted up, swaying and catching her balance on the balustrade. Then she was through the French doors and running around the balcony of the main hall, calling for Gillie. Stopping only long enough to jerk her day cap from her hair and toss it on her sitting room floor as she passed, she headed for the main stairs.

"Aria!" Gillie appeared on the balcony of the west wing. "What is it? What's happened?"

"They're home!" Aria proclaimed, only now realizing why her heart thumped wildly and her face burned with excitement, and why she rushed headlong for the front doors. It just felt right. He was home . . . he *had* to be home! No dour twinge of reason dared intrude on this feeling that gripped her.

Aria was already down the staircase when Gillie finally jolted into action and followed, catching Lottie as she exited the parlor and repeating Aria's news. Then she whirled, passed shaky hands up over her hair, and snatched up her skirts to run after Aria.

"Aria! Stop! You can't run—".

But Aria was running, across the grassy yard in front of the house and straight for the road leading to Oberon's gate. Far down the shaded corridor of trees, she could see riders, three of them, coming quickly. And she prayed breathlessly that one would be him. Then suddenly she could run no more—her lungs burned, her heart pounded ominously in her head, and her limbs refused to respond to her control. She jerked to a halt and stumbled, heaving for air and unable to tear her eyes from the trio of horsemen.

Strange, she later had time to muse, that the color of Tynan's powerful roan stallion, Rondelay, was the first confirmation of her unreasoning conviction. Then the shape of his broad shoulders, bent to the work of his mount, and his raven-dark hair became discernible.

She stopped in the middle of the road, feeling her spirits, her heart expanding—soaring. It really was him! She was dizzy . . . delirious with joy.

Rondelay jerked to a savage halt fifty feet away and Tynan pounced to the ground like a great, hungry cat, springing for Aria with her name on his lips. He swept her up in his arms, whirling her off the ground and around before he remembered and set her down with care.

"Tynan!" she half laughed, half cried. "You're home! You're safe!" She squeezed her arms about his neck mercilessly, reveling in the crush of his arms, the fierceness of his unreined hunger for her, for his home. Their embraces were fervent, frantic, and joyous, all at once.

"Oh, Tynan," she choked, "I prayed so hard you'd come home to me! I worried so when I didn't hear——" But his lips on hers absorbed the rest of her meaning without need of words. Then he showered her upturned face with kisses and tasted the saltiness of her tears.

"Aria, I missed you—I thought they'd never dismiss our unit." His voice was thick and gravelly.

"You're all right?" She pushed back in his arms to run inspecting fingers over his shoulders, up his neck and over his dusty hair. Through grime and sweat and dust, his hardened vitality was visible. But her palms flew over his chest and down the corded arms that held her securely. "Are you sure you're all right? Tell me!" Her persistent inspection brought a curl of laughter to his generous mouth.

"Just a few scratches, which I'll be happy to have you tend."

He grinned with a familiar lechery that sent a reassuring wave of warmth through her.

"Gladly!" She pulled his head down to hers and molded a perfect kiss against his lips.

"I'll hold you to that, wife."

Clinging to his broad frame, she hugged him over and over, laughing at her own giddy relief and enjoying his intense delight in feeling her against him. Finally, she let her hands slide slowly down his chest and lowered her eyes, glancing about her fingers with chagrin. "You feel so good . . . I don't want to let you go."

"You don't have to, sweetest. And I'll take the blame for your scandalous behavior." Grinning broadly, he cradled her against his side and they strolled slowly toward the house, passing the similarly entwined figures of Gillie and Jamison. Aria felt a rumble of amusement vibrating Tynan's ribs and looked up to find a devilish twinkle in his eye. "Jamison's been pure hell to live with these last weeks. . . . He's a desperate man."

"Then perhaps we'd best send Gillie home this evening." Aria laughed conspiratorially.

"Oh, no—I've seen enough bloodletting to last awhile," he rejoined. "Let Gillie tame the savage beast her way."

Aria shivered, enjoying the ripples of warmth his laughter created under her skin.

"You know," he gazed about him at the gentle beauty of his wife and his home, "I've never missed England the way I missed this place. I thought of you both constantly. And I thought of how precious life . . . and freedom are to me now." He studied her face, finding in it the key to his own higher impulses. She made him want to be better than he was . . . to set things right around him.

"I . . . I've decided to sign those papers of yours that horrified Skeen and Franklin so."

"Papers?" A puzzled expression flitted through her brow

before she realized what he meant. "Tynan! Really?!" She pulled him to a halt and hugged him thoroughly.

"Well," he offered self-consciously, "after all, how does it look for a man to spout freedom and liberty . . . and keep other men in bondage? There are quite a few in Philadelphia who feel very strongly about it; there'll be more jubilees in the years ahead. But I think it took you to make me want to see it. And you chose seven years. I've always had a fondness for sevens . . ."

"Oh, I knew you'd come to see it!" Aria's heart swelled with pride for her extraordinary husband.

Suddenly she remembered and pulled back abruptly, reaching into her snugly clad bosom. For his wondering eyes, she produced a heavy golden ring, set with rubies and the crest of the House of Penrith. Her eyes filled with liquid crystal as she reached for his hand. "You're home now. I said I'd have no need of your instructions."

But his muscular fingers wrapped around hers and held them still, while he searched her emerald eyes with his.

"Aria, I said I had time to think . . . and reason to consider what matters most to me. I have carried the past within me long enough. I've declared myself a colonial now, a rebel and an officer sworn to oppose the king's oppression. In this land I found love and a measure of happiness I never imagined could exist." His hard fingers stroked her damp cheek tenderly.

"Being here, loving you, has given me something to believe in, to strive for . . . to build. I want to help build a country where our children need never fear riders in the night . . . where we can prosper as we may and can grow old together in peace." He ran his palms in circles over her shoulders, sifting his thoughts carefully.

"The threat of royalist uprising is over. I've been asked to stand for office in the provincial congress, Aria. I have no need of an earldom I cannot see. You are what I want and need . . . you and this place." His light eyes shimmered with unspent emotion as they swept the house and barns and fields of their home and returned to her lovingly.

"You want . . ." Aria's throat was tight and her eyes were full. ". . . to send the ring to your brother." She blinked, clearing only enough vision for him to fill. Deep inside her loins came a strange, fluttery sensation that seemed to affirm Tynan's decision. Never had she felt such oneness with him . . . and now with the life growing inside her.

"Send it, my love," she whispered, touching his face.

Relief flooded his taut body as he pulled her into his arms once more and felt the welcoming depths of her love.

Epilogue

A low, sultry buzz vibrated the air around the trellised summerhouse in Oberon's garden. The smell of June honeysuckle wafted in and out, following the breeze through brick paths lined with lilies of the valley, budding lupines, coral bells, and bright cornflowers. Aria's eyes closed as she sat listening to the pulse of her home, appreciating its fragrant breath. This was her favorite place of all on Oberon, this secluded garden refuge.

The sound of distant hooves disturbed her peace and she raised her head to peer around the post toward the long drive in the front of the house. She glimpsed a horse and rider approaching Oberon, but the house quickly blocked the view. From the corner of her eye she saw Tynan striding purposefully from the stable to the house. Her cheeks warmed with admiration at the manly set of his shoulders. She never tired of watching him and never ceased marveling at the way the smallest things about him fascinated her.

She smiled wistfully, thinking of her outrage when she learned Tynan had abducted her. None of them could have known what lay ahead . . .

"I think he is asleep now."

Her head came up quickly from against a post and she smiled fondly at the picture Frederich Mueller made, cradling her six-month-old son, Seth, in his fleshy arms. Frederich's face was serene as he watched the babe's untroubled sleep; his eyes shone as they raised to meet Aria's.

"I think you're spoiling him, Frederich. He'll expect to be crooned and rocked to sleep all the time." She rose and reached to take the babe gently from him.

"No, little ones must have extra loving—to store up and save for de hard times of life . . . vhen it is hard to find." His warm brown eyes and fleshy face radiated that otherworldly certainty that Aria found irresistible.

"You may be right, Pastor Frederich." She looked at the cherubic form nestled trustingly against her breast and ran a loving fingertip from the cap of dark hair down around his cuddly cheek. "Who knows what times and hazards our children may someday have to weather?"

A fierce surge of protectiveness swept through her, subsiding into a lingering ache of love for her sturdy little son, Tynan's child. How could a mother, any mother, abandon her child? After feeling this trust, this warmth, how could her mother have sold her?

"Ve just teach and trust, Aria . . . and pray. It is all a mama and a papa can do. An' someday ve let go of them—into de vorld. An' still ve pray."

She opened her mouth to ask, but closed it and lowered her troubled eyes from Frederich's compassionate look. Had her mother trusted that things would somehow work out? Had Marian Dunning cared enough to pray for the child she had once carried as Aria now carried her son? Since Seth's birth, it had never been far from her thoughts.

Frederich helped her down the steps of the summerhouse into the sunshine. As they walked the long path toward the main house, he clasped his hands behind his back, observing her need for silence.

"Frederich . . . I'm so glad you came." She finally shook off her mood and focused determinedly on the joy at hand. "I couldn't imagine anyone else baptizing Seth. We've talked of you so often . . . wondered how you and Anna were getting on. Merrill Jamison thought of sending for you to perform the marriage for him and Gillie." She laughed quietly. "He said he liked the way you tied a knot."

"I vould have come, too—to make Jamison vedded." His finger shook savagely. "I told him he needed a vife, dat rascal."

"Well, he has one now," Aria said, beaming with revived humor, "and you'll get to meet her tonight when they come for supper. I think you'll like her."

They wound their way through the garden to the terrace outside the library and entered the house. Levina and Broadrick met them in the hallway. Levina wore an odd expression and took Seth from Aria's arms.

"Thank you, Levina, he's getting heavy." She rubbed her arms gratefully.

"I was just coming for you, madam," Broadrick pronounced, offering a gentle assist with the baby's blanket. Levina cast an approving eye in his direction and he drew himself up taller. "There's a visitor come . . . a woman."

Levina watched her a bit uneasily. "The master sent for ye. They're in the main parlor." She nodded in that direction.

"I wonder who that could be?" Aria frowned, straightening her bodice front. "I'll just see—" she nodded to Frederich, "then I'll check on dinner."

The parlor doors were opened back and the early summer breeze through the shuttered windows carried the sound of voices into the hallway. Aria's steps slowed as she approached, intent on her husband's familiar tones . . . and on others that plumbed the well of memory.

"—journeyed a long way to settle our account, sir—" The voice sent Aria's heart sliding toward her knees.

"There's naught that needs to be settled. All obligations between us are resolved." Tynan's deep tones were clear and free of irritation.

"Then my price was duly met and honorably rendered?" came the voice that awakened Aria's earliest recollections. It was a voice that recalled despair, the loss of an entire life.

"Duly rendered before the first available parson, as agreed. The man is here even now—it is easily verified."

Marian Dunning straightened and met his look without quailing. "You have married Aria." Relief freed her stopped breath. "She is with you here?"

"She is. This is her home you see about you, madam." His big hand swept the elegant parlor.

"And is she . . . content?" Marian tightened, but did not waver.

"She is."

The absolute assurance in his response wilted Marian's rigid posture a bit and she looked briefly at her gloveless, tightly clasped hands. "It was worth the journey just to hear that. She may not . . . want to see me. I will trust this with you, sir." She pulled a rolled piece of parchment from her worn reticule and extended it to him. "With this, honor is . . . satisfied." Her voice cracked as the ache in her chest reached her throat.

He made no move to accept the document, but looked past Marian to the door, where Aria stood, staring at her mother.

Marian turned to follow his gaze and stiffened as if struck. Her doe-brown eyes widened as they flew over her daughter's fully blossomed womanliness. In an instant she knew the earl had spoken the truth—her daughter was content to be with him. And her shoulders sagged as if a terrible weight had finally been lifted from them.

Aria stared at her mother, seeing streak of white under her plain straw bonnet. Her dress was the simple, brown linsey-woolsey of the frontier, adorned only with a plain linen collar. Fresh lines, etched by labor and care, were visible in her once delicate skin. But Aria's eyes fastened on her red and hardened hands. They spoke of the toil of living, not the ease of ill-gotten coin.

Aria's heart ached. Her mouth was dry and her hands grew cold in spite of the summer warmth.

"Why have you come?" Aria managed a steadiness of

speech that surprised her. She felt as though she stood on the very brink of a yawning chasm.

Marian looked down at the parchment in her hands, praying she would not disgrace herself when she spoke.

"I came to see . . . if you were settled . . . if you were well. And to bring you this." She extended the rolled parchment to Aria, who made no move to take it.

"Have you wasted your thirty pieces of silver already? I would have thought you more shrewd with your coin." Confusion tightened Aria's throat and she moved farther into the room, keeping a distance from her mother.

"Silver?" Marian stiffened, feeling her relief turning to despair.

"The money you took to deliver me into Tynan's hands. Either you wasted it quickly, or you set a shamefully low price on your daughter's virtue."

"I know not what you've been told—" Marian's pain-flecked eyes darted to Tynan, "but I took no coin from your husband for you. My payment was in other kind."

Aria blazed first at Marian, then at Tynan. "You deny you were paid your price for me?"

"I was paid—"

"Then I need hear no more." Aria wheeled and headed for the doorway, finding Frederich Mueller standing in it, blocking her way.

"Aria!" Marian moved toward her, then halted sharply, unable to stop the plea in her voice. "Daughter—" Aria could not take her eyes from the troubled understanding in Frederich Mueller's face.

Marian trembled as she moved to lay the rejected parchment on the table near her. "This is yours. Five thousand in gold and a small piece of land near the river . . . the one with the willows. That was all that was left from the settlement of your father's estate. It is your dowry to your husband." She took another step toward Aria but stopped herself, and her fingers tied themselves in whitish knots to keep her arms from reaching out.

Aria had difficulty seeing the loving rebuke she felt from Frederich's kind eyes. Memory and longing crashed over her in terrible suffocating waves. This was the woman who had borne her, loved her. This was the woman she revered as a child and had come to know only in the depths of shared misfortune. She was a mother herself now, experiencing the complex and sometimes conflicting emotions motherhood involved. Could she, who had once received forgiveness so gratefully, do less for the one who had given her life itself?

All this and more crowded into her mind and her throat as she watched Marian move toward the door, her head lowered to hide the shame that stained her pale face.

"Aria—" Tynan's voice was full and urgent. She turned to look at him and saw the swirl of strong emotion in his angular face. She could not know how keenly the pain in her heart was shared.

"Her price was our vows."

Aria stared at him, scarcely able to make sense of what he said.

"Mother—" she called, halting Marian just outside the doorway. Clasping and unclasping her cold hands, she searched for words, any words. "Where are you . . . living now?" The ache in her heart was painful to watch.

"I am with Lathrop still. Evelyn died last spring and now we run the trading post together."

"You came this long distance . . ."

"I needed to see you were all right." Her mother's voice caught. "And I needed to bring you the remains of your father's estate as the dowry he and I wanted you to have. A lady must always have something of her own—"

But Aria heard no more. Tears filled her eyes and vaulted down her cheeks as she opened her arms.

"Mama—"

Tynan watched them embrace with a strange, full feeling in

his chest. Then his gaze found Frederich's unabashedly tearful smile, and Tynan took a deep, cleansing breath and strode out.

It was several minutes before Aria reclaimed her senses and looked about them. From her seat on the sofa, she saw Tynan standing in the doorway, holding a sleeping Seth in his strong arms. There was a curiously tender expression on his face.

Marian rose, mute with joy, and touched the peaceful little face with awe-filled strokes. Tynan laid his son in her arms and led her back to the sofa.

"Aria—" Marian's chin trembled.

"Mother, I know why you did—" her eyes flitted to Tynan, "what you did. At first I was furious and hurt. But as time went by, the hurt eased. I think Tynan and I were somehow meant to be together. Who could say that your way wasn't best?"

Their hands met over Seth's little fingers and Aria watched with aching satisfaction as Marian discovered her grandson. The rightness of it flowed through her.

"I . . . Seth . . . needs his grandmother." She sought Marian's glistening eyes. "Will you stay?"

Marian looked to Tynan's wry smile and her fingers tightened lovingly over Aria's in reply.

Later in the sweet silence, she sought her handsome, enigmatic husband, threading her arms about his waist and lifting the love in her heart to his sight.

"Then I take it you're not angry with me . . . for not telling you exactly what price your mother extracted from me?" His grin was roguish and irresistible as his lips descended slowly toward hers.

"I should leave you twisting in the wind, Tynan Rutland," she murmured. "But I've pledged you my honesty. I don't think I've ever loved you more than now."